FLIP-A-MATION™
BEGINS ON
PAGE 73

FLIP FRONT
TO BACK.

©JMG

OH, TO BE A QUOZL . . .

The Quozl loved their sleek, wood-paneled space-ships, the ultimate in tasteful design . . .

The Quozl made sure their furry bodies were preened to perfection, and in the height of fashion . . .

The Quozl thrived on Quozl spirit. Didn't *everyone* in the universe want to be a Quozl?

NOTE: ANY SIMILARITIES TO OTHER SOCIETIES, PAST OR PRESENT, ARE PURELY COINCIDENTAL.

Quozl
"Alan Dean Foster has a knack for creating memorable characters—people you'd like to meet!"   —UPI

Other Books by Alan Dean Foster

QUOZL

Alan Dean Foster

ACE BOOKS, NEW YORK

This book is an Ace
original edition, and has never been
previously published.

QUOZL

An Ace Book/published by arrangement with
the author

PRINTING HISTORY
Ace edition/May 1989

ISBN: 0-441-69454-3

Ace Books are published by The Berkley Publishing Group,
200 Madison Avenue, New York, New York 10016.
The name ''ACE'' and the ''A'' logo are trademarks
belonging to Charter Communications, Inc.

PRINTED IN THE UNITED STATES OF AMERICA

10 9 8 7 6 5 4 3 2 1

This one's for Susan Allison,
who already has a title.
With affection.

1.

SOMETHING WAS WRONG.

No one on the *Sequencer* had been able to tell him exactly what it might be, but he could sense it. Very unscientific, he reprimanded himself. Contrary to all his training. But whatever it was, logic failed to vanquish it.

Nor was he alone in his feelings. The uncertainty was there in the recycled air for anyone with half a nose to sniff, was visible in the posturing of his fellow Quozl.

He asked questions of those who might know something. The directness of some of the replies, which would have been unthinkably rude under normal circumstances, was confirmation enough that he was not alone in his unease. The interrogated bristled at his straightforward inquiries and he fussed and hissed under his breath at their reactions.

There was no way you could dismiss it: everyone on board was on edge.

He checked his attire carefully before leaving his room. The thin, almost fluorescent plastic slats that formed rings around his thighs and upper arms flashed colorfully in the subdued light. He was clad in a snug but not constricting one-piece jumpsuit of mild purple with black speckling. With the seventh finger of his right hand he adjusted the small opening in back, twitched his short, thick tail to make sure the suit wasn't binding.

A glance in the mirror revealed that one of the four earrings in his right ear was loose. He tightened it, turned slightly, and raised the ear fully to admire the effect. He adjusted the bandana around his neck, the two scarves that encircled each upper arm, and lastly the yellow and pink sash that crossed from shoulder to waist. When going to question senior officials it was always best to dress in a respectfully subdued fashion.

There was no need to shave again. Two narrow curves revealed by the U-cut neckline of his jumpsuit marked him as an elite scout. The curlicues and triangles cut from his short black fur elsewhere were purely decorative. The pair of white stripes that marked him from muzzle to tail were natural and needed no tonsorial enhancement.

Time to get the blades in his shaver resharpened, he reminded himself. The delicate cuts on the backs of his hands were becoming harder to maintain. No possibility of replacing the blades. The ship could not recycle everything forever while maintaining peak efficiency, and there were items of greater importance that had first demand on the engineering department's resources.

Of course with planetfall due any day now it would only be a matter of time before the *Sequencer*'s exhausted reserves could be replenished a hundred times over. The wealth of an entire new world would be theirs to utilize.

Except there was a problem—or so the rumors claimed.

As he left his room and strode out into the corridor he found himself admiring anew the paneling that covered walls and ceiling. It was a near-perfect duplication of the wood of the Tawok. He smiled inwardly. Artists and builders had long shared the same dream; to fashion a starship entirely from wood. The ideal fusion of the aesthetic and the practical. It worked well in sculpture but not in equations.

The *Sequencer* was metal and ceramic and plastic, but its decorators had filled it with real wood and expert reproductions. The ship's interior was soothing to the eye and reassuring to the Quozl soul, the next best thing to contemplating a real forest.

As he left the residential area behind he found himself

wondering how the *Sequencer*'s sister ships were faring. *Passes-Over-Beyond* had left Quozlene orbit a year ahead of the *Sequencer*. *Races-Lower-Stars* was due to have entered underspace half a year after *Sequencer*. There was, of course, no way for them to communicate with one another, just as there was no way for them to communicate with home.

A variable term, home. It lay ahead of them now, not behind.

One settlement ship per year, each directed to a different system determined to contain habitable worlds. That had been the pattern for some time now. No one talked about what the inhabitants of a ship would do if the survey turned out wrong and the system they had been directed to proved to hold no inhabitable planets. Settlement ships could not be sufficiently equipped for second attempts. Even though this was common knowledge there was no lack of volunteers from perennially overpopulated Quozlene to fill the ships. It was an honor to spread the Quozl through the firmament, and a greater one to perhaps perish in the attempt.

Occasionally Looks-at-Charts worried about his lack of Quozl spirit and would have to retire to a chosen shrine to meditate. It was his failing to consider living better than dying, the amount of honor one might accrue in the latter notwithstanding. His advisors tried to comfort him by pointing out that his failing was one reason why he had been selected for training as a scout.

You have chosen a difficult profession, they'd told him. One you may not even have the chance to practice. You will suffer personal and possibly physical anguish as a result.

He turned a corner, wondering when the suffering might begin.

The passageway twisted and turned in simulation of an ancient Quozl tunnel. As he progressed he passed more and more fellow ship-citizens. Before fifth-generation Elders he lowered eyes and ears. Members of the sixth like himself he either ignored or eyed openly, depending on their sex or status. Youngsters of the seventh generation avoided him lest they receive a chastising glare or noncontact cuff for appearing too friendly.

He could have taken transport forward but much preferred to walk, delighting in the shifting smells and sight as Tawok gave way to Rebarl and especially the deep maroon and black Sasum. Its perfume flared his nostrils, pungent and rich as only honorific polishing and cleaning could make it.

Art filled the unwood places, occupying the mind's eye when honest grain and color were absent. Some of it was static, some kinetic. Looks-at-Charts studied it all with equal respect. Most of it was familiar but occasionally there would be a new piece, rendered by an artist of the present generation. Those considered to be masterworks he automatically bobbed before. Many had been carried and cared for lovingly all the way from Quozlene itself, parting gifts from the homeworld. Though their creators were long dead, their work lived on to inspire new generations of artists who might choose also to work in paint or sandbark or dyeshot.

He turned the next corner to the music of giggling and whispers. There were two of them and in his artistic perusing he'd almost run into them. Having interrupted their space rendered their laughter polite. One was brown-spotted cream color with brown facial and body stripes. Her companion was pure beige with white striping. Scarves and shaving placed them in food service. Not of the elite or of his class, but comely for all that. What Quozl female wasn't comely?

They were ready enough. A Quozl was ready most of its waking hours, ready and eager. Furthermore they appeared to be off-shift. Not much time in the span of a day, ample time in the span of love. All four green eyes that gazed openly back at him indicated he could have either or both of them. He wondered how much of their interest was piqued by his posture and how much by his rank and unusual occupation.

He automatically checked the chronometer on this workbelt. Plenty of time. When it was done with, all three parted satisfied, he forward, they back to work. As it always did, the encounter filled him with fresh Quozl purpose. Having noted their names and places of work he fully intended to look them up again sometime. Perhaps they could bristle together for several days running. They had been refreshing individually and in concert, a change from his usual routine.

He did not worry about the slim chance of having sired offspring. In the whole seven-generation history of the *Sequencer* there had been only two such incidents. The first had been an innocent error involving the ingestion of expired oocide. The second had been, insofar as the court which had judged the case had been able to determine, deliberate, and both parents had been ejected into interstellar space.

Hard to believe, but true. The records of the third-generation were there for all to peruse. Two Quozl had violated the onboard edicts restricting procreation. One incident in seven generations was not a bad record, but you still had to be on your guard, still found yourself sometimes wondering. If he did sire an unauthorized embryo and was determined to be the father, he would soon find himself embracing vacuum.

It was the only way. Penalties had to be severe lest chaotic coupling reign. The Quozl were incredibly fecund. Without restrictions the *Sequencer* would find itself fatally overpopulated within a couple of generations. Which was why there were settlement ships in the first place. Pressure existed on the homeworld to expand despite all the chemical restraints Quozl biologists had developed. Onboard births were permitted, but only according to strictly enforced quotas.

So the pair he had coupled with would not become pregnant. In a few hours they would be ready again and so would he. Without drugs to render them infertile both would surely have conceived.

It was appropriate that the symbol which adorned each settlement ship represented the empty female natal pouch.

As he entered the central recreation oval he was able to see the huge, complex sculpture by the adored artist Grand-cuts-Standover, a priceless gift from the citizens of a dozen large Quozlene cities to the generations that would crew the *Seqeuncer*. It dominated the open area, reaching to the very apex of the dimpled ceiling. The sculpture had been cut from a single massive Aveltmar tree, the roots and branches having been etched by a Master of Carving. Fountains hung from its shaped and tooled branches, water collecting in pools scooped from flaring roots. Benches and lounges were scattered about its base, surrounded by growing plants whose daily needs were attended to by meticulous gardeners. On the *Sequencer* those who took care of growing things had the same status as engineers.

That was only fair, since it was just as important to do that which helped maintain sanity as to do that which maintained engines. Simpler to care for plastic and metal than minds made of flesh and blood.

Quozl wandered through the open place or rested and relaxed beneath the massive carved tree: courting, fighting, or simply staring at the water. Engraved in the center of the thick Aveltmar trunk was a panoply from Quozl history, fourteenth Anarchic Era. Here a Quozl warrior clad in ancient armor took a spear in the belly. Blood and intestines spilled from the gaping wound, all realistically depicted. His companion was in the process of losing his head, his attacker's sword halfway through the neck, blood gushing in a frozen explosion from the traumatized veins.

It was much the same everywhere: multiple figures of Quozl and their Dermicular mounts fighting and bleeding and dying, crushed or cut to bits. Crowning the sculpture was a photographic rendering of the Water Clans General Soft-cries-Nightly trampling several children of the enemy under the hooves of his Dermicular.

Looks-at-Charts paused for a moment (you couldn't help but pause) to soak up the violent scene. The reddish wood of the Aveltmar made the blood and torn organs appear so real, lit by the indirect lights set in the ceiling. It was a powerful reaffirmation of the Quozl spirit, restful and relaxing to his soul. Refreshed and content, he walked on.

Not far before a figure stepped in front of him. The Quozl's scarves were bright blue and off-green except for the single yellow and green he wore tight around his right thigh. His jumpsuit was green with blue slashes crisscrossing the snug material. Like Looks-at-Charts his fur was dark, though his eyes were blue and not purple like the scout's. A single strap running across his chest supported an electronic snarp, its strings and switches glinting in the soft light. Looks-at-Charts couldn't tell at a glance if it was charged for playing, but it was clear regardless that High-red-Chanter was on his way either to or from work.

"It pains me deeply to interrupt your progress in this manner, but there is a small insignificant matter that requires mutual attention."

"It's no bother at all," Looks-at-Charts replied appropriately. "I am only sorry you find it necessary to waste your valuable time on unworthy communication. A brief note to my room would surely have sufficed."

"Electronic communication lacks eloquence." High-red-Chanter shifted nervously from one huge foot to the other. "Though I likewise regret the loss of time, I find it unavoidable."

"Since you have taken the time to interrupt your important schedule, the least I can do is pause to listen." Looks-at-Charts promptly assumed combat position, selecting the Aki stance, ears swept safely back behind the head and down, one arm tucked back and ready to block, the other held forward in preparation for striking. His knees were bent and his toes raised, ready to kick.

High-red-Chanter chose the Omo bracket, both arms held parallel to each other and the floor. It was less traditional, more daring. Other members of the crew swerved around them, chatting among themselves and ignoring the two potential combatants.

Looks-at-Charts suffered some embarrassment because of their exposed position in the middle of the walkway. High-red-Chanter should have confronted him in the park courtyard or off to one side. Now neither could leave until the confrontation ended.

Wasting no time, he took one step and brought his right leg up in a formal opening kick. It was delivered with precision, stopping a thumb's length from High-red-Chanter's stomach. The musician brought his left arm down to block the kick. Foot brushed stomach and forearm grazed leg. Both Quozl assumed new stances, the initial exchange having been properly met.

Looks-at-Charts had a pretty good idea what this was all about. Simply because every nonmated male on the ship was available to every nonmated female and vice versa did not mean there was no such thing as jealousy among shipmates. There was one lustrous-furred supple young thing who worked in Agriculture who had attracted more than passing attention from both kicking, punching Quozl. Her name was Tie-grow-Green and though she tried, she could not dispel the animosity that seemed to erupt of its own accord between scout and musician whenever she was discussed.

Frankly Looks-at-Charts was surprised that High-red-Chanter hadn't tried to force the issue before now. The musician was notoriously nervous and unreasonable. Looks-at-Charts drew inspiration from the unsurpassed sculpted tree that dominated the gathering area. He would not back down. There was principle at stake here. He struck with a clenched fist.

"I'll see your genitals broiled!" the musician snarled as he leaped and twisted. Looks-at-Charts could have brought his fist up hard but naturally did not. His fingers extended to flick the lowermost edge of High-red-Chanter's jumpsuit just as his opponent spun to bring the outside part of his foot around in a scything arc. The ship sandal kissed the shaven circle on Looks-at-Charts's left cheek.

High-red-Chanter was good, Looks had to admit as he changed position once again. The fight continued, the two Quozl circling and feinting and striking. The conversation was as important as the blows they threw. Passing crew avoided them. Rarely were any rude enough to stare. Neither of the combatants paid them the least attention.

Looks-at-Charts drew his inspiration from the wooden cascade of mutilated and eviscerated figures that dominated the great wooden artifact nearby, sought strength in the frozen waterfalls of blood so lovingly rendered from the soul of the tree. High-red-Chanter sang to himself, martial music both ancient and new. Looks-at-Charts recognized much of it. He appreciated fine art and High-red-Chanter was one of the most accomplished young musicians on the ship. Looks had often admired his work.

He was not as enamored of Tie-grow-Green as the musician was, but a challenge once issued could not be ignored. If he'd walked away in front of witnesses his status would have suffered. A scout wasn't supposed to walk away from anything. Lose that and the next female might not be so interested in coupling. His frequency of intercourse might fall from a normal, healthy four or five times a day to one or two. Eventually that would impact on his work performance. He had no choice but to accept High-red-Chanter's invitation.

Because of his scout training, Looks-at-Charts enjoyed advantages in skill and strength, though High-red-Chanter was more flexible in his movements. As was to be expected from an artist his language was also more elaborate. Looks appreciated the beauty of it even as he struggled to parry and thrust. Not that he was unskilled in the use of the spoken insult himself, but he spent so much time preparing for the day that might not come that his social skills suffered from neglect. His nouns were rusty and his tenses loose. High-red-Chanter scored repeatedly and Looks immediately realized that if he was going to emerge victorious from this contest it would have to be on the physical level.

So evenly matched were they that the contest might have continued until both withdrew from exhaustion, until High-red-Chanter risked a difficult double kick and flip maneuver. It was harder than stringing together adjectives to form a spear of vituperation. The complex leap should have been attempted only by an expert in the form. While willing, High was no specialist.

Even as he ducked to avoid the blow, Looks-at-Charts

admired the determination which had driven the musician to try it in the restrictive confines of a ship's corridor. High executed the flip and double kick impressively, but it took all he had simply to accomplish the move. At the end he didn't have enough to exercise proper control. The claw on his seventh and outside big toe skimmed Looks-at-Charts's left arm, which was held in the correct defensive position. Unable to manage the swing, High-red-Chanter could not stop himself from breaking the skin of his opponent, slicing through the dark fur.

Looks-at-Charts did not blink, did not wince. He saw the bright red blood foaming up through the bristles. A red mist formed over his eyes, indicating the onset of the fury which every Quozl is taught from birth to deny. He forced himself to recite the first line of the ancient First Book of the Samizene. Peace returned to blanket his emotions, the mist faded, the ages receded.

Landing on both feet and stumbling only slightly, the musician assumed a stance preparatory to throwing a choke hold. "The veins in your throat will grow stiff as the branches of a Samum, your blood will become as water. . . ."

He stopped as he watched blood run down his opponent's arm. Looks-at-Charts adopted a defensive posture even as he quickly raised a scarf to try and hide the wound. He was too late. High-red-Chanter had seen the blood. His expression tensed, lips held firmly shut over clenched teeth, then assumed a submissive position: head bowed, ears front and down, elbows out, and all fourteen fingers interlocked to show contrition. He was barely able to control the anger in his voice.

"I have drawn blood and broken flesh. I stand ashamed before you." He knelt on one knee, resting his backside on the protruding heel of a long foot. "Defeat comes to me like a bad dream in the night."

Having won, Looks-at-Charts felt terrible. "I rain apologies on you for this accident." Because of the embarrassment

he knew that High-red-Chanter would be impossible to interact with for days to come.

Looks-at-Charts's apology would only make it worse for the
musician, but there was no other way to handle it. His
clumsiness had cost him and he would have to live with that.

"This is not over," High-red-Chanter mumbled. "I will
challenge you for her again."

"It was nothing of importance. You magnify everything.
And you were winning. I wish it could have been otherwise."

"No, the miss was mine, as was the challenge." The
musician rose, having held the submissive position just long
enough. He was unable to meet his opponent's gaze. "I was
not skilled in that maneuver and should not have tried it. I let
my ambition and anger get the better of me. That will not
happen again."

"Yes, another time things may go differently." While
Looks-at-Charts's voice was full of sympathy, his stance
indicated his true feelings.

"It is thoughtful of you to say so." Anger burning within,
High-red-Chanter spun and stomped off into the recreation
area.

Looks-at-Charts waited until his rival had been swallowed
by the crowd, then resumed his walk forward. It was fortunate that the musician had drawn blood because on the verbal
level, at least, he had been winning handily.

Hundreds of years ago there would have been no attempt to
score status with a near miss, a passing strike. Then each
blow would have landed and more than blood would have
been drawn. Eyes would have been gouged, genitals crushed,
bones broken. That was the old way of the Quozl, the way of
the ancients. The way depicted in so much Quozl art. It had
been the only way of coping with the phenomenal Quozl
fecundity. Nature had tried disease and famine but in the end
it was the Quozl themselves who were the only ones able to
limit their population. They had chosen war. Centuries of it.

Then had come artificial methods of birth control, and the

Books of the Samizene to show the Quozl a new way, and the teachings of Over-be-Around and the great philosophers.

You could still fight, but combat became a ritualized art form instead of organized murder. You won by almost disabling, almost killing, almost cutting. To actually make contact more than fur-deep was to lose, both in status and in the fight itself. Hence High-red-Chanter's embarrassment at having drawn blood.

A poor fighter might try to win by deliberately courting contact, but a skilled opponent could always dodge and adjust. Fighting became a matter of control. It was necessary therapy for the calmest Quozl. One could draw solace from the violence that flowed through most Quozl art. All the old, dangerous, primitive tendencies had been sublimated. What could be studied did not have to be acted out, what could be seen did not have to be repeated.

Such fight-dancing was frequent. Had it been otherwise the ship's psychologists would have become concerned.

One simultaneously fought with words. That had been High-red-Chanter's strength and Looks-at-Charts's weakness. He had fought back as best he could, however, confident that the emotional musician would eventually make a mistake. Which was exactly what had happened.

Be not too proud, he told himself. His special training had stood him in good stead, but he had not received it to gain status among his peers. Fill a pouch too full and it will burst. He had learned more control than most Quozl because one day he might have to demonstrate that control under unimaginable circumstances.

He turned up the corridor that would eventually lead him back to his room, wondering whether to look for a coupling or simply some rest. The two techs from Agriculture had given him good and he wouldn't be ready to go again until he'd had something to eat. Proof arrived in the shape of an attractive colonial with black fur and yellow eyes whom he deliberately avoided. Fuel first. The fight had taken a lot out of him.

He considered watching a viewplay, perhaps an amusement or something similar requiring little mental effort. He could study the Samizene or simply sleep awhile. As a scout there was little for him to do except study.

Soon it would be different, he told himself. It was all but assured. What was hard to do was to maintain the proper air of indifference, to show control when sheer anticipation threatened to put you in the infirmary from exhaustion.

He was quite at peace with himself as he entered his residence, though he still felt some regret at the manner in which High-red-Chanter had lost the fight. Sprawling on the bed-lounge he idly called up recent work on his viewer. They were too familiar to him by now to hold his interest. He'd memorized them years ago: theoretical geography, adaptive botany, field survival, and basic surveying, all information based on facts provided by the citizens of the three worlds the Quozl had first settled. Many settlement ships had been sent out since, but thus far only the inhabitants of Azel, Mazna, and Moszine had progressed far enough to build ships capable of making the return journey to Quozlene.

As he scanned the statistics he was as amazed as ever at the variations that could exist within a single star system. A scout had to be ready to deal with all of them in addition to the unexpected. Three worlds plus Quozlene itself did not seem sufficient background to draw upon. There would be surprises. There could not be too much preparation. He and his colleagues Flies-by-Tail and Breeds-cloud-Out had committed everything available to memory.

The device could also synthesize scenarios by extrapolating upon known facts. For example, it could assume slightly less oxygen and more methane in an atmosphere and postulate the resultant vegetation accordingly. Such syntheses were amusing but insufficient. A mockup by its very nature must ignore certain important factors.

Such ignorance caused Looks-at-Charts to feel the weight of responsibility more than ever. It was going to be up to him and his associates to help decide where the *Sequencer* should land, where the colony would try to establish itself on the new world. Someone had to be first. Not that he wanted it any other way. In temperament and intelligence he was perfectly suited to the task he'd chosen and for which he'd studied so hard. His whole life had been aimed toward the moment that was fast approaching.

Stares-down-Canyons had died a cycle ago without having the chance to fulfill his dream. He had been fifth generation and Looks-at-Charts's mentor, drilling him in his studies while knowing all the while that unless the original calculations proved wrong he would never set foot on the new world, never have the chance to exercise the skills he had mastered. His patience and good humor had made the impossible seem attainable to the young Looks.

Stares should be here, Looks-at-Charts thought sadly. Not I. He recited several phrases from the Fifth Book which dealt with feelings of inadequacy and immediately felt better.

Landscapes and climates flashed across the viewer box, mirrored in his eyes. Bored, he switched to information on Mazna, always more interesting than statistics from Azel or Moszine because unlike them, Mazna had turned out to harbor hostile lifeforms. The first two colonies had been established with comparative ease. In contrast, Mazna had been a fight.

Details were so few, he mused in frustration. By now there must be dozens of other Quozl colonies scattered across the firmament, but none save the first three had advanced enough to return a vessel to Quozlene with helpful information. For all he knew, half a dozen such ships had arrived home subsequent to the *Sequencer*'s departure. Any one of them might hold the solution to a forthcoming problem. It was a solution he would never see. Communication between worlds traveled no faster than a settlement ship itself, though here were always stories and rumors of new scientific developments. It was intolerable.

Useless it was, and stressful, to sulk over such things. For all practical purposes Quozlene, Azel, and the rest did not exist. Nothing existed except the *Sequencer* and those aboard her. The ship was a ponderous giant, a slowly moving island of intelligence and life making its way through a dumb, ferocious cosmos. Isolation was their pouch, not Quozlene. Not for the past six generations. Sometime in the far future his great-great-great-offspring might succeed in building a ship to return with news of the colony's success, but he would not know of it, nor would any of his contemporaries.

More out of frustration than need he shifted the viewer from the education lines to the primary entertainment line. He found himself watching a depiction of the epic Fourth Dynastic War which pitted the Northern and Eastern United Clans of ancient Quozlene against the Southern. The depiction required days of nonstop viewing and he had yet to watch it all the way through. It was full of the kind of sweep and spectacle which entralled the colonists who had been born on the ship, and which for thousands of cycles had made Quozlene a living hell.

Within a short time he had witnessed less than half a dozen disembowelings and as many beheadings, interspersed with scenes of ritual torture and dismemberment, but he was not disappointed. Even in an epic some time had to be reserved for necessary explication. Some of the performers were legends or so the accompanying history of the making of the epic insisted. They were dead now, but their images lived and breathed and drifted within the depths of the viewer. They had achieved electronic immortality.

He found himself nodding off, the curved sides of his bed-lounge enclosing him pouchlike, the false wood walls arching overhead and the viewer humming softly high above his feet as it disgorged shrunken depictions of ancient massacres.

His mind's eye was filled with dreams of the new world. In them he was the first to stand on its rich soil, to survey a paradise compared to which Azel was a desert. A second Quozl stood beside him, sleek of fur and bright of eye, the most beautiful he'd ever seen. They coupled repeatedly while his communicator frantically asked for details.

Though he was not yet of age and had yet to qualify according to the standards set for procreation, he dreamed also of siring offspring, of fulfilling the central Quozl purpose of replication, of watching youngsters moving inside their mothers' pouches. Soon it would no longer be a fantasy. With a whole new world to fill, the chemical inhibitors everyone ingested in their daily meals would be removed and impregnation could commence unrestrained.

Unless their new home turned out to be another Mazna, hostile and threatening. In that case he, Looks-at-Charts, would show the way, beating back the flora and fauna until the colony was safely established. Nothing could stop him, nothing could hold him back.

They would raise a memorial to him. His offspring and his children's offspring would do him homage as the first to set foot on the new world. Looks-at-Charts the Great. Looks-at-Charts the Honored. Looks-at-Charts the Unsurpassed.

They would admire him as one whose taste was unequaled.

He could hear the acclaim, feel the roar of adulation wash over him, and he accepted it as his due even though he knew he couldn't really be hearing it because he was asleep, asleep and then he wasn't and it wasn't the whistling from thousands of throats that brought him awake but rather the insistent whine of his viewer.

Absent the epic and in its place a disapproving face staring back at him. Tell-no-Fury was addressing him in appropriately honorific terms, but he was not wasting time. That befitted the senior member of the Landing Preparation staff. Looks-at-Charts blinked double lids and sat up fast, his future glory a rapidly fading memory.

"I am terribly sorry to have interrupted your rest. Please forgive me," said Tell-no-Fury. Looks-at-Charts was properly ashamed for not having been available to respond. Technically he was on duty.

"It was unforgiveable and I can't find a proper excuse."

"There is no need for excuses." What Tell-no-Fury was actually saying was that he was good and mad but that he didn't have the time to waste on bawling the young scout out because he had something more important on his mind. As if this wasn't sufficiently apparent in his tone, both ears were turned down and forward.

"The meeting," he explained quietly.

Meeting. . . . Looks-at-Charts checked his chronometer and his eyes squeezed shut in shock. *The* meeting. His encounter with High-red-Chanter had caused him to forget. No wonder Tell-no-Fury was so upset!

"It is about to commence," the staff senior said dryly. "It will commence with or without you, but having noticed your absence I felt it incumbent upon me to ascertain the state of your health and to inquire if I might be of some assistance in the event you proved unwell."

"A thousand thousand apologies for my inexcusable tardiness!" It was the best Looks-at-Charts could manage under the circumstances. In this instance eloquence would be an unavoidable casualty. He would try to make up for it later. "I'll be there before your viewer cools."

He did not so much leave as flee his bed, forgetting even to shut his own viewer down. That would cost him later but presently he was only concerned with now. He ripped off his jumpsuit, got the armholes of his dress jumper on backward, cursed as he straightened them out, and adjusted his fur beneath the elastic. Then he closed his eyes and tried to calm himself, repeating the requisite phrases over and over in a soft murmur. When that didn't work he approached the foam figure of a Quozl in full ancient battle dress which stood near the doorway and struck it several times in the three vital areas. Feeling much better, he hurried out into the corridor.

II.

No RELAXING PACE this time, no casual stroll through the recreation area. He commandeered the first empty intraship transport vehicle he encountered and snapped directions. Leaning back and propping his feet on the rest bar, he straightened his ears as the wheeled capsule accelerated. The vehicle resembled an infirmary pill and moved through the ship's guts almost as fast, traveling through the narrow transport tunnel. He emerged close to piloting and guidance, having traveled from near the *Sequencer*'s midsection to a point close to its bow.

Ignoring the warning from the vehicle, he jumped out before it had come to a complete stop and tried to run without appearing hasty. His ears were burning but not from the machine's admonition.

How could he have slept through part of *the* meeting? There was no time to check insignia, brush his fur, or check his shaved patches, no time even to use a grooming razor.

As he neared the meeting chamber he slowed, wondering who would be present and who would not. Tell-no-Fury perhaps, Flies-by-Tail certainly among those he considered friends. The doors recognized him and parted to permit entrance, the fluorescent lines simulating the grain of Orkil wood pulsing brightly.

There was no mistaking the importance of the meeting. Stream-cuts-Through sat on the highest row, surrounded by her officers. The Captain looked tired, but then that seemed to be her natural state of being lately. Around the ribbed triangle shaved into her forehead gray was beginning to appear prominently. Stream-cuts-Through was fourth generation and something of a legend in her own time. It was rumored that in her younger years she had been noted for her readiness to interrupt the most intense coupling in order to deal with any problem involving the ship.

Eye-bends-Left sat next to her on the high table. There were four tiers in all, arcs facing the main viewscreen, and most but not all the chairs were occupied. Eye was the *Sequencer*'s Navigator, or more properly, the individual who monitored and took care of the computer which navigated the settlement ship. The presence of both Captain and Navigator suggested that this might be the meeting their lives had been pointing toward. It was no great surprise. The timetable was as much a part of everyone's life as eating and coupling.

And he'd almost slept through it.

Tell-no-Fury was not present, he saw as his gaze swept the ranked rows. All of his colleagues and most of his other superiors were, some forty in all. The youngest sat on the bottom row, their elders above according to age. All were freshly groomed. Scarves were twisted just so, earrings polished and gleaming. As he entered quickly he wished he could hide behind his own feet, which for a Quozl was not a physical impossibility.

A few faces turned in his direction, rapidly and politely looked away. Only Nose-sees-Carefully acknowledged his arrival, half raising her right ear in salutation. If observed by one of the Elders higher up the gesture would draw her a protocolic reprimand. Looks was grateful for the gesture and responded. They had never coupled and neither found the other particularly attractive, but they would have to find each other soon. Coupling to ensure compatibility was essential to any successful mutual enterprise, and they might find themselves working together.

Several of the Seniors were still taking their seats which meant that the meeting had not officially begun. Tell-no-Fury had warned him just in time. Stream-cuts-Through rose as he stumbled to his seat, trying to make himself as small as possible. Nose-sees-Carefully sat seven seats away from him, one row up. She did not look in his direction. He resolved to couple with her as soon as practical. Her gesture might have drawn the attention of disapproving Elders away from his ignoble entrance.

Had he arrived two moments later his disgrace would have been unavoidable. But if this was *the* meeting he was certain his tardiness would be overlooked.

Stream-cuts-Through's voice was high and strong despite her age. Since it would have been extremely impolite to stare at her while she was speaking, Looks kept his eyes on the viewscreen ahead. His posture was formal: ears erect and aimed forward, back straight, fur relaxed.

Her magnified image spoke to him from the screen. In ancient times a leader spoke to his or her audience from behind a translucent partition. Later it was done with mirrors. Now electronics placed the ritual respectful distance between speaker and attendees.

Her address was brief and to the point: Quozltime had finally come. Six generations of patience and hard work were about to be rewarded. Tomorrow at this time the *Sequencer*'s drive would begin shutting down for the first time since their ancestors had left Quozlene orbit. She paused to let that thought simmer before continuing.

"Already we have entered the welcoming sunstorm of charge particles emanating from the star that warms our new home. Tomorrow we will return to normal space for the first time in six generations."

There were no celebratory shouts and whistles and barks. No one rose to yell, no one made a sound. This was a moment for proper contemplation.

The Captain continued. The *Sequencer* appeared to have survived its long journey in excellent condition and was already being prepared for the final part of its mission.

She really was aging, Looks-at-Charts thought as he regarded her screen image. He wondered how long she would have following establishment of First Burrow to enjoy the new world.

Not that her presence would be necessary. Captains did not lead colonies. Captains guided ships through underspace. It would be up to the Landing Supervisor and the Council of Seven to administer the new social order. Stream-cuts-Through would be the last of her kind even as Looks-at-Charts would be the first of another. He sensed the passing of the spear, not so much from one generation to another as from Quozlene to a new world. Shiraz. It had been so named before the *Sequencer*'s drive had been ignited.

"As you know," she was saying, "it is not easy to do imaging of normal space when traveling in underspace. However," both of her ears bent forward and kinked halfway to indicate good tidings, "our technicians have had little else to do in Imaging for some time now, and they have been bending all their energy to the task of securing at least one special image for us to view. They finalized this objective only a little while ago. It is something for all of us to enjoy, a destination that no longer need be represented by an abstract point on a floating chart."

The viewscreen flickered and in place of the Captain was a world. Distant, heavily magnified, and computer-enhanced, but beautiful enough to take one's breath away. A world not unlike Quozlene itself, rich with bright color and cloud.

Politeness had its limits. As soon as the image appeared on the screen, several members of the audience could no longer restrain themselves. Whistles and hums of delight echoed through the chamber despite the frowns of some Seniors.

It was far away but at first sight was everything any colonist could hope for. Ample water and judging by the cloud formations, rain. That might mean trees, the soulmates of every Quozl. Not a nightmare desert world. Another Azel, perhaps, or Moszine.

The young Communicator on his right leaned over to whisper. "Look how little land, how much water!"

"No, there's plenty of land," countered Looks-at-Charts, disagreeing.

"I know what you are all thinking." The Captain gestured with an ear and the image flickered anew. "This is a view of the other hemisphere."

A few sharp whistles sounded and someone was discourteous enough to blurt aloud, "It's worse than the other! It's *all* water!"

The view of the first hemisphere returned. Given the extraordinary circumstances of the meeting, the interlocutor was not chastised. "Certainly Shiraz possesses more water than any world thus far encountered, but there is ample land for settlement. Preliminary calculations indicate that Shiraz will support a population of many billions if carefully developed, though we cannot tell precisely since we as yet have no way of judging such matters as the fertility of the oceans or the land, or even the exact composition of the atmosphere. That will have to wait for orbital measurements to be taken and for the first ground surveys to be completed." Looks felt the slightest of pressures on the back of his neck but didn't dare turn around to see if the Captain was staring in his direction. To make eye contact now with one's superior would constitute an unforgivable breach of courtesy.

One of the senior administrators seated on the top tier let out a sigh. "At least it's there." Those around him whispered similar sentiments.

"Having taken up entirely too much time," the Captain declared, "I turn your ears now to your Landing Supervisor."

She sat down and the Quozl next to her rose, his image occupying only the upper left-hand corner of the big screen. Lifts-with-Shout was so anxious to speak that he stood before the Captain had completely resumed her seat. No one remarked on the discourtesy because they were all dying to hear him.

One of the fifth generation, he was also one of the strongest Quozl on the ship, much more squat and powerful than the average adult. The deviation from the physical norm was

◇ 22 ◇

unusual, but then so was everything else about Lifts-with-Shout. Unlike his collegues, he had little time for ritual, meditation, or casual conversation. Only his remarkable mind had enabled him to overcome these deficiencies and reach his exalted position. For Lifts-with-Shout could organize anything, and above all a Landing Supervisor had to be able to organize.

It was whispered behind his back that he was a throwback. Jokes about his lack of social skills and grace were common. But even his most ardent detractors had to admit that he knew his work.

Looks-at-Charts paid close attention to everything the Landing Supervisor was saying, putting all thoughts of pleasure, meditation, or recreation out of his mind. It was time to be serious, and Lifts-with-Shout was all that, scarcely pausing long enough to apologize for the poor quality of the imaging and his own feeble skills.

He spewed a stream of information about Shiraz, using the image of the new world to show them principle features. Particular attention was paid to two large land masses joined by a narrow mountain range. They would scan these last. The main land mass would be their first choice for a Burrow, since it offered the greatest opportunities for rapid expansion of population.

Looks listened and filed everything the Landing Supervisor said away for future study. By the time they entered Shiraz orbit he would have memorized every word and gesture, having studied the recording of this meeting over and over.

When Lifts-with-Shout concluded he crossed both ears to indicate his satisfaction, thanked them for their attention to his wholly inadequate speech, and passed domination back to the Captain. Stream-cuts-Through rose a second time.

"The work of many fingers is about to come to fruition. The Akora sapling begins to put out first branches. Our roots are strong and go deep and the grain of our determination is hard and unbroken. This is a moment of great significance for all Quozl. I am told by Eye-bends-Left," and she gestured at the Navigator seated on her right, "that all preparations for re-emergence into normal space are progressing properly.

"Tomorrow we will break back into the real universe. Those of you who are section supervisors must prepare your populations for this. Our journey has been more tedious than dangerous, but this is one of the few maneuvers the *Sequencer* must perform that is potentially fatal. It will all be over quickly one way or the other."

At least there'll be some excitement around here for a change, Looks mused. Breaking from underspace into normal space was a complex operation, sure, but the Captain was deliberately overemphasizing the danger. That was part of her job. The thought that something could go wrong was of more significance than the expectation that something likely would.

When she had concluded, the ship's senior philosopher rose to call for a full moment of meditation, charging everyone in the chamber to clear their minds and spirits for the task ahead. Looks-at-Charts participated as fully as everyone else. It was not necessary for the meeting to be formally dismissed.

The presentation had gone on longer than he'd expected and he felt the familiar stirring in his loins. After coupling he intended to return to his room to commit Lifts-with-Shout's dissertation to memory and to drink in the image of his new home.

He and Burden-carries-Far were out in the corridor when they found themselves confronted by the Landing Supervisor. It was hard to believe when looking at him that he'd never set foot on any world, had never walked a surface made of something other than plastic or metal or ceramic. It was vitally important that Lifts-with-Shout *looked* competent.

"It's been decided," he said in his familiar brusque manner. "You two will take the first survey ship down."

Looks-at-Charts had expected as much but it was exhilarating to have it officially confirmed. The only surprise was that Burden-carries-Far was to accompany him. He'd thought his friend and colleague would command a second vessel. Obviously it had been decided to put as much talent as possible on the initial survey.

Looks was glad of the decision. Burden would be good company to share the great responsibility with. They had competed in study but never personally, had participated in multiple couplings together. Burden-carries-Far had jet-black fur except for white patches around his face and wrists. Members of the opposite sex found him especially attractive.

"I wish I could go with you," the Landing Supervisor was saying in an uncharacteristically soft voice, "but the initial survey is only a small part of landing preparation. The *Sequencer* must be made ready, not to mention her population. So I must remain here, though I will travel with you spiritually if not in person. I will know your work as well as you do, so see to it that you miss nothing and apply all your learning. I will be available to advise and to make the important decisions. You will have all the glory and none of the stress." Both scouts executed their most deferential and apologetic gestures.

"We know nothing of actual conditions on Shiraz?" inquired Burden-carries-Far.

"Impossible to tell from underspace. One prays for a world like Azel. You two will be among the first to know for certain. If Shiraz should be more like Mazna we will cope as best we can."

"What are your thoughts?" Looks-at-Charts asked his friend after the Supervisor had left them.

Burden-carries-Far inhaled deeply. "I think we have not enough information about which to wonder, and that I am ready for a coupling."

Looks was more than ready to go along with that.

They retired to a public assignation chamber for that purpose. Burden had chosen one decorated to resemble a Fifteenth Dynasty pleasure burrow. The effect was sybaritic, accomplished through skillful use of lights and artwork. Privacy coves were as abundant as the alveoli in a healthy Haghwick's lung. Not that privacy was necessary for coupling, but occasionally one liked to try something that might not work. A failure in public could be embarrassing, while in private it was likely to be ignored.

They encountered a pair of prowling computer technicians and after the formal, traditional exchange of greetings and commentary, plunged into a satisfactorily orgasmic quaternary that was better than anticipated because of everyone's heightened sense of tension and expectation.

When it was over and farewells had been executed, the two scouts left together. They joked about fighting to see who would be the first to actually set foot on the surface of Shiraz. Their competition was friendly and confined to words and gestures. Neither wanted to risk loss of face by initiating an actual combat dance. Looks-at-Charts tried several times to defer to his companion but the sly Burden would have none of it, knowing that if he accepted such offerings he would lose status.

The battle might not be to see who first set foot on Shirazian soil but who could succeed on staying inside, in which case they might both lose out to some thoughtless botanist or crew member who'd trip and fall headfirst onto the soil of their new home. It was not an impossible scenario. He and Burden would have to talk this over between themselves lest in their desire to act appropriately and without loss of status they fail in their primary objectives.

You could feel the heightened sense of anticipation everywhere. Everyone knew they were about to emerge from underspace. Everyone knew that Shiraz was, astronomically speaking, now little more than a falling branch away. Since Engineering and Navigation were the only sections fully engaged, the rest of the colonists were overflowing with nervous energy. Coupling proceeded at a frenzied rate, to the point where the Captain had to go on the *Sequencer*'s communications network to call for restraint lest secondary tasks be seriously neglected.

Or as she put it, "You must control your internal drives if the rest of us are to efficiently manage that of the ship."

Her sense of humor went a long way toward relaxing the most nervous among the crew. By the time Engineering actually commenced its countdown the atmosphere aboard had mellowed from the orgiastic to the merely anxious.

No one knew what it would feel like to return to normal space. They could only refer to the texts and try to imagine. And when it finally took place it did so in a fashion that, as so often happens with events anxiously anticipated, was greatly anticlimactic.

Looks-at-Charts was walking toward the center recreation center when it happened. As the final countdown issued from the wall speakers he paused for a deep breath. When it was done he felt no different. The interior of the *Sequencer* and his fellow Quozl looked no different. It was the universe that had changed. Once more he was part of real time, real space. There was that knowledge. That and the fact that somewhere before them, very near now, lay their new home. Shiraz. An entire world instead of a metal droplet floating through emptiness. They would make it Quozl.

Someday his children's children would refurbish the *Sequencer* or build another ship like her and return to ancient Quozlene to proclaim their success. The new generation would meditate at the place of Elders. Looks-at-Charts would not be among them. He would be one of those they would meditate upon. In addition to the more mundane elements necessary to the establishment of a new colony the *Sequencer* also carried with it a sense of history and of destiny.

Now that the transition back to normal space had been accomplished, the recreation center was filling up rapidly. There was no coupling taking place here. This was not a designated area. Instead it was a place to come to view entertainment portrayed on oversized viewers, to listen to localized music which changed as you strolled from one acoustic bubble to the next, to study art traditional and modern, and to invest your skill in a game or two. A great place to relax and meet other members of the colonial team.

The psychologists insisted on this. It was vital, they insisted, that a ship's complement not become socially stratified. That engineers mix with ergonomists. The ship's engines weren't all that had to be kept operating in tandem.

Looks thought he saw High-red-Chanter off in the distance manipulating a triple whirl. The globular machine spun and dipped like a drunken gyroscope as the two riders strove for position. You won by obtaining a predetermined tactical position—and by not throwing up.

As he moved deeper into the complex he spotted Flies-by-Tail chatting with two other females. There was a good chance she would be the one chosen to pilot the initial survey vessel. As she turned, her gaze settled on him and her ears danced eloquently. His first though was to invite her to the nearest coupling chamber, but now was not the best time. He meditated briefly, forcing down the familiar feelings. Perhaps on the surface of Shiraz, he mused. That would be another footnote for the history texts.

They greeted one another politely and she ordered cool refreshments from one of the ubiquitous service machines. The acoustic bubble she'd chosen was mid-level traditional mixed with a few unobtrusive electronics. Soothing but not stupefying. Around them Quozl burned off excessive energy. There was plenty to burn in the excitement of having returned to normal space.

"I saw the imaging," she said softly. "It looks to be a pretty place."

"Shiraaazzz." He stretched the concluding whistle, sipped from a long twisted drinking tube. "Hopefully it will live up to its name. If not we will tame it."

"Confidence in a scout is invaluable. Overconfidence can be dangerous."

"Isn't it the same with a pilot? I'm never overconfident."

"Never? In nothing you do?" Her ears curved in amusement and he read the hidden meaning. He was as adept as any mature Quozl at detecting the standard double entendres.

"In nothing I do. I know what I'm capable of. A scout has

no time for overconfidence, only assurance. When to move ahead, when to retreat."

"Advance and retreat, yes."

Blessings on this pilot, he mused. They thought alike. Yet strangely enough at that moment he wanted only to talk and relax. Nonetheless, he could not keep himself from eyeing with approval the delicate whorls and designs shaved into her golden brown fur. White streaks ran from her nostrils across her face and down to disappear beneath the top of her jumpsuit. It was a wonder, he knew, that given their unrelenting urges the Quozl had managed to raise any kind of civilization at all.

The Books of the Samizene had changed all that, with a little assist from first traditional medicine and then modern chemistry.

He felt confident and content. He'd spent his whole life preparing for the days to come, knew what was expected of him, knew what he had to do and how to go about doing it. His meditation was dense, his coupling regular and precise, and physiologically he'd never been in better shape. Assurance and high self-esteem radiated from every pore of his being.

So it was a great shock to his system when the whistling shriek filled the recreation chamber, completely drowning out the music and bursting every one of the carefully framed acoustic bubbles.

Games halted in mid-play. Dancers let their feet fall flat on the floor. Dreamtimers awoke with a start and every viewer collapsed in static.

One by one they began to react to the piercing signal. It took that long because it was a signal they had all studied as youngsters but had never heard outside their studies.

It was the General Alarm.

There were many alarm signals and many drills employing them: alarms in case of loss of hull integrity, alarms for depressurization, alarms for water leaks and accidental dispersion of toxic chemicals. They'd practiced and rehearsed how to deal with these theoretical situations and their respective alarms. But there had never been a drill designed to cope with a general alarm because it would have been disruptive to too many important ship's functions.

Which in all likelihood suggested that this was not a drill.

Hesitation was rapidly giving way to movement and action as those around him abandoned their amusements in the rush to their posts, moving in long, leaping Quozl strides. The few mothers with maturing infants went more slowly, careful of the offspring in their pouches. As they did so the General Alarm segued into a second modulated wail that was even more impossible than its predecessor.

Battle stations.

Battle stations? That was an anachronism, an archaic throwback to a primitive past designed to amuse instead of prepare. There was nothing in the universe to battle against. Looks-at-Charts began to slow as new thoughts formed in his head. Consider the situation. They'd just arrived in or close to Shiraz orbit. It was a moment of great import and great release for the majority of the crew, but it was not a game. How better to bring everyone back to reality than by putting an abrupt and shocking damper on their initial enthusiasm?

Quozl ran and dashed around him, pushing but not shoving. There was plenty of a excitement but no panic, no rudeness. No one was trampled or elbowed aside. Looks-at-Charts began to smile inwardly. If he was wrong he would be late reaching his assigned position. That would mean a reprimand. But if he was right . . .

The wailing faded, to be replaced by a calm voice he didn't recognize. He cheered it anyway because it proceeded to confirm his suspicions. A scout, he told himself proudly as others slowed to listen, must have good instincts and the confidence to act on them.

It had indeed been a drill, to alert and place a cap on the unrestrained levity. Time enough for that later, once the colony was in place and the First Burrow established. There were plenty of impolite murmurs and even a few curses from the crowd, but there were also signs of amusement. Leave it to Stream-cuts-Through to re-establish discipline in a fashion none could ignore, and relieve tension at the same time.

Battle stations indeed! Even criminals rarely resorted to actual physical violence, though every Quozl knew how to fight. But there was no one to do battle with. A criminal who resorted to violence would lose status among his own kind, let alone among the general populace.

The Quozl were alone in the universe, the sole intelligence, the keepers of conscious thought. Battle stations call existed to comply with tradition, not reality. There was no one for the colonists to talk to, much less fight.

His communicator whistled for attention. Acknowledging, he was instructed to report not to the main meeting chamber this time but to a smaller one up near Command. He frowned inwardly, then relaxed as he changed direction. Lifts-with-Shout would want to talk to the landing teams separately, in more intimate surroundings than the big chamber offered. Or perhaps he was going to be queried about scouting procedure now that it was at hand, or maybe a final, spontaneous test. It didn't matter. He was ready for anything. Hadn't he divined the actual reason for the General Alarm before anyone else? Or perhaps it was time to select an actual touchdown site for the survey ship. That thought made him walk faster.

He wondered if he dared joke with Stream-cuts-Through if she was present. He wanted to compliment her on the delightful absurdity of sounding General Alarm and battle stations. It really was funny, he told himself. No one had ever accused the Captain of suffering from an excess of humor, and here she'd gone and fooled the whole ship. That made the joke all the more marvelous.

As in the main meeting chamber there was a viewscreen on the left-hand wall, but it was much smaller. There were no rows of seats, not even a central table: only large comfortable chairs in which one could sink and relax. More akin to living quarters than a business room.

Stream-cuts-Through wasn't there when he entered but she arrived presently, her distinctive voice preceding her. Lifts-with-Shout greeted her. Burden-carries-Far sat on the far side of the room. What surprised Looks was that his friend was in animated conversation with Senses-go-Fade. What was the ship's philosopher doing here? Unless, of course, he was present to watch the two scouts as they answered questions and render a verdict on the state of their mental health.

The joke must have already worn thin because he saw no signs of amusement. Quite the contrary. Ears were either laid flat back and down or held stiff and formal. He could see the tenseness in Burden-carries-Far when his colleague turned and saw him. Was something wrong after all? All the confidence with which he'd entered the room abruptly vanished, to be replaced by a horrible thought. It was so horrible he blurted it out without properly presenting himself.

"Battle stations? I thought it was a joke."

It was a measure of the seriousness of the situation that Lifts-with-Shout utterly ignored the scout's awful breach of courtesy.

"No, it wasn't a joke."

Looks-at-Charts heard the door close, tightly, behind him. He barely noted that there was a guard stationed at the door. An armed guard. In all his years he'd never seen an armed guard on board the *Sequencer*. He wondered weakly if the guard was present to keep others out, or him and his companions inside.

"But it was rescinded," he mumbled, sounding not at all mature. "It was declared a drill." Nervously he fiddled with the big earring in his left ear.

The Landing Supervisor's ears crooked ever so slightly. "We reacted the wrong way at first, which is to say we reacted as we should have. That was a mistake, and unnecessary. It was decided rather hastily and on Senses-go-Fade's advice to retract the alarm in order not to panic the ship, since the majority of colonials will have nothing to do with this matter. They must be prepared to receive the information gradually. A parokim tree grows strong only when care is taken in planting."

"But 'battle stations'? That's just for tradition's sake."

"Some traditions have a way of haunting history." Everyone turned to Stream-cuts-Through.

Looks tumbled into a chair. "I still don't understand."

"I was present when the analysis was confirmed," said Burden-carries-Far from nearby. He was as tense as when Looks had entered. "We weren't out of unshifted space very long. Preliminary surveys were well under way when I entered Command. I had a question which I quickly forgot as the situation became apparent."

"*What* situation?" said an exasperated Looks-at-Charts.

"You can imagine the reaction among the onboard survey team," Burden continued with a touch of irony in his voice. "They were as anxious as everyone else to do the tasks for which they had been training all their lives. Instead they found themselves distracted and set to an entirely new work."

"They found something unexpected," Looks said.

Burden's ears went absolutely sideways, parallel to the floor. "At first nobody believed the information that was coming in, but they were right there the instant the *Sequencer* entered Shiraz orbit. Emanations from the surface, mostly in the form of primitive radio waves. Too much to be natural phenomena."

"As we enter nightside you can see it with the naked eye," an obviously troubled Lifts-with-Shout added.

Looks-at-Charts was uncertain. "See it?"

"Light. From population centers. Urban concentrations."

"Artificial illumination." Burden's ears twisted. "Once we saw that, even the most reluctant conceded the obvious."

"Could they be Quozl? Another settlement ship gone off course and come to rest here?"

A senior navigator spoke up from the far side of the room. "Settlement ships don't go 'off course.' Besides, the transmissions are all wrong. There are numerous languages in use down there, and none of them are Quozl."

"And there's another reason," the Landing Supervisor mumbled to himself.

Looks-at-Charts was both anxious and excited. Another intelligence! All the texts insisted that there was no such thing, that the Quozl were alone in the universe and would be so until the end of time. So it fell to the Quozl to fill up the inhabitable worlds with life. That was the Quozl purpose.

Now it appeared that unless all the signs had been misinterpreted they had company. Or competition.

His questions came too fast to sort out. All he could manage was, "What are they like?"

"We don't know," said Stream-cuts-Through softly. "Their multitudinous transmissions are verbal only, no visual. But we know that they cannot be like us."

"How can we know that?"

The Landing Supervisor eyed him sharply. "Because they are at war." All fourteen of the Captain's fingers were interlocked, tight with tension.

Looks-at-Charts tried to mull the implications, found too many contradictions not to question further. By now he had remembered who and where he was.

"I apologize for my ignorance and for my unsatisfied mind, but how can we know such a thing if we cannot even see what they look like?"

Burden explained. "Our instruments are not powerful enough to resolve individual creatures on the surface, but at their best they can detect the existence and movement of large mechanical devices and groups of individuals in motion. There are numerous and constant low-scale explosions, large columns of metal vehicles that come under attack, and at least two large population centers that are undergoing steady bombardment. All this from the most preliminary observations."

"You all understand now," said Stream-cuts-Through, "why this must be kept secret from the majority of the colonials. Information will be discussed at regular meetings here in this sealed room twice a day at times to be determined. Nothing will be sent over normal channels lest it be intercepted by unauthorized personnel. I look forward to hearing your suggestions and comments.

"As far as anyone not involved with touchdown and pre-liminary survey is concerned, prelanding procedures are proceeding normally. I need not add that anyone caught breaching this security matter will be dealt with most harshly. That is all." And she concluded by naming a time for the next gathering.

Like the rest of the landing team, from Lifts-with-Shout on down, Looks-at-Charts was forced to place his emotions as well as his dreams on indefinite hold. Preliminary survey personnel worked under guard and in double shifts to learn as much as possible about the unexpectedly dangerous world of Shiraz. Some of it was reassuring; much was not.

The Captain's first concern was for the safety of the *Sequencer* itself since there was no guarantee that the warlike inhabitants of their new home might not join to turn on alien visitors. That fear was quickly dispelled when it became clear that the natives were incapable of traveling or of sending vehicles beyond the lower reaches of their own atmosphere. Their aircraft were slow and limited in range.

Nor did they possess any sort of long-range detection devices. It appeared that the *Seqencer* was safe in orbit, unreachable and undetectable from the surface except possibly by means of primitive visual scopes. The staff debated briefly and decided that based on what was known of native technology, it was most unlikely they possessed optical devices capable of resolving an object as small as the *Sequencer*. And even if they had the scientific means to do so, it was unlikely they would be taking visual looks at space except for specific astronomical purposes. They were too busy shooting at each other.

Though the conflict appeared to be worldwide it was intense only in specific regions: principally in one part of the largest ocean and on two large land masses. One hemisphere was virtually free of actual combat. It was there that the study group concentrated its efforts.

They had to go down. Looks-at-Charts knew that as well as the Captain, as well as any colonial. The *Sequencer* was designed as a springboard, not as a permanent home. They could not return to Quozlene, could not go elsewhere. Inhabited or not, racked by artificial convulsions or not, Shiraz was now their home. They would have to make the best of the situation.

Nor was there any point in waiting to see what would happen below. If one used Quozlene as a model, then the primitives of Shiraz might well have been fighting for thousands of years, might continue to do battle among themselves for thousands more. It never occurred to the hastily assembled native modeling group that the conflict might only just have begun and might end relatively soon, in Quozl terms. They had no historical precedent on which to formulate such a model. There was war or peace. It was not a stop-and-go matter.

Stream-cuts-Through and the Command section were much more concerned with the technological progress the natives might make under the impetus of war. That had happened on Quozlene. If the natives followed a similar developmental pattern then they might at any time discover how to send weapons beyond the limits of their atmosphere and gravity and thereby threaten the *Sequencer*. It would be far better to establish the First Burrow and proceed in relative safety than to wait for that to happen.

It explained Command's initial reaction. Battle stations had not been a joke. It was only after the survey teams discovered the technological limits of the natives that it had been rescinded. But those limits might change at any time. Before that happened the colonists had to make a move.

It was incredibly frustrating to have crossed so much space only to find themselves thwarted, however momentarily, on the brink of triumph. Looks-at-Charts could not hide all his frustration. His friends noted it and he was forced to seek therapy and spend additional time in meditation. He had plenty of company. Fortunately the crew involved was either isolated from the general ship population or widely scattered among them, so no one not in on the secret became overly suspicious and security was preserved. The great majority of colonists went about the routine of preparing for touchdown unaware of the continuing crisis. There was no panic and security was preserved.

But the longer touchdown was delayed, the longer the *Sequencer* remained in orbit, the harder it became to conceal the knowledge that their new home was already tenanted.

III.

"EVENTUALLY WE MUST persuade these warlike natives to share their world with us." Senses-go-Fade had their undivided attention. The ship's philosopher did not speak often, and when he did he was often ignored. Not today, however.

"Despite the predominance of the oceans there is ample uninhabited land which the natives either cannot or choose not to make use of. Quozl can make a home anywhere. There are vast tracts devoid of the marks of agriculture or urbanization. The other possibility is that this race is still in its infancy and therefore its population is still immature. Regardless of the reason there is ample room for settlement."

"What we need at this point," said Stream-cuts-Through from her central chair in the tiny meeting room, "is not knowledge about Shiraz but about its inhabitants. We have decided that the natives cannot be like us mentally. But the Quozl once fought as they do. Might they not resemble us physically? The biologists tell me that intelligence is unlikely to develop a second time, as it has here, in a radically different physical form. However, just because we might look like one another does not mean they would necessarily welcome us with open arms. We would still be foreign to them. Another tribe to fight, much as the tribes below are in conflict.

"All this is hypothesis. They might also greet us with open arms and unprotected pouches."

"That's likely," said Lifts-with-Shout with a grunt. The Landing Supervisor was not an optimist.

"Precisely our problem." The Captain gestured with one ear in appreciation of the Supervisor's position. "We cannot afford to make a move based solely on guesswork, however admirable that guesswork might be. What hard information we have been able to assemble is taken wholly from long-range, extra-atmospheric study. We need more intimate knowledge."

Looks-at-Charts felt a thrill of excitement race through him but of course said nothing. His status did not permit it.

"There are ethical questions involved as well," said Senses-go-Fade. "While our technology appears to be superior, the *Sequencer* carries only small arms and few of those at that. We cannot simply push intelligent natives off the best settlement sites nor would we if we had the wherewithal to do so. Since we cannot fight them we have two choices left to us: we can cooperate with them, or we can avoid them altogether. Presently it seems only the last option is open to us. I regret this but see the necessity of it."

It would have been different with the ancient, immature Quozl, Looks-at-Charts knew. They would have landed, massacred the locals, taken their land and foodstocks. Civilized behavior had long ago closed off that course to them. It was no longer how the Quozl lived. They could not do anything like that and still remain Quozl.

With luck they would manage. He had studied the preliminary images until his eyes blurred and both lids felt like dead weights. There was so much empty land. They could hide, begin the colony in secret. Perhaps the warring natives would exterminate themselves. That would solve the ethical dilemma.

It would be nice to have friends, though. Nice to know that the burden of maintaining intelligence in the universe no longer fell entirely on Quozl shoulders. Nice to have company—assuming it was friendly and not hostile.

But how could they have achieved mechanical technology while continuing to war? It was enough to drive an intelligent Quozl insane, and it was doing just that to the members of the native study team. How could supposedly intelligent beings cooperate one moment and then turn to internecine combat the next? Shiraz was a place where reality was proving itself surreal.

"We must go down." Lifts-with-Shout was insistent. "We cannot continue to squat in orbit and peer through our scopes like a cycling from its mother's pouch. Each day the colonists grow more restless and that makes it harder to maintain security. We will not learn what we need to know of this world unless we walk upon it, please all to pardon my sharpness." His eyes flicked in the direction of Looks-at-Charts. "Our sensitive touchdown personnel will lose their optimal edge if we wait much longer. Their skills will atrophy from disemployment. It is time not to debate but to *move*."

The Supervisor's forwardness was socially off-putting, but invigorating all the same. Knowing their place, both scouts kept silent. But inwardly they were cheering their superior.

"Remember Mazna." Sense-go-Fade counseled caution with words and ears. "Full of hostile and dangerous, albeit nonintelligent, creatures. I agree we must move, but carefully."

Looks wanted to smash the philosopher's teeth down his throat, hang him up by his ears, crush his toes. Ancient emotions. He meditated furiously.

All waited for a pronouncement from Stream-cuts-Through. "I will call a Council of Seven. We will try to arrive at a consensus."

Looks-at-Charts spent the following day anxiously awaiting word. His status was too low to involve him in the decision-making process. All he and Burden-carries-Far could do was wait to follow instructions. It was the province of the Captain and the Council to decide whether to wait for additional orbital studies to be completed or to proceed with an actual visitation survey. Hard it was to wait, truly, but harder still, he reminded himself, to make decisions that would affect the future of the entire colony.

That didn't stop him from cornering the Landing Supervisor when Lifts-with-Shout emerged from the meeting room.

"Profuse apologies," the scout stammered, "for while I know it is not my place to inquire, my interest is somewhat aroused. Can you possibly hint, my Senior, as to which way the Council is tending in its deliberations?"

Lifts-with-Shout glared at him for appearance's sake. That did not bother Looks-at-Charts. What bothered him was that his Supervisor might choose to say nothing.

Instead he declared thoughtfully, speaking as though the scout was not present, "The vast empty spaces of Shiraz suggest that we can establish First Burrow safely and in secret. Not all are convinced of this, but most agree that we can linger here too long. You are not the only one who wishes to experience the sensation of standing on solid ground and inhaling fresh instead of recycled atmosphere.

"Once First Burrow is proclaimed then we can study the natives quietly and at our leisure, learning about them at close hand, as the child matures in the pouch. This feeling is bolstered by the realization that we have no other choice." The burly Supervisor carefully adjusted a leg scarf.

Looks-at-Charts waited a properly deferential moment. "Do we anticipate violence?" As a sign of respect he adjusted a scarf of his own.

"We do not. We *can*not. If contact proves unavoidable, violence must be abjured, regardless of the consequences. The damage to the Quozl psyche would be worse than anything the natives could do. You and your colleagues must keep that always in mind when you go down."

Looks-at-Charts forgot all his other questions. "Go down? It has been decided, then?"

The Supervisor looked back at the closed door. "Not yet, but it will come soon. They must decide that way. There is no other choice."

Looks-at-Charts breathed deeply but hid it from his Senior lest he be considered impolite. "When?"

"Perhaps as soon as tomorrow. One ship. You, Burden-carries-Far, others to be determined. A full complement."

It made perfect sense, Looks-at-Charts knew. One ship

first, in case of hostilities or unforeseen complications. Survey would take longer, but this way there would be insurance. For those on the *Sequencer*. Not for those who went down first. He reminded himself to lay out his finest attire.

The Landing Supervisor was checking his chronometer. "Who would you take?" he asked unexpectedly.

Looks-at-Charts thought quickly.

"Flies-by-Tail scores highest in simulations. She's quick and sure."

"What about the scientific complement?"

Looks-at-Charts dropped eyes and ears deferentially. "I am not so certain I am qualified to choose among experts not in my field."

"Don't be so modest. You all know each other. Come, I'm asking your advice."

"Since you ask, I would take Breathes-hard-Out as meteorologist and Walks-with-Whispers for geology. I beg indulgence for my poor selections."

"You need a xenologist."

Looks-at-Charts considered. The xenologist would have to be female, since the idea of taking an unbalanced crew was unthinkable. He didn't have to think long.

"Stands-while-Sitting."

Lifts-with-Shout was clearly surprised. "She is fifth generation. I applaud your respect but beg additional explanation."

"I know, but she's still active sexually and anyway, mating considerations and compatability should not be foremost in these determinations. The science group will need internal direction and she'll be senior to the others."

"Some say she is actually fourth generation."

"I don't care. I've met her several times and wouldn't mind mating with her myself. She'll be a steadying influence on the entire sextet, especially if the unforeseen happens and we stumble into any of the natives. I'd like to have her knowledge and experience with us."

"As you wish. I commend your choice, but make certain

◇ **42** ◇

everyone takes the proper coupling suppressants prior to departure.''

Looks-at-Charts acknowledged strongly. ''Time enough for that later if everything goes well. We don't want to be dealing with hormonal distractions on the surface of Shiraz.''

''No, we don't,'' the Landing Supervisor agreed. ''I disagree with none of your choices, and I'm certain the Captain will concur.''

It was all going smoothly enough, Looks thought to himself. They would land, engage in a flurry of studies, select a burrow-site, and bring down the *Sequencer,* all while avoiding contact with the combative natives. Glory without conflict. Their names would fill entire history texts. He was wholly optimistic. He had to be. They all had to be because there was nowhere else for them to go.

Lifts-with-Shout turned to leave but the scout begged a last question. ''Are we positive the natives have no means of detecting the *Sequencer* while we remain in orbit?''

''The group analyzing surface emissions is not positive of anything, but they are relatively certain. We will have to content ourselves with that. Another reason for making haste in securing a burrowsite.'' He hesitated and became for only a moment something less than a Landing Supervisor and more than a friend.

''That doesn't mean we want the survey team indulging in unnecessary risks. You and Burden-carries-Far are the two highest-rated scouts we have trained. It would be catastrophic if the ship were to lose you both. I would also be personally distressed.'' And he turned and hurried off before Looks could say anything.

It was a comforting thought to carry with him as he walked off to find his colleague. They had much to talk about before tomorrow.

''Who could have anticipated such a thing? Who could have imagined it?'' Burden-carries-Far was sipping from a tube, lying on his back with his feet propped comfortably in the air. The lounge was nearly empty except for the two scouts. Everyone else was on duty. *Their* work would start tomorrow. "What do you think they'll be like?"

"It's not our job to find out. It's our job to secure the immediate landing site and protect the scientific team."

"I know what our job is." Burden stared languorously at the ceiling. The contents of the tube were affecting him. "They might have cold blood and external skeletons."

"Not according to the techs co-opted for the native studies group. They say they'll probably look a lot like us."

"That lot of spring humpers?" Burden made a derisive noise. "I wouldn't place much reliance on their ravings. If only their broadcasts contained visuals!"

"Apparently their technology hasn't advanced that far, and we can't wait for them to develop visual to accommodate our curiosity. We must get down and in quickly. We don't even know what their climate will be like for certain."

"So you don't trust these long-range approximations either. I thought as much." Burden was clearly amused. "Me, I'm not making any evaluations until I breathe the stuff personally."

"Not that weather matters very much since we'll be burrowing," Looks muttered. "We have one thing in our favor: Shiraz is severely underpopulated. We ought to be able to find an adequate and hidden site without too much difficulty."

"All that water." Burden-carries-Far stared at the colored bubbles in his drinking tube. "If only we were river motiles." He let out a series of short, sharp barks. Listeners would have taken umbrage, but not inside a lounge.

"I wonder how long contact will be delayed," Looks murmured.

"If they're primitive enough to war among themselves I'd think the Council would try to avoid it as long as possible. Don't fret, my friend. There will be plenty to observe. I don't think we will lack for excitement. A whole new world lies before us, and the flora and fauna can't be very hostile. Not if these natives, primitive as they are, have managed to develop civilization."

"Not necessarily. Who knows what another sentient race might do, how they might think and act? You are theorizing as a Quozl. Shirazian thought processes might be utterly different. Reason says they should have exterminated themselves by now, not maintained their present level of barbarism."

He slept only with the aid of heavy meditation tapes. The magnitude of what they were about to do, the responsibility, was beginning to sink in.

In the morning the six members of the initial survey team were shown the drop site. It was located east of the mountains of the war-free northern continent, in high foothills. The land was almost unpopulated and the vast empty mountains would help to conceal the survey vessel's approach as it dropped down over the frozen wastes of the northern polar region. The nearest native population center was an enormous distance away.

Breathes-hard-Out wondered what they would do if their presence was detected by hostile native aircraft. Lifts-with-Shout replied that based on their observations of the ongoing native conflict, the fastest Shirazian craft hardly moved fast enough to stay aloft. As for the drop site itself, the study team would have preferred a couple of years to choose a place. They did not have that time.

The survey ship was small and narrow. Two sets of flexible wings folded tight against the fuselage for extra-atmospheric travel. Flies-by-Tail was already there when the others arrived. She'd been busy with the mechanics all morning, questioning them on the smallest details, making certain the backup systems for the backup systems were in full working order. At the last moment it would be up to her, not Lifts-with-Shout or the Captain or anyone else, to decide whether the team would drop or not.

Everyone wore full scout suits instead of the more comfortable but less attractive onboard jumpsuits. No scarves, but they were permitted a normal complement of jewelry. Looks-at-Charts checked his multiple earrings. They were not expected to do their work completely naked. The full suit was reassuring. He did not entirely trust the study team's assessment of Shiraz's mild climate.

It was also comforting to know that native aircraft had yet to be observed overflying the drop site. It was as remote as it was protected.

Burden-carries-Far looked nervous despite his usual bravado. Looks wondered how the Landing Supervisor and the others perceived him. They kept their opinions to themselves. The six were the best the *Sequencer* could put forward. Now was not the time to show lack of confidence.

He studied his companions for the historic journey. Breathes-hard-Out was tending to her shaving, plucking at contrary follicles to ensure she looked her best. She noticed his stare and ignored him, a sure sign their hormonal suppressants were doing their job. Stands-while-Sitting stood off by herself, silent and composed and slightly regal as befitted the senior member of the landing team. The only one unable to hide his nervousness was Walks-with-Whispers. The geologist was a worrier. It was not severe enough to compromise his brilliance, but Looks made a mental note to ensure that Walks was always assigned a companion, both on board and off. His anxieties could complicate matters in an emergency.

Except that there weren't going to be any emergencies, he reminded himself firmly. The first landing on Shiraz was going to be dull, predictable routine, nothing more.

He had a few words with Walks before they boarded.

"I'm fine," the geologist assured him. "Just think what we are about to do! I am to be the first of my profession to examine the surface of a new world, a world never before visited by Quozl. It is almost too much!"

Looks-at-Charts kept his reply deliberately low-key. "Why? Aren't rocks the same everywhere?" He was careful to remain clear of Walks's Sama space.

"They are *not*," said Walks with emphasis. His eyes flicked to the ramp that led into the ship. "No more time for talk, is there? Now is for real."

"And forever," Looks finished solemnly for him. "Don't worry. Everything will go smoothly."

"I know that," said the geologist as he turned to board, "but I wish there were no natives. No, that's not true. I wish they were *civilized*."

"Maybe they'll surprise us."

"I doubt it." Walks-with-Whispers started up the ramp, his sandaled splay feet slapping on the plastic.

The formal ceremony of departure was brief and affecting. Stream-cuts-Through was not present. She was in the command center overseeing every aspect of the drop.

Since the native's transmission-interception capabilities were still a matter for hypothesis it had been decided to limit contact between the *Sequencer* and the survey team. They would talk only as absolutely necessary until they returned. Then there would be ample time for conversation.

Looks-at-Charts had ridden the simulators hundreds of times to the surfaces of as many imaginary worlds, but despite the simulator's accuracy he discovered it was not the same. He heard Flies-by-Tail's voice, watched her delicate fingers touch the few critical instruments not controlled by the ship's brain, but it was different. Different because it was not a simulation. Reality, he thought, has its own flavor.

Then they were floating free, clear of the *Sequencer*'s artificial gravity, falling without seeming to fall toward the blue-white curve not so very far below. Burden-carries-Far sat on his right, unnaturally silent and introspective.

Both scouts were qualified pilots, but that was not their specialty. Both knew they could not have managed the descent nearly so well as Flies-by-Tail, and they admired her skill as the little vessel was swallowed by air. The trio of scientists were secured in back, each in a private room-lab, watching the drop on monitors. Looks felt sorry for them. It was not the same as being here, in forward command, watching Shiraz rise rapidly toward you.

Their new home was a vast gemstone awash in spilt milk, a water-filled pouch dotted with land. The *Sequencer*, the only home any of them had ever known, was reduced to a simple schematic on a small monitor screen.

Looks inhaled deeply, reflectively. The children of Quozlene were leaving the Pouch. How fortunate Shiraz would be to have them.

They bumped and slewed as they fell through the gratifyingly thick atmosphere, the four wings taking the buffeting efficiently, the counterdrive howling as it fought to reduce their velocity. Anyone watching their descent would see only a falling meteorite, he knew.

They could see the surface now. The instrumentation which had been hastily installed to alert them to the caress of a locating beam or transmission remained mute. No one was observing their approaching with anything more advanced then the naked eye.

Suddenly he was aware of the painful tension in his body. He'd been sitting so stiffy his muscles ached. He recited the relaxing exercises and concentrated on Flies-by-Tail as she brought them down. Thanks to the suppressants coursing through his system he was able to admire the smooth curve of her shoulders, the lean nape of her neck, and the delicate arch of her ears without anxiety. He focused on the top half of a particularly complex whorl shaved into the fur of her upper left shoulder where it peeked out from beneath the seal of her duty suit.

They were coming down too fast, toying with the safety margin, cutting across snow-clad peaks and the crest of a vast green forest. His Quozl soul leaped. *Real* trees. Hard-grained wood. He tried to isolate details among the green and brown blur beneath them.

He could feel his weight again. Gravity slightly less than that of the *Sequencer* and Quozlene. A noticeable but not significant difference.

Then they were down, hardly a bump or jolt as Flies-by-Tail coasted on the landing skids to a halt opposite the nearest trees. Through the port Looks-at-Charts saw they were tall and straight and nearly identical, but at that point their resemblance to the trees of Quozlene ended. Instead of leaves these growths were clad in some kind of green fur. It was difficult to be certain at a distance but they looked like nothing in any of the botany texts. Nor were they visibly kin to any of the growths discovered on the three colony worlds. Yet trees they surely were, however alien.

At least Burden-carries-Far kept his mind on his work. "We can't stay here. We're too exposed." He gestured forward with an ear. "There's an opening large enough to admit the ship."

Flies-by-Tail acknowledged and the little vessel rose on hovering jets as she maneuvered them toward the green wall. Dust accompanied the passage of the ship.

They were crossing a small meadow, water and green growing things dancing beneath the hovering jets. Then over a narrow stream which emptied into a small lake. On the far side of the lake was a reasonably flat open place bordered by a number of fallen trees whose roots had been undermined by an ancient flood. Flies-by-Tail managed to back the survey ship halfway under the largest. There was a bump as she struck wood, then a sigh as she cut the hovering jets. They settled to the ground beneath the natural lean-to.

The hardest thing Looks-at-Charts had ever done was to restrain himself while the necessary preliminary checks were run. Long-range measurements and estimates had to be confirmed, new tests done. Though it seemed to take an eternity, the first results appeared on the ship's instrumentation in rapid succession.

The air was breathable, the temperature tolerable. They would not have to wear cumbersome equipment. Flies-by-Tail looked longingly at the lake, wondering what the water of Shiraz might taste like—and what potentially upsetting microorganisms it might harbor.

The second disappointment was personal. As had been prearranged, he and Burden-carries-Far spun a random-numbers disc, and Looks lost. He did his best to conceal his unhappiness, congratulating his colleague, who was appropriately

◇ 49 ◇

apologetic for having won. Burden offered the honor to Looks, who formally declined, whereupon the joyful Burden sorrowfully prepared to open the hatch door and be the first to set foot on the Shirazian surface.

They donned side arms, a necessary precaution which had been learned the hard way on hostile Mazna. Such fears and worries as they held, however, vanished the moment the hatch was opened and the descent ramp extended itself.

The air was thick and warm, full of the scent of living things. They had to paused lest it overwhelm them, like a dozen rich desserts consumed without pause. The air was alive with whistling sounds, not akin to the noise the Quozl made among themselves but sweeter. Clicks and burrps came from deep within the high green plants that lined the sides of the lake. Looks-at-Charts studied the stream which ran almost directly beneath the descent ramp.

"Water. Fresh, not recycled."

"Water is water, I guess." Burden-carries-Far marched unceremoniously down the ramp and into the shallow stream, letting it flow over his sandaled feet and soak his fur. "Cold," he informed them, promptly violating every procedure in the texts by bending to scoop up a handful and conveying it to his mouth.

Looks heard Walks-with-Whispers gasp behind him, felt Stands-while-Sitting push against his back. "Don't do that!"

The scout flung droplets from his fingers and eyed her amusedly. "Nice taste." He turned and jumped the rest of the stream. "Let's get moving."

Looks-at-Charts hurried down the ramp, followed by Stands-while-Sitting. Flies-by-Tail watched enviously from the pilot's chair. She could not leave the ship until the scouts declared the immediate vicinity secured. Breathes-hard-Out would remain aboard to continue her atmospheric studies.

Walks-with-Whispers was a different matter. Neither scout particularly desired the geologist's company while they made their initial observations, but since there was no visible danger they could not insist he remain on board. After a good deal of verbal posturing and feinting it was decided that he could come and go as he required so long as he stayed within view of the pilot's chair. He agreed reluctantly but was soon so busy gathering rock and soil samples he'd completely forgotten the disagreement.

That left the two scouts and their senior xenologist free to tramp through the forest as they pleased.

It was a wonderful environment, Looks-at-Charts thought. Better than they could have hoped for. No wonder it had nursed intelligent life. The strange furry trees towered around them on all sides, their blood the source of heavy, pungent odors that managed to be simultaneously alien and reassuring.

It didn't take long to locate the source of the high whistling sounds they'd heard immediately upon arrival. They issued from small winged creatures that darted between the trees on lithe, dark wings. While the calls of the larger aerials sometimes resembled higher-pitched Quozl speech it was obvious they could not be the dominant species.

"I don't think anything so small and fragile could develop intelligence," was Burden-carries-Far's evaluation. Their opinion was confirmed when they saw a pair of the creatures settle into a mud and stick bowl atop one large branch. It was clear the structure was not the product of advanced technology.

More impressive than the flitting, mysterious noises that filled the alien woods were the smells. Shiraz was an aromatic paradise. There seemed no attempt by either the flora or fauna to disguise their identifying odors, as there was on Quozlene. Perhaps animals here did not feed as often by smell, or perhaps a different mechanism was at work. That was for Stands-while-Sitting and the scientific teams aboard *Sequencer* to decide. All he had to do was enjoy it. He almost forgot to monitor his appearance.

You could suffer sensory overload on Shiraz simply by standing in one place and letting the fragrances and sounds come to you, he decided. But they were instructed to cover as much ground as possible. Looks-at-Charts had chosen this direction for a reason, because of something he thought he'd glimpsed just prior to touchdown. It was a reason Lifts-with-Shout might not have agreed with, but they were out of touch with the *Sequencer* now and on their own until they returned. Besides, a scout was supposed to employ initiative when he thought the occasion demanded it. That was all he was doing.

Burden-carries-Far did not comment on his colleague's choice of direction. Stands-while-Sitting might have overruled him, but she said nothing, apparently quite content to let the two younger scouts take the lead while she immersed herself in examining their extraordinary surroundings.

Sweet old tail, thought Looks-at-Charts. She's as anxious to find answers to all our questions as any of us.

Though their suits contained emergency supplies sufficient to keep them going for several days, Looks had no intention of being away from the scout vessel that long. They would make their preliminary survey and then return. Flies-by-Tail would not be alarmed, however, if they kept out of touch for a while. They were supposed to use their hand communicators to contact her only in an emergency situation.

He had no intention of studying only trees and flying creatures on this visit. They had to find out more than that, no matter the caution of the Captain or Lifts-with-Shout or the Council of Seven. They had to learn something of what they were up against, of what they might have to deal with if events didn't proceed as planned. That was what he intended all along. He sensed that Burden-carries-Far would go along with him if the opportunity he hoped for arose. If not there would be a power dance to end all power dances.

Meanwhile he could delight in their new surroundings, knowing that all immediate decisions were up to Stands-while-Sitting. In a sense, he and Burden were along solely to convoy and protect her, though their own observations would of course also be of inestimable value to those anxiously awaiting their reports back on the *Sequencer*.

''See.'' Burden-carries-Far knelt to recover a sharp-edged, fist-sized brown object. He pointed to several identical modules hanging from the branches of a nearby tree. "Some type of seed pod."

"Or botanical defense mechanism," said Stands-while-Sitting dryly.

The scout half dropped it but at the last instant decided to hang on, unsure whether their experienced colleague was joking or quite serious. In any event the object did not explode in his hand or bleed toxic sap. He inspected it closely, then tied it to one of the scarves attached to his left leg. It bounced decoratively with each long stride.

Not to be outdone, Looks-at-Charts found some delicate bright flowers and secured them to the shoulder strap of his suit. He could smell them without having to turn his nose in their direction. Everything on Shiraz seemed more intense than on the ship: the colors, the aromas, the clarity of the air, everything. This new world glowed and stank with beauty. It would take olfactory specialists years just to catalog the local range of smells. What other wonders lay ahead, just around the next tree or slight hillock?

A while later they paused for a brief meal. Everything was proceeding according to plan, both that designed for them and Looks's own private one. They'd encountered no hostile fauna or natives, only beauty in abundance. An easy place in which to be seduced, he reflected. That would not happen. It was one reason why he and Burden had been chosen for this singular honor. They could not and would not be distracted from their duty.

They encountered plenty of active diurnal fauna as they made their way through the forest. In particular they saw many small furry creatures who made their homes high up in the trees and bombarded them with irritated chittering sounds. They bore a comical but only passing resemblance to tiny Quozl. There was also a slightly larger ground-dwelling creature whose ears superficially resembled those of the Quozl, though they were incapable of twisting and moving in the intricate signing patterns that were second nature to the visitors.

A larger quadruped provided considerably more excitement

when they chanced across it in a small clearing. Both scouts instinctively reached for their weapons only to be stopped by Stands-while-Sitting.

"Use your eyes and your studies," she whispered to them as she recorded the encounter with her imager. "It's clearly no carnivore. No cutting teeth or claws."

The delicate brown creature stared at them for a long while before turning to trot off into the brush. "See! There's another," said Burden, gesturing with both ears. A smaller, spotted version of the first animal followed close behind, provoking debate among the trio of travelers as to whether it was the young or a completely different species.

The argument had not been resolved by the time they reached the edge of the forest, right where Looks-at-Charts had guessed it would be. A broad open plain stretched out before them. The ground had been sliced with parallel grooves. Clearly machinery and not natural erosion had been at work here.

Stands-while-Sitting hesitated. "We should return to the forest."

"Nonsense!" Looks-at-Charts advanced confidently toward a fence fashioned of wooden stakes linked together by metal wire. "There's no danger here." He fingered one of the pointed barbs attached to the wire. "Look how primitive. Much simpler and more effective to pass a field between posts. They must not have that technological capability."

"Or perhaps each bard is tipped with a toxic substance," said Stands-while-Sitting thoughtfully.

Looks lost a good portion of his confidence, quickly inspected his finger. The barb had not penetrated through his fur to the skin. He inhaled deeply, then turned and made a gesture of abasement to his Senior.

"You're right. It was a foolish thing to do. I am unworthy of my training."

"None of us is perfect." Stands had come up beside him to study the fence. "So much newness is overwhelming. We do not always think before we act." Her gaze rose and she gestured to her left. "Since you are evidently bound to advance, let us do so over there."

A small stream had cut away the earth beneath the fence and they were able to crawl through without touching the lowermost strand of armed wire. Then they were strolling through the recently plowed field.

"I wonder what they grow here," murmured Looks-at-Charts.

Burden-carries-Far kicked at the hard earth. "From the looks of it I'd say not much. See how tough the soil is, how poorly mulched."

They continued to the top of a slight rise, whereupon at Burden's signal they all dropped to their bellies.

A structure stood in a clump of trees not far away. No, several structures, Looks saw at second glance. The largest had an arched roof and unsealed openings. The nearest was marginally more elaborate in design and execution. Sunlight reflected off windows or ports.

A cleared path ran from the east end of the building to connect to a much larger path that ran from south to north, vanishing over both horizons. There was no sign of movement.

Feeling the blood pounding through his veins, Looks forced himself to recite several passages from the Eighth Book of the Samizene. It calmed him sufficiently to rationally consider their situation. Clearly they were looking at a native dwelling, perhaps several of them.

"I wonder what to do." Stands-while-Sitting was torn between her innate conservatism and a desperate desire to have a look inside the structures below. Were any natives present their course would be clear: avoid contact at all costs. But the grounds appeared deserted.

They observed for a long time but the only movement came from small quadrupeds and fowl who clearly belonged to nonsentient orders.

"Perhaps it has been abandoned," suggested Burden hopefully.

"It appears too well maintained." Stands backed away from the crest of the little hill and considered. "Yet it seems the inhabitants are not present. We will return to the woods and spend the night there," she decided, "and come back in the morning. If after adequate observation we still sight no natives, then it might be propitious to proceed."

Looks-at-Charts was all for dashing down the opposite slope immediately, but without a valid reason to do so it was Stands-while-Sitting's decision that would prevail. She was Senior. And in this he was properly obedient.

IV.

THEY SPENT A restless night, not because of the alien nocturnal noises but because of the thought of what they might see tomorrow. Burden was up before the Shirazian sun, waking his companions and breaking camp.

They marched back to the top of the rise and waited and watched from there until the two scouts were writhing in an agony of impatience. Finally even Stands-while-Sitting had to admit that the place seemed deserted. They had to restrain themselves from running down the opposite slope once she gave permission to advance.

- Up close, the structure did not appear nearly so solidly built as it had from a distance, in spite of having been fashioned of that noble material, wood. The base was constructed of rough-hewn stone.

As they cautiously made their way around to the front of the building they were surprised by the presence of several small feathered creatures busily scratching and kicking at the dusty soil. They ignored Stands-while-Sitting as she recorded their activities, even when she came quite close. This behavioral pattern was quite different from that which had been observed among the small inhabitants of the deep forest.

"Tamed," commented Looks-at-Charts, "but for what purpose? Do you suppose the natives eat them?"

"They certainly don't maintain them for protection." Burden-carries-Far gave a desultory flick of his left ear.

To no one's surprise they discovered that the doorway was

sealed. Careful study suggested that the only thing holding the barrier closed was a simple metal lock. This was easily subverted. They entered with Burden in the lead and Looks bringing up the rear, the two younger scouts convoying their Senior.

At first the feeling of alienness was overwhelming, but as they walked around the outer room Looks-at-Charts began to relax. There were structures and artifacts whose purpose was easily divined. A soft mat covering the floor was intended to provide a more comfortable walking surface. There were objects to sit upon, which while not built to Quozl proportions were still usable for that purpose. These creatures, Looks mused, must have very short legs and no feet at all.

When they had completed a quick, cursory inspection of all the rooms in the building and had satisfied themselves that it was unoccupied, they began to examine specific artifacts in more detail. Small switches set in the walls produced light in glass bulbs. Other, larger bulbs contained smelly liquid which Stands-while-Sitting suggested could be ignited to produced additional light.

The food preparation area contained a large metallic structure which kept food cool. Burden-carries-Far was all for sampling some alien edibles, but his intention was firmly vetoed by their xenologist. It was one thing to be adventurous, quite another to act in foolhardy fashion.

"It smells quite palatable," Burden argued.

"That means nothing. They may contain all kinds of potentially lethal bacteria." Stands-while-Sitting did consent to letting them drink the water which was provided by a small spigot, as Burden had already sampled some in the wild and had as yet shown no ill effects from the reckless consumption.

They returned to the main room, where Looks let out a sharp whistle at the most important discovery so far. His companions rushed to join him in studying the flat images attached to the back wall.

The means of reproduction used was primitive and two-dimensional, but it was sufficient to give them their first look at the natives of Shiraz.

"They look like us and yet they don't." Burden's gaze moved in slow fascination from one image to the next. He shuddered slightly. "They're furless. That, or they shave their whole bodies right down to the skin."

"Look at all that clothing." Looks pointed to the nearest picture. "Perhaps they only shave their exposed parts and are properly furred underneath."

"I think Burden is correct," said Stands. "They may need the extra garments to protect them from the weather if they are naturally hairless on their bodies." She tapped one glass-covered image. "Yet they have some fur on their heads. Look how long it grows!"

"Perhaps it is a mating attractant," Looks suggested.

The faces were more alien than the bodies. There were two eyes, true, but they were much smaller than those of the Quozl. Instead of lying close to the face, the nostrils protruded in a long, bony structure and were the same color as the rest of the bare skin. Only the mouths were reasonably similar, though those of the aliens were slightly wider. In several of the images the natives displayed their teeth in hostile gestures.

As for ears, Looks thought the natives possessed none at all. It was left to Stands to identify the tiny, wrinkled structures located (of all places) on the *sides* of the skull as possible organs of hearing. Looks had thought them simply ornamental fleshy growths. They appeared far too small to serve any useful function.

"That can't be," muttered Burden-carries-Far. "How could they hear anything with ears like that?"

"It may be that their hearing and vision are not as acute as ours," said Stands-while-Sitting.

"Deaf and blind. Maybe dumb as well." Burden's ears twitched contemptuously. "They certainly don't look dangerous. See, this one is displaying its teeth. The cutting teeth are small and inoffensive. They can't have much biting power."

"Don't underestimate them," Stands warned him. "They possess perfectly effective weapons."

Burden was whistling his disgust. "I don't see how they can chew enough food to survive."

"Perhaps they don't. Perhaps their metabolisms are slower than ours and they require less nourishment. That would be an advantage."

A couple of full-length images offered clues to the rest of the natives' physiognomies. Each hand had five digits instead of the Quozl seven, which suggested inferior manipulative capabilities. One could not tell about the feet because in every image these were completely enclosed in some type of covered sandal. Two of the pictures were apparently of females. The Shirazians were truly alien. Instead of being protected inside the pouch, the female nursing organs were located on the chest and in clear view beneath heavy clothing.

"The females have slightly more fur." Burden examined the frozen images carefully. "The hips are wider, perhaps to allow for a wholly internal pouch."

With her recorder Stands-while-Sitting made careful copies of all the two-dimensional images. The scouts resumed their inspection of the building and its contents. But it was left to the xenologist to solve the riddle of the large boxy device that stood against the far wall.

Burden and Looks were debating the purpose of a large, vented, cavelike opening in one wall. The floor of its interior was swathed in ashes, but they contended as to whether the opening was intended for cooking or heating.

They were startled out of their argument by the sudden, sharp rasp of alien voices. These issued from the mysterious box. At the first sound Stands had jerked aside, but resumed fiddling with the front-mounted dials positioned beneath a now glowing transparent rectangle as soon as it became clear that the device was harmless. The rectangle was covered with alien squiggles. Some form of primitive writing, perhaps. Turning one dial caused a solid marker to move back and forth between the squiggles.

Looks-at-Charts eyed the box warily. "A communications device of some kind?"

"I don't think so." Stands-while-Sitting continued to adjust the dials, varying voices and volume. "I have addressed it in several ways and there is no response whatsoever. I think it is simply a machine to listen to."

They left it on as they continued their inspection. Several times the air in the room was filled with the realistic thunder of explosions, and sounds that were suspiciously like the screams of the injured or dying.

"Viewplays with sound only?" hypothesized Burden, pausing in his work to listen to one particularly tormented sequence.

"Possibly," murmured Stands. "But remember the orbital observations and resultant analysis. These primitives are warring with one another." She gestured at the box with an ear. "It may not be a simple simulation."

They lived with that sobering thought as they continued their work, inspecting, recording, and trying to commit everything in the structure to memory, until Stands-while-Sitting happened to glance out a window. She checked her chronometer.

"The day is ending, a shorter one than we are used to. We must leave."

The scouts were reluctant to abandon the dwelling. "Perhaps the length of hair is related to social status as opposed to gender," said Looks.

"No, I think it's the other way around," Burden-carries-Far argued as he turned toward the entrance. It was dim inside the building now.

"We will try to return tomorrow." Stands-while-Sitting's voice was thick with reluctance. "There is so much to try and absorb. This was not planned." She eyed Looks suspiciously as she spoke. "But having found the right tree we would be remiss in not girdling it completely." Her gaze turned to the talking box. It squawked noisily, imparting vital information they could not comprehend. She wished they could take it with them, but it would be missed, and it was really too heavy and bulky to haul all the way back to the survey ship. She moved to turn it off.

"I agree wholesoully." Burden started toward the front door.

He was halfway there when it was opened from the other side. Final sunlight poured in and made him shield his eyes.

"I thought I heard . . . ," roared an intense, painfully loud voice before breaking off in mid-sentence.

The vision in the doorway imprinted itself permanently on Looks-at-Charts's mind in the seconds of silence that followed. It was not horrible or frightening, just ugly. Like the two-dimensional images hung on the wall, it had fur growing atop its otherwise bald skull, and very little of it at that. Unlike the pictures they'd examined, it also had a massive mat of tangled hair exploding from its face. It was taller and more massively built than any of them. Looks realized with a start that the images they'd studied had given no ready clue as to the actual size of the natives. If anything, the design of the furniture seemed to indicate they were shorter, so the actual appearance of the native was quite a shock. They had no feet, as suspected, but their legs were longer than he'd imagined, and their torsos unconventionally large.

He and Stands instinctively held their ground while Burden reacted. Not knowing what else to do, he assumed a formal greeting posture, ears down and hands at his side. When the native did not respond, the scout attempted to make him feel welcome. With his right hand he reached for the native's face with all seven fingers, to demonstrate acceptance and friendship.

Instead of complementing the gesture by reaching for Burden's face with his five-fingered paw, the native raised the metal tube he was carrying and let out a deafening shout.

"Christ! Martians!"

A puff of smoke enveloped the end of the tube and the room was filled with the echo of an impressive explosion. Everything happened very quickly after that.

Burden-carries-Far halted with his still welcoming hand an arm's length from the native's face. He retreated a couple of steps and stopped, staring down at himself. Blood was leaking from a hole in his chest. Touching himself with the hand that had been extended in greeting, he let out a piercing, high-pitched squeal.

This upset the Shirazian visibly. Looks-at-Charts saw him start to bring the metal tube around to point at Stands-while-Sitting, who stood paralyzed next to one of the native chairs. As a scout he was instructed to act and leave thinking to those better qualified. In any event there was no time to think.

Drawing his side arm, he aimed at the native and fired. The weapon hummed softly and the Shirazian stumbled. As he did so he emitted a much feebler noise than had Burden-carries-Far. Directing his attention at Looks, he tried to point his metal tube with shaking hands. Incredulous, Looks fired again. The metal tube *boomed* and something flew to pieces behind the scout, who had to fire three more times before the native finally keeled over.

Some kind of natural shielding, Looks thought as he stood breathing hard and cautiously eyeing the fallen Shirazian. Or else their nervous systems differ from ours.

Closer inspection revealed that the native was no longer breathing. Only when Looks was certain that the threat had been dealt with did he allow himself to join Stands-while-Sitting in examining Burden's body.

He and Looks-at-Charts had practically grown up together since leaving their mother's pouches. They'd studied and played together, had gone through similar study years together, had coupled in parallel. He'd always been the bolder of the two. Now, in his eagerness to make contact, he'd done something terribly wrong. Precisely what they would have to wait to find out.

That didn't matter now. What mattered was that none of their medical training could bring him back to life.

"The hole passes completely through him," Stands murmured as she put down her scanner. "It penetrated his heart. I am sorry. He would have been a strong coupler."

"The strongest. The most elegant." Looks could hardly

muster a whisper. He rose and began the ceremony of passing only to find he could not go through with it. Burden had been too close to him.

He left it for Stands-while-Sitting to complete while he stood guard outside. But in the gathering darkness no more of the ferocious natives appeared. When she'd finished she rejoined him. Together they stared at the rising circle of Shiraz's moon.

"Perhaps this native dwelt here alone," she finally said.

Looks turned on her. "Without a female?"

"We know nothing of their sexual habits." She looked back through the open doorway. "We must take Burden-carries-Far with us. We cannot leave him here for some wandering native to find. All trace of our visit must be erased."

Looks-at-Charts considered. "That means we must remove the body of the native as well, since he was," he found himself choking on the word as the enormity of what he'd done began to sink in, "killed by a Quozl weapon that is certainly different from the one the native utilized."

"Can you carry it? I can manage Burden."

"I'll carry it," Looks-at-Charts assured her. "I have no choice."

With water from the food processing area and chemicals from their packs they obliterated all traces of Shirazian and Quozl blood from the room. Stands went through the entire dwelling to ensure everything was placed as they'd first found it. Then they left. Not as they'd arrived, in light and hope, but in darkness and despair.

It was one thing to insist he would carry the body of the Shirazian, quite another to actually attempt it. They'd gone no farther than a few steps when Looks had to halt and lower his burden.

"It's impossible," he wheezed. "It weighs as much as any two Quozl."

Stands-while-Sitting surveyed their surroundings. The large moon provided ample light to see by. "Let us look around and see what we may find."

◇ **64** ◇

What they finally found was a large platform mounted on two wheels. A pair of metal handgrips protruded from one end. They placed the native on the platform and Burden-carries-Far atop him. Then each of them hefted one of the handles, raising the platform off the ground at an angle and resting the majority of the dead weight on the two wheels. Using this device they were able to wrestle their grisly cargo up the gentle hill and into the plowed fields that led toward the woods. At regular intervals they paused to retrace their steps and obliterate their tracks and those of the platform's wheels.

The fence which had been so easily avoided proved a major obstacle on their return. They had to wrestle one body at a time over the wire, then the platform, and lastly themselves, being careful as always not to leave any torn fragments of clothing on the wire or any trace of their passage. It was morning before they reached the edge of the forest.

It was harder to push the overburdened platform through the forest, but they felt safer beneath the cover of the furred trees. Though the task before them required most of their energy and concentration both still found time to replay the disastrous events of the previous evening over and over in their minds.

The native had responded to Burden's gesture of welcome with instant death, without trying to communicate or ascertain what the Quozl scout was attempting to do. He'd killed instinctively. And Burden's side arm had been pouched at the time. Stands-while-Sitting theorized that the native had been startled by their unexpected presence in its dwelling, but that didn't excuse the magnitude and incivility of its overreaction. It should at least have waited to see what they might do in response to its arrival.

Unless this particular native was an aberration, a mental defective, it meant that Shiraz was a deceptive paradise. How could they make contact, make peace with creatures so murderously uncivilized? Who still warred among themselves and slew friendship-seeking strangers on sight? These were not encouraging thoughts to contemplate on the long march back to the survey ship.

Would it always be like this, Looks-at-Charts wondered? Violence and death upon confrontation? He voiced his concerns to Stands-while-Sitting.

"It cannot be. There are only a few thousand of us. You saw the lights of the native urban areas from orbit. They must number in the many millions, perhaps in the billions. Our weapons may be more advanced but they are designed only to cope with hostile unintelligent fauna. Though primitive, the projectile device the native used to kill Burden-carries-Far was perfectly effective. And you saw how difficult it was to put down. Any conflict with the Shirazians would surely result in our annihilation. Even if we succeeded in fighting back, the psychological damage to our own people would be as devastating as their deaths." She eyed him curiously. "How are you coping?"

"With difficulty. I put it out of my mind as best I can, but it isn't easy. And I have had specialized training. I understand your concerns. What can we do? We are stuck with Shiraz and its insane inhabitants."

"It is not for you and me to decide."

It might have been the most calming thing the xenologist could have said. Looks-at-Charts relaxed as he realized that the limits of his personal responsibility in this matter were finite. Final decisions would be up to the Captain and Lifts-with-Shout and the Council of Seven. All he and Stands-while-Sitting had to do was make their respective reports. Then he could turn himself in for treatment.

He had slain another intelligent being. The fact that it was not Quozl did not diminish the magnitude of the act. Right now he had no time to think. When he did he knew that his sanity would be at stake. The ethical conflict might do him in. Stands-while-Sitting's concern for his health was not misplaced.

There was also the shock of having seen his friend killed. There'd been no reason for it, no reason at all. It was significant that the native had been equipped with a killing device. Did they all carry such weapons with them wherever they went, much as he was never without scarves and earrings? Death as decoration? Who ever heard of carrying a weapon into one's own dwelling place?

"Barbarians whose technology has exceeded their social maturity," was Stands-while-Sitting's opinion. "They have not yet learned how to sublimate their violent tendencies in art and other forms of social discourse as have we. They operate sophisticated machinery with unsophisticated minds. Socially that creates a volatile situation. I wish we could learn something more of their psychology. That will have to wait until the philologists can decipher their language. One thing is clear: their violent tendencies are reflected in their behavioral responses. That's why they are so loud. The very volume of their speech is an indication of their unrestrained primitiveness."

"We know so little about them. How can we learn enough to cope without exposing ourselves?"

"Leave that to the experts. All I know is that the *Sequencer* cannot stay up, therefore it must come down. We are going to have to live here."

It was growing dark once again, the short Shirazian day springing dusk upon them like a fisher's net. They found a place to camp beneath one of the largest furred trees. The two-wheeled platform holding the bodies of Burden-carries-Far and the dead native stood outlined against the dimming light, a mobile icon of failure.

"There was no female present at the dwelling," Looks-at-Charts commented. "How can that be possible? Surely the native was sexually mature?"

"Perhaps their frequency of coupling is somewhat less than ours." Stands-while-Sitting was contemplating the alien woods, toying with one of the sharp green prongs that served these trees in place of proper leaves. "They might skip a day or two. Possibly that is where the native had been." She turned sharply to face him. "Speaking of which . . ."

It struck Looks that because of their preoccupation with the events of the last couple of days neither of them had remembered to take their daily suppressants. The familiar Quozl trill rushed through him unbidden.

There was no need for words in this strange forest. They comforted each other eight times that night. When morning arrived he felt much better than he would have if they'd spent the time reciting Samizene verses to one another.

The shock felt by those who'd remained with the survey ship was as great as if they'd witnessed the double killing in person. Walks-with-Whispers fainted and it required some effort to revive him. Flies-by-Tail and Breathes-hard-Out both needed treatment to settle their digestive systems and steady their respiration. It took some time before any of them could examine the two bodies in person without hyperventilating. Such was the Quozl reaction to the murder of two intelligent beings.

And his companions had all received training, Looks-at-Charts thought. How would an ordinary colonist react? With a cataleptic seizure? Stands-while-Sitting was right. They could not even think of fighting. Even if they managed to win a few fights, the victors would be mentally impaired beyond repair.

Having recovered enough to argue, Walks-with-Whispers insisted, "We can't return to the ship already. I've barely begun my studies."

"He's right," agreed Breathes-hard-Out. "I've just begun to chart the basics of atmospheric movements here."

"None of that matters anymore." Stands-while-Sitting spoke with the full Elder's intonation. "We cannot remain here." She indicated the body of the native. "This individual may be missed by his burrow-mates. While it was not our intention to secure a specimen, events have provided us with one. The facilities for study and preservation exist only on the *Sequencer*. If we delay returning, this invaluable repository of information will start to decompose."

Flies-by-Tail wrinkled her black nose. "It's already begun to decompose."

"My point exactly. We cannot risk being discovered here and we have already learned more than we expected to. More," she said solemnly, "than we wanted to. If this native's reaction to our presence was typical of what can be expected from others of its kind then we are all in danger even as I speak. Our presence on Shiraz is still a secret. Right now preservation of that secrecy is our primary task. We must leave unnoticed while we still have the chance." She took a moment to preen importantly, underscoring her determination.

The geologist and meteorologist continued to argue against an abrupt departure but it was not a question for serious debate. In an emergency Stands-while-Sitting had command. She was backed up by Looks-at-Charts and Flies-by-Tail. The scientists continued to grumbled even as rapid preparations were made to depart.

There was some discussion about when to leave. It was decided to lift during the darkest part of the night to render visual observation from the surface as difficult as possible. Except they were not leaving, not departing, thought Looks-at-Charts as he secured his harness. They were fleeing with their dead, leaving whatever optimism they'd brought with them in their wake. They were running away to preserve the secrecy of their existence.

It was not how he'd planned to return to the *Sequencer*. There would be no quiet glory, no solemn triumph. One of his best friends was dead and Shiraz was worse than they'd imagined. He would have a different place in the history texts than he'd envisioned.

If the burrow survived long enough to fashion any history texts, he told himself.

Because of the development of Mazna there was ample information in the texts on how to deal with inimical primitive lifeforms. There was nothing on how to cope with a hostile intelligence, not even theories. They would have to develop a plan as it was implemented, knowing that one wrong move could result in annihilation.

His pride surged along with the hovering jets as Flies-by-Tail lifted them off the moist earth and pivoted the little vessel. They were Quozl. He ought to have more confidence in his seniors, in Stream-cuts-Through and Lifts-with-Shout and the others. They would cope because they had no other choice. He found himself reciting the first part of the Ninth Book as they emerged from the forest and Flies-by-Tail activated the drive, sending them soaring into the night sky.

> *There is no end.*
> *There is no beginning.*
> *There is only the middle.*
> *For such small favors are we thankful*
> Now *is hard enough to comprehend.*

The decon crew that sprayed and checked them for alien bugs were bursting with questions they knew could not be answered. So were the ordinary colonists the survey team encountered in the corridors upon their release from quarantine. Only a few stared impolitely, insultingly. Most managed to keep their eyes on their business and not intrude on the surveyors' spaces, though there were some uncivil eye contacts. By mutual consent the survey team ignored these. No one wanted to deal with matters of common courtesy now. Other outrages were uppermost in their minds.

There had been communication with the *Sequencer* on the way back, however, and despite every safeguard it was impossible to keep all that had happened secret. So there was a perception, a feeling among the thousands on board the ship that something on Shiraz was not quite right, that their new home was not a garden world like Azel. No one knew precisely what was wrong. They only sensed that something was.

The worst rumors about Shiraz could not compare to the reality he and his colleagues had encountered, Looks knew. He ignored the soft-voiced queries of the escort that was supposed to shield him from questions as they convoyed him to the conference chamber. The Captain was there, of course, and Lifts-with-Shout, and Senses-go-Fade, and the rest of the command staff.

When it was his turn he delivered his report as unemotionally as possible. It wasn't easy to ignore the shocked expressions that stole over the faces of his seniors as he described the circumstances of Burden-carries-Far's death and the subsequent killing in self-defense of the Shirazian. It was with immense relief that he concluded, sat down, and listened dully while Stands-while-Sitting presented her report in concert with the audiovisual recordings she'd made while on the surface. The delight the senior staff would ordinarily have experienced at the sight of the true clear sky, the great fur-needled trees, the fascinating alien flora and fauna, was mitigated by what they had already been told. Thus the perceptible air of apprehension that came over the room when the first images of the native dwelling appeared on the projection wall.

Looks had prepared them as best he knew how, but the room was still filled with uncharacteristic expressions of shock and dismay as the interlude with the native unfurled. Stands-while-Sitting's recorder had been running constantly since they'd entered the native dwelling, and while the image skewed wildly with her movements, the recorder's stabilizer still held it steady enough to show the advancing Burden-carries-Far, the explosion at the end of the metal tube, and Looks's response.

Several of the Seniors required immediate medical treatment. There was a pause before the recording resumed, but the journey back to the survey site was all anticlimax.

When everyone had recovered sufficiently from the initial shock, the encounter sequence was replayed at normal speed, then slowly, and then was rotated to provide as many different perspectives on the action as possible. Only then did Lifts-with-Shout lean toward his pickup and speak.

"You are certain there were no other natives in the vicinity? That neither you nor the ship was observed?"

"We cannot be certain of anything," Looks-at-Charts pointed out, "but we have discussed the matter and believe that except for the single Shirazian we encountered the area was uninhabited. It was a solitary encounter that took place in a solitary dwelling out of line of hearing and sight of any other Shirazian habitation. In that respect we were fortunate."

"What of the world itself?" The Captain's voice was a grim whisper.

Stands-while-Sitting rose. "The water is mineral-rich but drinkable. The air is fresh and clean and the proportions conform to measurements made from orbit. As you saw, the smaller native flora and fauna appear harmless enough. The trees are unique, but they are true trees, as true as any on Quozlene. They are soothing to touch and to smell. This is a world worthy of worship. A world meant for Quozl."

"Except we didn't get here first," muttered Lifts-with-Shout. He stared at Looks-at-Charts. "You didn't by any chance bring the alien weapon back with you?"

"No." Wondering if they'd made a serious mistake, he glanced over and down at Stands-while-Sitting for support. One ear flicked briefly in his direction and he relaxed a little. "We thought it important to leave the native's dwelling as undisturbed as possible."

"It is unlikely that anyone," Stands-while-Sitting added, "would connect the native's disappearance with the presence of offworld visitors, but we thought it best not to leave reason for speculation."

"You did the right thing." Both of the Landing Supervisor's ears drooped sadly. "But in this instance I wish you'd done the wrong thing."

Looks-at-Charts replied calmly. "I had time to make a thorough inspection of the device. It hurls small metal projectiles with penetrating force. Primitive, but it kills as efficiently as any modern weapon. The devices the natives employ against one another are, I am told by staff, similiar except in scale."

"Horrible," muttered one of the senior staff members.

"Uncivilized," sniffed another.

"Once we called such actions part of our own civilization, until we gained the wisdom of the Samizene and matured." Stream-cuts-Through surveyed the chamber. "This is the first non-Quozl intelligence that has ever been encountered. Let us try not to judge them by our own standards."  There was silence in the chamber, polite silence as they waited.

"Obviously there can be no violence. That violence has already occurred is regrettable. Two intelligent beings have been slain." Looks-at-Charts had already apologized profusely. He did so anew, and the staff waited approvingly until he'd concluded.

"We cannot fight and we cannot run." The Captain turned her attention to Flies-by-Tail. "Were you able to tell if you were tracked either on arrival or upon departure?"

"We observed no natives in our immediate vicinity," the survey pilot replied, "and none of our sensing devices was activated. That is not proof, but it is encouraging. The area we visited was as isolated as the ship's survey staff believed it to be. We came close to no urbanized regions."

The Captain gestured with both ears. "Before setdown we need to learn more about their aircraft. Are any extra-atmospheric, what kind of fuel do they utilize, what is their speed and range, and how are they armed? We must ensure that the path to the burrowsite is not normally overflown and that the natives can pose no serious threats to the *Sequencer* so long as it remains our whole world."

A member of Lifts-with-Shout's landing group rose deferentially. "That can largely be ascertained from orbit, Honored Captain. If they are fighting one another they will have their most advanced weapons in frequent use. We can learn where they are being employed and study them with high-resolution instrumentation."

"Do so," said Stream-cuts-Through curtly. "We will study

your findings and make a determination as to how to proceed.'' Her gaze rose as she surveyed the tense assembly. ''You will all be provided with any new information as it is acquired, and will make yourselves available individually and as groups for short-notice consultation. I will explore actual options with Senses-go-Fade and his philosophers. Proceed we will, but only in accordance with the precepts of the Samizene.'' A unified murmur of approval rose from the assembled staff.

Lifts-with-Shout half stood. ''What should be done about preparations for touchdown and inburrowing? The colonists grow anxious. The less they hear, the more concerned they become.''

''And the more wild the rumors that circulate among them.'' The Captain acknowledged the Landing Supervisor's concerns with wide-spread ears and a double blink of the nictitating membranes that covered her eyes. ''First your people can assure everyone that Shiraz does not have an atmosphere of methane and argon, which is one rumor that seems to have circulated widely.'' A few amused whistles lightened the air in the chamber.

''You may as well begin. Emphasize thoroughness, downplay speed. Have everyone take their time to check and recheck. It's time we'll need. Commencing preparations will stop some of the rumors and mute the talk. I need hardly remind you that the proceedings of this gathering are not for general dissemination. At no time is it to be discussed with anyone not present.'' She flicked her gaze in the direction of Looks-at-Charts and Flies-by-Tail, the youngest Quozl present.

''Be especially vigilant while coupling. I won't have any member of my staff precipitating a panic.''

The two young members of the initial survey team deferentially dropped their eyes and ears.

They needed more time, of course. No matter how much time they took, Looks-at-Charts knew they would always need more. More knowledge of Shiraz and its mad inhabitants, more time to prepare the colonials, more time to consider the possibility of failure, something which the previous six generations had never had to contemplate. Many items were in short supply aboard the *Sequencer* after the long journey out from distant Quozlene, but none so precious as time.

Eventually the majority of ordinary colonists would have to be told, he knew. But the less time they had to reflect on the existence of a hostile non-Quozl intelligence on the world below, the less likelihood there would be of a panic. During touchdown everyone would be far too busy to mull over unworkable alternatives.

Landing Command pored over maps and statistics as they agonized over site selection. The place chosen for First Burrow had to be located in a region where the colony would have access to specific resources without drawing the attention of the Shirazians, and where they would be safely distant from the world-spanning native conflict.

The hastily assembled philology team distinguished itself by rapidly translating the most important of Shiraz's bewildering multiplicity of languages. Their reports proved that while the natives might biologically be related to the Quozl, mentally and spiritually they were vastly different.

Soon it was obvious to anyone with a smattering of elementary mass psychology that they fought among themselves because they had not yet come to terms with something as basic as their individual sex drives. They had no idea how to control them, channel the related energies, make use of the related cerebral aspects, or sublimate their violent tendencies in art, music, and other aspects of civilized behavior. Instead they regularly engaged in physical combat both on an individual level and as organized tribal groupings.

Even the most imaginative psychologists aboard the *Sequencer* were astonished. Controlling the sex drive was basic to the establishment of a mature civilization. That the Shirazians had achieved a high level of civilization could not be denied. That it was socially immature was equally unarguable.

"What is remarkable," declared a senior philosopher one day, "is not that they continue to war with each other, but that they have somehow managed under these biological circumstances to avoid exterminating themselves."

"War is a natural and understandable by-product of their lack of control and understanding of their own hormonal systemology," said a colleague. "It is the only means left to control the expansion of the population."

"It goes deeper than that," argued his senior. "Is is more basic to their civilization and affects much more than mere population growth. It affects everything about them. It would affect the way they would react to us."

The analysts could tell nothing about Shirazian art from the native's purely aural broadcasts, but they did record many samples of native music. It was clashing and discordant, full of the confusion that lay beneath the rest of their civilization. Such discoveries were discouraging, but there was no talk of giving up. They could not give up. Despite its incessantly warring, wild tribes, Shiraz was to be their home.

Pressed for a determination, Senses-go-Fade and the xenologists allowed as how if they landed and presented themselves to the natives there was a fifty-fifty chance they would be attacked and exterminated on the spot. The corollary was that there was a fifty-fifty chance they would be accepted and tolerated, if not welcomed with flattened ears. As these odds were not to the Captain's liking, it was decided to continue as planned. They would select a burrowsite, touch down, secure the colony as best they could, and deal with native contact only if and when it became unavoidable.

If the colony successfully established itself and throve, staff estimated that preliminary steps to make contact might commence in reasonable safety in one to two hundred of the local years.

V.

LIFTS-WITH-SHOUT'S LANDING STAFF'S first choice of a burrowsite was an island. Any island. But the larger ones were all occupied and the smaller provided insufficient resources and space for expansion. Nor for psychological reasons did any Quozl wish to live on a small body of land completely surrounded by water. The ship-born colonists knew of drowning only from texts. That did not mean any wished to experience the sensation in person.

The few extensive unpopulated regions were equally unpromising. Great tracts of empty tropical forest were not suitable for burrowing and based on the information gleaned from the settlement of Mazna, were the most likely to harbor dangerous diseases and lifeforms. The frozen polar regions were less hospitable still, as were those utterly devoid of vegetation.

Most promising were several places in the northern hemisphere which, while surrounded by large urban areas, were themselves practically empty. In the end staff settled on a mountainous region not far south in planetary terms from where the survey ship had set down. It had several notable advantages, first and foremost being that it was likely to be similar to the one area already studied firsthand.

The region contained no lush fertile valleys for the natives to farm. It was cut by deep canyons and wild rivers, and the best instrumentation on the *Sequencer* could find no evidence of habitation within a predetermined radius of safety.

A second survey visit was made. Like the first, its arrival and departure passed unnoticed by the natives. A third trip located a site as close to ideal as they were likely to find without far more extensive on-site inspection.

Several narrow valleys were cut by streams which emptied into a sizable lake. The valleys were largely indistinguishable from one another, which meant that anyone observing them from above was unlikely to remember individual geological features. One especially steep-sided valley was almost the exact width of the *Sequencer,* and much deeper. The land through which its watercourse cut was rocky and barren, unable to support tall stands of fur-needled trees which might damage the ship on touchdown. A modest waterfall was located far up the canyon. This distinguishing feature would be moved but not obliterated. Given the region's isolation it was unlikely anyone passing through would note the slight movement of the waterfall a modest distance to the west. The small river would provide excellent cover for the *Sequencer* once it was burrowed in.

For a while the ship would remain their only home, until expansion could begin. It had been designed to serve as such by its builders. The drive would be adjusted to provide power for the new colony. Instead of having to scramble to build dwellings of mud and stone, they would live in the same rooms they had lived in on the long journey outward from Quozlene. The ship was the colony's security, a bastion of familiarity and a reminder of home they would have no matter how extensive the colony grew. It was a gigantic, space-traversing pouch.

But once down, it would never be able to lift off again. There would be no second chance. Their first choice had to be the right one.

Landing Command produced topographic charts in three and four dimensions down to the smallest pebble. Every feature would be precisely reproduced atop the colony once the Sequencer was burrowed in. Artists would work alongside engineers and geologists and excavators.

Once it was announced that these final preparations for touchdown had begun and that a site had been chosen, the atmosphere on the *Sequencer* grew more relaxed. Everyone fell to assigned tasks with renewed enthusiasm and determination. Artists argued good-naturedly with the excavators as burrow-in procedures  were built up in stages on modeling screens. Looks-at-Charts knew their differences would be settled before touchdown commenced. They had to be. There would be neither time nor room for last-minute improvisation.

Meanwhile Lifts-with-Shout was always arguing for more time; more time for study, more time to prepare. Despite repeated delays there eventually came a day when Stream-cuts-Through decided they had spent enough of that precious commodity. Word was passed.

Touchdown commenced.

The two scout ships would go down first, to prepare the way. The *Sequencer* presented another problem entirely. It would be much easier for the natives to detect with the naked eye and completely vulnerable once on the ground with its drive shut down. It was therefore decided despite the additional danger involved to descend only during bad weather, when the primitive native search-and-detect devices would be at their greatest disadvantage.

Crew and colonists made ready. There came a time when there was nothing left to check. In an atmosphere of worry and apprehension instead of the great joy that ought to have been, the *Sequencer* made ready to descend.

Each survey vessel would land at one end of the narrow valley which had been chosen to receive the burrow so that their visual observations might confirm the measurements made on board the colony ship. If something untoward was discovered, the *Sequencer* could still veer off and reascend at the last moment. Flies-by-Tail and Looks-at-Charts were on one, Walks-with-Whispers and Stands-while-Sitting on the other.

Looks found that he missed the senior xenologist's reassuring presence and calm analytical manner, but he understood the practicality of dividing those who had actual knowledge of the Shirazian surface between the two survey ships.

He and Flies-by-Tail were themselves accompanied by four members of the landing team, all of them trying to hide their nervousness and unease. What to do if violent natives were encountered had been an anxious topic of discussion prior to departure. In the end it was decided that there could be no more killing, no more violence, unless the safety of the *Sequencer* itself was involved. Not because of the harm that might befall any Shirazians but because of the psychological damage such an encounter would do to the collective Quozl mentality.

Already heavy therapy had been required to stabilize the shaky psyches of Looks-at-Charts and his companions, and only their specialized training had enabled them to emerge relatively unscathed from the incident. Colonists who had not been the beneficiaries of such training would be much more likely to suffer permanent mental harm were they forced to witness such violence, which compelled Senses-go-Fade's staff to insist it be avoided at all cost.

Despite treatment, Looks-at-Charts still suffered recurring nightmares as a result of the encounter. The sight of drawn blood, the knowledge that he had taken an intelligent life, albeit in self-defense, were things that would stay with him the rest of his life.

And he had only been forced to kill one native. What if there had been several?

The survey craft bucked and heaved as it descended. The turbulence was far worse than on the previous flight, as was to be expected since they were making touchdown in the midst of a massive thunderstorm. The heavy clouds would serve to mask the *Sequencer*'s presence. Thoughtfully he checked his freshly shaven whorls and spirals, his immaculate fur, the scarves and jewelry that indicated his personality and status. The site might prove difficult and the weather inauspicious, but he would arrive well-groomed. Anything less would have been unQuozl.

Under the expert direction of Flies-by-Tail, the survey ship fell through wind and rain. The presence of hostile, primitive fauna and flora notwithstanding, the weather was enough to prove that Shiraz was no paradise world like Azel. Lightning  reached for the little vessel and its sister ship while the wind hindered instead of helped their descent. Black clouds obscured the view out the front port. Flies-by-Tail concentrated on her schematic screens, letting the ship fly itself as much as possible, inputting only when absolutely necessary.

The mountains that enclosed the landing site were jagged and unforgiving. The natives would not have to intervene to cause a disaster. There was no room for error on the part of Stream-cuts-Through and her staff. If they set down a little too far to the right, a shade too heavily north, the unbalanced *Sequencer* would slip and crash, leaving nothing of the Quozl dream but a memory.

The surface exploded into view with astonishing abruptness, drawing whistles of surprise from the inexperienced team members. In the dark and rain it was like returning to the primordial pouch. Mountain peaks loomed threateningly close, their peaks puncturing the low-lying clouds.

Then they saw a deeper slash through the rocks where wind and water had riven: the landing site. A flash of light vanished southward, barely visible. Flies-by-Tail saluted their companion survey craft before bending to the task of bringing them down safely. There was little room to maneuver, not enough time to reduce velocity. One moment they were airborne, riding the buffeting gale, and then they were rattling over the gravel that formed much of the valley floor.

Contemplative silence was supposed to prevail immediately after touchdown. Instead the team members chatted excitedly, gesturing through the port at slick granite walls and the tiers of spiny-leaved trees that climbed the eastern talus slope. As for the intermittent brush, the survey ship had sliced over and through it easily.

An exhausted Flies-by-Tail positioned the little craft according to instructions. With the engines cut, a rumble of a different kind filled their erect, alert ears, penetrating the walls of the ship. Shirazian thunder.

Harnesses were hastily unfastened. All-weather sandals slapped against the deck as the team prepared to go outside. Weariness notwithstanding, Flies-by-Tail made ready to join them. Her body was limp but her tone upbeat as she joined the others near the hatchway, pressing close to Looks-at-Charts.

"Someone should be here to say 'Welcome home,' " she whispered. When a glance at his body posture suggested she could safely invade his Sama, she reached out to caress his cheek with six fingers. The excitement of the moment was sufficient to override the standard suppressant dose she'd taken prior to departure. Looks felt himself responding and deliberately moved away. A shared touch was one thing; now was not the time or place for the rest.

The final check run, they opened the hatch. Shiraz greeted them with cold wind, icy rain, and a blast of stroboscopic lightning. Looks was comforted by the inclement weather. It would take pretty sophisticated instrumentation to detect a descending vessel in this muck. If their preliminary observations were accurate, the natives did not possess it.

Striding down the ramp, he braced himself against the wind as he turned northward. There was no sign of their landing craft, which suggested it had made planetfall successfully at the opposite end of the valley. Behind him the four members of the survey team were struggling to assemble their equipment. Their task was twofold: to confirm readings and measurements made from orbit and to stand ready to provide last-second corrections if necessary. Though they wore protective oversuits, the howling wind and beating rain still made their work uncomfortable.

"What a wonderful place," he mused aloud. "No doubt

our offspring, may they be honored and respected, will bless us profusely for choosing it.''

''We had no choice.'' Flies-by-Tail stood close to him, watching the landing team struggle with their instruments. ''We had to come down somewhere unpleasant. At least the Shirazians are like us in that respect.''

''We don't know that,'' he corrected her. ''They may have other reasons for avoiding this place, reasons we cannot imagine or suspect.'' He blinked away rain. ''Although I do not think they would come here for the benign climate.''

It helped to concentrate on the trees that began growing halfway up the valley slopes and continued to the cloud-concealed crests of the mountains. Trees, even alien trees, were reassuring sights, harbingers of warmth and productivity and a generous nature. Such strange trees they were, unlike anything on Quozlene or the other settled worlds, with their narrow sharp-tipped leaves and deeply ribbed bark. He wondered if the vegetation in the temperate regions to the south was much different.

Despite his protective jumpsuit and his well-groomed fur he found he was cold. The wind ruffled his fur and let the rain penetrate to the skin. Lightning arched across the sky, jumping from one mountaintop to the other, a billion-volt bridge. Accompanied by Flies-by-Tail he walked a little ways away from the ship. Since none of the landing team was asking his advice there was nothing for him to do except stay out of the way unless needed.

''Not such a terrible place,'' he murmured hopefully. ''If it were other than isolated, cold, and difficult to reach, it would be overrun with Shirazians.''

''The crucial point.'' Flies-by-Tail had her ears down to protect her cheeks, her arms folded over her chest.

As he looked at her he was startled by the realization that her training was now redundant. Had this been a normal colonization she could have looked forward to many years of convoying survey teams and scouts across the surface of the new world. Instead they were going to have to hide in their burrows, unable to travel freely across the surface much less through its blue skies. If they were to function as productive members of the new colony, Flies-by-Tail and the other pilots would require extensive retraining, training they might not take to with ease or enjoyment.

Come to think of it, what would be his fate? Would any exploration of the surface be permitted in his lifetime? He refused to consider the other possibility.

"I'm sorry," he heard himself murmuring.

She looked at him in surprise, her nictitating membranes shielding her eyes from the rain. "For what?"

"For the thoughts I was having. They were selfish and egocentric. I am abased."

"You are forgiven," she said softly without knowing what she was forgiving him for.

They stood close together watching the survey team work, four of his fingers toying idly with her tail where it protruded from the seat of her suit. He was thinking of Burden-carries-Far and how they had argued over who would be first.

Both had achieved important firsts, both regrettable. Burden had been the first Quozl to be slain by a member of another intelligent species, while Looks had been first to kill in turn.

As his spirits fell, something else rose. It was unQuozl, he tried to tell himself. Wrong time, wrong place. But despite the suppressants he could feel his body coming alive. Flies-by-Tail's eyes glistened blue-gray through the rain. He let his mind dwell on the husky whisper of her voice as his fingers worked the smooth fur of her tail.

Perhaps, he thought, the time of firsts was not yet over.

"I realize that the weather is less than ideal and the ground here hard, but possibly . . . ?"

She met his gaze straight on. From that point, as was the way of Quozl, additional words were unnecessary.

So another first was perpetrated, though only two knew of it. Yet there was more to it than that. Looks later thought of it as a kind of memorial service for Burden-carries-Far. It was the type of memorial he would have approved of.

After they had concluded and were slipping soaked but content back into their suits, Looks told Flies-by-Tail of the discussions he and his dead colleague had engaged in over the years. She concurred somberly that what they had done was as fitting a memorial as any Quozl could ask for.

They talked until interrupted by an all-pervasive rumbling overhead. It was deeper than the thunder generated by Shirazian lightning. Tilting their heads back they could see that one cloud had broken through the underlayer of storm and was descending slowly on a cushion of lambent air.

Slowly the *Sequencer,* massive as a small mountain, was coming down.

If the drive failed now, or if someone in Engineering made a mistake, the great ship could be lost or, at best, severely damaged. If it swerved too far north or south, either of the survey teams would be crushed to the thickness of individual molecules. But neither drive nor crew erred. All had waited too long for this moment.

Slowly the ark eased into the notch between the craggy flanks of two mountains. The cushion created by the drive turned the river that ran thought the valley into a dense mist that hissed in all directions, fleeing the descending mass.

Lightning flashed repeatedly above the descending vessel, lessening as the great bulk settled to the groaning earth. The metal walls of the ship rose a third of the way up the side of the flanking peaks, filling the valley from side to side.

New calm came over Looks-at-Charts, accompanied by renewed confidence. The ship was down. None had perished as a result of the landing. As near as anyone could tell, the natives had not sensed its arrival and were ignorant of its presence. How long that would last none could predict, but for now, for the present, he and Flies-by-Tail and Captain Stream-cuts-Through and the rest of his brethren Quozl were alive and safe. The ship was down. Now they could begin to make this small piece of Shiraz their own.

As for tomorrow—tomorrow would bring its own Samizene. Today was time enough. Who could say what might be theirs tomorrow?

Even had natives been living nearby they would not have heard the touchdown, so skillfully had it been accomplished. The valley's parameters have been calculated with exquisite precision, so that the ship's sides had barely scraped rock as she descended. The silvery glow faded from the vast underside. Conscious of the fact that the ship's superstructure could barely support its own weight under the influence of real gravity, the engineers shut down the drive. For the first time in generations, the *Sequencer* was silent.

Now it was the turn of Geology and Engineering to deploy their waiting troops. They swung into action as the storm continued to rage around the ship.

Looks-at-Charts was conscious of the special privilege that had been his; to be in a position to watch as the *Sequencer* mated with its final resting place. Her journey was at an end, that of the colonists' was just beginning. Six generations in all had lived and died within her protective hulk, thousands who had spent their lives engaged in maintenance and repetition, just to make this moment possible. He and his generation would not let their ancestors down. They would not fail. They were Quozl. He brushed at an earring.

The *Sequencer* would not rise again. Indeed, it could not, now that they had committed themselves by shutting down the underspace drive. They were no longer citizens of the ship but of this world, no matter how its bizarre inhabitants might react to their presence.

He could imagine anxious colonists clustered around screens hoping for views of their new home. At this point they were probably being treated to a long lecture by Senses-go-Fade or

one of his assistants designed to prepare
them for the shock of permanent burrowing. The geologists and engineers had an
easier task than the philosophers. All they
had to do was move rock and metal, not
minds and attitudes.

You could see them now, already blast-
ing out huge quantities of rock and debris.
The big levitators were coming out, sucking up the crumbled
stone and soil and depositing it around the *Sequencer*'s flanks.
Like some monstrous, prehistoric burrowing creature it slowly
began to sink into the earth, attended by a horde of tiny
workers. It would serve the colonists as First Burrow, as
home until the first tunnels could be constructed. Tunnels
which would lead not to the surface but into the hearts of
the two mountains that formed the valley.

They would dig in as their primitive ancestors had, expanding carefully and safely beyond the sight of the Shirazians. All
they would see of the strange fur-spined trees would be their
roots. The engineers would excavate rooms and galleries,
tunnels and theaters and farming chambers.

They'd found their world. In addition they would now need
secrecy, and time.

The providential storm lasted eight days, ebbing and surging like a wave without clearing completely for more than a
few minutes. It was more than the engineers needed. When
the clouds parted on the ninth day there was nothing to
indicate that an enormous starship lay entombed beneath
thousand of tons of rock and earth. Above the buried vessel
the landscape had been reproduced with extraordinary precision, down to the smallest bush and smoothest stone. Anyone
viewing it from above would consider it unchanged. It would
take precise measurements to reveal that the level of the
valley bottom was now several hundred feet higher than it
had been a week earlier. Even the twists and turns in the river
that now flowed on top of the hidden starship had been
reproduced with admirable fidelity.

The most professional observer would shrug and put down the difference in altitude to errors in the old maps.

Only after ensuring that the surrounding countryside was deserted did Stream-cuts-Through and Lifts-with-Shout and a chosen few specialists tunnel out to inspect the surface. They compared what they could see with the recording made by the first survey team.

Meanwhile the ship's philosopher-meditators worked overtime to soothe the frazzled nerves of the less stable settlers. For the most part they were taking it well. Many had prepared themselves to live out their lives on board the *Sequencer*. That they would now do so underground did not involve any profound psychological readjustments. The younger colonists were more forcefully affected, since they had entertained reasonable expectations of setting up housekeeping on the green surface of their new home. With therapy and patience they would come to terms with the future that fate had dealt them.

As the colony settled in, Looks-at-Charts was permitted to spend time on the surface, gathering invaluable information while convoying small groups of scientists and educational specialists. Since orbital observation indicated that the Shirazians were primarily diurnal, such excursions took place exclusively at night. At such times he was conscious of the great privilege that had been awarded to him. Most members of the colony would never be allowed to set foot on the surface of their new home.

As time passed they learned much more about their new world. Only rarely did Shirazian atmospheric craft pass within range of the ship's detectors, and never directly over the burrowsite itself. There was nothing to suggest that the natives suspected the presence of the *Sequencer* and its expanding population in their midst.

Some discoveries were as pleasing as they were surprising. The geology team located water in ample quantities at a modest depth, water of unmatched purity and taste. There would no need for the extensive and complicated pipeline which had been planned to tap the waters of the nearest lake.

While not especially rich, the rocks enclosing the burrow contained metals in quantities sufficient to supply the colony's needs. It was also stable and dense enough to permit the excavation of tunnels and rooms without the need to add internal bracing or supports. This enabled the engineers to expand far more rapidly than would have been the case in softer terrain.

Artists resumed their work, often inspired by the images and recordings brought back by the small exploration teams. Farming expanded from the ship into surrounding galleries. Life was good, if tense. Above the buried ship the native fauna returned in numbers. It was as though the arrival had never been.

Caution remained the byword of the colony, however. The requests made by Looks-at-Charts and the other scouts and scientists for permission to travel farther afield on the surface were repeatedly denied. The continued safety of the colony required only knowledge of their immediate surroundings. It was far too soon to risk discovery merely for the chance to add to the sum total of general knowledge about the new world. The violent death of Burden-carries-Far was still fresh in many minds. That he was followed not long after touchdown by Walks-with-Whispers did little to alleviate the Council's concerns. The mental confusion and depression brought on by the death of a colleague and the concomitant slaying of an intelligent native had in the end been more than the gentle geologist could handle.

So wide-ranging exploration was out of the question for now. Be content to live and expand First Burrow. Thus said the ship's philosophical staff. Reckless surface expeditions could be left to future, more self-assured generations.

The colonials busied themselves turning *Sequencer* into an arcology. A year later when Looks-at-Charts and Flies-by-Tail decided to mate, the Burrow was firmly established.

They immediately applied for permission to birth and were

as quickly turned down. It was expected. They would have to wait their turn and hope that their application found favor with the prognosticators. The speed with which new facilities were added determined the permissible rate of population growth. If controls were eliminated, the colony would find itself overrun with infants in less than two cycles.

The colony had been in place a year and not a single native had ventured close to the site. Meanwhile much was learned about the Shirazians from constant monitoring of their broadcasts. Knowledge expanded exponentially when they began experimenting with their first crude visuals.

Studies of these confirmed many of the theories first proposed by the xenologists. Continual intertribal conflict was the rule among the natives, though it was intermittent among the most powerful tribes. The latter maintained shockingly extensive stocks of weapons in the apparent belief that future conflict was inevitable. Even on ancient Quozl such a waste of resources was unheard-of. The philosophers risked madness in their arduous attempts to rationalize such bizarre behavior.

The Shirazians bred without restraint but their civilization was preserved by the fact that their rate of reproduction was much lower than that of the Quozl. Every study, every observation, only served to confirm what had been determined earlier. The natives' sex drives ruled their lives and society, and not the other, proper way around.

Applying this principle made it possible to understand almost any native action, no matter how incomprehensible at first. It explained how an obviously technologically mature society could still engage in tribal conflict. Unable to understand and deal with their own psychosexual urges, the ruling males resorted to bloodletting and physical violence as a means of demonstrating dominance. No wonder Shirazian society was such a hopeless morass of misunderstandings and mutual tension. Endocrinologists and psychologists had not yet learned how to merge their disciplines. Chaos was the inevitable result.

As for the childbearing females, they were as confused as their mates, but unable to cope with a situation they instinctively sensed as counterproductive and immature. This was the result of their physical inferiority, a physiological imbalance that Quozl scientists decided must be the result of an aberrant evolutionary
process. Since male and female Quozl were always nearly of similar size and strength, relationships between the sexes had proceeded from a position of equality. And since female Quozl carried their infants in pouches which did not restrict their physical activity, they had no need of continual male protection. It was clear that the Shirazians were more to be pitied their condition than feared.

Study of increasingly sophisticated visual emissions confirmed everything. Shirazian young were born directly into the world without having enjoyed the protection offered by a nurturing pouch. As the extensive musculature required to carry a nursing infant was not present or necessary in human females, they had not developed in the manner of their Quozl counterparts. This not only allowed but indeed demanded that the males establish dominance over the females, thus upsetting what otherwise would have been a natural balance between the sexes. Aberrant Shirazian society had its basis not in voluntary decisions but in genetic ones.

Nor was there any reason to hope for change, unless the females somehow managed to overcome their inherent physical disadvantage enough to assert themselves to the point of putting an end to the nonsensical intertribal wars, or the males matured enough to realize they had to gain control over their hormonal imbalances.

As if that wasn't enough to complicate ordinary intraspecies cooperation, there was also the matter of the bewildering multiplicity of languages. As one xenologist put it, the wonder was that any Shirazians remained alive at all.

Looks-at-Charts followed the studies and viewed the many

recordings with interest in the hope that one of the hasty expeditions he led might encounter a few less violent natives. That was unlikely, but he'd always believed in preparedness. Flies-by-Tail survived the demise of her profession and built a new career as a nursery attendant. Both survey ships had been placed in long-term storage. They would not take wing again for at least a hundred years lest they be observed by the natives.

Looks-at-Charts argued on behalf of his mate for one long-range night flight to observe the nearest urban native settlement. Each time the request was made it was turned down. It was too risky, and they could learn enough about such places by monitoring the Shirazian broadcasts. Secrecy was always more important than knowledge. Looks-at-Charts vehemently disagreed, but he was not a member of the Council. He thought them much too conservative.

Yet as everyone was to learn, the intelligent natives of Shiraz were not the only inhabitants of the new world who could pose a danger to careless Quozl.

VI.

IT WAS THE second year of burrowing. Looks-at-Charts had been permitted to take a study team slightly farther from the colony than had ever been allowed before. Two years it had taken to cross from the valley of the Burrow into the one to the south. It was just as Looks-at-Charts had feared: the second valley looked exactly like the first, differing only in topography.

They did find some new small fauna, however. Something also found them.

Looks-at-Charts heard the screams, the high-pitched desperate whistling, as he was watching the antics of one of the small arboreal quadrupeds. Native visual broadcasts had identified these as squir-rels. It blustered theatrically, bawling him out in its active nonlanguage.

It was the warm season, a beautiful day. Looks was glad Landing Command had relented enough to allow the occasional diurnal expedition. The continued absence of Shirazian presence had made the advisors a little bolder. Looks had taken to wearing a full complement of jewelry and scarves on such journeys. The scientists took little care with their appearance and so he felt it incumbent upon him to uphold the high Quozl standards.

There were also two attractive females among his charges and he wanted to look good in the event their thoughts turned from study to coupling, even as he knew that Flies-by-Tail would be availing herself of similar opportunities back in

First Burrow. Between the comical antics of the squir-rel, the warmth of the Shirazian sun, and his aroused thoughts, the last thing he expected by way of interruption was screaming.

The two geologists working nearby looked up from their excavation. Once they had completed their studies the hole would be carefully filled back in and the surface returned to as close an approximation of its original appearance as possible.

They had been camped on the slope for several days and in that time had seen nothing to differentiate it from terrain previously visited. Certainly they had encountered nothing threatening. But the screaming could not be mistaken. Looks-at-Charts instantly recognized the voices of the team's bota-nist and its zoologist. As he listened the shrieks came again, echoing through the woods.

He turned and ran, his large, elongated feet carrying him uphill in great bounds. His every sense was alert, ears erect and aimed forward to catch the slightest unfamiliar sound. He felt the weight of his side arm at his belt. For one of the few times in his life he ignored the way he looked.

Now he could hear the other voice. The deep, throaty growl made his fur stand on end. It was far too massive to be made by a Quozl, or even a native. It was known from studying the emissions the Shirazians called "nature pro-grams" that the planet was home to large carnivores, but the study teams had never encountered one.

A stream notched the slope. He cleared it in one bound, sending dirt flying from where he touched down on the other side. A single figure emerged from behind a large tree to intercept him. It was Dawn-stands-Blue, the botanist.

She was inhaling unevenly and he took a moment to steady her. In response to his questions she could only turn and point weakly, eyes full of fear.

"Show me," he demanded, deliberately shocking her with impoliteness.

It worked. Her ears twisted as she pointed more carefully. Leaving her behind he raced uphill in the direction she'd indicated. She watched him for a moment, then staggered off toward the camp.

Beside a large boulder he found the bleeding, torn corpse of the zoologist. It was not quite completely decapitated. A few ligaments still connected the head to the neck. As he stood over the body with drawn side arm, a new odor reached his nostrils. It was thick and musky and alien. He hesitated. As he did so, another boulder nearby suddenly rose to face him. It growled.

The creature was immense, many times the mass of a Quozl. Here was a real monster, the stuff of underspace nightmares. It hovered over the pitiful form of the dead zoologist and gazed at Looks-at-Charts out of intense brown eyes.

Then it lunged. Since it was clearly not a member of an intelligent species Looks did not hesitate. With those teeth and claws it did not need intelligence to protect it.

Taking careful aim, he fired repeatedly. His first shots only enraged the monster without visibly affecting it. Looks continued to fire as he dodged. The monster was faster than it looked. It could have run down a native, but not a Quozl. Still, Looks knew that if he allowed himself to be cornered against the rocks, or lost his footing for even an instant . . .

He was starting to worry about the charge in his side arm when his shots began to affect his attacker. The monster shook its head, then turned and shambled off into the trees. Looks expected it to take the body of the zoologist with it but was relieved when it did not.

Too confident, he told himself as he stood there trying to catch his breath. We grew too confident. Shiraz is still not home. Reciting a few stanzas from the Tragili Battle Epic helped to calm him. Because the surface study teams had never had any trouble didn't mean there was no trouble to be had. The only consoling thought was that since this was the first hairy monster they'd encountered, they must not be common to this region.

Only when he was sure that the creature was not lying in ambush behind the trees did he bend to inspect the zoologist's body. It looked like a whirlpool puzzle, its borders sound but the interior scattered every which way. He tried to remember some songs of parting, sang a few phrases in his wholly inappropriate voice, then turned to walk slowly back in the direction of the campsite.

It was his fault. Even though he'd been watching over the others and the camp itself, the death of the zoologist still fell on his shoulders. Their safety was his responsibility, and he'd failed. It was likely this would be his last surface expedition.

Because he felt that, he took the time despite his grief to drink in the beautiful blue sky, the massive clouds, the astonishing variety of tiny arthropods which populated the surface of Shiraz, knowing he might never see them again. Then he forced himself to walk straighter, to banish any suggestion of servility from his posture. Pridefully he adjusted his leg scarves.

There was no reason for him to grieve. He'd been far luckier than his fellow colonists, the great majority of whom could view the surface of their homeworld only in recordings made by the occasional surface expedition. They would never smell its air or its vegetation or observe its largely innocuous fauna in its natural habitat. Only a select few would ever have that privilege.

A privilege he would now have to forfeit.

The others were waiting for him. He saw the relief in their faces and posture when he emerged from the trees, simultaneously wondering why they still had any confidence in him.

"We know what happened." The geologist gestured toward the slowly recovering but still traumatized botanist.

"Then you all know what must be done."

It was painful and slow. The zoologist's corpse could not be left to decompose because of the unlikely but still finite possibility the remains might be chanced on by a wandering Shirazian. Therefore, everything had to be packed and removed back to the colony for disposal and all traces of its existence expunged from the vicinity, including loose fur and any bloodstains.

They took turns trying to console him, explaining that there was nothing he could have done and that the zoologist bore the primary responsibility for his own demise because he'd wandered too far from the camp. Though he believed none of them, he accepted their condolences politely. It helped to reinforce his sense of community, which had been badly damaged by the accident.

Only when they topped the crest of the ridge that divided the valley they'd been exploring from the one that was home to the colony did they stumble across the corpse of the monster. They smelled it long before they saw it.

"You were a better shot than you thought," said one of the geologists.

"I wish I hadn't been."

The geologist eyed him uncertainly. "I do not understand."

Looks approached the massive body. "Now we have this body to move as well. Our weapons are different from those employed by the natives. If they were to find this corpse they would know immediately that it had not been slain by one of their own. They would become curious."

"Unlikely," commented another member of the party.

"I agree. Unlikely, yes—but not impossible. We can take no risks."

"It is not a risk," the geologist argued. "The evidence indicating manner of death will be obliterated by the local scavengers." He looked around nervously. "They should be at work here already."

"You do not understand. We are not allowed to make such judgments. Besides, do none of you see that here we have a biological specimen beyond value?"

"That may be," another argued, "but it is of no use to us because we have not the means for dragging it back to the Burrow."

"We must." Looks-at-Charts was insistent. "Not because of its value to Bioresearch, but because it is a memorial to Sees-while-Dreaming."

That took them aback. They could argue that trying to move the monstrous bulk was impractical, but Looks had outflanked that argument by tying the recovery of the corpse to the death of its discoverer, the dead zoologist. He'd trapped them. Now he tried to ease their practical concerns.

"We have the one lifter."

"It might carry that," agreed the botanist tiredly, "if handled with the skill of an artist."

"The lifter is full," another geologist pointed out unnecessarily.

"I know. You will have to dump all your specimens." He gestured with both ears and a hand in the direction of the floating mass of rock and soil.

The geologists debated the matter among themselves. As a nonscientist, Looks-at-Charts had no vote in the matter. The botanist was in no condition to argue rationally and so excused herself from the argument.

It was finally decided that Looks was correct. The value of the animal outweighed the value of all their specimens. They would salvage the most important of these and carry them in their packs. The lifter would be used solely to support the monster and their unlucky companion.

And most importantly, the deceased zoologist would have a proper memorial. That was the unvoiced but unanimously accepted rationale.

They went about the business of dumping their laboriously gathered specimens and arranging them to blend with the immediate landscape. Then they loaded the monster and struggled to balance its bulk atop the lifter. It took all of them to manage it. One Quozl corpse did not disturb the balance.

Only then did they sing a final song of farewell to their mangled colleague and proceed in the direction of the Burrow.

The biologists' ecstasy at receiving the corpse of the monster was boundless. The colony's chief geologist made certain the origin of the gift was not forgotten in the general excitement.

"We left behind most of ours gains from this journey."

The head biologist acknowledged the other department's loss. "We will see that you are granted your fair share of our expeditionary time. It will be more than worth it."

Looks-at-Charts listened with one ear to the polite politico-scientific banter while wondering where Flies-by-Tail was keeping herself. He was about to leave when the chief biologist drew him aside.

"I know how you came by this prize and that it was outside the means and quota set up for regulating the taking of surface specimens, but in this instance I do not think you have to worry."

"It might have been avoided," Looks insisted. "I could have run off and returned later. Or I could have driven it away without killing it. I acted in haste."

"You acted instinctively, to preserve lives. Those of the expedition team as well as your own. You thought you had only driven it away in the first place. You knew nothing of this creature, of its habits or inclinations. Had you fled, it might have pursued, and others might have perished. That's why you are a scout."

There was admiration as well as reassurance in the Senior's voice, and it helped more than Looks cared to admit.

"Someone sometimes has to make decisions based on rapid analysis of a situation. We cannot always take time for thought and meditation. Soul-searching cannot precede every action. Particularly when one is confronted by incipient death. Tell me, Looks-at-Charts, how much longer do you expect to practice the profession of scout?"

"Not very long, not after this." Looks-at-Charts spoke ruefully, his ears down over his face. "I know the procedure. There will be a formal hearing. Everyone will agree, just as you have, that I acted correctly and within established parameters. That will do nothing to change what took place, will not resurrect the dead. I will be 'asked' to retrain for another profession.'' ·

"I will place my influence on your side." Seeing how downcast the scout was he added, "And I will do something more. I will tell you something we have only recently learned. Only two know of it. As yet it remains only theory. You will be the third to have the opportunity to ponder its meaning, and its potential.

"You are aware that we are finishing up our work with the native specimen you and your companions brought into the colony prior to touchdown cycles ago?"

Looks-at-Charts's ears straightened. "I had heard rumors to that effect."

The memory of that incident still affected him powerfully, though through meditation and therapy he had learned to cope with it. The dead Shirazian had brought no army of vengeful colleagues to the mountain valley. It was fortunate he had been a member of another tribe.

Through his dissection the Quozl had learned much about native physiology. While the biologists would dearly have loved to have a female specimen to compare with the single male, no one proposed an expedition to acquire one. Unthinkable thought. They would sooner have slain themselves.

What had the chief biologist learned? Something so unique only a select few could be entrusted with the knowledge? Looks-at-Charts scanned the room. No one was paying them the slightest attention. The other scientists were swarming around the huge carcass of the dead carnivore.

"Everything else we have learned from our work with the native male has been made available for study by others," the biologist was whispering. "This I and the one who first formulated the theory have decided to suppress. It is more than controversial."

Excitement and anticipation collided inside the scout. As the biologist intended, it helped to mute his despair.

"What is it? Something inconceivable? Do they have unsuspected mental powers, or physical capabilities we have not yet observed? It must be something we have not been able to discover from monitoring their programs or all would know of it."

"Truth. What is strange is that everyone in the colony is unconsciously aware of it without having considered it. When eventually we make contact with the natives it may prove to be our salvation— or our deaths. It is something we can control only marginally, and the secret itself we cannot control at all. We are helpless. Everything will be determined by how the Shirazians react to the revelation."

He gestured for Looks-at-Charts to enter his Sama, to come as close as possible without actually making contact. Looks complied, twisting an ear close to the biologist's mouth, all but caressing the fine fur there.

As the biologist spoke Looks realized the theory was like nothing he'd imagined. And yet the scientist was right when he'd declared that everyone in the colony was aware of it unconsciously. Looks listened calmly despite the emotions running through him, careful to betray none of his excitement to the others in the room. When the biologist finished he turned and walked off without a formal farewell, leaving Looks to stand alone with his thoughts. He remained a while longer before departing in search of Flies-by-Tail.

The scout was stability and calm outside, utter turmoil and astonishment within. He could hardly walk straight for the wonder that filled him. That, and a surging curiosity he had not expected and could not put aside. It was a curiosity that could never be satisfied, which made it all the more frustrating to contemplate.

If he was fortunate to live long enough, then someday he might at least see the knowledge become common among the colony. He wondered what they would make of it, even as he wondered how the natives would react to the revelation.

Assuming the work of the biologist who'd made the discovery was accurate, of course.

He hoped that it was, and hoped that it wasn't, and saw why the chief biologist had decided to withhold the discovery from the colony at large.

It was sufficient to tear it apart.

There was no such thing as a patrol. It was unthinkable, for example, that anyone might try to sneak out of the Burrow in contravention of every colony law and regulation. Only the privileged few were permitted access to the outside. The rest of the colony lived and loved and meditated within the buried body of the *Sequencer* and the network of tunnels and sub-burrows that the engineers were constantly pushing out in all directions from the ship itself.

The settlers seemed content. After all, their lot was an improvement on that of their ancestors. They accepted the need for remaining concealed and went about their business, secure in the knowledge that their Seniors would make the best decisions about their future.

Not only did they have the spacious *Sequencer* for a home, they now also had tunnels and new excavated chambers to explore, with more to come. They did not miss the sun and the sky because neither they nor their parents had ever known such things. They could view the recordings brought back by the surface expeditionary teams and perhaps fantasize, but they would never consider breaking the law to see for themselves the wonders of the surface.

For education as well as amusement and an entirely different view of the world above they could watch the broadcasts of the humans, as the Shirazians called themselves. Detail study of these transmissions was a part of every young Quozl's education. When contact was finally made, the Quozl would be familiar with their hosts' society.

Contrary to his expectations, Looks-at-Charts was not stripped of his privileges nor shorn of his duties. It was not his fault that his team had wandered into a valley that was home to monsters, nor was he responsible for the two members of his team who had strayed from their assigned work location. He was still allowed to visit the surface as escort and guide.

Flies-by-Tail never accompanied him. She was not qualified and her abilities were in demand elsewhere.

Having explored the valley to the north of the colony site, Looks-at-Charts determined to lead the first expedition to the next one to the south. Another river flowed through the gap in the mountains before emptying into a small lake.

Only three accompanied him. Looks preferred small groups so he could keep his eye on all of them. Oftentimes the scientists were like cubs, oblivious to the world around them, interested only in their play. They expected him to look after them.

The botanist and zoologist could hardly restrain themselves. Little research had been down so far on Shirazian aquatic lifeforms, yet human broadcasts indicated life existed in abundance in lakes and other large bodies of water. They anticipated a plethora of discoveries.

The hike over the intervening ridge was not difficult. Once down the opposite slope they found an easy descent the rest of the way to a healthy, roaring stream.

The last thing any of them expected to hear as they made their way downriver was music.

But music it was, and familiar at that: a brash, martial piping. Looks-at-Charts gestured for his charges to wait in a clearing while he reconnoitered, since he was the only one carrying a side arm.

As he advanced he wondered at the source of the music. Perhaps it was some kind of Shirazian animal skilled in mimicry, which was repeating music it had overheard played by a member of another expedition.

The sounds led him through the trees and up a steep slope, until he found himself staring at a small, natural amphitheater. The acoustics were excellent, the notes bouncing off the smooth granite. It explained how he and his companions were able to hear the melodies so clearly.

Two Quozl occupied the center of the formation. While one played the slute, the other pirouetted and leaped gracefully, dancing patterns in the sand that had been deposited by the spring runoff. In the warm growing season the amphitheater was probably filled with water instead of music.

He didn't recognize the female. She was half white, brown fur being confined to her legs, arms, and muzzle. As if her natural coloring wasn't pale enough, she had shaved more than a third of her body. She wore scarves and jewelry on the left side of her body only, an unorthodox arrangement the significance of which puzzled the fascinated scout.

The male manipulating the slute Looks-at-Charts did recognize. He was shorn as radically as his female companion. He wore no scarves at all, only earrings and other jewelry. The music he made was traditional, devoid of contemporary embellishment.

There was no danger here. Only disobedience.

Leaving his weapon holstered, Looks-at-Charts picked a path down into the basin. "High-red-Chanter!" His voice echoed through the amphitheater. "I hope you have permission to perform outside."

The dancer halted in mid-pirouette. The tremolo of the slute stilled as both performers turned to confront the intruder. High-red-Chanter removed the mouthpiece of the instrument from his teeth. Neither of them bolted, which was an encouraging sign.

But what in all underspace were they doing out on the surface, unescorted, unarmed, and so far from the nearest Burrow entrance.

"I do have permission." High-red-Chanter recognized his old rival. "It is nothing to cause you embarrassment, scout."

"Your reassurance consoles me." Looks leaped the last body length to the sandy surface and approached the pair. The female stood slightly to one side, watching him warily. High glanced at her, his ears moving eloquently.

"Thinks-of-Grim, this is the scout Looks-at-Charts. But you probably recognize the first Quozl to kill on the surface of Shiraz."

Looks stiffened but did not respond to the challenge. He'd anticipated something other than a hearty welcome from the musician. Old humiliations were hard to keep buried.

Beneath the single hostile sally, High-red-Chanter and his companion wore an air of stolid indifference. It was as if anything their visitor cared to say was of no consequence. Under the circumstances that might be construed as a kind of madness, but Looks knew it was premature to affix labels to the performance he'd just witnessed and the subsequent attitudes displayed by the performers.

"You said you have permission." It was a polite rejoinder which High could have accepted. Instead his reply was cruelly brusque.

"I do."

Blunt to the point of insult. Looks-at-Charts held his temper and considered leaving with the situation unresolved. This was not something he was obligated to pursue. He could depart with a farewell, leaving them to their music and dance, and file a formal report. Let Lifts-with-Shout and the Elders deal with it as they saw fit.

But he found he could not simply walk away. Something held him there: curiosity, old memories, a sense of responsibility perhaps. He could not have said. So he opened himself to further execration.

"Who gave permission?" There, he thought, pleased with himself. I can be as impolite as you.

It didn't faze the musician. "The Second Book of the Samizene. The Scroll of Aesthetics. The Talker Soliloquies. The entire artistic history of the Quozl."

The scout's ears dipped. "I don't understand."

"I wouldn't expect you to." High-red-Chanter's mouth

twitched to reveal a couple of teeth. Looks felt his blood rush. The ancient challenge was almost enough to make him charge. Almost. Only training, experience, and great self-control kept him safely within his own Sama.

"You are not an artist," High continued. "Merely another cog in a machine."

"We are all cogs in the colony. If it survives, that is more important than anything else. You are troubled by false individuality. You need help."

Ears bobbed negatively. "Not we. As artists we can no longer abide by the foolish, arbitrary rules and restrictions that force us to dig in the ground like bugs."

"The Quozl have always lived underground," Looks-at-Charts pointed out. "There is no shame in living as our ancestors did."

"Not if that is the only choice, but it is not."

Looks tried another tack. "The decisions of the Council are not arbitrary."

"They are whenever art is concerned. Since they chose to conspire to deny us choice, we must make one for ourselves."

"You're crazy, the two of you."

"We're artists, the two of us." High-red-Chanter said it as if it explained everything. In a way it did.

Looks-at-Charts's conscience required him to say one more thing. "You have no official permission to be out here, do you?"

"We have aesthetic permission, historical precedence." The female spoke for the first time. "It is there in the Second Book for any to see. We have spiritual permission. Those are the only permissions we need."

"That's not for me to decide. You realize I must note your presence here in my official report."

"We would not expect otherwise from you." High managed to turn compliment to insult by way of inflection. "Report whatever you wish. It will not matter."

"It will when you return to the Burrow."

"Who spoke of returning to the Burrow?" Obviously relishing the scout's confusion, the musician continued. "We aren't going back. We're going to start our own Burrow. A place of free choices. Out here life is not predetermined as it was on *Sequencer*." Extending both arms and all fourteen fingers, he pivoted slowly and addressed the sky. "A world is not underspace!"

"Honest aesthetic sentiments I'm sure," Looks replied carefully. This was worse than he thought, much worse. He couldn't leave now. "But if you don't return you risk exposing yourselves to the natives, thereby putting the entire colony at risk."

"We risk nothing of the sort." The musician halted and lowered his arms. "We will live as well concealed as any colony. We know our responsibilities as well as our limitations. We have with us an ample supply of suppressants which we have been hoarding since we oversubscribed more than a year ago. Nothing will be put at risk."

For the first time Looks-at-Charts noticed the pair of handmade, cleanly fashioned shoulder packs lying off to one side beneath a protective overhanging rock. He sighed, locked eyes with the unrepentant High.

"All this is nonsense. No one breaks from this Burrow. No one defies Landing Command."

"Four years we have lived on this world," argued Highred-Chanter, "and not a single native has been sighted in the vicinity of the Burrow. The colony remains safe no matter the wanderings of two inspired Quozl. We will not be seen. Two are less conspicuous than thousands even if they happen to be living on the surface.

"It may happen that we will eventually become bored with our self-imposed isolation and will voluntarily return to the colony, but right now we burn for freedom. We need the stimulation new sights, new smells, new sounds can provide. Recordings are not enough. If we do not obtain these things we will perish creatively."

"There are many other artists in the colony. All content themselves with their surroundings."

"How do you know? Have you asked any of them how they feel? It does not matter anyway. What matters is that *we* are not content. We seek space beyond our individual Samas. We required it."

"You will not be allowed to find it. You must know that you will be returned, forcibly if necessary."

"Those who would punish us must first find us," High said haughtily. "I do not think Command will try to because dozens of tracking Quozl would be too conspicuous. We've been planning this for some time. Trying to locate us would be more of a danger to the colony than letting us go. We have kept it to ourselves and have encouraged no one else. Let any others who are disillusioned find their own path to freedom."

Looks-at-Charts examined the musician's words. This was no irrational act, as he'd initially thought, but something which had been thoroughly planned. It might be as High-red-Chanter said, that Landing Command would decide it was less risky to leave them be than to try and bring them back.

He advanced to the outer limits of the musician's Sama, remained poised there on the thin edge of tolerance.

"There is one other possibility you have not mentioned."

"What might that be?"

"That having found you and learned of your intentions, I might force you to return with me. That would eliminate the need for any large-scale search." His right hand rested meaningfully on the butt of the weapon holstered at his waist.

High-red-Chanter glanced at the side arm, then searched the scout's face. "We are not going back and neither you nor anyone else can compel us to do so."

"I could shoot you."

"That's true, you could." The musician's ears bobbed as he displayed his amusement. "Having already killed I suppose you could do so again."

Looks-at-Charts had been expecting the insult and so it did

not shake him. "I am no killer. I am a scout who knows his duties and responsibilities, much as we both know the laws you choose to defy. I do not kill."

"Then how can you expect us to take your threat seriously?"

"I said I didn't kill. I did not say I couldn't shoot you. As the security of the entire Burrow is at stake I believe I can make myself shoot to incapacitate you. Medical could make repairs later."

He could see that High didn't believe. "You threaten violence. I know you, Looks-at-Charts. You're still Quozl. If you shot us you'd suffer severe mental damage."

"It would risk such damage, and I have the ability to override my conditioning. It was part of my training. If I were you I wouldn't insist on a demonstration of that ability."

It shook High-red-Chanter. Looks could see it in his expression though the musician struggled to hide his emotions. It was a victory of sorts.

"If you shoot us you'll lose everything you've worked for. Command would never allow anyone who'd demonstrated deviant tendencies to travel to the surface again."

"*You* speak to me of deviant tendencies? It wouldn't matter. I would resign voluntarily. It might cost me my mate. Friends would shun me. My parents would turn their faces away in shame should they encounter me in a corridor. Not even the mentally impaired would want to couple with me. Such reactions would be proper. I am prepared to deal with them all to ensure the safety of the colony."

"Yes," murmured Thinks-of-Grim, "I can see that you are crazy enough to go through with such actions."

"I do not think it is my sanity that is in question here." He unsealed his holster and started to draw his weapon. "Therefore I must insist that for the sake of the Burrow and the future of all Quozl on Shiraz you . . ."

He never finished the sentence.

When he regained consciousness he found himself lying on this back staring up at a semicircle of concerned faces. They were not those of High-red-Chanter and Thinks-of-Grim but of the study team he'd been guiding. They helped him to his feet, then evacuated his Sama as he stood alone surveying the otherwise deserted granite basin. The packs were gone, along with their owners.

"We came searching for you," said the zoologist. "I know we should have waited for you to return but much time passed. We grew concerned and came looking. For this breach of regulations we apologize profusely."

"You are forgiven for you zeal," Looks replied absently. At the moment formalities did not interest him.

"You must have fallen." The expedition's botanist indicated the slight slope behind them.

"I did not fall. I was struck." He proceeded to tell them about the source of the music which had intrigued them.

"High-red-Chanter's mind is gone but there's nothing wrong with his reflexes, nor those of his companions," he concluded. "He engaged me so deeply in conversation that I forgot to monitor the location of his mate. I was so concerned with my own potential for violence that I failed to consider she might be capable of it herself."

Word of the artists' perfidy stunned the scientists and much mutual meditation was required before they regained their psychospiritual equilibrium. Only then were they able to discuss what had happened in a calm and rational manner.

"Do you think we should go after them?" the botanist asked. "There are four of us. We might force them to return."

Looks-at-Charts extended both ears parallel to the earth. "We cannot. We are not authorized. Besides which, we've no idea which way they've gone nor do we have any equipment which might aid us in tracking them. Furthermore," and he noted with irony that he was repeating High-red-Chanter's own argument, "we cannot risk being detected by the natives."

The zoologist was staring off into the forest. "Surely we can't let them go. They could jeopardize the entire Burrow."

"I tried to explain that to them. They are convinced they can remain hidden from the natives." He touched the front of his head, came away with blood on his fingers. He eyed it as if it was an illustration from a medical text and not the reality of his own body. One Quozl had bled another. Truly the two artists were insane.

"This is not for us to decide."

Unlike the time when he'd been forced to kill the native, this time he was calm and relaxed. He'd done what had to be done and failed, but at least he had tried. And it was not he who had committed violence.

"No one will blame you for what has happened." The geologist spoke most sympathetically. "You failed because you acted properly. Had you not come upon them their flight would have gone unremarked upon. Now the authorities can determine how to deal with it, before it is too late."

"It may already be too late." Looks-at-Charts took a step forward, felt himself swaying. Instantly two of the scientists moved to support him. The geologist inspected his forehead. The rock had struck him just above the left eye.

"You could have been killed. This is proof enough of their madness." She eyed her companions. "We must make a report. Our own work can wait."

"By all means," agreed the zoologist fervently. "Let us return to the Burrow as rapidly as possible."

They had no choice, of course, but Looks-at-Charts still found reason to regret their action. Perhaps this one time it might have been better to have acted insensibly.

Lifts-with-Shout was beside himself when he heard the news. The aging Landing Supervisor was all for sending out an armed party to track down the two miscreants. He was vetoed by the Captain and the Council of Seven. Exactly as

High-red-Chanter had predicted, they decided the risk was greater than the possible gain.

"Human atmospheric craft are slow and primitive," the Captain was saying, "and they pass close to this region but infrequently, yet we cannot chance one sighting a sizable search party. We must balance this and the small chance of tracking the two against other possibilities.

"High-red-Chanter and Thinks-of-Grim are artists. They do not have survival training." She glanced in Looks's direction as she said this but he kept his gaze properly averted. "They may very well perish at the claws of the native fauna or die of food poisoning. When the cold season arrives they are quite likely to die of exposure." The Quozl had learned that the cold season on this part of Shiraz was very cold indeed, characterized by immense drifts of frozen water and bone-chilling temperatures.

Looks-at-Charts confirmed that neither of the renegades was heavily dressed, though of course he had no way of knowing what they carried in their packs. The packs were not large enough for them to carry much.

One of Lifts-with-Shout's subordinates rose to speak. "They are at the mercy of a hostile alien environment, with only what they can carry to help them. I cannot see how they could survive the cold season. Any tools they did not steal they must fashion with their own hands." He let his gaze wander around the conference room. "Although much of the local flora is edible or neutral, some is toxic to Quozl systemology. The renegades have no botanical training. They may have taken records and information with them, but that is not the same thing. Our work is still very incomplete. They must survive all alone and," he could not keep a sneer out of his tone, "propagate their art."

"I think they will return," said a member of the philosophical staff. "As Quozl we know that the company of others of our own kind is absolutely necessary to maintain mental health. Even should they succeed in coping with the Shirazian surface and climate, they will still suffer from loneliness. I give them half a year before the absence of another Quozl face, the whistle of another Quozl voice, or the dip of an ear drives them back to the Burrow.''

Senses-go-Fade rose and his subordinate sat back down. ''Perhaps it might be so save for one thing. High-red-Chanter and Thinks-of-Grim are artists. Such individuals are capable of unusual things.''

''Not so much.'' The one who'd sat down refused to abandon his thesis. ''They will go insane, if they aren't already.''

Looks-at-Charts sought and was granted permission to speak. ''At first I too thought they were mad. On reflection I realize this was not the case. They were calm and in control of themselves, though passionate as to their intentions.''

Stream-cuts-Through pointed both ears in his direction. ''What would you recommend, scout?''

Looks had already decided how to answer the question if asked. He didn't hesitate. ''This is difficult country, full of sheer cliffs and uncrossable watercourses. Two unarmed Quozl are unlikely to get far, especially while burdened with supplies. The single native specimen available to us displayed no natural equipment for climbing or extended journeying. If anything, he appeared less equipped by nature to withstand extremes of cold than the average Quozl.

''Based on what we already know and on my own personal observations, I think it safe to assume that the natives avoid this region. The proof of this is that we have found no evidence of their presence since the First Burrow was established. I consider it, therefore, highly unlikely that these two fools will travel far enough to come in contact with even isolated natives.

''Should this occur, we might reasonably expect the natives to react much as did our solitary specimen: with violence. They would then know of the existence of two Quozl only. They would learn nothing of the existence of the rest of us, of the colony, or even of our origin. I have studied their broadcasts. There would be much initial excitement, which would rapidly fade as soon as native authorities decided the two artists were alone.

"Weigh that against the chance that an armed search party might encounter a prowling native or two. At first I thought we should go after them. I no longer believe this. Let them go. Let them slute and dance for a while. The surface of Shiraz will take care of them."

Stream-cuts-Through and Lifts-with-Shout did not vote. Instead, they let the experts make the decision. It was decided the best thing to do was to do nothing. They would all meditate in the hope that the renegades would return. They would be punished for their actions, but welcomed back as well. They were still Quozl.

When all was done, the Captain made an eloquent speech praising the two artists for their daring and boldness. This was proper. As for maintaining secrecy it was decided to ignore but not deny, since the relatives of the two who had vanished would surely ask questions. It would be treated as a matter for the mental specialists. That would discourage interest on the part of the general population. If the Council did not make an issue of it, the colonists would assume there was nothing much out of the ordinary to discuss.

Looks-at-Charts found himself reciting one of the multiple chants for the souls of the departed. High-red-Chanter had been no friend to him, but he and his paramour were still Quozl, of the Shirazian Quozl. They deserved sympathy, if not respect.

While he chanted on their behalf he mused on what a pity it was that he'd been unable to shoot the both of them.

The colony continued to expand and grow at a carefully monitored predetermined rate. Tunnels were dug in the cardinal seven directions as well as downward. Elaborate ventilation systems sucked fresh air from the surface of Shiraz to cool and invigorate the lowest levels. Chambers were built according to patterns first developed on Azel and Mazna.

Meanwhile scouts led by Looks-at-Charts and his successors continued to escort study teams to the surface. Expeditions ranged farther and farther afield without finding any evidence of native presence. The native war ended and was soon followed by other tribal conflicts, though on smaller scales. The Shirazians seemed congenitally incapable of cooperating among themselves. The philosophers debated such contradictions fruitlessly.

During the intermittent tribal peace that followed, the local natives developed and expanded, but none of their destructive pathways came anywhere near the Burrow. The landing team had chosen the touchdown site better than they could have known.

Following the death of honored Stream-cuts-Through, permission was given to the native study team to install a well-camouflaged antenna atop the northern peak, to better monitor native transmissions. Language studies in particular benefited from this development.

It was learned that the natives had developed fission and fusion weapons. This was serious, since their uncontrolled use might result in the accidental destruction of the colony. Yet after a short testing period they were put away and not utilized in any of the intertribal conflicts. Another puzzling development that enriched the work of the philosophers. The Shirazians were not only alien, they were as alien as could be imagined. Having developed a superior weapon of war, they chose not to employ it. The ancient Quozl would not have hesitated. Nothing the Shirazians did made any sense.

Yet their technological development continued apace, with the study team wondering what they might achieve if they could ever quash their propensity for conflict. Trails in the sky were found to be made by advanced native atmospheric craft that flew far faster and higher than those the Quozl had encountered at touchdown. Their visual broadcasts acquired color and sharpness if not depth.

There came the day when the presence of an artificial relay satellite was detected. It was followed by others, by a rapid increase in the number of transmissions, and by visits via primitive propulsion craft to the planet's single satellite. The Quozl watched and meditated, and all the while the colony slowly grew.

Meanwhile their mountain fastness remained as isolated and unvisited by the native population as ever. In the double generational gap that followed touchdown, only one sighting was ever made of a native in the vicinity of the Burrow.

Actually there were four of them. The study team that made the rare encounter numbered five and was led by the aged but still virile Looks-at-Charts. They concealed themselves as they observed, hardly daring to breathe, ears held flat against their necks to present as low a profile as possible. They should have fled, but could not bring themselves to do so. The natives gave no indication that they were in any way aware of the nearby Quozl presence. The team stood alert and ready to flee quickly, but unless circumstances forced them to do so they determined to stay as long as possible to take advantage of the unprecedented opportunity for observation.

"Surely their intent is not to establish a burrow here," insisted a zoologist as he peered through his observation scope. "See how flimsy and small their structure is."

"Obviously temporary," the xenologist agreed.

The site was kept under observation around the clock, even at night when activity was limited. The team intended to miss nothing, not knowing when such an opportunity might come again. The study of electronic broadcasts was highly informative, but nothing compared to observation in the field.

It was pleasant to learn that the natives traveled in the manner of Quozl: an equal number of males and females. They were thoughtful enough to perform many of their daily activities outside the shelter, which enhanced the team's ability to record. Among these activities was one the natives called swimming, which they executed in a nearby lake. This was fascinating to the study team, which had seen such movements performed on recorded broadcasts. It was much more interesting to witness it in the wild. The activity itself smacked of insanity, which was only in keeping with the rest of Shirazian society.

The natives remained for several days. Special excitement was provided by one pair who on two separate occasions abandoned the communal habitat to couple amidst the trees in the middle of the night. The trees played no part in the coupling and the pair appeared to ignore them completely. This was disappointing to those team members who had hoped to record at least one behavioral pattern analogous to that of the Quozl.

The team observed for a long time until it struck them that no pause was involved and that coupling had concluded for the night. The realization was met with general disbelief.

The senior zoologist peered through the dim light in the direction of the scout. "Do you suppose they truly have finished and that really is all?"

"It would seem so." Looks-at-Charts was as astonished as the scientist.

Her assistant continued to stare through his scope, hoping in vain to spot additional activity. "Perhaps this pair is not healthy."

That assessment acquired some credence until the following night when the second pair emerged to couple. They finished faster than their predecessors. Confusion among the team members deepened. If the first pair had been unwell, then the second had to be on the verge of death. Yet the quarter appeared normal and healthy in every other way.

"Most of them choose to live at sea level," the geologist pointed out. "Possibly the altitude of this valley is affecting their biorhythms. Or it might be something in the atmosphere."

"I doubt it." Looks-at-Charts spoke with confidence even though this was hardly his field of expertise.

If there was something in the air, a gas or pollen or anything similarly detrimental, it did not affect the Quozl. Looks proved that by coupling with the senior zoologist half a dozen times before the sun rose. Neither of them experienced strain or illness as a result of the activity. There was nothing wrong with the air.

"It seems impossible for them to have populated the planet to the extent that they have if what we just witnessed was typical." The junior zoologist spoke in conference later that day, after the natives had collapsed their portable shelter to return the way they'd come.

It was again the geologist who incongruously first proposed the obvious.

"If their frequency of coupling is so much less than our own, then their fertility rate must be higher. Keep in mind that in our study of their transmissions we have seen little use of artificial contraceptives."

Looks-at-Charts gestured acknowledgment with both ears. "Perhaps only a single coupling is sufficient to ensure pregnancy. That would go a long way toward explaining its infrequency."

"Another partial explanation for their continuation of inter-species combat." The junior zoologist could not contain his amazement. He added hastily, "This is not for us to decide. We are simply a field team, here to gather facts and record observations. Final determinations will be made by those more qualified than ourselves."

To which all five of them were in traditional agreement.

Such observations rendered the Shirazians no less alien, but helped to make their alienness more comprehensible. It was becoming clear that while technologically advanced, they were emotionally, sexually, and spiritually immature. What could result from such racial anomalies *except* constant frustration and hormonal-induced conflict? The pessimists among the Quozl researchers felt that cooperative contact would never be possible, that the secret of the colony's existence would have to be kept from the natives forever.

But they kept this opinion to themselves.

VII.

Runs-Red-Talking delighted in instruction, especially the coupling sessions. He always had more energy than he knew what to do with anyway. Despite this his attitude during such classes was as serious and constrained as those of any respectful young Quozl. Coupling was serious business the intricacies of which could not be left to chance. So he paid close attention to the lectures and demonstrations and tried to envision what it would feel like to be sexually mature.

There were some things difficult to envision, information he was able to comprehend intellectually but not emotionally as he trained for adulthood. An instructor could only explain so much. Analogies helped but they were not reality. It wasn't like trying to imagine levitating or seeing through walls. There was more than mere philosophy at issue because his own body was involved. Still, no matter how hard one tried or studied the references there was still much missing. One could learn how to do anything, but you could not will the body to do something it was not yet capable of.

At least he was convinced it would not be painful.

As he left the meditation chamber he inspected himself thoughtfully. He was proud of the single half swirl with attendant stars that had been shaved into his upper right arm, of the bright gold and purple scarf that trailed from his left leg. Earrings were not permitted, not for several years yet. He longed for their weight and jingle. All part of the maturation right he had not yet achieved.

Meanwhile he and his companions could only admire the intricate designs etched into the fur of the adults, the blaze of color and jewelry they wore. Young Quozl lived on energy and envy. He'd already chosen and discarded in his mind a thousand earrings and scarves and other forms of bodily decoration. This was encouraged by his elders. It was good practice.

He was third-generation Shirazian. Easier to say that than to use the ridiculous native word for the planet. The natives were as dull and unaesthetic as they were warlike. So why had he always found them so fascinating? When a study session had ended he would run and rerun recordings of the natives and their incomprehensible activities long after his friends had fled in pursuit of more pleasurable activities.

Rains-cross-Grain and Appears-go-Over spotted him shuffling along solo and altered their paths to intercept him. Though they knew each other well they still took the time to perform the traditional greeting and Sama-sharing ritual. It was good practice and a lot of fun, especially when someone made an embarrassing mistake or left out something important.

No one forgot anything this time, however, and they continued their walk together.

Rains-cross-Grain was his closest female friend while Appears-go-Over was male and larger than either of them. He stood out because physical disparities were uncommon among the Quozl. How the natives coped with such variety among themselves was a source of unending wonder to those who studied such matters. It offered another rationale for their barbaric combativeness. Male and female Quozl, Runs knew, were always of more or less equal stature. Exceptions like Appears-go-Over were rare. Conscious of his differentness, Appears always walked hunched over to try and minimize his size.

They were taking a walk through First Burrow, which was centered on the entombed hulk of the *Sequencer*. The mother ship which had safely carried their ancestors through underspace to Shiraz was a fascinating place to explore, full of chambers and machines that no longer functioned because their work was now obsolete. Once it had been the entire settlement. Now it was only the axis from which the colony expanded.

Work was proceeding apace on Burrows Three, Four, and Five. Two had been completed the previous cycle. The tunnels which would link the new Burrows with the first two were finished while Four was in the process of receiving population. These were what young Quozl thought about, not the *Sequencer* and the long crawl and touchdown. Consideration of those was best left to historians. Runs and his friends were intent on their future.

As for the natives, they were no more aware of the colony's presence now than they'd been the day the *Sequencer* had entered their atmosphere. The country in which the Burrows were located was as little visited as ever. With luck life might continue in this fashion for hundreds of years, until the Quozl were so firmly established on Shiraz that nothing could threaten their survival.

So well was the colony doing that it was rumored plans were afoot to send several hundred well-equipped settlers on a nocturnal march to settle the valley to the north. This was territory familiar to the colony, having been visited many times by exploration teams.

Some philosophers wondered why the natives shunned this region. It was true that the climate was severe, but transmissions showed Shirazians dwelling in more hostile climes. They were adaptable, like the Quozl. Possibly it had something to do with the lack of farming land on the sharp-sided mountains. Apparently the natives had not yet learned how to grow all the food they needed underground.

They could have learned from Quozl agronomists, who made good use of the pure, clear water available to them and the artificial light provided by the engineers. New tools and machinery were fashioned from metal and hydrocarbon deposits the geologists found in abundance beneath Shiraz's surface. Food for growth and material for expansion were not lacking. Shiraz was a rich world.

"Personally," Rains-cross-Grain was saying, "I have no desire to visit the surface myself. It looks cold and dirty." She brought both ears flat against the sides of her head to emphasize her feelings. "We have everything we need right here, just as our ancestors did. Besides, the surface is home to terrible creatures."

Indeed, everyone knew the tale of the monster which had killed the hapless zoologist only to be slain in turn by the great explorer Looks-at-Charts. Runs-red-Talking always felt a surge of pride whenever his famous if distant relative was mentioned. Several times he had heard Looks-at-Charts lecture before he finally managed sufficient courage to approach and introduce himself. He did so acutely conscious of his inferior status and attire.

Looks-at-Charts had been gruff and distant, as was only proper, but he had corkscrewed an ear once when no one else was looking, and Runs had all but levitated with delight as a result of the acknowledgment. He'd bragged about it for days afterward. He knew he was unworthy of any special attention or consideration but felt singled out anyway.

"I wonder how I might react were I to encounter such a creature," mused Appears-go-Over.

"You'd run," said Runs-red-Talking with assurance. "It would only be the sensible thing to do. Haven't you studied it down in the surface museum? The size of the animal! All teeth and claws and voracity."

Actually Runs had always wondered if the monster slain by Looks-at-Charts was all that ferocious, or if it had simply been stuffed and mounted that way to frighten adolescents and infants. It wasn't necessary. Most Quozl had no desire to visit the surface. The weather was often terrible: freezing in the cold season, too dry in the hot, and there was always the danger of meeting one of the homicidal natives and getting yourself killed.

He found himself saying unexpectedly, "I wouldn't be afraid of a visit to the surface."

Rains-cross-Grain looked at him sideways. "Then you're as crazy as the natives."

"It wouldn't be so bad."

"Looks-at-Charts says otherwise, and he ventured out with proper equipment and backup support," she argued. "You're not a scout and you have no access to anything."

"You don't need anything." To his shock he sounded almost belligerent. "Everyone knows what the surface is like. I know I couldn't use any equipment, or even one of the restricted survey maps, but there'd be no danger so long as you stayed in the Burrow valley and memorized your exit location."

"You'd die up there." Rains-cross-Grain gestured conclusively with both ears, pointing them straight up.

"I think not," he replied haughtily. "Why should walking across real soil be any more dangerous or difficult than walking a tunnel? You simply have to remember reference points and landmarks."

"I still say it can't be done without the right equipment."

Runs moved very close, until he was just outside her psychological imperative. "Are you challenging me?"

His straightforward response upset her. She looked to Appears-go-Over for support. "I was merely postulating a scenario, not seriously suggesting it be tried." He backed away and together the three of them turned a corridor corner. By way of apology he adjusted her scarves.

They passed two adults, and three pairs of ears dipped and bobbed in simultaneous genuflection as a sign of respect. The adults ignored them, though they would have reacted immediately had the strolling adolescents not been properly deferential.

Rains-cross-Grain had recovered from the abruptness of her friend's reaction. "Though I still have to believe that anyone who ventured outside without appropriate support and supplies couldn't possibly survive"—she hesitated, said finally—"overnight."

"Of course they could." Runs spoke analytically now and without his earlier passion. "The same water we drink in the Burrows runs freely across the surface, there are edible native foods, and for an overnight stay you wouldn't have to eat anything anyway. I think you could stay out on the surface for many days all by yourself." Even as he finished the statement he wondered if perhaps he hadn't overdone it a bit.

He had. That was too much for the tolerant Rains-cross-Grain.

"No one could do that. Not Looks-at-Charts himself would dare such folly."

Runs gazed unwaveringly into her pale lavender eyes, a wild, jaunty tone in his voice. "I would."

"Don't talk like that. This is a ridiculous conversation." Appears-go-Over was clearly upset with both of them. "Talking nonsense is a waste of time. You speak like you'd really try it. Even if you wanted to, you couldn't."

Runs-red-Talking knew whereof his friend spoke. It wasn't a matter of avoiding the guards. There were no guards posted at any of the exit tunnels. There was no need for them. Anyone who left the colony without authorization and thereby risked exposing himself to the natives risked the most extreme discipline. Only camouflaged, experienced, properly equipped exploration teams were permitted to go outside. The thought of embarking on a casual stroll touched on the sacrilegious. No one had ever tried such a thing.

That was precisely what so intrigued Runs-red-Talking. You didn't need special training or equipment to go outside. All you needed was the will.

Appears-go-Over wasn't through. "You mustn't speak of such matters."

"Why not?" wondered Runs. "If I went would you expose me?"

"Of course not." Appears made it clear that betrayal was not a word in his vocabulary.

◇ **124** ◇

Rains echoed him, but her assurance was glazed with sarcasm. "We'd dare not make a report because we might be held partly responsible for your madness."

"You're right anyway." Runs laughed it off. "It would be a stupid thing to even consider. I wonder why we've wasted so much time discussing it."

"Because you wouldn't shut up about it," Rains reminded him.

He lunged playfully in her direction and she darted out of his way. They laughed freely in the absence of adults, dancing and making bold gestures they were as yet physically incapable of concluding. The absurd business of taking a stroll on the surface was quickly forgotten.

Runs believed his friends when they said they would not betray him, but it was best to be prudent in such matters. If he went ahead and did what he'd almost decided to do, there was always the chance that one of them might tell and that as a result a group of adults would appear to drag him back home before he had the chance to see or hear much of anything. So he carried on quietly, pretending to have put the whole matter out of his mind.

He planned carefully, waiting awhile to make certain his friends had forgotten the conversation, casually monitoring the surface weather reports when no one was looking, preparing himself as best he could so that no one would suspect what was growing in his mind.

So long as they were polite and properly respectful of their elders, young Quozl were indulged to excess by the adults. They had free run of the colony. Friends often stayed for days with other friends, informing their natural parents and supervisors only upon their return. For such excursions they were sometimes chided, but never disciplined.

Given such lax supervision it was not difficult for Runs-red-Talking to accumulate a tiny store of supplies. They were not designed to encourage surface exploration and they were not what a properly equipped expedition would have carried, but they would have to suffice.

He had a small container for carrying water, concentrated vegetable tablets to sustain him in the event that edible surface growths proved scarce, and an extra oversuit. The surface could be cold at night in this first part of the second half of the year. He also took his school recorder so he could make notes. Why, there was no telling what great discoveries he might make. Looks-at-Charts might honor him personally.

He was not in the least worried about encountering natives. The colony had been in existence for three generations and in all that time only a single quartet of Shirazians had come close to the Burrows. He was, however, mildly worried about dangerous animals. Studies of native transmissions had identified the monster mounted in the surface museum as a grizzly bear and he did not want to meet one behind a tree. The bear was no figment of an overly active meditation session. It was very real, and the surface might be home to other, even worse horrors.

But if you wanted to be an explorer you had to take risks. Besides, what he was planning was nothing compared to what Looks-at-Charts and the first survey team had chanced. In contrast to them he knew what the terrain was like in the immediate vicinity of the Burrows, having intently studied the records made by numerous expeditions. He knew something about the flora and fauna as well. If the first team had advanced in ignorance, could he not follow in their footsteps steeped in knowledge?

He began in the midst of sleeptime, walking quietly, slipping past preoccupied night workers, passing through the shadows cast by encounter room sculptures, ascending into the upper tunnels. Study chambers and living quarters fell behind, as did workshops and industrial warrens. On past the towering cylindrical shafts which hummed softly as they inhaled air through camouflaged vents and compressed it for injection into the colony's extensive respiration system. Until at last he stood before An Exit.

It was just a door. Its exterior, he
knew, would perfectly duplicate its sur-
face surroundings, be they solid, liquid,
or even gaseous. There was no alarm,
there were no guards. There was no
need for either since no Quozl would
dare to defy the law which prohibited
unauthorized surface excursions. No responsible, informed, *adult* Quozl, that is.

But I am just a juvenile, Runs told himself. I am not old
enough to fully comprehend such matters, therefore I cannot
be severely punished for my lack of understanding.

In any event it would not matter, for he quite intended to
return before his absence could be discovered or traced.

Working furiously and earning the admiration of his relatives and friends for his relentless industry, he completed all
necessary preparations well in advance, so as to be ready the
instant the right moment presented itself. His natural parents
thought he was visiting with a distant uncle. His uncle was
convinced he was staying with a cousin. The cousin believed
Runs was sojourning with friends and the friends knew for a
fact he was meditating. By the time anyone could trace that
carefully constructed circle of deception he would be back
wondering what all the talk was about, insisting all the while
that he'd done no more than go for a stroll through the
botanical collection in Burrow Four.

To prevent accidental openings the door was secured man-
ually. Runs took hold of the control wheel and twisted.
Nothing happened and for an instant he experienced a delicious irony. Were all his elaborate preparations to come to
naught simply because he wasn't strong enough to manage
the door? It was the one thing he hadn't considered.

He was on the verge of despair when the wheel creaked
and turned. A panel moved aside, revealing a sequence of
brightly lit buttons behind. He fingered them in the sequence
he'd memorized. That was very helpful of the study team
which had made the recording. It showed the team departing

on a meteorologically intensive mission to the surface. All one had to do was freeze the recording to study the correct lock sequence. There was no reason why anyone would want to, of course, so no one had thought to expunge the sequence from the recording, for which he was very grateful.

Counterlifts whispered metallically as the barrier rose on concealed hinges to reveal the forbidden world outside. All he had to do was step through.

It took him a long time to locate the hidden external switch. It looked for all the world like a twig growing from a real tree.

It took a moment for the door to close, swinging down silently to blend perfectly with the surrounding rock and vegetation. It looked no different from its surroundings and to make sure he could find it again he marked the place with his spray, a primitive but efficient method. No native would notice it. They were decidedly lacking in matters of olfactory sensitivity.

He'd chosen a night blessed by a full moon. Real wind brushed back the fur on his face and he immediately sampled the air, wary of nocturnal carnivores. His blood pounded.

Having not encountered Rains-cross-Grain or Appears-go-Over in several days he doubted either would remark on his absence. Rains had never repeated her challenge and in all likelihood had forgotten the entire discussion.

He had no difficulty choosing a course by the light of the moon. The ghostly landscape was bathed in silver, magnificent and alive. What you did not get from the otherwise thorough recordings brought back by the study teams were the smells, the odors, the aromas of their adopted home. He inhaled deeply, savoring every sharp, musky, sweet smell as he played at matching them with creatures or plants remembered from his studies.

Whistling softly and chanting to himself, he headed down the gentle slope outside the exit in search of a suitable place to greet the forthcoming sunrise.

VIII.

"HEY, DAD!"

Chad's father had the cowling off the seaplane and was standing on a stool, bent over the gaping engine compartment. The plane's pontoons bumped gently against the narrow, handmade dock. It was hot today and he harvested sweat from his forehead with the back of his free hand as he turned to face his son. A socket wrench dangled from his fingers.

"Boy, can't you see I'm busy?"

"I know, Dad, but you said maybe we could fly into town today for groceries. Mom said she really needs that Crisco and some milk and eggs."

"Yeah. And you really need cookies and some ice cream." He nodded toward the single-story log cabin that stood stolidly a hundred yards upslope from the lakeshore. "I'm sure your mom has some cookies hidden somewhere. As for ice cream, you know we can't keep ice cream here. There's no freezer in the little fridge. I wouldn't mind having some ice cream around myself, but we need all the space in the chest to store block ice. For that matter, I'd like to have a freezer, a bigger generator to run it, and the money to pay for them both, but this year I'm afraid we'll have to do without any of 'em."

"Ahhh, that's what you said last year." As the pouting eight-year-old kicked at something crawling hastily across the dock, his father sighed.

"Maybe we can manage it next year, if I get that promotion. Right now I have to get this fixed or we won't go anywhere for anything. Why not take a hike somewhere? Watch the fish. Shoot a moose."

Chad tried not to smile and failed. "It's too hot."

"Then go swimming."

"Water's too cold."

"Baloney. It's warmed up by now. Go bother your sister, then, but leave me alone until I finish this. You want me to make a mistake and have us fall out of the sky on the way for groceries?" He ducked his head back beneath the engine cover.

"That won't happen, Dad. You know more about planes than anybody." He turned and started toward land.

A voice came from inside the engine compartment, softer than before. "Maybe in a day or two we can fly out for some ice cream."

Chad spun around. "Really, Dad? You mean it? For sure?"

"If the weather holds and we don't get a thunderstorm pattern."

"All *right*! I'm gonna have a Popsicle, ana Dove Bar, ana strawberry icee, ana . . ." The sugary liturgy faded like a solitary soprano's in a cathedral as the boy turned and sprinted up the hill toward the cabin.

His mother was in the kitchen manipulating meat loaf, her fingers slick with grease and ground chuck. Chad burst in and forgot to catch the screen door before it slammed behind him.

"MomDadsaidIcouldhavesomecookies!"

His mother looked across at him. Her hair was secured behind her in a ponytail. He never saw her wear her hair like that in the city. Only during the summer when they were at the cabin.

"He didn't say anything of the kind," insisted another voice, oozing snide. "He's just making it up."

"I am *not*!" Chad glared in the direction of the little den. His fourteen-year-old sister, Mindy, was sprawled on the sofa perusing a garish magazine featuring on its cover a long-haired young musician clad primarily in trendy rags. The lettering shrieked across the room.

"Mindy, knock it off." His mother looked back down at him. "Chad, *did* your father say you could have cookies?"

"Well, not exactly." Chad didn't meet his mother's gaze.

"What do you mean, 'not exactly'?"

"He sort of said we probably *had* some cookies. I don't see the point in having them if we can't eat 'em."

"You may have *one* cookie."

"Ah, but Mom! I'm going on a hike! I need my strength."

She neither smiled nor wavered. The law, he'd learned long ago, was the law. But she was concerned if not compliant.

"Got your backpack ready?"

"Sure. My pack's always ready." It lay on the bed in his room. There was another bed in the room, often occupied by his older sister, but as far as he and the fates were concerned it was *his* room.

Just as it was his cabin, his floatplane, his lake, and his mountains. Legal niceties did not concern him. There was legal and there was self-evident.

"There are some tuna sandwiches in the fridge," his mother was saying. "Take one and an apple."

"Geez, Mom." he was already pawing through the old refrigerator, scanning the Saran-wrapped sandwiches for the one displaying the least amount of crust. "I don't want an apple."

"No apple, no cookie."

"All right, all right." He hid the sly expression on his face. "One apple, two cookies."

This time she had to smile. "Two it is, but you'd better eat that apple."

"I will. I'll save it for later."

She didn't ask if he was taking water. He knew enough to stick close to the lakeshore. In addition there were several small streams from which he could drink. The pristine mountain wilderness area where the cabin was located had thus far avoided contamination by pollutants. They'd been coming here ever since her husband inherited the place and none of them had ever been made sick by the water. If anything it was probably one of the healthiest, most unspoiled places left in the country, or so Jack always insisted.

"You be back before sundown," she said unnecessarily. Chad knew the rules. Despite his age he was an experienced solo hiker, precocious and careful. He'd been taking short walks on his own since five. By the time he was twelve he'd be going out overnight. She tried not to think about the passage of time as she turned back to the chopping board and began sweeping minced onions into the ground chuck.

Chad carefully packed his sandwich, the apple, and the two largest sugar cookies he could find, slipped the brown sack into his pack, and headed out the front door before his mother could change her mind.

His father was still slaving over the plane engine, occasionally utilizing words which Chad knew he ought not to be hearing but which he was by now familiar with. Words he never dared use in the presence of adults or his blabbermouthed sister, who would gladly repeat them to his mother in the expectant ecstasy of seeing him punished. His father didn't introduce him to cursing. The Bible took care of that. He would gladly have suffered fire and brimstone and plagues of locusts in place of a fourteen-year-old sister. Unfortunately that was the affliction the fates had chosen for him.

Yet when he could get away from her, away from the cabin where she holed up with her magazines and poetry for most of the summer, it no longer seemed so important. Nothing was more important than anything else when you were eight, precocious, and intensely curious. Everything was new and fresh: the next tree, the next rock, the next beetle making its laborious way through the gravel that lined the lakeshore. The tadpole swimming in the sunlit water. The ghost birds that you couldn't see who left their songs hanging like windblown transparencies in the evening air. The world was a wonder.

As much as he enjoyed his explorations he was still disappointed no one else came to build a cabin by the lake. His father explained that it was no longer permitted and that if Grandpa Carson hadn't built his before the government regulations had been put in place concerning this region, they couldn't live here for the summer either. Besides which not everyone could afford or knew how to fly a floatplane. The rugged, precipitous terrain that enclosed the lake made that and walking the only ways in. There were plenty of other lakes, some much prettier, all more accessible. So few people came here.

The isolation was what made their annual summer stays so pleasant to him, he'd tried to explain to his son. Flying big planes was hard work and he delighted in the solitude they found here in one of the least-visited parts of the country. The lake was narrow and twisty, difficult to land upon. Only the fact that he was a professional pilot enabled them to visit here with comparative ease, and he still had to make every approach with the utmost care.

His mother also enjoyed the peace and quiet while his sister wanted only a place to read and practice her poetry. Chad had snorted derisively at that. What could you expect from an older sister, or from any girl? Poetry!

Except Mom. Mom wasn't really a girl. Mom was—Mom, and that was different.

He wondered how far he'd get today. His parents insisted that whenever he went off by himself he keep the lakeshore within view. It limited his options considerably.

There were so many streams he wanted to follow, so many talus slides worth scrambling up. His father wouldn't listen. This way, he'd explained patiently, if Chad hurt himself (as if he could possibly hurt himself!) it would be easy for them to find him simply by following the shoreline. So he kept the cool water within sight, according to the rules, sometimes teasing the limits by walking uphill until only a tiny patch of blue was visible through the trees and delighting in the little thrill this near denial of parental authority gave him.

It really was hot today, he mused, but so long as you stayed in the shade of the huge pines and furs that grew right down to the water's edge you were okay. You could play tag with the sunlight, skipping from one path of shadow to the next.

He studied his watch, of which he was inordinately proud despite the fact it only cost three bucks. He'd made good time since he'd left the cabin and judging by the angle of the sun and his own stomach it was time to stop for lunch. The cabin lay far behind him, well out of sight, along with the float-plane and the little dock his father had hammered together out of rough-cut pine and split lengths of six-inch log.

He took a bite out of the apple and, contractual obligations thus satisfied, attacked the sandwich with gusto.

Runs-red-Talking knew he was taking a chance nibbling unclassified alien vegetation, but he'd taken so many chances already this one additional small one hardly seemed worthy of concern despite the fact that no one knew where he was. Should he suffer any kind of poisoning that would prevent him from making it back to the Burrow, there would be no one to come looking for him. He was prepared for that.

He'd planned for this trip as well as anyone in his position possibly could, studying the recordings made by authorized expeditions and committing to memory whatever seemed potentially useful. For example, there was a certain variety of weed which grew in profusion on the mountain slopes. While not particularly nutritious, it was quite edible and wonderfully fresh-tasting in comparison to the processed food available in the colony. There were also a number of edible flying creatures. All one had to do was convince oneself it was all right to eat a living being that had not been preprocessed. He kept reminding himself that there was native fauna which would have no such hesitations where he was concerned.

Such thoughts made his first night's rest uneasy. The second night (for now that he was out he had no intention of returning immediately) was better, though a tremendous piercing racket woke him abruptly just before sunrise. His fur did not relax until the noise was swallowed by the night, and he was surprised at how quickly he fell asleep again.

He encountered nothing as monstrous as the massive nightmare whose stuffed form graced the museum, but he did espy something long and tawny-hued crossing the talus slope opposite him on four padded feet. Its lower jaw hung slack, enabling him to see the prominent canines, but it was far away and failed to sense his presence. It kept climbing until it disappeared.

He had no map. It would have been dangerous to make one, since its discovery would have revealed his intent to any thoughtful adult. What information was available on the ground he was traversing, mostly from the initial pretouchdown survey, he had committed to memory. Like everything else known about the surface, it was available to any who wanted to study it.

He did not have to debate which direction to take. He chose the path he did, not because it was inherently any more interesting than any other, but because it enabled him to follow the course of the river which ran above the Burrow. Regardless of what else he might encounter, he would be assured of a constant supply of drinking water.

According to the report filed by a single expedition member more than a year earlier, the river fed a large lake in a sheer-walled valley to the east. The report was never confirmed because the interests of that particular expedition lay elsewhere, but it struck Runs as a useful goal. He would walk to the lake, sample its waters, and return.

Three days out from home he caught his first glimpse of it

and experienced the rush of excitement which signified that he was about to cross from Quozl-mapped territory into unknown parts of Shiraz. The slope he was descending was gentle and easy. He could have raced down it at high speed, easily dodging between the widely spaced tall trees, but it was so much more pleasurable to take his time and touch each tree as he passed. Their rough, deeply scarred unQuozlene bark was a constant amazement. He could easily sense the sap moving through xylem as the tree pumped it skyward.

Artists and administrators fought constantly over Shirazian wood. The artists wanted to cut more of it while the administrators worried that such cuttings might be noticed from the air. The philosophers tried to mediate, with the result that only fallen trees and dead wood could be brought back into the Burrows. So the artists continued to fume while the administrators continued to worry.

Runs bent to heft a fallen branch worth a week's meditations to a skilled carver. He tossed it aside with the casualness of the suddenly wealthy. He had around him, as it were, wood to burn.

From his studies he believed that the tall plants which formed a meadow at the western end of the lake would prove not only edible but tasty. The habit of Shirazian vegetation of concentrating metals in their roots and stems added spice to their natural flavor. The forest of succulents he eventually encountered were no exception. They grew in such dense clumps that he was able to leave the shore and walk through the thicket itself. After a while the slope sharpened, the plants fell behind, and water tumbled musically over slick boulders in its rush to reach the lake.

Soon the cold would return to this part of Shiraz and all this beauty would disappear beneath a blanket of frozen water. Then the pace of exploration would slacken and only specially equipped expeditions would dare its frigid surface.

He knelt to examine a seed pod which had fallen from a nearby tree. It was still intact, having not yet been disturbed by the small chisel-toothed quadrupeds that made their homes

high in branches and tree hollows. They
were not the only ones who found the
contents of such pods appealing. As he
walked he used his teeth to peel back
the thick seed covers, spitting them aside
so he could suck out the nourshing nut-
meats within. They were a real luxury in
the Burrow. Ever since he began his
journey he'd gorged himself on such treats. His store of
tablets lay untouched in his pack. He was confident the trail
of kernels would not be noticed by any passing aircraft.

Not even the Head of Council feasted so well. Only the
members of the exploration teams had shared such delights.
He ate what he wanted and tossed the remainder aside.

As he followed the river he searched for signs of the
peculiar amphibious creatures which inhabited its shores.
There was nothing like them in the old records and they had
charmed and fascinated expeditionary zoologists. Usually
they sat without moving, their throat sacs pulsing, until
something disturbed or intrigued them and they leaped into
the water. They filled the night air with the most extraordinary chorus.

One particularly fine specimen did not run when he approached, choosing to maintain its perch even when Runs
stepped into ankle-deep water. His hands relaxed on his knees
as he stared.

The creature flicked a golden eye in his direction, tensed,
and hopped off into the reeds. Runs mimicked the posture
and hopped right alongside it. As soon as it landed it flung
itself into the tall thin growths a second time. Runs heard it
splash somewhere up ahead. Automatically he checked his
legs. No doubt this tranquil backwater was home to numerous
water-borne parasites, but expedition zoologists had yet to
identify any that found Quozl flesh palatable. Most could not
make their way through dense Quozl fur.

He crouched to follow the amphibian when another sound
made him freeze. It was much more frightening and expres-

sive than the mysterious yowl which had momentarily kept him awake that first night.

"Hey, a frog!"

Runs-red-Talking spun wildly in the water, his ears erect for maximum reception. He was surrounded on three sides by tall reeds whose stems reached no telling how deep into the murky water. The lake itself lay somewhere not far ahead. That left him with two choices: to retreat into the reeds and hope he didn't stumble into water over his head, or to make a dash for the dry land on his right. While he was trying to decide, the decision was made for him.

"Maybe over th—"

Unless his language studies had been for naught, Runs knew that the native had ceased in the midst of an incomplete thought. His first impression was that for a Shirazian it was very small. Even making allowances for its nonexistent ears it appeared unusually tiny. He was struck instantly by the nakedness of the arms and face, made even more grotesque by the unruly knot of fur which adorned the skull. Long strands of the stuff hung down the back of the native's neck.

Its back was distorted by a huge growth, until Runs realized that it was not organic but instead a kind of flexible container not unlike the one slung over his own right shoulder. The legs were tightly bound, a practice which struck Runs as foolishly confining. Perhaps it had something to do with the nakedness of Shirazian skin. It might be ashamed to reveal itself.

Finally there was the typically impossible Shirazian footgear, which not only protected the bottoms of the feet but also completely enclosed them in stiff, unyielding material. It was as impractical a piece of design as could be imagined. They made Runs uncomfortable just to look at.

Both lawbreakers gaped at each other for a long moment before the native made a noise. It was astonishingly loud. Runs's ears folded in response. As it spoke, its naked facial muscles jumped wildly, as out of control as the Shirazian libido.

"Wow! What are *you*?"

Runs-red-Talking had spent many days immersing himself in native language study, usually finishing at or near the top of his study group, but in the shock of the moment his knowledge deserted him. Unable to formulate a sensible response, he settled for familiarity. Reaching out  and forward with his right hand, all fingers spread and extended, he penetrated the native's Sama in the vicinity of its face.

He had completely forgotten that it was precisely that gesture which had resulted in the honored scout Burden-carries-Far's death at the hands of another native.

"What is your name?" Even as he mouthed the words he felt a chill, wondering if he would be understood or if his response would be dangerously misinterpreted.

In any event, the native did not respond in a hostile fashion. It did not appear to be armed. Taking a moment to reflect on its diminutive size, Runs decided it was either a juvenile or very young adult. Regardless, it reacted eagerly.

"Hey, you can talk!"

Somewhat to his surprise Runs found he could understand the words. They were no different from what he had encountered in his studies.

"Sort of," he said, wishing the native would moderate its tone.

It looked at him slightly sideways. Perhaps one eye was more efficient than its companion, Runs thought. "You sound weird. Like a cat that's trying to hum."

The short native promptly emitted a series of rapid barking sounds, issued like its words at deafening volume. Runs winced as he tried to make sense of them. Remember! Why can't I remember?

Then it came to him. The last sounds were not whole-thought communication but rather amusement expressed aurally. Instead of indicating laughter normally, via gestures and expression and body language, the Shirazians employed highly individualized variants of the barking sound. Runs was pleased. If the native was amused, it could not be angry. He lowered his right ear to indicate that he understood.

"Hey, that's neat!" How did they stand such loudness, Runs wondered? His ears throbbed as the native continued, pointing with a five-fingered hand. And how did they build anything with only ten fingers? "What else can you do with those?" He fingered one of his own pitiful organs of hearing.

Runs was at once excited and confused. Was the juvenile Shirazian so different from the adult form? This one was openly friendly.

Of course, creatures like that existed on Quozlene itself, as well as Mazna. Species whose grubs or larvae were quiescent when disturbed but whose adult form reacted violently to contact. And like the Shirazians, the adults also varied wildly in size and shape from one another. Diversity gave rise to competition, which implied eternal conflict.

Had he betrayed the colony to such beings? Yet if this one was truly a mere juvenile . . . He searched the terrain beyond. It appeared to be traveling alone.

That made no sense. Studies proved that Shirazian juveniles stayed close to their parents or in restricted areas. What was this one doing out here by itself?

Like himself, he thought with a start.

It had not been wandering aimlessly. He could see it was healthy and well-fed. Nor did it act lost. Though it was difficult to identify juvenile gender since the females were pouchless, he guessed from bearing and hip displacement that the one confronting him was a male.

It made no sense. There had to be adults in the vicinity. He had no wish to sample the mature form's violent propensities. The longer he remained, the greater the chance the adults would put in an appearance and the more ingrained this encounter would become in the juvenile's memory, though studies suggested their attention spans were brief. A few apparently had no memories whatsoever. Occasionally this trait carried over into the adult form. It seemed especially common among important Burrow leaders, who frequently appeared to act from instinct instead of rational thought.

As all this flashed through Runs's mind, the juvenile reached out with unexpected speed and grasped the extended fingers in his own. The breach of courtesy stunned Runs. You never invaded another individual's Sama below the chin line unless you planned to kill or couple. Logic insisted that this native intended neither.

"Hey," it declared in its booming, painfully loud voice, "you're *warm*. In fact you're really hot. Have you got a fever or something?"

You could tell a lot from visual and aural broadcasts, but one thing you could not learn was body temperature. To Runs-red-Talking the native felt as one dead. Yet it was obviously healthy. Runs realized he'd just made an important if accidental discovery. No one had taken measurements of the single dead native specimen's body temperature until it was too late. Here he stood, clutching one that was alive and well. He wondered if the adults felt equally frigid.

Not that heat was absent. It was simply feeble.

"Don't look so afraid," the juvenile was saying. "There's nothing here to be frightened of. What's your name? Where did you come from? Not from around here, I'll bet."

Around here. Runs wrenched his fingers free of the astonishingly powerful grip and turned to flee, his legs animated by sheer panic.

"Hey, don't go! Wait!"

His feet cleared the ground in great, measured strides. He had to get away before adults appeared on the scene. They might want *him* for a specimen. His only chance lay in the hope that the juvenile might forget about the encounter. Native juveniles were wont to do such. What could this one tell its adults anyway? Runs jumped the last rivulet and turned upstream, not pausing to think, not realizing he was making a straight line for the Burrows. He was not the fearless explorer he'd imagined himself to be: only a terrified youngster who'd run into far more than he'd bargained for.

The last words of the native juvenile to reach him were "Boy, can you run!" Then he was beyond hearing range.

He didn't slow down until he reached the crest of the first ridge. Utterly exhausted and out of breath he collapsed and rolled onto his back, trying to recover his strength. He was bruising his tail but paid it no notice. His mind hurt worse than his body, aflame with the knowledge of what he'd gone and done. It didn't even matter that his clothing was an unQuozl mess.

Suddenly it no longer seemed so daring, a mere prank, a challenge from a friend to be casually taken up. The odds had beaten him. He had been the one to actually encounter a native when all the previous expeditions had managed to avoid such contact.

When he could breathe freely again he sat up and stared downslope. He'd covered a lot of ground and there was no sign of the juvenile. How the natives could even balance themselves, much less run, on those narrow, tiny feet was something which continued to amaze Quozl biologists. There had to be some concealed mechanism for maintaining equilibrium they had yet to discover. But they could not run very fast. A quozl infant could outdistance all but the best of them.

Only then did it occur to him that he'd best take a roundabout route back to the colony and pay some attention to obliterating his tracks so that he could not be followed. As he started to do so it struck him that he knew only one way back home, the way he'd come. He knew only a single set of landmarks. He could not take a circuitous route for fear of becoming hopelessly lost in these mountains.

He agonized over his choices for the rest of the day before resignedly starting back the way he'd come, carefully utilizing branches to wipe out any tracks he left, trying to keep to the rocks wherever possible. Where streams presented themselves he deliberately walked along them, forcing himself to suffer the watery chill. It took longer, but by the time he was

◇ 142 ◇

within a day's hike of the Burrow he was convinced the natives would not be able to follow him.

Chad burst into the cabin, ignoring the delicious aroma of fresh meat loaf browning in the woodstove. His sister spared him an indifferent glance before turning back to her magazine and boosting the volume on her Walkman another notch. The earphones rode her head like pink limpets.

"Hey, Mom, hey, Dad, guess what?"

His mother didn't turn from her work. "Your father's out back."

He hesitated long enough to hear the familiar sounds of logs being split by the heavy, double-bladed axe. His mother stood by the sink stirring a large pitcher of cold tea. Maybe they didn't have ice, but the stream water they piped to the cabin was plenty cold.

When she saw he wasn't about to leave she finally turned to him, a tolerant, maternal smile on her face that he planned to quickly erase. "Did you have a nice hike, dear?"

"Did I ever! Boy, wow! Mom, you'll never guess what I saw."

"What did you see, Chadee?" She began filling glasses from the pitcher.

"I saw a . . . !" He hesitated. His excitement had rapidly outpaced his eight-year-old's powers of description. "I don't know *what* it was. But it was neat. It had long ears and big feet and . . . !"

"A rabbit." His mother set glasses on the table, one facing each side.

"No, Mom, no!" Why couldn't adults ever *see*? "It wasn't a rabbit. Its face was different and it was a lot bigger."

She remained unperturbed. "A jackrabbit. Your father says you don't usually see them up this high, but sometimes . . ."

"NO!" That did it. She stopped what she was doing to

stare at him. He spoke as earnestly as a saint. "Mom, it—wasn't—a—rabbit. It had a tail, yeah, but it was kind of pointy, not fluffy like a rabbit's. It was as big as you are, and it had real big eyes, and its teeth were like mine." He opened his mouth and pointed to the incisors in question. "And it walked real straight, and it wore clothes, kind of like a girl's bathing suit only with pockets and stuff ana belt, and it ran like he . . ."

His mother fixed him with a penetrating gaze. "Chad, you've been listening to your sister's stories too much."

"*It's not a story, Mom*. I really saw it." Suddenly one of those grandiose realizations that occasionally occur to children struck him with the force of the school bully's fist. It was the immediate, sure, and certain knowledge that even if he were to bring into the cabin the entire advisory staff of the American Academy of Science together with the ghosts of Einstein, Franklin, and Curie, their combined arguments on behalf of what he'd seen would not be sufficient to convince Mrs. Alice April Collins of 15445 Chandler Boulevard, Burbank, California, of the truth.

So what he did instead was look across at the table and mumble softly, "Maybe it was a rabbit. Is lunch ready?"

"Soon," said his mother, completely dismissing the incident from conversation, though he could hear her muttering under her breath. "We've got to get Mindy to stop telling him these scary bedtime stories."

Chad's older sister was a terrific pain in the ass, but she did have a talent for spinning the most wonderful tales. Particularly at night when it was dark and rainy and thundering outside and she could do her utmost to terrify her little brother. Chad yelled and complained when in reality he actually enjoyed his sister's yarns, the more frightening the better. He could repeat them to his friends at school, wishing that he could be as good with words as she was. Sadly he was much more straightforward and a lot less imaginative. Math was much more to his liking. As his father put it, he was a steadying influence compared to his wildly imaginative sister.

So he knew he wasn't suffering an unpredictable outburst of artistic inventiveness. He'd seen the creature and had even talked with it, if you could call that funny humming-whistling speech. It had bolted and run, faster than even Jimmy Stevens in the sixth grade could run. It had big feet and long legs, too long for its body. He knew what it was.

An alien. Or maybe some weird medical experiment that had escaped from a hospital or a zoo or a military installation somewhere. It wasn't an animal. Funny talk was still talk, and it had been dressed, in strange oversized flip-flop type shoes and a bright shiny suit. The latter didn't offer much protection in the mountains, but he supposed that if you were covered with fur you wouldn't need many clothes.

Then there were those ears. Like rabbit ears, only thinner and with the edges curled toward each other, like a wet piece of cardboard. They tapered to points and when they bent it was almost as though they were jointed instead of wholly flexible. And the big eyes, staring back at him. Fortunately little teeth. He remembered neither fang nor claw. But he did remember one other thing.

"Hey, Mom?"

"What is it, Chad?" She was hovering around the sink again.

"Do you know of anything that has seven fingers?"

She hesitated and frowned at the sink, for the first time curious instead of simply dismissive. "Seven fingers? No, I don't think so. You could ask your father, but I don't think there's any animal with seven fingers."

"No big deal. Just asking." He slid into his seat, selected a piece of bread from the stack in the middle of the table, and reached for the raspberry preserves.

"We're running low. Leave some for everyone else."

"Hey, Mom, I'm hungry. I've been exploring, remember?"

"I remember. Just save enough room to explore your vegetables."

He nodded as he ladled seeded red gel onto a whole-wheat platform. Seven fingers. Seven plus seven was fourteen. Having fourteen fingers would be almost like having a whole extra hand.

Or maybe his mother was right and his sister's stories *were* having an effect on him. He shrugged inwardly. His teachers said he could stand a little imagination.

He was almost finished with the bread when his mother spoke to him again. "Go and find your sister."

"Aw, Mom. You know where Mindy is."

"And so do you. Go and get her."

"Okay, but she won't listen to me. She'll just make a face and say I'm interrupting her and that she wants to finish whatever junk she's listening to."

"I'll finish *her* if she makes me wait supper. Tell her I sent you."

"Right," he said, having been officially deputized. He put down the half crust of bread, having sucked the preserves off the edge, and headed for the den.

His mother found strange thoughts shouldering aside concerns about overcooked beans and an inadequate supply of jam. Why *seven* fingers? Why not nine or ten or eleven? Had Mindy been telling the story, they would've been tentacles, with big toothy suction cups. She shrugged. Why not seven? As good a number as any.

She found herself staring at her own spread left hand. Dishwater wrinkles. In two years I'll be forty. The big four oh. If she kept on that way she'd end up brooding all through supper. So she put it, together with all philosophic consideration of additional digits, out of her mind. By the time supper was over she'd forgotten the entire incident.

Chad couldn't wait to get back to the reed marsh at the southwest end of the lake. But though he looked everywhere and spent the whole day, even risking his father's disapproval by returning after sunset, he saw no sign of the creature. Nor the following day or the day after that.

Maybe he *had* imagined it. His sister would have understood, but he didn't tell her because she'd only laugh and make fun of him. He never mentioned it to his mother again and not at all to his father.

He visited the marsh every day for the next several weeks until he'd half convinced himself that what he'd seen was a figment of his imagination, a bear cub or something that shock and surprise had embroidered. He'd imagined it talking, imagined trying to shake hands with it, imagined the look of intelligence in its eyes. Nothing could run that fast anyway. It could even have been some other kid playing a practical joke on him, a prankish hiker. Like that guy who'd gone stomping around Washington in his fake Bigfoot suit, getting his picture in the papers and on tv until somebody spotted him changing in a gas station rest room. But if it had been a practical joker he was fast enough to make the Olympics.

By the time they left the valley to return to Los Angeles and the new school term he'd completely forgotten it.

Well, almost.

Runs-red-Talking unerringly found his way back to the Burrow. The camouflaged entrance to the underground world of the Quozl was exactly where he remembered it. Finding it was a great relief since he'd reached the end of his endurance, supplies, and the excuses he'd concocted to explain his absence.

Every pebble was as he remembered it, every bit of forest detritus firmly in place. No one had passed this way since he'd employed it during his flight to freedom.

He adjusted the twigs that comprised the concealed switch and stepped aside as the section of surface unhinged itself, rising to reveal the smooth-sided tunnel beyond. He paused for a last long look at the surface of Shiraz, inhaled a final lungful of unrecycled, unprocessed air, and then darted inside.

As the door shut he savored last glimpses of the shrinking

outside world. Then he reached for the contact that would secure the barrier. His fingers never touched it.

"Stay your hand, youth. There is no need to lock the door since we were just going out."

His heart plummeted as he whirled. There were four adults, all laden with journey packs and full equipment belts. Two males, two females, one of the latter carrying, judging from her slightly protruding pouch.

You can't be, he thought wildly. It's almost sunrise outside and diurnal expeditions are dangerous. Dangerous and infrequent—but not unknown. How lucky he was, how fortunate, to have encountered one of those rare daytime study groups.

He wanted to strike out in anger, to slay them all here in this place to preserve his terrible secret, to cover his foolishness with their blood. Being Quozl, what he did was apologize.

Profoundly, abjectly, in the most affecting and honest inadequate language he could muster, his ears lower than low, his eyes locked on the tunnel floor. Because they realized the seriousness of what he'd done they politely allowed him to go on, until hoarseness invaded his throat and stole his words.

If they had only arrived a few moments later, after he'd left the tunnel. Or a few moments earlier, before he'd come inside. But they'd seen him enter. They knew he'd been outside, on the surface. If not his actions, then the soil and grass adhering to his sandals would have been proof enough of that. He'd cleaned them as best he could, but final cleansing would have had to wait until he'd reached his living quarters. Now it didn't matter. Nothing much mattered anymore.

"Given my lowly station and insignificant age I realize that this serious breach of the law must be reported," he managed to wheeze. "I expect to pay for what I have done with all I have to give. I can ask only humbly that you take my immaturity into account and realize that this childish action was taken on a dare from my fellows, and that no real harm has been done."

The leader of the expeditionary group made a double gesture of resignation with his ears. This breach of Burrow security was more important than their plans. Their work must now be delayed while this unbelievable incident was reported. All his careful ceremonial shaving would be for naught.

There were only three of them on the mount of inquiry, but they were intimidating enough. One was of his sire's generation, the second an Elder, and the third one of his contemporaries. The usual assemblage for debating a juvenile offense.

Landing Command said nothing about the inquiry while of course following it with the utmost interest. One of the conditions of Runs's punishment was that he say nothing of his excursion to his friends or parents or anyone else. Landing Command and the Council were concerned now about damage control, not revenge.

Runs could see that it required a considerable exercise of will on the part of the Elder to maintain his seat, when what he really wanted to do was charge down the imitation rock slope and batter the youthful offender to a harmless pulp. He spent much of the inquiry reciting passages from the Samizene to calm himself. It was the first time in his life Runs had actually felt physically threatened by an Elder, and for a while the whole bloodthirsty history of ancient Quozlene passed through his mind.

It got so bad that the Elder eventually had to disqualify himself lest he embarrass his generation. The one who replaced him stared directly at Runs for the remainder of the session. It made Runs acutely uncomfortable, to the point where he feared his falsehood might be discovered.

Because while he admitted to having broken the law by visiting the surface, and to having spent a number of days outside, and to having traveled a considerable distance, he neglected to specify exactly where he'd been, admitting quite truthfully that he didn't know. Which was to say he didn't know in terms of actual measurements. No one was able to ask if he'd visited a certain lake because he'd been the first Quozl to do so. His inquirers did not possess referents sufficient to assess the extent of his iniquity. They fumbled around the fringes and believed them extreme enough. It did not occur to any of them, nor to Landing Command, that a single ill-equipped juvenile might have traveled farther in a particular direction than any of their highly trained explorers. Of course he hadn't wasted time on study. His interest had been solely in covering distance.

Of his encounter with the native juvenile he said nothing. He did not lie, he merely did not volunteer. No one asked him if he'd encountered a native, of course. The odds weighed massively against it. No one considered that odds existed to be beaten.

They questioned him calmly and steadily. Had he left anything behind? No. What had he hoped to gain from such a foolhardy and dangerous excursion? Enlightenment. Did he realize he had jeopardized the security of all the Burrows? He did not deny it.

"Yet you went ahead anyway," said his solemn contemporary.

Runs felt slightly more comfortable talking to one his own age even though he knew that individual was the most likely to recommend the severest punishment, because he belonged to the generation Runs had shamed. The elder generations he had simply endangered.

"It was the ultimate in foolish things to do," he murmured. "I will never forget it nor be able to expunge the shame from my soul. This private agony I will carry with me to my death."

"We are concerned neither with your shame nor your death." The female Elder shifted on her seat, adjusting the wrinkled, aged folds of her pouch. "We are worried only about the safety of the colony, which you have risked for your own infantile, selfish ends."

"If I may, in my embarrassment and sorrow, say but one thing in my defense?"

They looked at each other and eventually nodded in unison.

"I was but one to visit the surface of our home. There are many who expose themselves to possible observation. Scientists and researchers and other revered Elders."

"You speak of the experienced, those who travel in camouflage and know how to keep hidden."

"I studied their movements and methods," Runs told them earnestly. "I would not have gone out otherwise."

"Your caution is appreciated," said the Elder sarcastically. "Perusal of recordings is not experience, memorization not knowledge."

Runs-red-Talking bowed his head and said nothing. The Elder studied him. "We will consider what is to be your punishment."

They were in an awkward position regarding what he'd done, though he was so scared he didn't realize it at the time. If they applied something of sufficient magnitude to fit his crime it was sure to be noticed and remarked upon by his friends and relations. The result would be the need to explain why he was being treated so severely, which was precisely what the authorities wished to avoid. It would have been much easier to punish him for a lesser crime, like defacement or disrespect.

With reason winning out over emotion, the result was that he received the most severe tongue-lashing of his young life. That was all. Anything more might have provoked questions, something to be avoided at all costs. So he found himself released without restrictions, for which he was properly astonished and grateful. He took no joy in it, reveled in no private glee, because he knew how severely he'd offended.

He knew he would be closely watched for future evidence of deviant behavior, that his every activity would be monitored and analyzed. That did not concern him.

Indeed, from that day on he was a model citizen, not

visiting the upper levels even on perfectly innocent errands, avoiding upside like a plague. Eventually surveillance was reduced. All colony resources were limited and trained personnel had much to do besides keeping watch over a harmless, very inconspicuous youngster. Round-the-clock observation gradually gave way to daytime checks and thence to random visits, until at last officialdom's involvement with him was lost to time and monotony. Each report was the same: No dangerous or deviant behavior recorded.

Since his journey Runs-red-Talking hadn't gone anywhere near a Burrow exit, nor had he expressed the slightest desire to any of his acquaintances to do so. As he matured he opted for an unremarkable career in mechanical maintenance and repair. He appeared completely content with his training choice and his everyday life. Oh, he studied native transmissions, but so did everyone else. They were a diverting amusement. The authorities pronounced themselves pleased with the course his life had taken.

So was Runs-red-Talking.

IX.

IT SEEMED TO Chad that nothing was permanent, that the world existed in a constant state of flux. Certainly the change from twelve to thirteen was significant, more so than any of the preceding birthdays. Like any youngster he quickly forgot that each birthday was more important than its predecessor.

But this time he was right. There was something genuinely magical about turning thirteen. He was no longer a child: he was an official teenager, something that Mindy had held over him for years. No longer. Of course, at eighteen she considered herself an adult, more of an adult than her parents. Though no woodswoman, she'd resigned herself to continued participation in the annual summer visits to the lake. As her mother was fond of pointing out, in a few years she would find herself immersed in other interests and other lives, and would do as she pleased. For a little while longer, her participation as a family member would be greatly appreciated. Chad was of a different opinion but knowing how little weight that would carry, wisely said nothing of it.

Mindy's interests had expanded beyond music and writing to include boys. No, not boys now. Men, in their twenties, impossibly old men as ancient as his dad, Chad mused. He paid little attention to them. His sister was pretty and they came and vanished in brief thunderstorms of aftershave and flowers.

At least the mountains never changed. The engine hum was loud in his ears as he pressed his face to the glass and gazed down at the familiar sweep of forest and gorges. Not many people would dare fly these canyons, with their narrow sides and treacherous downdrafts. He'd taken his father's flying skills for granted, but no longer. He now had some idea of the talent required.

He was old enough to recognize certain peaks and valleys and individual bodies of water as they flashed by beneath. Not roads. There were no roads in this country, never had been, and if the federal government had its way, never would be. Just animals and birds and the occasional rugged backpacker. And the Collins family, who had a deeded acre with cabin and the means to reach it. Too small an exception for the government to take issue with.

His father banked the Rutan sharply and dove toward the lake like a carrier pilot at Midway. You didn't have time to worry because in seconds you were leveling out and bouncing across the deep blue waters of the lake. Chad strained for the first sight of the cabin, relaxed only when it came into view at the head of the little bay. It was unchanged, as immutable as the surrounding mountains except for the annual improvements his parents added. There had been heavy snowpack in the mountains this year. That meant high water, fast streams, and good fishing, according to his father.

Having given up on Mindy years ago, he was always trying to get Chad to go fishing with him. Occasionally Chad would accompany his dad, not to fish but to wile away the hours lying on his back on the floor of the boat, toying with the water that seeped in, reading comics or paperbacks while his father did all the work. The real treat was the basket of sodas that hung over the side, refrigerated to an icy coldness by the lake.

The annual vacation was the only time he and his sister had unlimited access to candy and junk food.

Chad was never bored at the lake. As he grew, his parents allowed him to roam farther and farther from the shoreline. He'd never had any trouble in the mountains, and unlike L.A., there were no kidnappers or perverts to worry about.

Bears and mountain lions were scarce and avoided every attempt of Chad's to encounter one.

It didn't take long to unload the plane. Everyone knew what was required of them. For the last several years Chad had participated instead of immediately dashing off into the woods. After the unloading came the cleaning, sweeping the floor, dusting shelves and furniture, removing tarps and cobwebs. His father fired up the generator and checked the lights, grumbling softly whenever something refused to cooperate, making a list of what needed replacement or repair. His mother cleaned the bedrooms in tandem with his sister, then went to work making the kitchen serviceable. In no time they were ready for another two months of kickback-donothing, as his father called it.

As man-crazy as his sister had become, Chad was surprised she continued to make the trek to the cabin. The isolation, she'd explained, was good for her work. She had determined to become a writer. So far her successes had been small and isolated, but encouraging. Poems in a small literary magazine that brought praise but no money, a pair of short stories to a magazine nobody bought, one novelette for which she received the munificent sum of two hundred and fifty dollars, and rejection letters full of suggestions.

She spent the days cooped up in her room, her typewriter intriguing the mice and squirrels, working on The Novel. She had a lap-top computer with a big screen and spare batteries which Dad carefully recharged for her.

The isolation was vital, she insisted. At the lake none of her beaus or suitors could get in touch with her. There was only the two-way radio in the plane. To mollify them she used the phone in town, on the rare occasions when she accompanied Chad and Dad on the bimonthly supply flights.

Chad was delighted with her hobby. She no longer pestered him as she had when they were younger. He was something to be tolerated now instead of actively tormented. As far as he was concerned she could spend the whole summer in her room without ever emerging. This adulthood thing had changed her for the better, though he regretted no longer being able to tease her. Now she merely ignored him instead of getting mad. Growing up certainly altered people.

It was at supper one week later when Chad finally broached the subject, as they were finishing the last of the barbecued chicken.

"Dad, you're always calling me a big boy."

"You are a big boy." His father spooned mashed potatoes and gravy.

"I've never had any problems hiking, right?"

"That's right. You're damn sensible. That's why your mother and I trust you to go off by yourself."

"Okay. So," he took a deep breath, "do you trust me enough to let me camp out overnight?"

The next load of potatoes never reached their intended destination. His father glanced in his mother's direction. She said nothing. A positive sign.

"We've already let you camp out." He resumed eating.

"Yeah, but just on the porch or down on the dock. I want to take some real hikes so I can see some of the back country. I've already been everywhere around here. I can do it."

"You don't know how to cook, and even if you did, you don't have any of the equipment."

"I don't have to cook. I can carry enough stuff. I don't eat much when I'm hiking. It's only for a night or two, Dad," he pleaded.

Like ghosts from a dimly remembered history of sibling torment were his sister's words. "You'll get scared."

"I will *not*. I know these woods. I've never seen anything bigger than a fox and unlike *some* people I know, I'm not afraid of the dark."

That brought Mindy's face up, eyes flashing. Then she simply sighed and shook her head sadly. Maybe his sister was no longer his avowed enemy, but she wasn't any fun anymore, either.

"I promise I won't get scared." He forced himself to keep calm. "And if I do, well, hey, that's my problem, isn't it?"

"Not if you run off somewhere in the dark and go over a cliff," his mother said grimly.

"Ah, Mom, c'mon! I'm not going running in the middle of the night and I'm not gonna fall off no cliff."

" 'Any' cliff," she corrected him.

"I know how to pick a good campsite, and I know how to make a fire. I'll have my flashlight and sleeping bag. That'll be plenty."

"What about the tent?" his father asked him. "I think you're strong enough to pack the tent."

"My sleeping bag'll be enough. It's got a rain flap and I'd listen to the weather on the radio first and if there was any chance of rain at all, I wouldn't go." He looked at his mother. "I'd only go if it was supposed to be warm and dry."

"It still gets cold at night."

Lo and be thankful, his father finally took up his side. "His sleeping bag is down. He'll be warm enough."

"But what about animals?" Chad held his breath, aware the discussion had been taken out of his hands.

"Like he said, he's never seen anything bigger than a fox. I think he'd be okay for a night or two, Alice. He's got to start sometime. It'll teach him responsibility, being out on his own." He looked back at his son. "It'll be interesting to find out if he really isn't afraid of the dark. The whole thing will be a real learning experience."

"I admit the weather's good, but don't you really think he's a little young?"

"Yes, he is, but he's damn smart for his age and I know he won't take any unnecessary chances. Will—you?"

Chad shook his head violently. "I won't do anything dumb, Dad."

"He'll go in one direction only. As fast as he hikes, it won't be hard to find him if there's any trouble."

"There won't be any trouble, Dad," Chad said quickly. "What kind of trouble could I have? There's nobody else around here and I'm not gonna try and climb any cliffs or anything. I'm only going on a longer walk. What could happen?"

"You could break a leg, that's what could happen." His mother shrugged. "Overnight only, the first couple of times at least, and you be back well before sundown the second day. Then we'll see."

"All *right*!"

"You watch yourself out there," his sister said, and to his great surprise, she smiled at him. Having spent his whole life engaged in sibling combat with her, Chad didn't have the slightest idea how to react to affection on her part.

He was so excited he rose with the sun the next morning. His mother was ready for him. Despite her concerns and objections to his forthcoming foray she'd prepared more sandwiches and medicine than any one boy would need short of an extended trek into the depths of the Amazon Basin, all of it neatly packed and ready to go.

"You be careful out there," she warned him as she opened the door to admit the first burst of sunshine. "Remember: no mountain climbing. Just walk where it's open and easy. Eat sensibly, not just the candy and cookies. And drink plenty of water." Ignoring his protests she adjusted the cap he wore. "Stay out of the sun as much as possible."

He backed away, rearranging the cap so that the brim once more covered his neck instead of shading his face. "Mom, I'll be fine. Really."

"Be sure you're back on time."

"Hey, I can tell time by the sun, Mom." Of course he also had the ten-dollar watch which had replaced the three-dollar job of years earlier. "Don't worry."

"I won't," she lied. "Which way are you going?"

"Down along the lake, then up the stream."

"Which stream?"

"The big one, to the west. Maybe I'll discover its source."

She couldn't repress a smile at that. "Maybe you will. If you do, what will you name it?"

"I dunno. Lessee. The Nile? No, that's been used." He was grinning broadly. "Congo? Nope. I know! Maybe I'll call it—Alice April Springs."

"That would be nice." She was surprised at the lump that formed in her throat. "Go on now, if you're going. You don't want to waste the sunlight."

"No. Thanks for the food an' stuff, Mom." He kissed her quickly, slipped his thumbs under the shoulder straps of his pack and hiked it higher on his back, and strode off accompanied by the spirits of Cook and Hillary.

His mother walked out on the porch and watched him until he turned west to follow the lakeshore, vanishing behind the trees. Damn him, she thought, for growing up so fast. I'm running out of kids.

As he matured, Runs-red-Talking grew solemn. His change of personality was surprising to his friends and relatives. Instead of playing, he spent most of his free time in meditation. This pleased his instructors if not his companions. He just wasn't fun anymore. Gradually they stopped inviting him to join in their group coupling practices and chase games in the lower Burrow levels.

Not that he was abnormal; simply quiet and introspective. Several philosophers noted his expanding knowledge of the Samizene and suggested he make supervisory meditation his profession, but he preferred to work with his hands. The quality of his repairs was unsurpassed, especially for one so young. Instead of fixing something, he meditated over it until he was certain of the solution. Only then did he begin to work. As a result he was somewhat slower than the other repair techs, but when he fixed something, it stayed fixed.

In his attention to studies he displayed greater maturity than his colleagues, for whom young adulthood was still a time of play. While they devoted themselves to dance and the arts of personal adornment he pored over schematics and recordings that dealt with circuitry design and replacement.

Shops in Burrows Two and Three were now turning out advanced components without the help of the *Sequencer*'s original designs. Runs dedicated himself to learning everything about them, the better to be prepared to fix them when they failed. He had a genius for locating trouble before it occurred. His intuition saved potential downtime and won him numerous awards. Those who had scoffed at his dedication were now praising him.

He was tinkering with a stalled scooter when its attractive owner ran a hand down his back to tweak the tip of his tail. Her name was Half-stripe-Missing, and she was no stranger to him.

"Why not come visit me tonight?"

Runs glanced up at her. She'd been a frequent coupling partner for half a season and he was not yet tired of her, nor she of him.

"I can't. I have scheduled meditation. I am only a third of the way through the Milian Cycle."

"The Milian Cycle can wait. I cannot." Half-stripe-Missing was little interested in philosophy.

"It's something I must do," he said simply.

Her ears flipped down to cover her eyes, then straightened in a gesture whose meaning none could mistake. "You're a strange one, Runs-red-Talking. Even when you are coupling I sense disinterest. I don't understand you."

"That's not surprising." He tried to inject some levity into a conversation that was disintegrating rapidly. "Sometimes I do not understand myself. Burrow Three's philosopher says . . ."

"You rely too much on philosophy and not enough on action." It was rude of her to interrupt but he did not counterattack. Instead he stepped aside, replacing his tools in his workbelt. She made no move to re-enter his Sama, for which he was grateful.

"There. All fixed."

"Thank you." She climbed back atop the battery-powered vehicle. "Now try repairing yourself. I'm going to find Stands-blue-Razor and see if he wants some company for a while. Meditate on that!"

"I'm sure he'll be delighted to see you," Runs murmured.

It was not the response she'd hoped for. She was soon gone, as was the pang of regret he always felt at such times. It wasn't that he was uninterested in her; simply that he had more important matters to attend to.

Having been reserved well in advance, his favorite meditation chamber awaited him. The empty, domed room was four body lengths in diameter, the prescribed size to permit maximum contemplation. Walls, dome, and floor were stained beige. Except for the meditator the room was occupied only by a single circular woven mat which had been manufactured in Burrow Four. It was a near-perfect copy of the traditional sij bark meditation mat. As sij trees grew only on distant Quozlene, this one was made of plastic.

He squatted on the mat and carefully placed the small bowl he'd brought with him off to his left, within arm's reach. It held nutrition cubes of many colors and values, arranged for maximum visual impact. Next to it he placed a cone-shaped bottle, precisely two finger lengths from the bowl. It contained a refreshing liquid.

At his tone the door shut tight behind him. No one would dare disturb him now. Settling back on his heels in the ancient contemplative posture, he silently regarded the wall before him. His hand fell to touch the mat by his right knee. A small display screen rose from the floor.

As he chanted, it displayed the subject for today's study. The chamber darkened as airy music issued from concealed speakers. Peace came. Floor, walls, and dome vanished, to be replaced by blue sky and drifting clouds. He was floating over a forest on Quozlene, trees reaching for him with hauntingly familiar branches and soft leaves encountered only in recordings.

As he drifted lower a small village hove into view. It was filled with Quozl busy at their daily tasks. All wore ancient costume.

Tilting to his left he found himself over water. In the sheltered cove the village fishers were taking leave of those who would remain behind. Males and females leaned on poles, pushing the wide, flat-bottomed boat out into the shallow waters of the bay. There was much elaborate waving of jewelry and scarves.

Abruptly he found himself in the boat, perceived but ignored by those around him. He could smell his ancestors: their unscented muskiness and pungent genitals. It was nearly lost in the rank odor of gutted fish and oil. The designs shaved into their fur were crude and primitive.

He watched thoughtfully as they set their nets. After a while he rose to pick up the cone bottle and bowl of concentrates. Walking through his ancestors, the gunwale of the boat, and the bay beyond, he advanced until he was halted by a solid obstruction: the far wall of the meditation chamber.

A panel came away beneath his skilled, trained fingers, to reveal a dimly lit hole in the middle of the ancient sea. Beyond lay a service crawlway layered with conduits. Bending to slip through the opening, Runs carefully replaced the panel behind him.

His shoulder pack lay a short distance away. He added the contents of the meditation bowl to the pack, poured the liquid in the cone bottle into the flexible fluid container that would ride close at his side. Behind him the instructive tale of the Milian fisherfolk unraveled unobserved. It was an important story, worthy of extensive contemplation. None would dare break in and interrupt him.

At the end of the crawlway he had to remove another

panel. The gap seemed too small to admit a nearly adult Quozl, but Runs-red-Talking had spent many hours in physical training enhancing his flexibility.

Pushing his pack ahead of him he advanced rapidly along the tunnel. He knew the way well enough by now to travel without light, marking his progress by counting to himself as he crawled. When a second shaft intersected the first, he turned down it, wriggling forward like a fish in a water-filled tube. Smooth metal pressed tight around him. His hips barely fit.

The narrowness of the tunnel didn't bother him. Claustrophobia was an alien concept to people whose ancestors had originally lived in burrows beneath the earth. It took some time for him to reach the first main tunnel, where he was welcomed by a blast of cool air. It was a relief to rise on hands and knees. After pausing to run through several stretching exercises he continued on his way. Only when he was finally able to stand did he remove the service belt from his pack and secure it around his waist.

When he reached the first intake he started climbing, fitting his feet into the narrow service steps slotted into the side of the spacious shaft. Fist-sized service lights provided just enough light to see by. He ascended carefully yet rapidly, conscious as always of the fact that it was many levels to the bottom. Cooled air rushed past him, drawn from the surface by multiple vacuum fans far below.

He passed numerous side shafts that fed air to the different levels of the Burrow. All were of lesser diameter than the main intake. When he could climb no higher he stopped, his heart beating against his ribs, certain as always that this would be the day he would be found out. But the only other sound in the shaft was the rush of air past his ears and the deep hum of the intake machinery.

Above lay a circular section of selectively permeable plastic designed to blend indistinguishably with the surrounding surface of Shiraz. Air could get through but nothing else. He had reached the topmost step.

Overhead, the preliminary intake fan whirred at high speed and in near-absolute silence. The huge but light blades could slice a careless Quozl in half without slowing. They could be halted for repair work, but doing so without authorization would invite the attention of puzzled inspectors. Runs-red-Talking had no intention of alerting his co-workers to his whereabouts.

Beneath his jumpsuit he wore a thin, undetectable harness of his own design. From his pack he removed the service gun, attaching one end of the plastic wire spool to his harness and the other to a suction dart. Taking careful aim, he fired. The soft discharge was lost in the whir of the fan.

The dart struck the far wall and adhered to the smooth metal. Runs checked the ring where the line attached to his harness a last time, took a deep breath, reciting a favorite line from the Sixth Book, and stepped off into nothingness.

His braced legs absorbed the shock as he slammed feetfirst into the far wall. There was the usual moment of terror when he feared the dart might not hold, the sigh of relief when it did. He began climbing, pulling himself up the line until he hung close to the dart. After reeling in the excess he rested a moment, catching his breath, hanging in emptiness suspended solely by the thin wire.

Removing a small tool from his service belt, he ran it over the wall of the shaft in a predetermined pattern until he was rewarded by a soft *click*. A small hatch popped open to reveal a gap in the otherwise unbroken metal. Runs pulled himself inside, reaching out and back to exhaust the vacuum from the dart and remove it from the wall. After securing the hatch behind him he turned to begin crawling up the slightly sloping tunnel.

No metal or plastic walls enclosing him here, only the bare rock he'd laboriously tunneled through over the preceding cycles. As he progressed, the acuteness of the slope he was ascending increased.

There was no electronically operated, camouflaged door at the end of the tunnel. After exiting he spent several hours replacing the dead leaves and branches that concealed the opening. A quick inspection of his surroundings confirmed his solitude. There was no one outside and he had not been followed. Nor would  he stumble into an official expedition leaving or returning by way of one of the now monitored exits, as he had so many years ago. He followed their schedules religiously and departed on his own journeys only when he knew no other Quozl was likely to be abroad.

He had his own exit, carefully excavated and maintained using common repair and maintenance equipment. His alone. It belonged to him and the spirits with whom he meditated, and they weren't going to expose him.

It was night. Everyone knew and respected his off-duty marathon meditation sessions. Sometimes they lasted for several days. His piety was oft remarked upon. When finished he would emerge from the meditation chamber fit and refreshed. None realized it was not meditation on the Milian Cycle which so rejuvenated him, but rather his delightful, solitary walks across the invigorating, unique, remarkable, and highly proscribed surface of Shiraz.

His Shiraz, as he'd come to think of it.

X.

CHAD'S CONFIDENCE WENT down with the sun. All well and good to assure your parents of your unmatched courage, quite another to find yourself out in the woods alone, miles from the comforting confines of the cabin. He was alone in the forest with the animals who had lived there since before man. Would they take exception to his presence?

Now that it was growing unimaginably, impossibly dark he wished he'd brought the tent despite its weight. Though the walls were made of insubstantial fabric, they would serve to shut out the night. His sleeping bag and rain flap would only block out the darkness behind him and over his head. Movement on either side or below his feet would be inescapably visible.

During the day the woods had been full of color and song. Now things were on the move that did not speak to each other, small shadows with flashing eyes that darted furtively from rock to tree. The crickets and the owl, the frogs that lived in the nearby stream, these were familiar, comforting sounds. It was the noise of brush being shoved aside, of leaves rustling as spirits squirmed past them, of great unseen wings beating the air, that sparked a young imagination which refused to rest.

He hadn't planned on building a fire. His sleeping bag would keep him cozy-warm and fire-building was hard work. His tuna-fish sandwich supper required no heating. But he built a blaze anyway, hurriedly gathering bits and scraps of wood and dumping them atop a bed of pine needles. He sacrificed a dozen matches before the miniature pyre reached for the sky. The relief he felt in the presence of light was no less than that of early Cro-Magnon.

The fire was not big enough to make any truly dangerous animal hesitate, but it was sufficient to force the shadows back into the trees. They were the real threat.

The stream behind him ran fast and deep. It would shield him from any unnameable horrors trying to approach from that direction. Its watery roar was comforting. With the fire at his front and the water at his back he climbed into his sleeping bag and began skinning a Hershey bar. He would eat the sandwich next, deliberately reversing the usual order. The gesture of independence made him feel better.

It was a moonless night and he wasn't sure whether to be grateful or disappointed. The shadows kept their distance. He tried to concentrate on the impossibly bright stars which spilled like sugar across the black velvet sky. After a while the brightness blurred and ran together to form a pale opalescent veil over his eyes.

The sound of splashing woke him. He blinked in the uncompromising light of morning, shooting up in bed so fast that he knocked the rain flap askew.

Turning to the river he saw nothing. The noise could have been made by a large rock tumbling downstream. The sun hurt his eyes and he blinked them clear, dizzy from waking up so quickly. Nothing came stomping through the stream toward him; no grizzly, no runaway elk. There was only the roiling glassiness of the water itself.

As he turned to check the smoking residue of his fire he heard it a second time.

Again he saw nothing, but this time he struggled determinedly out of his sleeping bag and into his jeans, walking toward the river until he was standing on a flat piece of granite that protruded into the water. The current had excavated a deep pool here. It would be a swell place to swim if you didn't mind the cold. Absently he bent to gaze into the depths.

With a shout he leaped backward. Then he cautiously returned to the edge. Whatever was down there wasn't coming after him, gave no sign of ascending. It lay on the bottom, staring back up at him while thrashing its limbs uselessly. Tiny bubbles rose from its small mouth in a steady stream. It looked almost familiar. No, he decided, it *was* familiar. He'd seen it once before, long ago, when he was just a kid. It was the creature he'd never quite been able to convince himself had been a figment of his imagination. Or else it was another one just like it.

"What are you doing down there?" He yelled at the top of his lungs in hopes of being understood above the river's roar. The creature continued bubbling at him. "Are you all right? Are you hurt? You're gonna freeze if you stay down there." He felt no fear, only concern. "Well, if you just want to lie down there, that's okay with me."

This statement resulted in many more bubbles and a rather more energetic waving of the slim, furry arms. Same as before, he noted: seven fingers on each hand.

"I'm not coming in after you." Chad was insistent. "Do you want to come out? If you do, then why don't you start swimming?"

It struck him that perhaps the creature didn't know how to swim. At thirteen Chad didn't realize that another animal's lung capacity might be inadequate in relation to its weight to create natural buoyancy, something humans took for granted. It did occur to him that it might be injured and that its wounds might not be visible.

He knelt to splash river on his face, banishing the last vestiges of sleep. Steeling himself against the cold, he lay flat on the rock and shoved his arm as far into the water as he could. The chill raced up his shoulder.

Nothing made contact with his hand. Then he felt soft

digits flailing against his own. Getting as good a grip as he could manage, he pulled. The creature rose slowly until a grimacing Chad was able to sit up and get his other fingers around the alien wrist.

The long-eared head burst the water like a leaping dolphin's, coughing and spitting and choking exactly as Chad would have if he'd been stuck underwater for too long. Chad realized that the creature hadn't been lying there on the bottom of the pool for fun and relaxation.

Clinging to the thin wrist, he started working his way across the rock toward dry land. Still expelling water, the creature dug at the surface with its right hand, trying to help.

Once clear of the water, Chad got both arms beneath the alien's and heaved. It was much slimmer than he was but surprisingly heavy. The tight clothing it was wearing left its arms and legs bare, with a reinforced slit in the back to permit the small tail egress. Heavy earrings dangled from the drooping ears. Brightly colored lengths of fabric hung soggily from thighs and upper arms. Its saturated fur made it heavier than normal.

"We gotta get you over by the fire." Chad spoke between clenched teeth, struggling with the alien's weight. "Come on, help me. Stand up."

The huge sandaled feet impeded their progress as Chad half dragged, half carried the creature through the grass to his campsite. He lay the heavy alien on his sleeping bag and left it there as he went to try and coax the remaining coals back to life.

Water continued to dribble from one corner of the creature's mouth. It lay with both arms at its sides, sucking air in a ragged, broken rhythm that gradually grew smoother. It was definitely alive and improving. The huge eyes remained shut. Lying there vomiting water it was not half so impressive as Chad remembered it, but then very little is as impressive at thirteen as it is at eight.

"Hang on." He worked furiously with the fire. He was delighted and not a little surprised when the twigs and dry pine needles he kept adding burst into flame. He kept adding fuel until he could feel the heat. Then he took the bottom of his sleeping bag and dragged it and its load as close to the fire as he dared, turning it sideways so the alien would receive the maximum amount of heat. Unpacking a granola bar for breakfast, he sat and nibbled on it as he waited.

"I hope that makes you feel better."

The huge eyes finally opened. "It does."

"So you *can* talk. I didn't think I'd imagined that, either."

"I've been studying your language for a long time. It's not difficult. Only the volume is hard to deal with."

"Yeah, you do talk awful soft." Chad immediately dropped his voice to a whisper. "I guess with ears like that you don't need to shout, huh?"

The alien's left ear kinked in a certain manner, but Chad was oblivious to the humorous significance of the gesture. "Thank you for lowering your voice."

"You're welcome. You sure looked funny lying on the bottom of that pool, kicking like crazy and going nowhere. Why didn't you come up? Did you want to drown?"

"Drown?" The creature seemed to hesitate. "No, not drown. I was . . ." A long, slim arm lifted to gesture in the direction of the fire. "I saw your camp. You were sleeping and I intended to study and depart, but I thought I recognized you by the light of your fire."

So it was the same one, Chad thought. He didn't know whether to be gratified or disappointed.

"I wanted to be certain," the alien was saying, "so I tried to find a place where I could view you more clearly without exposing myself. I walked into shallow water, thinking to conceal myself within, but I failed to pay sufficient attention to where I was stepping."

"Hey, don't feel so bad. I've done that a lot myself. But why didn't you float?"

"Float? We do not float as you Shirazians do. We sink.

◇ **170** ◇

Our body density is such that in proportion to our air retention capacity we . . ."

"I get the picture."

"It was a most peculiar sensation. As you can well understand we do not voluntarily immerse ourselves in water over our head unless we have at hand a means for instantly raising ourselves above the surface. We have studied your sport called swimming. It does not relate to us."

"I'll bet. You called me what?"

"A Shirazian. That is our name for your world."

"Kinda nice." Chad rolled the alien sounds around his tongue. "Has more flavor than 'Earth.' "

"You must not think very much of your world to call it dirt."

"Hey, *I* didn't name it. Don't get on my case. Don't you guys ever take baths? You are a guy, aren't you?"

"I am male, yes. We have other means of cleansing ourselves."

"You sure know a lot about us."

"We've been watching your television broadcasts and listening to your radio for some time."

Chad laughed and Runs-red-Talking drank in the peculiarly distinctive sound. "Mom's always telling me there's nothing educational on tv. I always knew that was a crock."

"When I was lying on the bottom I tried to call to you."

"All I saw was bubbles, and my ears aren't as big as yours."

"Yet you correctly identified the situation and saved me. I am eternally in your debt. I will meditate many times for you."

"Yeah, well, forget it. Look, I know you're from another world. Which one, huh? Not from the solar system, I bet. There's nothing habitable in the solar system. No matter how big your ears are."

"Truth, I am from much farther away, but I cannot tell you

exactly where.'' Regardless of his savior's youth, Runs knew such questioning skirted dangerous territory. He made a weak attempt to adjust his attire.

''Are you alone, or are there more of you here?'' Chad was looking past the sleeping bag and its half-drowned occupant, his eyes scanning woods and river beyond.

Runs-red-Talking was beginning to realize that despite the debt he owed this young Shirazian there was much more at stake here than an individual friendship. He would have to watch what he said from now on. Go cautiously, advised the Samizene. Go with care.

''I am the only one here now,'' he replied truthfully. To change the subject he asked, ''Why are you here alone?''

''I could ask you the same question. I think we might get the same answer.'' Chad used a long branch to stir the fire. Bits of flame ascended to oblivion. ''I like being on my own, exploring on my own.''

''Exploring?'' The alien's ears twisted sharply. ''You are right. I feel much the same way. My Elders, however, do not approve of such things.'' He wasn't sure ''Elders'' was the proper word to use in this context but it was the best he could think of.

''Yeah, my 'elders' aren't too hot on the idea either.''

''You must not tell them about me,'' Runs said solemnly.

''I tried that before, the first time we ran into each other. They wouldn't believe me then and they wouldn't believe me now. So why should I tell 'em?''

The response was nearly too facile, Runs reflected, but what else could he do except believe and trust? He sensed no guile in the youth. He would have been more certain of his feelings if the Shirazian had been a tree. Trees never emitted false emotions.

''My name's Chad. Chad Collins.'' He extended a hand. Runs studied the five fingers, hesitated, then reached for the boy's face with his own hand. Chad intercepted the gesture and shook entwined fingers.

''Don't look so weird. It's a greeting.''

"Slightly different." The chill was slipping from the Quozl's bones as the fire continued to warm him. "But why do you display your teeth in a hostile gesture?"

Chad continued to grin. "It's not a hostile gesture. It's a smile."

"Smile, yes. A concept I did not encounter except in the abstract. It is much more difficult to deal with in the flesh. Among my people the showing of teeth is considered a threat."

"Like with dogs, huh? Okay, I'll try not to smile too much. What's *your* name?"

"I am called Runs-red-Talking, as near as I can translate into your tongue."

"Weird."

"No, what is 'weird' is that none of your names appear to mean anything. How can you have a name that is just a sound, signifying nothing?"

"A name's just a name." Chad shrugged indifferently. "What else can you do with those ears?" The organs in question bent forward sharply as Runs held them stiffly parallel to the ground. They then described a perfect pair of arcs, meeting behind his head and pointing directly backward.

"Rad. Where's your spaceship? Somewhere around here?"

"No. Not around here." Traditional Quozl skills of verbal circumlocution served him well in his conversation with the native without forcing him to lie. Truthfully enough, the *Sequencer* wasn't "here" but several valleys and ridges to the west. "Here" had the virtue of being by its nature an imprecise geographical term.

"You live near here?" Runs inquired.

"Not really. We come up for a couple of months every summer. Nobody actually lives here. The government won't allow it. This is all wilderness area. Nobody's allowed to build a house or even bring in a car. Our cabin's an exception

◇ **173** ◇

because my grandfather built it before the government declared this area wilderness, see?''

''Not really.'' Runs was dubious. ''You are going too fast for me. I have trouble enough with your language without having to comprehend complex concepts as well.'' Besides which I must look horrible, he thought, untangling an earring.

''Sorry. Our home, the place where we live, is in Los Angeles. That's a big city way south of here.''

''I know Los Angeles.''

''You talk like a girl with a sore throat,'' Chad commented unexpectedly. ''What do you do? Are you in school?''

''Everyone is always in school.''

''I don't think I'd like living with you guys.''

''I work at repairing things that break.''

Before either of them realized it they were deep in conversation over the virtues of continuing education.

''To stop learning is to die,'' Runs insisted.

''I'm not talking about stopping learning. I'm talking about getting out of school,'' Chad shot back.

''To leave school is to leave life.''

They argued and talked away most of the day, until Chad realized that he was really going to have to hoof it to make it back to the cabin before dark. He could have risked remaining out for another night but he knew his mother wanted him back the second day the first time he camped out alone, and he was going to need her goodwill in the weeks to come.

The idea that he was totally dependent on his parents' permission for movement was utterly foreign to Runs-red-Talking. Even at a very young age the Quozl had unrestricted access to all the Burrows. How else was one expected to learn one's surroundings if you were not allowed to explore them? Chad fully agreed, but as he explained, ''I'm human, not Quozl.''

They agreed to meet at the same place in a week's time with the understanding that if either did not appear they would try again on each day thereafter. To Chad's surprise it sounded as if his alien friend might have more difficulty making the rendezvous than he, for all his talk of freedom of movement.

The meeting was managed, however, and many subsequent to that, not only that summer but in those to come. When the floatplane began its dive toward the lake each July Chad was hard-pressed to restrain himself. To his parents he seemed more enthusiastic than ever, perhaps due to his growing ability to remain out in the forest for longer and longer periods of time.

"Our city boy's turned into a real woodsman," his father remarked as he went about his fishing.

Human and Quozl watched each other's growth and maturation with mutual fascination. While at first Runs was taller than Chad, the teenager quickly outpaced him, until he stood a full head higher than his alien friend.

"Our development proceeds differently from yours and does not encompass your unsettling variations. When I was a new youth I knew almost exactly how tall I would be when I reached adulthood. It was very reassuring. Your disparities of size promote competition among you." An ear dipped in a gesture of consolation. "Were I you I would find it very unfair. You place unsupportable values on mere size."

"I agree with you, but there's nothing we can do about it."

These days they had ample time to talk. By now Runs-red-Talking was one of the most respected repair specialists in the Burrows. His work was much in demand. For one who spent so much time engaged in extensive meditation he accomplished a great deal. He was careful not to vary his routine even during the cold season when he never visited the surface. It would not do for someone to observe that his piety was seasonal.

At seventeen Chad no longer needed his parents' permission to camp out for four or five nights at a stretch. They were convinced he planned to climb every mountain in the region. In reality he learned only enough about the land surrounding the lake to answer the occasional question and thus maintain his protective cover.

During their meetings Runs-red-Talking revealed little about himself, and that only gradually even though he'd come to trust his human friend. He knew that had he so desired, Chad could have exposed him many times over the previous cycles. That he had not done so was a source of personal satisfaction to Runs. When he returned to the Burrow he had difficulty containing his amusement at the pontifications of the surface study teams. They had only confusing and sometimes garbled transmissions to work with. Unlike him, they could not seek clarification of some supposition from an actual native.

Despite this he remained humble. One brag would bring him down. But oh, how he longed to correct many of the "experts'" misconceptions!

Chad was told that his friend lived in a Quozl colony, though Runs said nothing about its location or size. Chad accepted his friend's reluctance to disclose additional information with equanimity. He listened intently to what was proferred and forced himself to be content with that, realizing that were he to try and pressure Runs the limited supply of information might cease altogether. For his part Runs sensed his friend's burning curiosity and applauded his restraint. In that respect he was very Quozl.

"If it was known that I had met with you and told you even this much," he explained one morning, "I might even be killed."

Chad tucked at the hem of his flannel shirt. "I thought you told me that your people no longer believe in violence."

"Oh, we believe in violence, but only in the therapeutic, abstract sense. In art and conversation and music. Physical contact, even moving too close to another person, is forbidden. Except during coupling and mutually agreed-upon moments, of course. It would not be regarded as violence, or even as killing, but rather as a cleansing. I do not wish to be cleansed."

"No shit." Chad sat thoughtfully. "If they found out how much I knew, would they 'cleanse' me too?"

"An interesting question." The position assumed by the Quozl's ears indicated internal debate was taking place. "The philosophical and moral barriers that would have to be surmounted to permit such an act are extensive. They would also realize that you would be missed by your parents, if no one else."

"Not necessarily. My parents might think I fell into the lake, or off a mountain."

"But my people would not think that way."

Chad digested that. "How long do you think your people can keep this up?"

"Keep this up?" Sometimes human language could be as full of unique and incomprehensible similes and analogies as that of the Quozl.

"Keep knowledge of the whole colony secret from the outside world," Chad explained.

"That is a problem for the Elders and for the Burrow leaders, not for you or me. You are the only human who knows of our existence. No others even suspect. The secret has been kept for nearly half a human century."

"Why'd you tell me about the colony?"

"I could not keep it from you forever. You are intelligent. Sooner or later you would have divined I could not exist here by myself."

"Maybe, maybe not. Maybe I'd have stayed stupid and believed you if you'd told me you were some kind of interstellar hermit. Maybe," he said thoughtfully, "you *wanted* to tell me."

"That question is for the philosophers. Ah, look!"

Chad followed the arm movement. A doe and fawn had come to the stream edge to drink. Now they paused to stare in the direction of the two bipeds. The moment stretched into multiples, the four mammals regarding each other intently.

Then there was a faint *crack* from the forest: a pinecone falling or a clumsy burst of speed by an unseen rabbit. The doe whirled with a startled leap, the fawn skittering awkwardly in her wake.

"Deer," commented Runs-red-Talking. "Female and offspring, also female."

"I guess." Chad eyed the woods dubiously. "How can you tell the fawn's sex at this distance?"

"It is something we are predisposed to recognize." He turned back to Chad. "We have never yet discussed coupling."

"Coupling?"

"Sex. Intercourse. The reproductive process. Though we have learned much about you this is one subject your broadcasts deal with only inconclusively. Tell me please, Chad, how many times a day do you normally couple?"

His friend looked elsewhere. With interest Runs noted the startling and unexpected shift in facial skin tone. "Have I offended you?"

"No. It's just that, well, I never actually have."

"Have what?"

"Coupled, dammit!"

"Ah, I have offended. You appear sexually mature for your species. Have you an injury?"

"You people are real subtle, aren't you? No, I don't have an injury. We just mature differently than Quozl, I guess. I mean, physically everything's there and ready, but emotionally it's different with us. Not to mention socially. I can tell that much. How many times do *you* do it?" he finished aggressively.

"It depends on one's work schedule. A normal frequency for someone of my age and position would be nine or ten times."

"A day?" Chad's eyes got very wide.

"Yes." Clearly Runs was puzzled by his friend's reaction. "This would be regarded as abnormal by your people?"

"According to everything I've heard, yeah." He hesitated, asked uncertainly, "*Every* day?"

"Except on meditation and rest days when activity would be greater or lesser, according to individual preference."

"How do you find the time to do anything else?"

"The actual activity does not take very long. Two to six minutes, I would say, is average. Time does impose its own constraints."

"That makes a little more sense." For some inexplicable reason Runs thought his friend looked relieved.

"I am glad. Another difference between us." As the subject quite clearly made Chad uncomfortable, Runs-red-Talking decided to switch to another. "Tell me your thoughts about war."

"That's a funny thing to want to talk about after discussing sex."

"Why? The two are closely connected."

"Why do you want to talk about that?"

"Because we find the existence of an intelligent, technologically advanced species still battling on the tribal level a fascinating contradiction. The Quozl used to fight all the time, with unending ferocity, but that was long ago. It wasn't until we matured as a race that we discovered other means of controlling our population. Among the Quozl the sublimation of violence is the healthiest of art forms. Your attempts to do likewise are curiously flawed. For example, your television broadcasts show male violence but rarely any blood or actual damage. Hence their therapeutic value is nonexistent. They are worse than useless and in fact encourage serious combat."

"Television's not designed for 'therapeutic value,'" Chad told him. "It's designed to entertain and amuse. That's all."

"A tool turned inside out. The more I learn about you the more puzzling and intriguing I find you. This intertribal combat is unhealthy and counterproductive. It retards your growth."

"Not to mention the fact that people die," Chad murmured.

"That also." Runs-red-Talking rose and began chucking pebbles into the pool which had nearly claimed his life. He could skip stones better than anyone Chad had ever seen. His extra fingers gave him additional control.

"You don't seem to realize an obvious fact of elementary psychology, which is that if sufficient violence is supplied in the form of entertainment in tandem with social disapproval of the actual act, tribal violence will diminish."

"I guess people don't see that." Chad found himself studying the Quozl's slim lines, the sleek fur and delicate arms and fingers, the gentle, contemplative face. "It's hard to imagine you guys fighting all the time. You don't look like killers, and you certainly don't act like it."

"Appearances can be deceiving. That expression, I believe, is also current among your people." Whereupon he leaped into the air wearing an expression adopted from a Fourth Imperial mural by the revered artist Hands-over-Sand: eyes bulging, ears pointed straight back, face distorted to the left to display the lower incisors to the maximum. He held his right hand outstretched, fingers crooked to reveal nails that could have been shaped into claws. His other arm was kept back and curled to deliver a follow-up blow as he kicked out sharply with the blunt end of his enormous right foot. All this was done soundlessly, in the accepted manner of combat.

Chad didn't react silently. He let out a yelp as the huge foot flew toward his face. It was large and heavy enough to crush his nose if not the cheekbones supporting it. It flashed just past his right eye, the wind of its passing a whisper in his ear. A fraction of a second after, the fingers of the right hand caressed his forehead while the fist that was the left brushed his nostrils.

Then Runs-red-Talking was standing behind him adjusting his bodysuit at the crotch. His expression was as bland as before.

At the first instant of attack Chad had stumbled and nearly fallen. Now he straightened and tried to compose himself, aware that if the attack had been for real he'd doubtless be a bleeding, unconscious pile on the ground. He was trembling slightly.

There was no undertone of satisfaction in Runs-red-Talking's voice as he executed gestures of apology. "I am sorry beyond measure for startling you. I thought that since my words were not achieving the desired affect, a demonstration would be both more economical and more effective."

"It sure as hell had an effect," Chad mumbled. "What the hell was that all about?"

"A brief exhibition of ancient fighting technique, another revered art form among my people. Many centuries ago those blows would have been intended to make contact, not to pass without touching. I would have used this," and he indicated a small metal tool attached to his workbelt, "to slice you from ear to ear. Once we delighted in bloodshed, until we discovered the elementary immaturity of its physiological underpinnings."

"But you don't fight anymore," Chad said confusedly.

"Of such things we make dances and nonverbal communication. Much can be expressed through violent movement, nothing through actual violence. No one actually touches anyone else. Such contact would constitute an unforgivable breach of manners. The achievement lies in the coming close *without* touching."

"What about the guy who gets 'touched'? How does he react?"

"With extreme embarrassment for the other person's predicament. You cannot imagine the suffering of the one who makes contact."

"What if I hit you?"

"You could not, I think. Your reactions are not rapid enough."

"Well, when your back was turned, say, and you weren't paying attention. Would you hit back?"

"Only if I felt my life in danger. If not, I would simply leave and you would no longer be my friend. I could no longer think of you as civilized. You would make of yourself the kind of representative of your species that most believe is the accurate one."

Chad unclenched his fist. "I had a hunch it might go something like that. No wonder your Elders are so frightened of contact. If my government or another decided to fight them, they couldn't fight back."

"Oh, they could, and they would. Remember that I spoke of my reaction being otherwise were my life threatened. But it would be difficult and there could be no final victory. If we lost it would not matter and if we won we could no longer look at ourselves. We would lose our lives or our souls; either way we would lose. That is why the Elders so fear possible hostilities."

"You can't keep yourselves hidden forever."

"We've done so until now. Life underground is not ideal, but it is sufficiently fulfilling for most. As we expand and add Burrows it becomes better. If what we have suspected and what you have told me about this region is true, we could continue to grow for centuries before any other humans divined our presence. The Council feels we can maintain our secret for as long as is deemed necessary."

"Except for me."

"Yes. Except for you."

"I could tell on you, you know." Chad studied the river. "I could give away the whole thing."

"Yes, you probably could." As always there was no change in Runs-red-Talking's expression. It was eerie conversing with someone who never smiled, never frowned. Only those remarkable ears moved constantly, often accompanied by sweeping, intricate gestures of the nimble, long-fingered hands.

"But you won't do that."

"How do you know? How can you be so sure?"

Runs-red-Talking gazed at him out of large, melancholy

eyes. "Because I know what kind of person you are."

"Humans can be unpredictable. We do a lot of stuff on the spur of the moment."

"You are not a candidate for self-damnation."

"I think not either." He rose and nodded in the direction of a patch of dense reeds growing beyond the deep pond. "What say we go see if there are still frogs over there?"

XI.

THE MEETINGS BECAME more than a ritual. Time reduced them to the ordinary. Until the year Runs-red-Talking appeared clad in a type of bodysuit Chad had never seen before. Instead of the familiar dull operator's brown and yellow, the Quozl blazed brightly in garb of emerald green sewn with patches of black and pink. Scarves and earrings matched perfectly, as they always did. As camouflage it was an utter failure, but as an alien fashion statement it was dazzling.

Nor were the only changes in his attire. New whorls and lines had been shaved into his face and upper arms. An entirely different pattern had been scalloped from his thighs. Even the knuckles of his toes had been carefully worked over by an artist's razors.

"Got a hot date?" Chad inquired the first time he set eyes on the new Runs. "You look impressive."

Runs extended his right hand to conclude the by-now-familiar human gesture as he greeted his old friend. Then Chad relaxed as the Quozl extended all seven fingers and placed his palm directly over the human's face, gripping lightly for a moment with the fingertips.

They ambled over to the campsite where Chad's tent offered protection from sun and rain.

"What have you brought for me to learn this time?" As usual, Runs could hardly contain his excitement at these first meetings of each new summer. To Chad he displayed nothing in the way of emotion.

"Have a look around. See what you can find." He didn't smile. While his Quozl friend understood the human smile, the toothy displays still made him uncomfortable. So Chad did his best to dampen his instinctive reactions.

Runs found the plastic bags, used his long fingers to swiftly unseal them. Small brown objects tumbled from the first into his waiting palm.

"What are these?" He lifted the handful to his face. "They smell strongly of other woods."

"Mixed nuts. None of them grow around here. You've had the peanuts before but the rest will be new to you."

The Quozl examined each nut in detail before popping it into his mouth and chewing experimentally. "They're all delicious," he said when he'd consumed the entire packet. "But then, everything you have brought me has been delicious. We had hoped to find edible foods on Shiraz. We did not expect to find cuisine." He expelled air in the form of a high-pitched whistle, which Chad had come to know as a sigh.

"It's hard for me to enjoy these delights knowing I can share none of them with my friends."

"Hey, you're not alone. I've enjoyed everything you brought for me from the Burrow gardens, but I can't go spreading the stuff around either. It's a damn shame. We could do a lot for each other's agriculture. Not to mention what you guys could do for tree farming. I've seen you around trees. It's weird."

"The Quozl have always had a deep spiritual relationship with trees. It was gratifying to learn that those which grow here are no different in that respect from those of home." He held up a large curved nut. "What did you call this one?"

"A Brazil nut."

He placed it in his mouth and chewed blissfully. "Wondrous." As he swallowed he tried to peer into the depths of the tent. "Did you bring any more tuna fish this time?"

"Some."

"A few of the engineers have discussed the possibility of constructing a subterranean accessway from Burrow Seven to the river that flows above the colony. If the problems could be solved it would allow us to engage in a limited amount of aquaculture. Expeditions have tested the local fish and found the flesh nutritious and tasteful, as is everything else on this world, though we are not so fond of the flesh of the larger animals. I have tried more than anyone else, thanks to you, and I find this holds true. I do not know why it should be so. But all the fish is excellent, whether saltwater or fresh. It would add great variety to the Burrow diet.

"We still prefer our plants. I think we are further removed from wholly carnivorous ancestors than are you."

"I remember us discussing that before." Chad opened another bag of food for his friend to sample. "You've completely lost any canine teeth, for example."

Runs was staring eagerly at the new bag, which was larger than its predecessor. "What have you there?"

"We call 'em snack foods. You've had some before. Potato chips, crackers, pretzels, hapi mix, a nice assortment. My mother got kind of upset with me for opening a whole slew of bags and taking a little of each. She tolerates me, though. Everybody thinks I'm turning into a real eccentric because I'm always going off by myself so much."

"Very interesting. I am credited with great spirituality since I spend more time in meditation than anyone except senior philosophers." Had he adopted the gesture he might have grinned. Instead his ears twitched rapidly in the movement Chad knew to translate as amusement.

"My companions marvel at how I manage to stay in such excellent physical condition when I spend so much of my time immersed in deep contemplation. They cannot know that my body is being exercised as thoroughly as my mind. Here, I have something to show you. I thought to make it a present." He swung his own shoulder pack around and placed it on the ground. "I am not sure it is a good thing to do. We can discuss the ramifications."

Chad watched and waited while his friend unpacked. Runs-red-Talking was big on ramifications.

From the interior the Quozl withdrew a handful of interlocked rings. They were fashioned of wood, each a different color and grain, and had been polished until they gleamed like brass. One was umber, another dark brown, a third light brown shot through with golden splinters, while a fourth was a startlingly bright blue. The fifth was black with white spots, the sixth a silvery gray, and the seventh and last an absurd translucent pink.

Placing the rings between them he proceeded to demonstrate how you could create different sculptural shapes by twisting and locking the rings into position. Or they could be worn as jewelry. At a gesture, Chad picked them up.

"Are these as expensive as they are pretty? Hey!"

He nearly dropped the ring set as the black loop began to quiver slightly in his hand. None of the others vibrated but each exhibited a distinctive tactile quality. Runs tried to explain as he named each of the rings in turn.

They had been brought all the way through underspace from distant Quozlene.

"I'd like you to have it."

Chad was overcome. "I couldn't possibly." The look and feel of the alien wood held most of his attention. It was difficult to turn them, to feel them slip through his fingers, and concentrate on what his friend was saying.

"The problem I have is that someone else might see them. Your parents, or your sister, or your friends."

"None of them are botanists. They'd think it was just an interesting puzzle I'd picked up in a store somewhere. Unless I let them spend time with something like this." He caressed the black ring, feeling it jump slightly under his fingertip.

"Can you guarantee that will not happen?"

Chad slumped slightly. "No, of course not." He extended his arm. "Here. You'd better take 'em back. They're beautiful and I'd love to have them and I appreciate the thought, but it's an unnecessary risk."

"I thought you might say that." Runs turned the taking back into a ritual that lasted several minutes. Then he indulged himself in the snack foods Chad had brought for him to try.

Not all were appealing. While the term "snack" seemed appropriate, in several instances the word "food" did not apply at all. He much preferred the mixed nuts.

"Tell me about the fancy suit. Is it some special occasion? Talk about risks: if anyone was looking in your direction they'd be able to spot that getup halfway across a valley."

Runs looked down at himself. "I thought it safe enough to emerge without changing. The weather is cloudy and there have been no recent atmospheric overflights. I did not believe there would be anyone about to see me."

"I was thinking about your own people, the expeditions you're always sending out. You're right about the woods, though. They seem empty." He pointed to the black circles and cutouts. "What about the patches? I haven't seen any of them before. Are they significant of something?"

"Indeed. I have sired."

"Sired? You mean you had a kid? You?"

"With an old friend and mate. We were finally given permission to conceive. You know how carefully we limit our population."

"Yeah, I remember you talking about that. A kid's a real privilege. You must be pretty proud."

"I am. You should see him, nesting in his mother's pouch, hardly bigger than your thumb. He will grow rapidly, much more rapidly than a human child which is of course born in a more advanced state of maturity." He blinked. "You have not yet sired?"

Chad raised both hands. "I'm not even going steady right now."

◇ **188** ◇

"Well, then, how is your coupling frequency?"

Chad looked away. "You've got to understand about that. We just don't do it as often as Quozl. We're not designed for it. We don't talk about it as freely, either."

"I did not mean to offend."

"You didn't offend." Runs's habit of apologizing for everything was difficult to get used to, Chad reflected. "You are not responsible for your biology, I'm not responsible for mine."

"I know, but it still seems rather a shame."

"*You* think it's a shame!"

While they argued Mindy crouched in the bushes opposite the tent, hardly daring to breathe. She'd lost her brother's trail once but had managed to find him again by hurrying to higher ground. He hadn't traveled half as far as she'd expected.

Two days he'd spent camped by the shore of the river, sitting near his tent and peering up the canyon without straying. That behavior was strange enough, but she hadn't begun to observe strangeness. That arrived in the leaping shape of something short, gray-white, and furry, a big-footed whisk brush clad in opium green. Trailing brightly hued scarves and tinkling earrings it shook hands with her ingenuous brother, whereupon he began feeding it nuts and pretzels as the two of them sat down to immerse themselves in nonstop conversation.

Now *that* was strange.

Her powers of identification might have failed but there was nothing wrong with her imagination. It didn't resemble anything she knew and it moved much too naturally to be someone in a suit, acting out a role. Half an hour's close scrutiny was sufficient to convince her that her brother's companion wasn't from around there, and she didn't mean Idaho. It looked exactly like something from another world, though rather more cuddly than she would have designed it. The fact that it spoke excellent English and dressed like a refugee from a Carnaby Street fashion closeout only added intrigue.

They were still chatting amiably but she was too far off to overhear the actual conversation. If the creature carried a weapon it was inconspicuous and her brother seemed completely relaxed. She felt safe in assuming it could not be too dangerous.

She *had* to get closer if she was going to hear anything.

"Make no mistake about it," Runs-red-Talking was saying. "That's why the Books are so important to us."

"How many of them are there?"

"Hundreds. You could not begin to master them in several lifetimes. The best one can hope for is a respectable sampling. They cover every aspect of Quozl life and more are being added all the time. The Samizene is not static: it is an evolving organism imbued with self-regenerating immortality. You do not study it. It breathes into you through your mind, you inhale the spirit with your eyes." He broke off abruptly, staring past his friend.

Chad turned, saw nothing, looked back. "Something on your mind? You see something?"

"No, Chad, I do not see anything. But I can hear something. It moves clumsily, and it exhales tension."

Chad turned and concentrated. "I don't hear a thing. But of course with those ears you can hear a lot better than I."

"I can also see better and smell more intensely. These things I have learned over the years. Among the Quozl, the most sensitive human would be considered sensory-deprived."

"Yeah, but you guys can't swim worth a damn." Frustrated, he climbed to his feet. "I swear I can't see anything moving in there."

"Some large animal: bigger than a squirrel, smaller than a deer."

Suddenly color flashed between two bushes, enough for Chad to recognize. He cursed himself silently. "That's no large animal. That's my sister." He took a step in her direction, hesitated. "You'd better hide in the tent."

Runs's ears bobbed negatively. "She has been here long enough to have noticed me, I fear. If she had not been watching there would be no reason for her to continue hiding. Yet if there is any chance . . ." He bounded into the depths of the tent.

Chad let the rain flap flop against the opening, walking toward the line of trees. "All right, Mindy, you can come out now." When she made no move to emerge he added, "I saw you. You've got that stupid green shirt on, the one with the red stripes. At least if you're going to try and hide in the woods you should pick something without bright red stripes."

There was a long pause, then she rose from behind another bush, slightly to the right of the place he'd guessed. "I wasn't hiding." She was smiling at him, unable to eliminate the slightly superior tone she always used when they talked. As she advanced toward him he saw that her attention was focused on the tent. His heart sank. Runs-red-talking was right.

"What is it, little brother?"

"What's what?" He spoke irritably. "And don't call me that."

Ignoring his request she nodded at the tent. "Your friend with the big feet and the oversized ears."

"Why'd you follow me?" he asked her, attempting to postpone the inevitable.

"I got curious. You know me and my curiosity. You kept talking about all the exploring you were doing, all the wonderful new places you were visiting, but every time you left the cabin you went off in the same direction. Every summer.

"For a while I thought you had a secret camp where you'd found some gold. As you got older I found myself wondering if you'd run into some pretty backpacker like yourself and the two of you were making a regular yearly rendezvous you wanted to keep secret from Mom and Dad.'' She indicated the tent. ''Is it a girl?''

''No. Runs-red-Talking is a he, not an it.'' He let out the heaviest sigh of his life. ''Come on. I guess I might as well introduce you.''

He led her back to the tent, pulled the rain flap aside. ''Might as well come on out, Runs. You were right. She saw us.'' Something stirred inside the shelter. Mindy was bent over, trying to restrain herself.

''His name is Runs-red-Talking?''

''As near as he can approximate it in English. I can say it properly but my Quozl's not too good. Too high-pitched and too soft for my palate. He says I just sound like I'm grunting, a lot of the time. But I'm getting better.''

''*You* can speak *its*—pardon me, his, language?''

''We've been friends for a long time.''

He heard his sister's sharp intake of breath as Runs emerged from the tent and straightened. To Mindy, Runs would seem expressionless and solemn. She didn't know how to interpret the subtle movements of hand and eye, ear and fur.

For his part Runs studied her with open interest. ''You are the first female of your species I have encountered in person, so I suppose some good will come of this.''

''His English is as good as yours, Chad. How did you learn our language?''

The Quozl turned questioningly to his friend. ''You might as well tell her what you feel she can handle,'' Chad said tiredly. ''She'll badger me to death if you don't tell her.''

''I will tell her, and freely, but,'' Runs turned back to Mindy, ''you must swear to tell no one else of this meeting or of my existence. Your brother has kept such a promise for many years. Can you do no less? If not, this encounter must end now and forever.''

''No, no,'' Mindy assured him quickly, ''I swear. I swear it. Why should I tell anyone? It's a big secret, right? Our secret.'' Her eyes swept over the Quozl. ''I like your jewelry.''

Runs-red-Talking tilted his head to one side, staring at her. "And I have observed in my studies which I can now confirm that despite the insignificance of your own organs of hearing, you decorate them as much as you are able, though among humans this civilized habit is largely confined to the females."

"Maybe we can trade earrings. No, we can't do that. It might risk your secret, right?"

Runs-red-Talking made no secret of his relief. "I am glad to see you may be counted upon to help preserve our privacy."

"Why would I want to share you? This is too good." She chose a place and sat down, crossing her legs and locking them together with her arms. "Now take your time and tell me all about yourself and the rest of the—what did you call them, brother?"

"Quozl. The Quozl." He didn't know whether to be furious with his sister for having followed him or relieved that she so readily accepted the need for continued secrecy.

"What do you want to know?" Runs asked her.

"Everything!" She smiled reassuringly at him.

"I do not have the time in this life to tell you everything, but I will endeavor to satisfy your immediate curiosity. We will begin with the business of smiling." Chad hunted for the thermos of cold fruit juice while Runs lectured Mindy.

While he spoke, Runs-red-Talking was considering alternatives. Short of slaying the female there was little he could do. The inherent logic of it notwithstanding, he doubted his human friend would understand such a course of action. The next step involved killing them both. That held dangers of its own. Their parents would miss them and come searching, possibly along with others of their kind much better equipped for tracking. They might find more than evidence of assassination: they might begin to learn who was responsible. Under no circumstances could he expose the colony to such a danger.

It really mattered not because he didn't want to kill Chad

and he was morally and spiritually incapable of harming either of them. He could not even intrude on their Sama without first asking permission. He had no choice but to discard the thought, which he never broached to his human friend.

Chad had to admit that his sister handled the return home perfectly. She did nothing to suggest that anything out of the ordinary had transpired during her absence.

Their parents did express surprise when she told them that instead of spending her days writing on the porch or in her room she was hencefoth going to accompany her brother on his week-long forest forays. At the same time they were delighted to see brother and sister, who had fought for so long, getting along so well. Mindy allowed as how she was learning things about the forest she'd never imagined while Chad reluctantly admitted it was good to have some company on his long trips.

Everything went smoothly from then on until the last week of the summer. Chad set up camp and waited with his sister by the side of the river, but when three days had gone by without Runs-red-Talking emerging from the woods he found himself growing uneasy.

He was splashing cold water on his face when Mindy came up next to him.

"Has he ever been this late before?"

"No." Chad fumbled for the towel, wiped his eyes. "Never. Never more than a couple of days."

"Maybe something happened to delay him longer."

"Not by choice. One of the things the Quozl make a fetish of is punctuality. He told me that several times."

"Okay, so he's late. It's too early to panic. He can't exactly let us know what's going on by letter. It's probably something so ordinary it's dumb, like locking himself in the bathroom. Or maybe he just got busy with something else important and forgot."

"For a few hours, possibly. Not for three days. It's not like him at all. You're right, though, when you say something might have happened to him. Something involuntary. What if he ran into a cougar, or a sow bear with cubs? Both of us always worried about that."

Mindy's reaction showed she hadn't considered those possibilities. "God, I hope not."

Chad looked back at her in some surprise. "I didn't think you cared about him, personally."

"There you go again," she said in exasperation, "putting words in my mouth, thinking for me. Did I ever say anything like that?"

"No. You just always struck me as a lot less interested in him than in the stories he told you."

"You're crazy. I like him as much as you do."

Finding the discussion suddenly distasteful, Chad turned to stare upstream. "Something's happened to him, I know it."

"He could be sick. Quozl do get sick, don't they?"

"I suppose. Funny, that's something we never talked about." He relaxed slightly. "Maybe that's all it is. But this still isn't like him."

"Nobody plans on illness. He's probably more worried than you are. He can't have his doctor or whatever they use send us a telegram." She settled a pan over the small propane stove. "Nothing we can do except wait and hope he shows up. If he doesn't we'll leave and come back in a week. That's the pattern, isn't it?"

Chad nodded. "That's the way it's been set up."

Runs-red-Talking did not appear the following day, or the next, or the one after that when they were packing for the hike back to the lake. Chad tried not to worry too much. His friend's absence might be due to something as ordinary as a sprained ankle. That would seriously incapacitate a Quozl. Or he might be having problems on the job, or with his family. They would find out in a week when they returned to the meeting site.

XII.

THERE HAD BEEN no mistakes in planning, neither had he grown careless. Instead he'd been caught out by that most dangerous trap of all: coincidence. Had he arrived earlier they would not have seen his shaft hatch opening. Had they been working instead of taking a group meditation pause he would have heard them and waited until they'd departed. He decided that the physicists were wrong. The universe was held together not by gravity, but by ifs.

Passing Quozl turned to stare, which was extremely discourteous and only added to the extent of his humiliation. He was in no position to stop and chide them. They couldn't really be blamed for the breach of etiquette, he knew. No one was ever escorted anywhere by an armed guard. There was no need for armed guards in the colony since an offender had nowhere to run to.

Only Runs-red-Talking had found that.

So startled passersby stumbled as they encountered the unprecedented spectacle of a single quiet Quozl being hustled along by four Shamers hefting side arms. They did not understand because Runs-red-Talking did not look dangerous. They had no idea how wrong they were.

None of them said anything, and the instant they realized what they were doing they turned away in embarrassment. But Runs could feel their furtive glances following his progress, could imagine many ears straining to pick up the least bit of conversation from his escort. The Shamers said nothing, however. Not because they had nothing to say, but because they were genuinely afraid of talking in his presence. The exact nature of the technician's offense was unknown to them, but its seriousness was not. On a scale of severity, they had been told, what he had done existed high above in a rarefied region of illegality all its own.

The escort did not accompany him into the chamber. Obviously they believe I am sane enough not to commit suicide, Runs mused as he entered. In that they're correct. I have neither reason nor desire to kill myself. He was less certain of his elders' feelings on the subject.

The room was small and informal. They were in Burrow Seven and everything was new: the wall decorations, the bells that hung in a corner and tinkled with imitation wind, the beautifully rendered false toki wood paneling, the seats and cushions and mats of elaborate design.

These were fully occupied. Some of the faces he recognized, others were new to him. They were talking among themselves, pointedly ignoring his arrival. One directed him with utmost indifference to a backless cushion set on the floor in the center of the room. The soft, indirect lighting shifted to focus on him. He did not cower under the attention but kept his ears and back straight, his posture attentive.

If his inquisitors were pleased they kept the opinion to themselves. There was an air of exhaustion about them, as though they'd been engaged in strenuous debate prior to his arrival. He had time to identify each of the Burrow Masters as well as five of the seven members of the Elder Council. There were also scattered representatives from several scientific departments. All this pomp and status just for him. He was not flattered.

A few had trouble concealing their anger. That did not bother him because it was expected. He had forfeited any right to consideration or understanding. When the conversation quieted and they began to turn to face him he launched into a short speech in which he effectively renounced any claim on their mercy or sympathy. A few sighing whistles were his only response. Now, he knew, would come the questions.

"How long has this been going on?" That from the Master of Burrow Four. It was not necessary to explain what he meant by the question.

How easily this could have been avoided, Runs thought. He remembered making his usual hike, enjoying questions and a multi-day visit with his human friends, and then returning. Remembered opening his concealed hatch and firing his harness line across the shaft, climbing out and preparing to close the hatch prior to swinging across the gap.

Only to look down and see an entire shaft cleaning crew staring back up at him, dangling from their own harnesses. They'd been engaged in a silent meditation break, until the noise of his activity made them look up. A human would never have heard or sensed his presence, but four sets of Quozl ears had detected him immediately.

He could not flee multiple witnesses. As he hung helplessly in harness, several powerful work lights caught his face, locking his features in the crew's memory. After that there was nothing for him to do but cooperate.

He harbored no delusions about his future as he replied to the question.

"For a while."

"Don't hedge with me!" The others present eyed the Master of Burrow Four approvingly. In the privacy of the chamber they could be as impolite as they felt. "Generalities will not save you. I want details."

Runs kept his head down. "I do not mean to evade."

"Anger I could deal with," said the Burrow Master. "Hatred I could understand. I could cope with frustration or even simple insanity. But for one to endanger all the Burrows through sheer stupidity and greed, that I have difficulty comprehending." Though he spoke calmly he could not entirely mask his suppressed rage.

"I apologize for everything, inconsequential though that may be." Runs looked up at the Burrow Master. "I have visited the surface each warm season for the past four cycles."

He was ready for the guarded inhalations, the involuntary whistles of astonishment his revelation produced. They'd suspected, from study of his handiwork, but they could not be certain of the time frame. Now he had quietly confirmed their worst fears.

No, he told himself. Confirmation of those was yet to come.

"For so long." The Master of Burrow Two looked resigned. "You must have learned a great deal about the surface world." Instead of replying verbally, Runs-red-Talking acknowledged with subtle adjustments of both ears. "You must have acquired much knowledge. Not to mention these."

He held out a handful of small objects. Given their easy disposability, Runs had felt fairly safe in bringing them back with him. But his room had been searched before he'd been allowed to return to it, following his apprehension, and they had been discovered. The items in question were not of Quozl manufacture.

"Where did you get these and what are they?"

"Human food." Runs did not answer the first half of the question.

It was a feeble attempt at delay. "Which you found in your travels, I suppose?" Runs did not reply. If they would deal in their own assumptions he might yet be saved.

One did not become a Burrow Master by proceeding on assumptions. "We have run some preliminary correlations with the surface study section." He carefully placed the bags of potato chips and cheezos to one side. "It is just possible that such perishables might remain undisturbed on the surface long enough for you to find them untouched." He displayed a cluster of globular fruits attached to a complex set of stems.

"These, however, were found unprotected by artificial vacuum. Through exhaustive study of Shirazian lifeforms we are familiar with these. I am told they are called grapes. Our specialists assure me that if anything like this was to be left exposed on the surface for more than a few moments the local fauna would rapidly consume it. Yet these are untouched.'' He placed the grapes alongside the three bags of junk food.

''Each of these flexible containers is stained with oils acquired from recent contact with human skin. Are you going to ask us to believe that you simply wandered into an unoccupied native camp and helped yourself? You have been careful, but everything you were wearing at the time of your apprehension has been subjected to the most intense scrutiny. Similar oils were found on the straps of your shoulder pack. These were compared chemically to the oils on the packaging. They match.

''From this we must infer that you have had a personal encounter with humans. I would give away all that I possess including my life to be told this is not so.'' Still Runs held his peace, forcing the Burrow Master to proceed to the inevitable. ''You may tell us the truth now, for what that may be worth to you. If we doubt, you will be subjected to encouraging varieties of sedation.''

That was it, then, Runs knew. If they didn't believe him they would inject him with drugs under whose influence he would tell all. By doing so voluntarily now he might retain a minimal amount of status. Self-consciously he adjusted his attire. It would not do to look bad while confessing.

''There were two humans involved.''

''Only two?'' inquired another Burrow Master quickly.

''Only two. Both young adults, male and female siblings.''

''Two young adults traveling by themselves so near our valley?''

Runs acted to defuse their skepticism. ''They do not travel alone, and they have come nowhere near the colony site. I meet with them three valleys to the east. I can show you the place on a surface map.

''There is one native family, two parents and these two

◇ **201** ◇

offspring, who,'' he struggled to translate a unique human concept, there being no Quozl word for "vacation,'' "regularly visit this region in the warm season for an annual meditation time. The same four come every cycle. The same four, and no others.''

"How can you be certain of that?'' asked someone Runs did not know.

"Because I am assured of it by my human friend Chad.''

"And you believe him?'' inquired another.

"Through four cycles of contact I have had no reason to doubt anything he has told me, so I see no reason to doubt this.''

"You have then engaged in contact for four cycles?''

"Longer than that.'' Why hold anything back now? Runs asked himself. "Chad and I first met when we were both juveniles. That was ten cycles ago.''

"Yes, that incident is recorded. Surveillance on you should never have been relaxed, but you gave every indication of having been healed. That mistake cannot be rectified. See what the cost has been!''

"You are all so afraid.'' Runs kept his head up. They could not think less of him no matter how he acted now.

Someone else he didn't recognize spoke, ignoring the challenge implicit in his posture.

"So you have had annual contact with two humans via your own illegal exit—which of course has been permanently sealed—for four cycles?''

"I was meditating on the surface instead of in chambers.''

"Your comparison fails. What have you and your humans talked of?''

Runs saw that the speaker held high status with the surface studies section. She was leaning forward intently, both ears pointed straight at Runs.

"What do they know of the colony?''

"Very little. They know of its existence and that it is home to more than one Quozl. They know we live underground but not where.''

"It is enough," mumbled another representative of the scientific community. "Since first we settled on Shiraz the natives have made many advances. If they know we are in this vicinity they now possess instruments capable of locating us."

"No," a colleague objected politely. "We can build devices which will fool their detection equipment."

"It doesn't matter." Runs spoke hastily. Let them think him lacking in the social graces. They could not think worse of him than they did already. "Both young humans are sympathetic as well as intelligent. My relationship with the young male in particular is very close. I have spoken often of the need for maintaining secrecy about our existence here and they concur. They will not speak of us to anyone else. In that I am confident."

"Well, then," declared the Master of Burrow Two, "we can all relax, can't we? If the renegade Runs-red-Talking is confident, what have we to worry about?"

"Nothing is certain," Runs countered.

"Do not quote the Samizene to me, you pouchless worm!" The Burrow Master half rose in her seat. Taking note of the aghast expressions on her colleagues' faces she slowly sat back down. "I apologize. Forgive me my outburst. I am ashamed."

It was not her feelings she was ashamed for, of course. Everyone else in the room harbored similar feelings toward Runs-red-Talking. But she had spoken violently, had let the primitive Quozl within take momentary control. When proceedings resumed, the atmosphere in the room was more solemn than ever.

"I can only say," Runs told them, "that my friend Chad has revealed nothing of our existence in the four cycles I have spoken with him. His parents do not know, nor do his friends, much less the authorities."

One of the other Burrow Masters commented emotionlessly. "If that is truth, then could we not ensure our future safety by eliminating these only two humans who are aware of us."

The highest-ranking philosopher present spoke quickly, preempting Runs's ready reply. Runs had previously considered the same argument, but it was better to have one of his peers deal with it instead.

"Morality aside," the Elder Quozl said firmly into the attentive silence, "we would be murdering two intelligent, warm-blooded beings who have done us no harm. They are guilty of nothing. Potential for damage is insufficient reason for killing. Were they to disappear they would surely be sought after by their parents. This is an abomination that cannot seriously be considered."

"Their sire pilots aircraft. He would surely be missed," Runs added. "The location of their meditation site is well known to friends and relations."

"I would consider it nonetheless." Burrow Master Leader spoke for the first time. "If we could be certain beforehand of complete success. But as our insane citizen so astutely reminds us, nothing is certain. Against that we have his insistence that these two young natives will not speak of us to others of their kind. Consider also: if we somehow succeeded in carrying out their elimination and it was discovered by the natives that we had committed such a deed, how would they react? Among themselves they sometimes tolerate murder, but I do not think they would react favorably to the knowledge that we had done so. I firmly believe that under such circumstances we could never make peace with them." He gazed down at Runs.

"What will happen if you never meet with these two humans again? Will they grow discouraged and forget you?"

"They might. They may also try to find me, fearing that I have suffered injury. I have never been so late for a rendezvous before."

Burrow Master Leader picked at something in his fur. "I was afraid you would say that. Humans are curious. Their persistence is still a matter of some debate. Regardless, we must deal with the fact that there are two of them who know of the colony's existence. I wonder how long they will refrain from telling others what they know without you to constantly remind them of the need for continued silence?"

"Are you suggesting, I ask this with utmost respect," said one of the other Burrow Masters, "that we permit this contact to *continue*?"

"While we decide how to deal with it, yes. Make no mistake: I disapprove of what has occurred as strenuously as anyone. But it has happened. That is fact. We must cope with the consequences. Wishes are fulfilled only during meditation. This is reality. It is a critical moment in our time on Shiraz and we must deal with it through reason, not desire." He looked back at the center of the room and said, utterly unexpectedly, "While we do that, you may leave."

Runs-red-Talking blinked. "Leave? Just—leave, Honored Elder?"

"Return to your work. Engage in some true meditating, at which you are sadly deficient. I do not need to speak of what will happen to you if you attempt to reach the surface."

The disbelieving Runs sat a moment longer, wondering if he ought to compose a speech of thankfulness. Then he realized he was not being exonerated, only excused until such time as final decisions were made. In some respects that was harder for him to deal with than an actual sentence. Possibly, he thought as he rose to depart, this was to be part of his punishment, leaving him to go on living as normally as possible knowing all the while that at any time his life might be forfeit.

But the Burrow Master Leader had talked of letting him continue contact. Could he live on hope if nothing else?

As he rose, the Elders and Burrow Masters and representatives of the scientific staff continued to argue among themselves. He was ignored completely, a sure sign of dismissal. Dismissed to return to work, to friends, to coupling and meditation. He departed in a daze.

Of his earlier escort there was no sign, but he did not delude himself. Dismissed he'd been, but hardly forgotten. He knew he was being watched. Let him stray however honestly near a ventilation shaft and his perilous freedom would come to a rapid end.

Humans would have treated one of their own who'd done such a thing very differently. They were never able to live up to their own ideals. A vast gap existed in human civilization between what they believed and how they acted. It was a gap that Quozl could help fill, if someday that was permitted.

Human history suggested that they tended to exterminate their own best thinkers. It was as if they could not stand the beauty inherent in their own thoughts. Compared to the average human, Runs-red-Talking was stable.

His hopes were certainly premature. The Council might still opt to find a mechanism whereby they could justify killing him and his human friends. He prayed for the Burrow Masters and the Elders, with whom any final decision would rest, to spend much time in meditation.

The rest of the day he tried to relax by viewing the most depraved, violent recordings he could obtain from the central library. Only afterward did he feel calm enough to return to his assigned work. Sensing that something was different his friends eyed him curiously, but asked no questions. If he wished to impart information he would do so freely. None would be impolite enough to force inquiry. He might be acting the way he was for personal reasons, in which case the questioner would find himself embarrassed by persistence.

Surely nothing would be done without him first being informed of what had been decided, he thought. He was too central to the matter. But no contact came the following day, nor the next, or the one after. Life went on shrouded in a fog of uncertainty.

So much time passed that he was actually surprised when

the summons finally came: a request slotted indifferently atop his morning schedule. No guards came to escort him. They weren't needed. He went quietly and of his own volition though he knew he might be going to his death. That was to be expected. Had he tried to run or hide he would have shamed those who  had requested his presence, and though they might be his executioners he could not do such a thing. It would cost him status. Different he might be from those who sat in judgment of his actions, but he was still Quozl.

There were fewer in the room this time and their composition had changed: only three Burrow Masters and greater representation from the scientific community. It puzzled him but he had no time to ponder it. The change could be either to his benefit or detriment. Scientists would not react as emotionally as administrators, but neither would they exhibit any sympathy on the personal level. They were permanently outside his Sama. There were also two philosophers present instead of one. To plead tradition, or to justify his execution?

As he squatted on the central mat he tried to divine something of their intentions by studying individual postures. The atmosphere seemed less hostile. Or was that only wishful thinking on his part?

The senior member of the surface study team spoke first. That indicated that the scientific staff was in charge of this meeting, not the administrators. It did not make him feel much better.

"By all rights and laws you should be excised from the community," she began. Runs-red-Talking thought he had composed himself but at her words a chill still rattled his spine. Her tone was as black as the inside of her pouch. "However, the situation is akin to a complex molecule. Remove one part and the entire structure collapses.

"If you were removed you would be missed by your human contacts. If they are removed they will be missed by their parents. If the parents are removed they will be missed by their friends. And so on unto cataclysm." She bent both ears to the sides, one long finger tracing a thin spiral shaved into her left forearm.

"The inescapable result is that if we break any link in this chain of awkwardness you have forged, we may draw more attention to this region than we dare risk. Then again we might not, but we have no reliable scientific model on which to base predictions. The alternative to breaking the chain is to keep it as short as possible. That means you, unfortunately, and your two young human friends.

"I wish only that we could peer into their minds and hearts to learn if they truly mean to guard the secret of our presence."

It didn't take Runs long to digest this declamation. What the senior was saying, basically, was that they all hated him for what he'd done, they'd much rather see him dead, but that they risked cutting their own throats were they to do so. Therefore, not only was he going to be spared excision, so were Chad and Mindy. And perhaps even more than that. He remembered the promising if reluctant words of the Burrow Master Leader.

He spent several minutes apologizing elaborately, several more humbly requesting permission to speak. "They will say nothing of us to any other humans. I am certain of it. I would wager my life on it."

"You already have," said the senior scientist. "You have not yet won, neither have you lost. Your wager hangs perpetually in the balance, defying gravity and reason. A puff of indecision either way could topple you."

"I have known the young male for more than four cycles. The elder female sibling I do not know as well but she is eager and insistent."

"It matters not," said one of the Burrow Masters. "The philosophers and the logicians have made the choice for us. Personally I disagree, but I bow to the intellect of those who know better." That was what the Burrow Master's words said. His posture suggested that he felt quite differently. Runs would have to be very careful. He had made enemies.

But they can't do anything to me, he thought with wild excitement! I am the first link in the chain they dare not break.

"What, gracious peers, am I to do?"

"You will go back." Everyone turned to another member of the surface study team. "You will maintain your two contacts. You will *not* expand on them. You will pay particular attention to anything that even suggests either of your friends has spoken of us elsewhere, at which point we will be compelled to consider additional steps. It is hoped that your evaluation is correct and that such steps need never be implemented.

"The colony has acquired a disease which cannot be cured but which hopefully can be contained. You will at every opportunity reinforce and re-emphasize the need for strictest secrecy, reminding these young humans that our very survival here is in their hands."

"How shall I respond when they question me about us?"

A younger member of the scientific staff rose in his chair. "Tell them as little as possible about our level of technology and the size of the colony. As to our art and social system you may answer freely. Tell them nothing of our military posture."

"We don't have a military posture."

"They may infer otherwise. Correct this if necessary. We are peace-loving, harmless, exhausted refugees who wish only to live out our lives in tranquil isolation. We are incapable of fighting."

"Your pardon, Honored Elders and peers, but I do not understand."

"It is not for you to understand," said the Master of Burrow Six. "It is for you to comply."

"No, he will react more effectively if it is clear to him."

This from the senior member of the study team. She looked over at Runs. "We must make contact with the natives of Shiraz sooner or later. History, reason, logic dictated that it be later. Runs-red-Talking decided it should be otherwise." He looked properly ashamed.

"As we cannot go back and alter what has occurred, we must try to make the best of it that we can. You have made contact with two young humans. Very well. If they keep our secret the damage is minimal. It may be that we will now be forced to reveal ourselves sooner than planned. In that event it would be useful to have two humans available to act as intermediaries. That they are not trained in such matters is evident from the information you have supplied. That they might be trained in such matters is a thought worth meditating on.

"Hopefully all of us—myself, you, your humans—will expire of old age with the secret of the colony still intact. Should that not come to pass it would help to have at least two humans who could testify to our nonthreatening posture."

"There is good in everything," opined one of the two philosophers present. "From now on you will record your meetings. These recordings will provide much useful information. You will be given questions to ask. Here there may be despair, but there is also opportunity.

"Let these two young humans learn about us while we learn about them. When open contact comes in the future we will not have to rely on interpretations of human entertainment transmissions to tell us how humans react in specific situations. We can try out actual scenarios on real specimens."

Runs balked at hearing his friends described as "specimens" but was in no position to express moral outrage. At the same time he saw the barely repressed eagerness in the members of the scientific staff. They understood the need for secrecy but at the same time they were desperate for accurate information about humans and how they lived. Here was an opportunity, albeit unexpected, to learn about the natives of Shiraz without revealing the existence of the colony.

With a start he realized that as deeply as they espoused secrecy, a few hungered for contact as much as he had.

"I will do the best I can," he informed his inquisitors. "I am a repair technician, not a trained observer, but I . . ."

Apparently there was no end to the morning's surprises.

"You will not go back alone. Members of various study groups will accompany you. They will be few, as we do not wish to alarm the humans. If what you have told us is true they will be delighted to meet other Quozl. They know there is a colony. It does no more risk to our existence for them to encounter others, and may even reinforce in some way in their minds the need to keep our presence a secret."

Rationally Runs had no reason to object. Emotionally it was different. He had done something unique. Chad and Mindy were *his* friends. He had done the difficult work.

Better to share than to die, he reminded himself. It would be stupid to try and keep the humans to himself. Why should he be jealous of other Quozl? Didn't he want increased contact and exchange of ideas? Not only was he to be spared, his contacts were to continue. What more could he hope for?

"We must hurry," he found himself saying. "The warm season is drawing to a close. Soon my friends will be leaving this region with their parents, not to return until the next cycle. If they are worried about me they may decide to begin a search."

"Never fear," said the senior staff member. "You will go to meet them soon. Remember as you do so that you are now acting in an official capacity on behalf of all Quozl. You will receive instruction and training for your new task. You will be provided with an innocuous new title and job description that you can mention to your relatives.

"You have betrayed them as you have betrayed all of us. The continued safety of the entire colony lies loud in your ears." She bent hers to emphasize her words.

"You all worry needlessly. Once some of you have met and talked with my two humans you'll see how groundless are your fears."

"You have not studied their transmissions," said another member of the study team somberly. "If there is one thing certain about humans it is their unpredictability. I do not see why your pair should be any different. Unlike Quozl they frequently act in an irrational manner."

"Make no claims of absolutes for us," said the Senior reprovingly. "Remember the tale of High-red-Chanter and Thinks-of-Grim before you credit us with what we may not deserve."

Like everyone else in the Burrows, Runs-red-Talking knew the story of the two Quozl who had disappeared on the surface many cycles ago. It was an accepted fact that their bones lay decomposing somewhere not far from the colony site, if they hadn't been devoured by Shirazian scavengers.

"I do not think that this one," she was saying in reference to Runs, "is irrational in that fashion."

"My profoundest gratitude be yours, Honored Elder." At that moment Runs would have laid all his jewelry at her feet.

"No, not irrational," she concluded. "Merely stupid."

Her closing comment did nothing to restrain his joy as he was dismissed. No more hiding in the woods or risking his life to cross the ventilation shaft. The next time he went to meet with his friends he would do so via one of the official exits, in the company of other important Quozl. They might be empowered to kill him if they believed the situation required it, but he would see to it that he did nothing to alarm anyone. He and Chad and Mindy would talk as they always had while others listened and recorded.

As he strode rapidly toward his living quarters he took time to enter an aggression chamber and demolish a number of armored Quozl images, sending blood and viscera flying. When he emerged he felt confident and refreshed, kowtowing to Elders and favoring passing youths with a generous eye. Only one thing had come out of the meeting that mattered.

He was going to be able to see his friends again.

XIII.

"WE'RE NEVER GOING to see him again."

Chad turned away from the water to watch his sister as she shook the thermos bottle containing water and fruit-mix powder. There was a spark of fall in the air today, an intimation of severe storms to come. Soon they would have to leave the mountain fastness for the balmy ozone of L.A.

"He wouldn't just vanish forever without saying goodbye." Chad was insistent on that point without knowing why. How did he know what a Quozl would do. "He's pretty resourceful. He'll get in touch with us somehow."

"Something's happened to him for sure." Mindy set the thermos on the picnic table. "What if he finally miscalculated and fell down that shaft?"

"I just don't see that happening to Runs." Chad came toward the tent, avoiding those rocks that were clad in slippery moss and algae.

Or maybe I refuse to see that happening, he told himself.

His sister suddenly looked up at him. "Do you suppose it's me?" She was doodling on her sketch pad. In addition to her writing skills, Mindy was an artist of middling ability. And I can't create a decent birthday card, Chad thought ruefully.

"I don't think so, Mindy. If he had second thoughts about you, after all these years, I think he would have said something before now."

"That's what I thought, but I wanted your opinion." She studied the afternoon sky. "We're due back the day after tomorrow. Dad's talking about packing up in a couple of weeks. He's been talking to the old-timers in Boise who say it's going to be an early winter. They say that every year, but Dad's getting older. He's afraid of getting caught in a fall snowstorm.'' She looked upriver. ''What if he never shows up again? What will you do?''

''He made me promise never to try and find his home. I wouldn't even know where to start, which direction to take. I don't think he trusted me that much.''

''Maybe it was for your own good,'' a high, breathy voice said by way of interruption. ''Aren't you going to offer us something to drink?'' Brother and sister whirled in the direction of the unexpected greeting.

''Runs!'' Chad moved to greet his friend, halted when he saw that he wasn't alone.

Three other Quozl accompanied him, another male and two females. All wore subdued clothing with a minimum of jewelry and flash scarves. They were clad as inconspicuously as it was possible for a Quozl to be without feeling naked.

It was easy to tell male from female. Besides subtle differences in attire, the suits of the females had slits marking the location of their pouches. Both were shut, indicating that neither was carrying an infant. They also had slightly more muscular legs, necessary for supporting the weight of a maturing youngster for a full year or more.

Runs wasted no time introducing his companions, who studied the two tall humans with undisguised interest.

''I don't understand,'' said Chad. ''I thought your secret was . . .''

''Found out,'' Runs informed him. ''After careful consideration of all alternatives it was determined that not only should contact be maintained with you and Mindy, but that it should be expanded to include members of the colony's scientific staff. This in no way mitigates the need for continued secrecy on your part.''

''We understand,'' said Mindy.

''I think that's great.'' Chad stepped forward and reached

for the face of the nearest Quozl. She instinctively brought her left hand up as if to strike at his throat. Anticipating as Runs had instructed him, Chad twisted his arm as if to knock hers aside without invading her Sama straight on.

Her eyes widened. Turning to her colleagues she chattered excitedly in Quozl as they discussed this sophisticated reaction on the part of a clumsy, ignorant native. Chad watched them debate, until finally she turned back to face him afresh.

If anything, her English was more polished than that of Runs, though her voice was no less whispery. "Where did you learn that?"

"From my friend." He indicated Runs, who looked properly humble.

Unable to restrain herself any longer, Mindy stepped up alongside her brother. Her sketchbook hung from her left hand.

"So you're going to study us?" The female's ears bobbed in a gesture Mindy had learned to identify. "Great! Let's all sit down and get to know each other."

It wasn't how Chad would have handled it, but he deferred to his sister. She'd always been the one with the instinct for the social graces.

It must have translated well because the Quozl readily complied, taking seats as best they could manage around the fold-up plastic picnic table. The cold fruit juice was passed around and eagerly sampled.

Runs downed his without hesitation, having enjoyed such delights previously. He took care not to try and dominate the exchange. It would have cost him status, and his was so low it could not survive further damage. Expeditions such as this one would never exonerate him, but they would go a long way toward making his presence acceptable to his peers.

With Runs to help explain, the encounter went smoothly, except that Chad and Mindy managed very little sleep since the three newcomers kept them awake long into the night with endless questions about everything from human foods to international relations. The time passed all too quickly, with Chad and Mindy promising to return to the campsite for a longer visit in one week.

When they returned, after restocking their packs and reassuring their parents, they found the Quozl already camped by the river awaiting them. On the basis of what they'd learned from the previous encounter, the Quozl scientists were able to prepare their questions beforehand. Composing suitable replies kept brother and sister busy every waking hour. In many ways it was akin to meeting Runs-red-Talking for the first time, Chad mused, only multiplied by three.

The Quozl sometimes seemed guarded in their response to his own questions, though he always received an answer. He supposed some suspicion on their part was understandable. Mindy disagreed, finding them always open and trusting.

Though offered the use of the tent, the Quozl chose to sleep outside beneath their thin wraps. Their fur protected them against the early morning chill, though it was not thick enough to cope with an Idaho winter. While they could stand and indeed preferred cooler temperatures than humans, they still had their limits.

The Indian summer was drawing to a close the day they looked on in amazement as Chad frolicked in the deep pool where Runs-red-Talking had nearly drowned. Runs was brave enough to wade out in the water up to his high waist, but his companions would advance no farther than ankle-deep.

"We are not aquatic by nature or inclination." The senior female in the party spoke as Chad emerged to dry himself. "We utilize water for grooming and cleansing, but the idea of immersing oneself totally in deep liquid for purposes of recreation is utterly alien to us. Your ability to 'swim' is one we do not possess and, frankly, do not envy." With her ears she indicated the depths of her revulsion.

Chad toweled away recalcitrant droplets. "Runs and I have spent a lot of time discussing our different tastes. I wouldn't find squatting in a small dark room very relaxing. Like many humans I suffer from something called claustrophobia.'' He tried to explain.

The Quozl was dubious. ''But you know that the walls aren't going to close in around you.''

''I'm just telling you what it feels like. For a clinical explanation you'd have to talk to a . . .''

A scream interrupted him, made the four of them turn toward the tent. The noise came from beyond, from the edge of the forest.

''My God.'' Chad fumbled frantically with his sandals. ''That sounded like Mindy!''

''Something has frightened her,'' said Runs worriedly. He thought of the stuffed monster moldering in the surface study museum. ''Perhaps a bear. What do we do if it is a bear?''

''We run out into . . .'' Chad caught himself. The Quozl couldn't swim. ''Can you climb trees?''

''Climb a tree?'' The senior female sounded doubtful. ''We can do many things with trees, but climb? What a novel concept.''

Their ancestors were not primates, Chad reminded himself. Their fingers were designed for delicate manipulation, not strong gripping. And their legs were impossible.

His sister emerged from the forest, followed by a rapidly moving bipedal shape. It wasn't a bear. All of them recognized the other male Quozl. He was running alongside Mindy, paralleling her sprint without breathing hard, and apparently talking rapidly.

She stumbled to a halt and to Chad's immense surprise, clutched at him for protection.

''What's the matter, what's wrong?'' he was thoroughly confused.

''He . . .'' she gulped air, ''that animal—I was sketching in the woods and he attacked me!''

''He attacked you?'' Her words still made no sense. ''What

do you mean, he 'attacked' you? Are you telling us that he tried to hurt you?'' Chad was not alone in his disbelief. He was flanked by a trio of dumbfounded Quozl.

Mindy was calming down. ''Well, no. Not exactly, I guess.''

''Not exactly? You *guess*? Mindy, we're not characters in one of your stories.'' She was avoiding his eyes. ''Say what you mean.''

''All right.'' Her face came up and she stared hard at the Quozl. ''He tried to put the make on me.''

''Say what?''

''Do I have to act it out?'' Sarcasm had replaced the anger in her voice.

The Quozl under scrutiny, Turns-theme-Over, was a respected member of the surface studies staff. As he responded he was careful to stand well clear of what he perceived to be Mindy's Sama. His voice was controlled and devoid of emotion, but his ears were frantic.

''I fear I have been the progenitor of a misunderstanding.''

''Misunderstanding mild!'' Runs had to recite his very favorite stanzas to keep himself under control. ''If you have violated Sama . . .''

''Wait a minute, everybody slow down!'' Chad considered the words of the Quozl and of his sister. They involved a subject which the Quozl dealt with much more openly than humans. It was something he'd been reluctant to discuss with Mindy. After all, she was his sister. Now he saw that he'd been remiss.

All of which notwithstanding there was something peculiar about what had or had not happened. Turns-theme-Over was an alien, for crissakes.

The Quozl tried to explain himself, but in Quozl fashion it took him an hour just to get past the requisite preliminary apologies. Chad could sense his bewilderment. He had no idea what if anything he'd done wrong. When he had finally calmed down some, Chad took over for him.

"What exactly," he asked his sister, "did Turns-theme-Over do?"

Now that the initial shock had faded, Mindy sounded uncertain. "Well, he touched me."

"Touched you where?"

She bugged her eyes at him, then replied. "Here, and here."

"What makes you so sure the contact was of a sexual nature?" Chad was surprised at his own openness. All those conversations with Runs-red-Talking had done some good. No therapist could have achieved more with a gangly, shy teenager. "Turns-theme-Over is a specialist in human affairs. He might simply have been trying to obtain information of a statistical nature."

"This may come as a surprise to you, little brother, but that's a line I've heard before."

Turns-theme-Over was anxious to defend himself, grateful as he was for Chad's intercession. "Again let me plead misunderstanding." He sounded honestly hurt and concerned. "I don't see what I did to cause the human to react in such a fashion."

Runs allowed a touch of sternness to creep into his tone. "Are you not, after all your studies, familiar with the strange human taboos in this area?"

"Forgive me." Chad knew what it took for the senior scientist to request forgiveness of Runs, a Quozl inferior in status to himself. Turns was truly apologetic. "I had grown so relaxed in their company I had forgotten. That is why research into this matter is so important, so that we may come to fully understand each other."

"That doesn't mean your studies can be carried out on a personal level," Chad admonished him.

Green-by-Shadow spoke up. "We have firsthand knowledge of male human anatomy." Chad was familiar with the story of the unfortunate first encounter between human and Quozl. "No similar opportunity has henceforth presented itself for examination of the other gender. Turns-theme-Over's actions may be explained if not excused by his professional enthusiasm.''

"He was enthusiastic, all right." Mindy stepped away from her brother, hands on hips. "I'm not taking my clothes off for him or anyone else."

It was growing more and more difficult for Chad to treat the situation seriously, now that it was clear that his sister had not been injured.

"Why not? Don't tell me you're embarrassed to undress in front of a Quozl?" He indicated Theme-turns-Over. "He's interested in you as a specimen, not a partner."

It was Chad's turn to be surprised.

"I must confess to more than mere objective curiosity." Theme-turns-Over kept his gaze averted from Mindy. "We are both warm-blooded, fur-bearing species, though humans only marginally. Interest in this subject among the Quozl extends to all relevant fauna. It is our nature."

"I'm not one of your fauna," Mindy protested. "You can try jumping all the deer and elk and porcupines you want, but keep away from me."

Cheese and crackers, Chad thought dazedly. Theme-turns-Over *was* sexually interested in his sister. What an absurd notion.

Wasn't it?

"It will be as you wish." Theme dipped both ears apologetically. "I will not transit your Sama again." He sounded so pitiful Mindy relented.

"Hey, don't feel singled out. I would've reacted the same way to a guy."

When Runs had taken his colleagues to hunt for amphibians, Chad confronted his sister.

"I'm sorry he upset you, but don't you think you overdid it? You embarrassed him so severely in front of his peers he'll probably never show his face outside the colony again. Nothing could have happened. The Quozl are a completely different species. They're not like us at all, even if you want to throw in theories about convergent evolution.''

"Turns-theme-Over is no bug-eyed monster, either," his sister shot back. "Have you ever stood back and taken a good look at them? They're almost our size; two legs, two arms, two ears."

"Bilateral diffusion. So what?" His gaze narrowed and he stared hard at her. "Don't tell me that now *you're* curious?"

"Aren't you? Don't you ever look at the Quozl females and wonder?"

"I look at a Quozl female and all I see are feet the size of baseball bats and a pouch big enough to hold the rest of the team's equipment."

"That's what I'm talking about: equipment."

"No, I'm not curious. They don't look even faintly human."

"I know," she agreed. "That's what's so strange about it."

"I don't know what you're talking about." Just like when they were kids, she'd managed to take over the conversation.

"That's because you're only eighteen."

"Maybe I am only eighteen, but I'm the one who knew about convergent evolution!"

They went on arguing among themselves, ignoring the wading Quozl while the Quozl politely ignored them. Turns-theme-Over never repeated his actions and they were not alluded to again. That did not mean the subject never crossed anyone's mind.

Thoughts were no offense to courtesy.

XIV.

IT WAS RAINING but not heavily. It only rained hard in Los Angeles in January and February. A March shower was to be savored.

He'd gone to the market to pick up his weekly allotment of groceries. When he finished he'd return home to the microbiology project which had occupied him for most of a month now. Or maybe he'd just take the rest of the day off, hit a museum or take in a film or visit his mom. His dad would be in the cockpit of a 747 somewhere between L.A. and Bangkok. Seniority with the airline brought prestige, better pay, and choice of assignment.

The only trouble was if he dropped in for a visit she'd expect him to stay overnight, and he much preferred his west L.A. apartment to the old Santa Ana homestead. Santa Ana was also a long run for his battered Ford.

It was a new market, which meant less than half the floor space was devoted to food. The rest was given over to hardware, electrical supplies, automotive parts, drugs, toys, greeting cards, and expensive inedible items. Easter was coming up. His aunt had two little girls and he wondered if he could find room in his meager budget for a plastic bunny or candy duck. The Easter display was hard to miss, a double-wide aisle groaning beneath the weight of barnyard chocolate.

The stuffed animals occupied the end of the aisle, an eight-foot-tall hillock of polyester rabbits and rayon chickens. Too many of them wore clothes or carried miniature pails and shovels. There was one large, appallingly anthropomorhized fuzzy duck that looked tough enough to withstand Amy's and Annie's ravening fingers for at least a couple of days.

His eyes strayed from the possible gift and his fingers clenched unconsciously on the handle of the shopping cart. He stared.

On the shelves to the right were licensed characters draped in holiday garb. Mickey was there, and Donald, and Bugs and Daffy and Tweety and a herd of Easterized Garfields, marching in ranks through fields of polyethelene grass, waiting to graze on unsuspecting pocketbooks. Some he didn't recognize.

Crammed in between a perpetually put-upon coyote and a double-suited Hobbes was a figure with big feet, long flexible ears, a flat face, oversized eyes, short tail, and straightforward expression. It wore a tight bodysuit of familiar design, though the color pattern was new to him. This he recognized instantly.

It was Runs-red-Talking.

The longer he stared the more surreal the stuffed toy became. After a while he was sure the plastic eyes had begun to follow his movements accusingly.

Two rug rats were coming toward him, dragging their mother and gesturing excitedly at the pile of toys. Before they reached him he grabbed the toy which had caught his attention.

It was about a foot high. The strangely shaped ears flopped down over the face. Ignoring the arrival of the screaming kids he turned it around to examine the back. A tag protruded from a sewn seam.

Made in South Korea
20% Rayon 80% Polyester
Contents non-toxic, non-flammable
Reg. U.S. Pat. Off. 2556439906

Of more interest was a plastic card secured to the left foot, which enthusiastically proclaimed:

This is an Authentic
QUOZL!
He's come all the way from far-off Quozlene
to be your very own!
His name is
SEES-INTO-YOUR-HEART

That was wrong, Chad thought absently. A Quozl name was formed of three parts, never four, never two. The error did not keep him from reading on.

QUOZLS make great companions.
They'll never let you down.
They'll never hurt you
because they don't know how to fight.

That was wrong too, Chad thought, his brain running on automatic pilot. They just choose not to. He scanned the rest of the card.

This QUOZL has lavender-gray eyes and wears
the green-gray suit of Botanical Exploration
Collect ALL the QUOZLS
for a complete colony of your very own!
LOVES-YOU-COMPLETELY
SNUGGLES-CLOSE-FOREVER
WATCHES-OVER-YOU-ALWAYS
LAUGHS-HIMSELF-SILLY
And all the rest!

Just when he was sure he had passed beyond shock into numbness he turned the card over and read:

Very slowly Chad placed the stuffed, expressionless Runs-red-Talking back on its shelf. His mind was operating at maximum which went partway toward explaining why his eyes were temporarily unfocused.

The instant he put the toy back the eleven-year-old boy who'd been wrestling with a corpulent Sylvester the Cat dumped it to point wildly.

"Look, Mom, look! A Quozl! I want it."

"You already have that one. That's the technie," his sister sneered.

"No, I don't!" He flailed at the toy until he got his fingers around it. "This is Sees-Into-Your-Heart. He's a botantist." He gazed up at his mother. "I gotta have him, Mom. I'll have the whole surface studies team if I get him."

"No, you won't," his sister insisted airily, "because the surface studies team is always changing."

"How would you know? You're always watching that stupid *Dance Fever*."

"Don't fight." Easter shopping had taken its toll on Mother. "How much is it?" Price tags, Chad thought dazedly, had long since replaced McGuffey's Readers as the starting point for literacy in American society.

"Ten ninety-nine," the boy reported promptly.

"All right," said the woman tiredly. It would buy her a cheap couple of days, until the novelty wore off, Chad mused. "But no more Quozls, understand? You've got enough."

"Aw, Mom," the boy began, "you can't have enough Quozls!" Suddenly realizing that the one he clutched had yet to be paid for, he hastily added, "But this'll be enough, I know it will."

"It better be. Come on." She shoved her burden up the aisle. "We still have to get the turkey."

Runs-red-Talking got jammed ears-first between two half-gallon containers of two-percent real chocolate milk and a giant box of Tide. Chad watched him go. Mother, menagerie, and groceries vanished around a display of Sugar Frosted Flakes.

As soon as they were out of sight he began pawing through the mountain of toys. Sure enough, there were two more. Kisses-You-Every-Night and Likes-to-Be-Close. Neither name had appeared on the botanist's name tag. Maybe these two were recent additions to the kiddie Quozl pantheon. Obviously the line was successful. He picked up Likes-to-Be-Close, at once fascinated and repulsed.

It was grossly fat. Every Quozl he'd met was lean and trim, nor had Runs-red-Talking ever alluded to obesity among his race. Furthermore, the toy wore an idiotic grin wide enough for most Quozl to construe as a death threat.

Returning it to the display, he hunted some more until he encountered a perfect Runs-red-Talking clone. After making certain all its identifying and descriptive tags were intact, he put it in his own cart, atop the frozen lasagna and bag of bagels. It gazed forlornly back up at him, an unnatural smile permanently affixed to its glistening face. It was a miracle he didn't run into anyone as he headed for the nearest checkout.

What the hell is going on here? For years he'd guarded the secret of the Quozl and their colony. Had someone else seen a Quozl elsewhere? Had the subtle Runs-red-Talking neglected in all their conversations to mention that there was another colony somewhere else on Earth?

With a shock he recalled the story of the Quozl musician High-red-Chanter and his equally deranged mate who'd fled the colony soon after its establishment. Since they'd never been seen or heard from subsequently it had been assumed by the others that they'd long since perished in the high, cold mountains. What if the Quozl were wrong and the two renegades had survived? If they'd survived maybe they'd been observed. Maybe they'd talked to someone else.

Maybe he and his sister weren't the only humans to have made contact.

That seemed the only possible explanation. At least, it was the only one he could think of at the moment. He didn't want to think about it, didn't want to believe it. The great secret was a secret no longer. The colony's existence was common knowledge, if the toy tags were to be believed.

He slowed, physically as well as mentally. Maybe the secret wasn't out. Could a secret be half revealed?

After all, it wasn't as though he'd encountered a newspaper headlining the colony's location, or seen this week's copy of *Newsweek* with a picture of Runs-red-Talking being interviewed by Barbara Walters. His gaze fell to his cart. Stuffed animals. Anything more significant than that would have been on the evening news, or on the front page of the *Times*. It wasn't.

Could some psychic be seeing the Quozl in dreams?

Screw that. He was a scientist—or a scientist in training, anyway. Someone somewhere had seen and talked to a Quozl. There was no other explanation. The problem now was to find out the details: who, how, where.

The television show would be the logical place to begin. He never watched kidvid. For him and his fellow graduate students, Saturday mornings were a time for sleeping in or fleeing the megalopolis for hiking trips in the south Sierras or beer runs to Mexico. But tomorrow would be different. Tomorrow he would not sleep in. Tomorrow he would use the alarm clock that heretofore had been a Saturday morning virgin.

"Thirty-three sixty, please."

"Huh, what?" He blinked at the cashier.

"Thirty-three sixty."

Another part of his brain had taken control, placed him in line, and methodically removed his groceries from the cart. They had subsequently been totaled, which was exactly how he felt. The cashier eyed him uneasily.

"Are you feeling okay?"

"Fine. I'm fine." He dug for his wallet.

"Paper or plastic?" the bagboy inquired.

"Plastic."

The stuffed clone of Runs-red-Talking went headfirst into a bag laden with cereal and snack food.

He left in such a hurry he forgot to buy a paper.

He hardly slept at all that night with the result that the alarm had to struggle to wake him. Unlike most mornings, however, he was alert and anxious after the fifth ring. No need to heat coffee, no need to sip juice, no reason for breakfast or reviewing the day's activities. Instead he fumbled into his robe and the bathroom. Throwing cold water onto your face was something drunks did in movies. He discovered that it was not just a literary conceit but that it actually worked. One more shock to add to the others.

Drying himself, he went into his living room and switched on the tv.

There it was in the guide: *Quozltime,* 8 A.M. every Saturday. No wonder he'd never noticed it before. He didn't begin to function as a human being until after nine-thirty, later on weekends. Flipping to the proper channel, he confronted a multitude of screeching cats pursuing pudgy mice. In the usual reversal of logic, the mice turned the tables on their pursuers. He'd never been able to enjoy cartoons. Too rational a mind, he knew. Sitting in the broken, oozing couch that was his favorite piece of furniture, he waited while the hands on the wall clock crawled toward eight.

The animation in the commercials was a hundred times better than in the show he'd been watching. Each was flashier than the next, all designed to sell two things: toys and sugar. As eight o'clock neared he found himself leaning forward, his clasped hands falling between his legs. He heard nothing but the tv; not the couple upstairs, not the traffic outside.

When it finally took over the screen, it was so matter-of-fact in its blandly colored limited-animation format that he could only untense and lean back in the couch. Silently he watched two-dimensional Quozl parade across the screen: fat ones, short ones, skinny ones, displaying none of the uniformity of size and build that was a Quozl hallmark. The females wore makeup and had absurd long eyelashes. They walked and talked and danced to an irresistible theme song. One wore dark sunglasses. Others whizzed about on cute little air scooters that to the best of Chad's knowledge no more existed in the Quozl colony than they did in downtown Manhattan.

It wasn't all pure invention. Quozl ear gestures and finger movements were rendered with some accuracy. The body-suits, omnipresent jewelry, and flash scarves had been drawn with regard for the originals. Not every name was overpoweringly saccharine, though none were familiar to Chad. No Runs-red-Talking cavorted inside the tube.

The colony itself was a product of pure imagination. Instead of existing underground the animated Quozl lived in simple surface structures located not in Idaho wilderness but close to an unnamed small American town. They consorted exclusively with adolescent humans. The only adults were either villains who appeared to motivate the plot or clumsy parents whose sole function was to get in the way of the efficient Quozl and kids.

Instead of declaiming eloquent phrases rich with meaning and subtle overtones in their high, breathy whisper, these Quozl spoke sappy, infantile English at a volume sufficient to drive any real Quozl to distraction. Of more interest was the story line itself. It spoke of a particularly introspective Quozl who had meditated and meditated to the point where he'd thought himself into a state of noncorporality. It was an interesting tale with an intriguing moral.

He'd thought exactly the same thing when Runs-red-Talking told it to him by the bank of the snow-fed river high in the mountains.

It was pure fiction, but the show treated it as fact. Quozl and children ran around in a panic trying to aid their newly ethereal friend, and then a monster materialized because the show, as opposed to the plot, demanded one. It was black with yellow eyes and came floating out of inner consciousness or wherever it was the unfortunate Quozl had dematerialized into, so naturally he was able to save his friends before they saved him, and by this time Chad was no longer interested in the feeble story.

What held his attention were the Quozl movements, their attire, their attitudes, and the rhythms of their speech. It shifted unpredictably from accurate observation to pure invention. There was no avoiding the obvious: while much of the show was fiction, it was constructed on a foundation of knowledge.

That did not include the way the Quozl interacted with each other or their young human companions. There was enough actual physical contact, touching and holding and hugging, to precipitate a war among real Quozl. The concept of individual Sama space apparently did not translate well to children's tv.

Mercifully it ended, with children and Quozl happy and content and singing at the tops of their lungs. As they danced and sang over the closing credits, Chad watched the names and titles go whizzing by at incredible speed. Many of them were oriental. But despite their unfamiliarity and the velocity at which they flashed across the screen, one name stood out clearly in tandem with a title.

Mindy Mariann Collins
Story Editor

He sat there for a long time, until a clutch of jut-jawed, half-naked heroes and heroines wielding lasers and other assorted weapons had disposed of half a dozen similarly clad evildoers, the latter distinguishable from the good guys and gals only by the hue of their armor and the fact that their eyes were devoid of pupils. A real human being appeared on the screen and began to talk about tide-pools. The shock was sufficient to jolt  Chad back to real time. He picked up the remote and switched off the box.

His sister. The entire improbable business had nothing to do with the long-departed High-red-Chanter and his mate. It was his sister. This was how she dealt with the trust of Runs-red-Talking and the colony. This was how she kept the great secret—by splashing it all over the airwaves every Saturday morning, indoctrinating the youth of America in the ways of the Quozl. Everything Runs-red-Talking had told her, everything she'd been able to glean from her brother's previous four years of contact, all the long conversations she'd held with members of different surface study teams, was all there on the screen rendered in cheerful pastels for anyone to see and absorb.

No wonder she'd done so much sketching.

He knew she'd been making a living writing for television, but she always named a company, never a show, and he'd never bothered to inquire deeply, being too wrapped up in his own studies. He regretted his lack of familial curiosity even as he wondered how long this had been going on. Probably the show was produced right here in L.A., though there was the matter of all those oriental names. Perhaps actual production took place in Japan, or Taiwan. It was time to find out.

His first thought was to call the local network affiliate which showed the program, until he remembered that it was Saturday. Business offices would be closed. He'd have to wait until Monday morning. There was an optional one P.M. seminar but that could wait. Everything could wait.

For lack of anything better to do he dressed himself, wondering how his sister was capable of such complete betrayal. Revealing the secret to a friend or two he could understand, but to put the entire colony on television? Beyond belief!

Too late to do anything about it now. The genie was out of the bottle. She'd delivered up the Quozl for more than thirty pieces of silver, much more.

Was it all the result of artistic frustration? He could remember Mindy yelling aloud when unable to compose the right sentence, or when she couldn't think of the proper word, or when a page didn't read back right. Could recall her endless efforts to finish a novel. All those years of struggling to make it as a writer, of humiliating visits to their parents to ask for still another loan whereupon her mother would sigh and come up with another few dollars, another pitiable check, insisting quietly and unconvincingly that this would be absolutely, positively, the last time they could help her out. The rejections coming in the mail, one close upon the posting of the next.

She'd sold a couple of short stories to magazines that paid in copies and criticism, two or three magazine articles for three-figure paybacks, and one lamentable concept for a slasher film that never got beyond the talking stage. Yet she struggled on. To her mother she showed perseverance, to her father unremitting stubbornness.

Then the big breakthrough which he heard about only casually. A writing job with some big production company. No movies, just television, but nice, steady, well-paying work. If Judas were alive today, Chad thought grimly, would he have a piece of the ancillary rights to the story of the crucifixion?

Story editor. He wasn't sure what it meant but it sounded impressive. A credit all to her own, that lasted a few nanoseconds longer than most of the others.

Come to think of it, she had said something during a holiday dinner about writing specifically for children's television. Since she hadn't elaborated he hadn't inquired. To him children's television meant *Sesame Street* and *Reading Rainbow* on PBS, not Saturday morning cartoons.

He slammed the door as he exited his apartment, wondering how he was going to restrain himself for the duration of the weekend. He considered confronting her immediately. She had a fancy house somewhere out in the west Valley. But it would be better to beard her in her lair, at the studio where she worked, where she couldn't flee as easily. Find out where she performs her perfidy, he told himself. Confront her there. He exited the building fuming. Despite the fact that he was not an especially impressive physical specimen, the pedestrians who saw his face made it a point to give him plenty of room on the sidewalk.

There was nothing else he could do, not even anyone to share his fury with. Not that it mattered anymore. Why try to conceal the Quozl's existence when everything there was to know about them was right there for anyone to see every Saturday morning at eight o'clock? The greatest secret on Earth sandwiched in between screaming ads for syrupy cereals and plastic avengers.

It was easy to find out where she worked. All he had to do was call his mother and ask. Controlling his tone while he put the question was much harder.

So it was that on Monday morning next he found himself pacing the false tile floor of the reception area in a new, slickly decorated building in Encino, when what he should have been doing was dissecting microorganisms at UCLA. As if that wasn't bad enough, they made him wait.

For years he'd had to listen to his parents brag to their friends of their daughter's success in the fiercely competitive world of television. And what about their son, the brainy one? Oh, him. He was working on his advanced degree. Still. If only they knew, Chad thought, that his sister's achieve-

ments lay in her ability to plagiarize and adapt, not in origi-
nality and invention. That her clever tales were stolen from
alien storytellers and her character designs sketched from life.

The office whose confines he paced like a caged bobcat
was decorated with framed animation cells taken from the
company's many programs and features. Most were utterly
unfamiliar to him, depicting superheroes, funny animals, and
distorted children. A few, however, were taken from the
Quozltime show and these drew his attention. The unnatural
shapes, the amplified speech and cute names and other changes
did not surprise him. This company was not in the business of
making documentary films.

The magazines arrayed on the coffee tables were alien to
him: *Variety, The Reporter, American Cinema, Animato*. As
he paced the room people came and went, sometimes drop-
ping off packages at the receptionist's window, other times
making pickups, occasionally vanishing into unknown regions
through a single back door. None of them wore a suit or tie.

After a while the receptionist glanced out at him and said,
"You can go back now, Mr. Collins. Straight down the main
corridor to the end, turn right, last door overlooking the
courtyard."

He hesitated at the doorway. "What number is her office?"

She smiled at him. "There's no number. Her name's on
the door."

Her name is on the door, he thought. Why not? Wasn't she
the story editor? She did more editing than anyone imagined,
he reflected as he strode past tiny rooms overflowing with
piles of books, drawings, posters, sketches, and magazine
cutouts, past people hunched over angled boards beneath
intense little lights. Strange machines hummed and whirred
and bulbs strobed unexpectedly.

Few of the doors were closed. Among them was the one
with his sister's named emblazoned across it. Automatically
he raised a hand to knock, then said the hell with it and
walked in.

It was unexpectedly spacious, an enclosed palace compared

to the cubbies he'd just passed. There
was a couch, a few chairs in skeletal
Danish Modern, an equally spindly desk.
Framed cells hung on the walls. Not all
were from the *Quozltime* show. The big
glass window provided a view of a sunken
courtyard lush with palm trees, philoden-
dron, and hibiscus, a rectangular tropics

circumscribed by a sea of concrete. The carpet beneath his
feet was shaggy contoured white, in imitation of a dozen
flayed polar bears.

The two garbage pails were empty because everything was
piled on the desk. Some of the items he recognized from
childhood: a favorite doll, a tired sneaker. The desk was
in the shape of a large "U." A typewriter rested on the
right, a computer keyboard and terminal to the left. His
sister sat in the middle, surrounded and protected by her
electronic flanks. She looked up with a startled smile when
he entered.

"What a surprise! You should've called so I'd known you
were coming, Chad."

"So you could've met me somewhere else?"

"Actually I'm surprised it's taken you this long."

"I've been sort of busy," he replied laconically. "You
don't get a Ph.D. in biology by faking your lab results, and
unlike certain other professions, you can't borrow the basics
from other people."

"This isn't how I wanted this to start off, but since it
already has, why don't you at least sit down and make
yourself comfortable?"

"I may never be comfortable again, thank you. I'd rather
just stand. If I sit down I might get my strength back, and if I
get my strength back I'm liable to punch something."

"It's a wide desk. I don't think you've got that much
reach. I'm not worried, Chad. You can talk about it all you
want, but you're not the violent type."

"I'm glad you're not worried. Would you be worried if I

went straight to your boss and told him what you were doing?''

She smiled. "And what *am* I doing? What would you tell my boss?''

Hard to hide pure bluff. It gleamed like polished coal, with its own unmistakable inner light. He couldn't tell her boss a damn thing, of course.

"How could you do it?'' was all he could finally say, staring evenly over the desk. "The Quozl," he lowered his voice, "they trusted you. Runs-red-Talking and Blue-watches-Time and all the rest. They trusted you with everything: their history, their stories, their very existence. And you betrayed all that. For money.''

She wasn't smiling anymore. "Did I?'' She picked up a pencil and began chewing on the eraser, a childhood habit she'd been unable to break. Between the typewriter and the terminal he wondered what use she had for a pencil.

"Am I supposed to argue with you?'' He looked away from her. "You've given away the Quozl. You've told the whole world of their existence. All those sketches you made, all those notes you took, it was with this in mind all along, wasn't it? You were never really interested in the Quozl for their own sake, you were only intrigued by their commercial possibilities. Have they been profitable for you?''

"Not much use in denying it,'' she told him evenly.

"How long? How long have you been writing about them for others?''

"Ever since that first summer. The idea of using them and their stories as the basis for a kidvid struck me the instant I saw them, but I wasn't sure what approach to take or how to write a pilot and bible. I had all winter to think about it.

"By the end of the second summer I had enough material for a proposal. I took it to my agent. She thought we might get a movie out of it. It didn't kick around very long before Barbara Hammer, who's in charge of production here, had it on her desk. She called me in and asked for three scripts. That took another winter. The show sold immediately. We're into our second season and gearing up for the third. *Quozltime*'s been number one in its time slot ever since it went on the air.'' There was wonderment in her voice.

''Nobody expected it to do what it's done. The spin-offs, the ancillary rights have been unreal. We've got companies, *big* corporations, bidding against each other for a slice of the action.''

''I saw some of the stuffed toys.''

''Oh, good. Nice, aren't they? Have you seen any of the McDonald's glasses yet?''

McDonald's glasses! He turned back to her, more numb now than angry. ''It really doesn't mean anything to you, does it? Your betrayal, what you've done? It means nothing to you at all. You talk of money, not trust. As far as what's going to happen to the Quozl, you could care less.''

''On the contrary,'' she said with unexpected passion, ''I care very much. But you tell me what's going to happen to them. You're the bright kid, the one who always brought home the good grades, the one Mom and Dad always patted on the head. You tell me.''

''They're going to be overrun. They're going to be put under heavy guard and watched all the time and poked and prodded and examined. The government will quarantine them until it can make up its collective mind what to do with them. Then the xenophobes will start squawking about an invasion, and the rednecks will start loading their hunting rifles and making reservations for flights to Idaho, and the televangelists will scream about godless aliens, and . . .''

''Calm down. None of those things are going to happen. Because nobody knows anything about the Quozl except what they've seen on television. The government doesn't know the Quozl exist. The rednecks and the televangelists and the xenophobic types don't know the Quozl exist.''

He gaped at her. ''I don't want to shatter the neat little

illusion you've constructed for yourself, but you've put them right there on Saturday morning television for everyone to see. It's only a matter of time before the dangerous types figure everything out.''

''Really? Before they figure out what, Chad? That a Saturday morning kid show about friendly aliens is based on reality? How are they going to do that? As far as any other human being is concerned, the Quozl are nothing but a product of one writer's imagination. Mine. How many of the shows have you actually seen? Not many, I'll bet, or you would've been here sooner. How many?''

He found himself studying one of the courtyard palms. ''Well, only one, so far.''

''One. If you'd been watching since the start of the first season you'd know that none of the episodes say anything about a Quozl colony hidden in the Idaho mountains. None of them mention their arrival on Earth. That's one of the beauties of children's television. You put something on the air and it exists as of that moment. There's no need for history or explanation. Even if I had mentioned the actual colony it wouldn't matter because nobody would take it seriously. This is *kidvid,* Chad. Not *Masterpiece Theater*.

''The Quozl in the show live near a small town in Southern California. I used Ojai for my model, but it could be anywhere. They interact freely with kids and act like overgrown adolescents themselves. They're about as much like the real Quozl as the Care Bears or the Smurfs.'' She rocked back in her chair.

''They're no more real to this audience, no more betrayed, than if Sylvester and Tweety Pie were thought to be living secret existences in Greenwich Village. They're less real to the kids who watch the show than are Henson's Fraggles. They're not even puppets; they're two-dimensional drawings. As for the adults, the only time they think about Quozl at all is when their kids are bugging them to buy the latest book or action figure or stick-on.''

He stared at her. "You can't believe it's going to stay that way forever."

"Why not?" Her smile was back. "Chill out, little brother. The Quozl's secret is as secure as it ever was. Nobody suspects their existence now any more than they did twenty years ago. The Quozl are cartoon characters that *I* invented. Nothing more. You're the only human being who knows otherwise, and you're not going to tell. So what are you so worried about?"

"I'll tell you what I'm worried about! I'm worried that . . ." He stopped in mid-worry. The inescapability of her logic was oppressive.

If he or anyone else was to suggest that the Quozl were anything other than animated fictions they'd find themselves locked up for observation.

"You're not going to get away with this."

"Of course I am. I've been getting away with it for three years and I'm going to continue to get away with it for as long as the show runs. If we're lucky, five or six years. Then the Quozl will fade away like most other kid shows. It won't matter because by then I'll be an established name in the industry."

She was perfectly right, of course. There was no way he could stop her, no way he could punish her. "You're not going back to the lake," he told her lamely. "You're not going to see Runs or any of the others ever again."

"Of course I am." Her smile widened. "I need material for the next season. We've already been picked up, by the way. The third year's the key when it comes to residuals. Do you have any idea how much money we're talking about here, little brother?" She leaned toward him and he drew back as if from something covered in spines.

"Look, you've been crawling back and forth to school in that beat-up old junker of yours, running on regular and prayer. That's when it wasn't in the shop and you had to find a bus. Why don't you go buy yourself something new? Pick out whatever you like and have the dealer charge it to me. It's the least I can do. If it hadn't been for you I'd never have found out about the Quozl and there'd be no show. I'd still be trying to sell that stupid novel and magazine articles at a hundred bucks a pop. How about,'' she asked him with a twinkle in her eyes, ''a nice new Corvette?''

She couldn't have broken his train of thought any more effectively had she shot him. He swallowed.

''That's a thirty-thousand-dollar car.''

''No problem. It'll put a dent in my bank account, but like I said, you deserve it, and with the show already renewed there'll be plenty of money coming in. Those stuffed toys you saw, the game board, the action figures and drink glasses, I've got a piece of all that.''

''As the 'originator,' '' he said sarcastically.

''Yeah, that's right, little brother. I've bought Mom and Dad a few things.''

He nodded. ''You sent them on that trip to Europe last year, didn't you?''

''Sure. They could always get places because of Dad's job, but they could never afford to stay in the nice hotels, eat in the good restaurants. This time they could. I took care of that. Why shouldn't I take care of my little brother as well? If you don't want the Corvette, how about a new Taurus or RX-7? You can use the difference to get yourself a new tv, a vcr, or a computer that didn't come out of a cereal box.

''I should have made the offer before, but I was always afraid you'd ask where the money was coming from. No reason for holding back now.''

''You're so altruistic, so thoughtful. I may puke. I'm not taking any of your tainted money, Mindy.''

''Tainted?''

''You're exploiting trust for money.''

She sighed tiredly. ''I thought we'd settled that. There's been no betrayal. The secret of the colony is safe as ever.

As for the money, if you don't want it, that's up to you. I can't force you to take what's due you. It'll stay in my own account. Is that more fair?''

"It's not more fair, it's just . . ." He stopped, confused. His sister had always been so much better with words than he. He'd come into the office with his mind made up and she'd subtly and quietly demolished a number of his certainties.

Several of them had been replaced by the image of himself gliding smoothly through Westwood Village, lowering power windows at a touch and letting the advanced Delco stereo blast across paralleling lanes of traffic while the blonde California girls turned to admire the sleek vehicle and its suave pilot. Not an easy image to toss in the garbage. He saw himself going wherever he wanted to on the weekends without worrying about breaking down every tenth mile or needing money for repairs. Angrily he shook the dream aside.

"I'm not buying a Corvette with that money."

She shrugged. "Up to you. I can get eight and a quarter, compounded daily."

"I think . . ." Determination flushed out of him in a green flood. "I think I'll get the Mazda instead."

He tried not to look at the sly grin that spread across her face. "That's my baby brother. Keep some money in the bank for emergencies. Much more sensible. You were always so sensible, Chad. In a pinch I always knew I could rely on that."

"I'm only doing this," he said sharply, "so you can't use the money."

"Naturally. You'll punish me as much as I'll let you."

Having voluntarily relinquished the moral high ground, he resorted to the only avenue left to him. "Make this year the last one, Mindy. You've made a lot of money, you've made a name for yourself. You won't need to do this anymore. It's got to stop."

"It'll stop, Chad. It'll stop when the network declines to exercise its option and the products stop selling. Meanwhile no harm's being done to the Quozl. If you can prove otherwise, do so. If not, then go buy your car. I've got work to do." She turned to face the computer terminal and switched it on, began typing with the ease of long practice.

He watched her as her fingers flew over the keyboard. "I just want to say one more time that I think what you've done is terribly wrong. It's dishonest, it's immoral, and it's the greatest betrayal of trust I've ever seen."

"You're young," she replied cryptically without looking up from the screen. "Wait 'til you've lost in love a few times. Until then don't talk to me about betrayal. Anything else?"

"Yeah," he mumbled, turning away. "Do I have the dealer call here or should I call you and leave his number?"

XV.

HE'D BEEN IN the complex devoted to surface studies many times before. As the principal intermediary between the natives and the colony his advice was in constant demand by the scientists and researchers who had made humanity their special area of interest. He was more or less at their beck and call.

He knew many of the senior and junior specialists by name, but not the young technician clad in blue and white who met him at the entrance and escorted him inside. She turned him over to Short-key-Leaps, the startlingly black-striped head of department. While Runs waited curiously, Short concluded what he was doing and then gestured for the younger Quozl to follow as they made their way deeper into the complex. Runs remained a respectful distance behind the Elder, asking no questions, keeping well clear of the other's Sama.

Short-key-Leaps entered a back room new to Runs that was filled to the point of constriction with gleaming, newly manufactured equipment. A Quozl of his own generation glanced over at them as they entered but did not hold the stare long enough to be guilty of discourtesy. Runs was immediately attracted to her. She did not respond at all. Her tail remained limp behind her, both ears stayed bent forward. It was an expression of noninterest that bordered on the insulting, but he displayed no reaction. There had to be a reason for her unQuozl-like indifference. His thoughts knotted as he came up alongside Short-key-Leaps.

"Trouble, Honored Senior? Are there humans in the vicinity?" That was the constant concern, that natives other than his friends might unknowingly come into the main valley and somehow stumble across one of the camouflaged entrances or air vents, or encounter a study team caught on the surface.

"That is not the problem," the Senior told him, simultaneously informing him that a problem indeed existed.

Short-key-Leaps wore a wonderful left-balanced necklace matched by the three earrings in his opposite ear, all fashioned of a local wood which Chad had identified as sugar pine. Like anything made of Shirazian timber it was extremely valuable. Great care had been lavished on the carving and polishing.

As the Senior spoke, the female left her seat and moved to lock the only door. This action was so extraordinary and unexpected Runs could not find the proper words to employ in reference to it. As she returned to her position, Short-key-Leaps whispered to her in passing. She bent an ear by way of acknowledgment, resumed her seat, and nudged contact points on the console in front of her. As a small viewscreen brightened she spoke in an efficient monotone.

"I am Tries-simple-Glow. It is my task to study native entertainment and information transmissions, which I have been doing for many cycles. It is important work, full of surprises. Just when you think you understand the natives something utterly unexpected occurs to alter your preconceptions."

Why was she lecturing him on human habits, he wondered? Him, Runs-red-Talking, of all people! But with a Senior present he dare not interrupt to question her. He wondered idly if she found his attire off-putting.

Patience, he told himself. Her intent will clarify along with the images.

"For many cycles it was difficult to pick up native visual transmissions, until the concealed antenna was positioned atop the north ridge and the humans began utilizing satellites to relay their signals. This improved our access to information enormously, but because of the proliferation of such signals it is very difficult to monitor all such transmissions. In past cycles particular transmissions were singled out for especial study. This resulted in the unfortunate concurrent neglect of other transmissions.

"Those signals were checked and recorded for future examination at less frequent intervals. They consist mainly of harmless entertainments and diversions of much less interest than the information and serious cultural broadcasts."

"Sometimes the most innocuous is constructed upon the most critical," the Senior observed philosophically.

"One such diversion caught the attention of a beginning researcher. It was checked against possible similar diversions. A match was made. The information was processed for advanced study. This diversion has been my particular area of interest for the past several cycles. It is one of those transmissions which recur at predictable intervals, which makes continued study feasible. It is what the natives refer to as a 'wild feed' and was found during a chance emission search. Otherwise we would still be ignorant of its existence."

She adjusted a control, bringing the screen to life. Shortkey-Leaps stared intently at the viewer. Runs felt it incumbent to do likewise.

What he saw froze his genitals to his pubic bone.

Drawings. Moving drawings done in typical native style. Drawings that depicted the Quozl interacting with humans. To his horror he saw one that quite resembled himself. Others looked like scientists he had taken to meet with his friends Chad and Mindy. Still others resembled no Quozl who had ever lived.

The broadcast was a mix of reality and nightmare, documentary and dream. The drawn Quozl spoke with the deafening volume of humans and employed humanlike gestures and facial expressions. They even "smiled."

As he watched, the miniature drama began to take shape

and he experienced a second shock. The story being depicted was familiar to him. It was based on the time a nightlight scanner had exploded in the hands of the scientist using it, resulting in a comitragic attempt to render joint human-Quozl first aid.

The story went on for some time, interrupted periodically by the image chapters humans called commercials, which Chad had explained to him were flashy, fast-moving, expensive sequences designed to convince observers to buy things they did not need at prices they could not afford. Human commerce was as much a mystery to the cooperative Quozl as was human intelligence.

Eventually, mercifully, the screen went dark. He felt no relief. There was no escape from what he'd seen. The images had burned themselves into his mind.

Short-key-Leaps and Tries-simple-Glow were both staring at him, without the slightest pretext at courtesy. "I have not told the Head of Council or the Burrow Masters yet," Short informed him. "No one knows of this except myself and Tries-simple-Glow. They will have to be told eventually, but Tries and I thought it might be instructive to obtain your reaction first."

"Can anything be said?" he replied dully. He launched into the most elaborate and lengthy apologia he'd ever attempted. In verbosity and eloquence it far exceeded the speech he made to his peers when his solo surface sojourns had first been discovered.

Now he understood the formality with which Short-key-Leaps had treated him and the outright coolness of the female. But it wasn't his fault, he wanted to shout! It made no sense. Chad would never do such a thing. Nor would Mindy. Both had promised. There had to be another explanation.

If only he could think of one.

While he wrestled with conscience and memory, Tries-simple-Glow had recalled final images to the screen. One chosen from previous study gleamed brightly, fixed immovably so it could not be ignored. It was a short list of human names.

Short-key-Leaps pointed to one. "That is the name of one of your two human contacts, is it not? Our semantics program identifies 'story editor' as one who supervises the writing of many stories."

Runs could read English perfectly. "The name 'Chad Collins' is not present?"

"He is nowhere mentioned," Tries informed him.

"Then this outrage," he said evenly, "is wholly the responsibility of his sibling."

"Merely because his name is not mentioned in context does not mean he is blameless," Short-key-Leaps insisted. "He may have given advice and made suggestions. The fact that his name does not appear means nothing."

"It must mean something," Runs argued, "or it *would* appear."

"It doesn't matter. What matters is that your humans lied. One of them, at least, if not both."

"I cannot believe it."

"The proof is recorded for anyone to see." There was bitterness in Tries-simple-Glow's voice, much more in the rapid movements of her ears.

"How widely is this broadcast being viewed?" Runs asked tiredly.

"We have no way of knowing." Short gazed thoughtfully at the screen. "But Tries believes it is seen by many. Otherwise the natives would not go to the expense of relaying it to many receiving points via satellite."

"How long has it been available for observation?"

"Quite some time, apparently," said the female technician.

"Has there been any recent increase in the number of humans visiting the vicinity of the colony?"

"For one whose future is precarious you ask many questions." Short glanced at the technician. "It is something

Tries and I have wondered about ever since she made her initial discovery. The answer to your question is no. Surface teams report no unusual native presence in the area of the colony site."

"We believe that is because this program is presented as pure entertainment directed at young humans," Tries said. "None of it is conveyed as fact. Any adult viewing it would have no reason to think of it as anything other than fiction."

"This mitigates but does not eliminate the danger this severe breach of security poses. We must decide how to present it to the Burrow Masters and what steps to take." Short-key-Leaps was watching Runs closely.

Those "steps" would surely involve his future, Runs knew, wondering if he would ever see his friend Chad again. He still thought of him as his friend until proven otherwise. Of his sibling Mindy, Runs was less certain. The broadcast had identified her as a participant in the treason.

He could not find out what had happened without talking to them, and he feared greatly that necessary meeting would not be permitted.

It was a very small, intimate gathering. Short-key-Leaps was there together with Tries-simple-Glow. There were two researchers from the surface studies team and the Masters of Burrows Four and One.

Next time it might be only two: himself and his executioner.

"So what are we to do now?" Burrow Master One wasted no time. "The humans know of our existence and our secret is no more."

"Not necessarily, Honored Elder." Short-key-Leaps gestured with an ear in Tries's direction. She rose to explain.

"It is clear," she said by way of conclusion, "that the humans consider these images and stories pure imagination. I have carefully reviewed more than twenty of them, and the location of the colony is nowhere mentioned. In addition, they are directed solely at preadolescent natives. It would appear that adults are involved only to the degree necessary to create the episodes and advertise"—she had to explain the uniquely human term—"products, primarily toys and nonnutritional foods."

The Master for Burrow Four spoke up. "Can we do anything to stop it?"

"It is possible to interrupt the transmission," Short-key-Leaps informed them, "or with time destroy the satellite relay. However, as I am sure you can see, this would only result in the humans moving the transmission to another relay and rapidly working to locate the source of the disruption. I believe such an action is out of the question.

"It would solve nothing, since so many broadcasts have already been seen. We cannot repeal what has gone before." Short-key-Leaps glanced for support in the direction of the two senior researchers who had accompanied him to the meeting. Both sets of ears responded affirmatively to his wordless inquiry.

"Furthermore, I am informed that at this point it might be in our interest to see that these broadcasts continue."

The two Burrow Masters relieved themselves of their confusion; Four with gestures, not all of them polite, and One with words. "That assertion requires more than simple explanation, Honored Mind."

"I request elaboration from my colleague Places-peers-Cleansing."

Short resumed his seat while another elderly Quozl rose. Runs thought his use of wire strips to line his right ear particularly modern.

"My associate and I have recently been granted access to the research materials accumulated by Tries-simple-Glow. We have been examining them intensively, studying their contents and debating their meaning.

"Our conclusions are, somewhat to our own surprise, unrelentingly positive. These fictional Quozl are portrayed as friendly, peaceful, affectionate, and helpful. They are also shown to be clumsy, comical, foolish, childish, and incapable of complex speech or thought. Lest one feel insulted, the young humans are often similarly pictured. To be brief, Quozl are shown to be not only harmless but positively benign. In our minds this far outweighs the many other inaccuracies.

"This is the image of the Quozl that is being presented weekly to millions of young natives. While it may not be true, it is useful. Eventually we must make contact with the natives. Open contact, not furtive and limited as now exists. It had been hoped this could be put off for another two hundred cycles. However, it is clear that events," and he glanced in Runs-red-Talking's direction, "have rapidly outpaced our desires. We must therefore adapt as best we can to developments over which we can exercise no control.

"As these broadcasts are presented as fiction and as they are directed at children and since they are unremittingly positive in tone, my associate and I believe we should do nothing to try and curtail their dissemination. When wider contact comes it may be with adults who spent their maturing time believing the Quozl to be clumsy, harmless clowns.

"If this course of reaction is accepted by the authorities, it is further recommended that we attempt to take a forceful role in additional developments."

Runs could hardly believe his ears, which for a Quozl was tantamount to a confession of unconsciousness. The Burrow Masters were no less dumbfounded.

"You are saying," muttered One, "that we should provide additional information to assist our betrayer?"

"Where revelation is concerned, we have lost the initiative." The Elder spoke forcefully. "If we cannot stop it, let us at least try to steer it in those directions which may prove most salutary to us. Screened information can be supplied to the two humans through our," and he all but choked on the word, "ambassador."

Instead of feeling flattered, Runs-red-Talking wished desperately for a deep, warm pouch to crawl into. He was to be raised to the status of ambassador. How wonderful. It explained why he felt vilified, despised, and universally disliked by everyone in the room.

He tried to find some solace in the knowledge that contact between himself and his friends would not be cut off. When the next warm cycle began he would be able to find out exactly how this terrible thing had happened. Only, several respected Elders did not necessarily believe it was so terrible.

In fact, they seemed to think that all the deceit, lies, and lawbreaking on the part of him and his friends might ultimately result in developments beneficial to the colony. If so it would be the result of remarkable good luck rather than careful planning.

How long would that luck hold? How long before the next betrayal, the next unintentional revelation resulted in something harmful to himself and his fellow Quozl? He would have to have a very long talk indeed with Chad and Mindy. Long and intense.

If one kept throwing triangles, sooner or later they would start to show up points-down.

XVI.

THE FIRST MEETING the following summer was comedy instead of drama. The Quozl instinctively danced all around the subject uppermost in everyone's mind while the two humans had no idea that knowledge of Mindy's betrayal was thoroughly documented in alien archives. There was no hiding the fact that something was wrong, however.

For one thing, Chad did all the talking while his sister hung uncertainly in the background, saying nothing and glancing furtively at her brother and the members of the study team. Runs-red-Talking had become adept at interpreting the extraordinary range of human facial expressions. He knew things were not as before but was too Quozl to come out and ask why things had changed.

As for Chad, he saw that the amount of ear-twisting and dipping was unprecedented. With the directness of his kind he inquired as to the reason. There followed a fair amount of verbal sparring until it was discovered that each side was proceeding to the same destination.

Chad was stunned and Mindy delighted to learn that not only weren't the Quozl mad, but they had decided to help with her stories. Their emotions underwent a sharp reversal when Runs explained that this had been decided not by choice but by a feeling of necessity and that the elders were anything but pleased. They were going to assist her because they felt it was the only option left to them. It was a stern lecture and Runs was as upset as Chad had ever seen him. Mindy appeared properly abashed but her brother could tell it was all for the Quozl's benefit, all for show. He knew she wasn't upset. Embarrassed perhaps, but not upset.

Now that all the little secrets were out in the open the atmosphere at the riverside camp lightened considerably. The study team went about its recording and gathering while Mindy sketched and observed and pressed them for information. Chad and Runs were left largely to themselves, which pleased them greatly.

They sat on the big rock that stuck like a finger into the current. Water churned around its upper edge, flowed swift and gentle around its base. Runs dangled his long feet in the cool water while Chad squatted nearby, engaged in the peculiar human game of throwing pebbles into the depths of the stream.

"They must have been furious."

"Oh, they were extremely distressed. Extremely." Runs spread his toes, let the water flow between them. "You can imagine the shock when in the course of examining routine human transmissions one of our people found that we were the subject of regular broadcasts to millions of your homes."

"I was just as shocked and surprised. As soon as I found out I laid into Mindy but good! Didn't matter. She'd thought it through long ago and she was ready for any argument I could muster. That's the trouble with a secret. Once it's out, it's out."

Runs's left ear dipped in agreement. "Our Elders were driven to the same conclusion. There is only one tunnel for them to travel."

"It wouldn't matter if I could make Mindy stop. The show would continue with another writer at the helm. She doesn't own the property. That's how she put it, anyway. It's controlled by the company she works for."

"She explained it all," Runs said. "There are many strange economic concepts new to us. What matters is that it cannot be stopped unless your offspring choose to view these transmissions no longer. Tell me, honored friend, what do you think of the Elders' opinion? Might the presence of this transmission in so many human households someday help to ease the strain of contact between our species?''

''How should I know? Most of the time I live in a half-centimeter-diameter lens. I have trouble understanding the actions and reactions of my own kind. It's a big jump from laughing at cartoons to learning that the characters they portray happen to be real aliens living right next door. I can't imagine what will happen.'' He tossed a big rock into the water, watched the current swallow the resultant ripples. ''They didn't punish you for what you've been doing all these years?''

''There would be no point. The secret was out, the damage done. The Quozl are a practical race. So long as I am of more use to the colony alive, everyone will work to ensure my health. I have knowledge and experience to offer. Behind my ears I am cursed and damned, but none would be so impolite as to make such feelings known to my face.''

''We're more direct.'' Chad glanced over his shoulder to where Mindy and two Quozl botanists were engaged in examining the plant specimens they'd gathered. ''Look at her. From the way she acts you'd think she'd never done anything wrong. Pure as the driven snow. I think it has something to do with working in Hollywood. From what I've heard, the moral guidelines there are made out of rubber instead of metal. Everybody has words to live by. I think the one uppermost there is expediency, followed close behind by rationalization.''

''It strikes me as a most peculiar subtribe,'' Runs admitted. ''Mindy speaks of creativity but lets many others alter what she creates. I do not understand the paradox. It would be like praising sculpture while hacking it to bits. Why praise it in the first place, and if it is so praiseworthy, why take it apart?''

"You'd have to ask my sister. Look at your friends, talking freely with her."

"Not so freely. They will help without revealing anything vital." Runs pulled his feet from the water, let them dry in the sun. "Despite all that has occurred or perhaps because of it I cannot help but feel that eventually we will have to pay for what has happened. Myself, you, your sibling. There is ample fault to be distributed here and not many to bear its weight."

Chad looked into large Quozl eyes. "Whatever happens, it need not affect us."

"No. Our friendship cannot be broken. It may be that this transmission's popularity will soon wane and our concern will lessen with its passing."

"Unfortunately fictional Quozl are very popular with human children. I saw some of the spin-offs, as they're called. Apparently anything with a Quozl on it these days sells."

"Yes, both you and Mindy have spoken of this phenomenon. It would be very interesting to have samples of these products."

"I'm sure we can get all you want," Chad told him sourly. "No doubt my sister gets a discount. You know," he said thoughtfully, "she's making a lot of money off you. So's the production company. It's not fair. She's profiting off your stories."

"We feel no deprivation."

"I know, I know, but it still bothers me."

"Because of the rewards she is reaping or because you do not share in them?"

Chad eyed his friend sharply, thinking of the car and the stereo and the other benefits of his sister's largess. "I've shared in some. I needed certain things Mindy was able to provide, so I took them. If I hadn't, she would have used the money." Not that I protested too hard, he reminded himself uneasily. "If I could undo what's been done, I'd give everything back."

"A secret is like an egg," Runs mused philosophically. "Once broken, it cannot be made new again, but if properly handled, the contents can nourish."

"Like a tiger by the tail. Once you grab hold, you can't let go."

"Yes. We cannot undo what these transmissions have done, so rather than stop them, which would do no good, we supply your sister with information on which to base her stories so that we can control their content to some degree. I wonder where it will all lead? I have mediated on it, to no avail."

"Me, too," said Chad feelingly.

"Do not sound so regretful. It is not all give and no take. We learn from visiting with you, from your replies to our questions. Some wonder openly if it would be possible to converse with your parents."

"I don't think that would be such a good idea," Chad replied slowly. "I know my mother wouldn't react quietly. Dad I'm not so sure about. He's used to talking with foreigners. But it would double the number of humans who know of your existence."

"Which is why it was decided against. The Council anticipates wider contact yet are simultaneously terrified of it. They are constantly considering and discarding proposals. You must understand that they have no precedent from which to proceed, and the Quozl have always relied on precedent. Humans are much more versatile when it comes to dealing with the unknown or the unexpected." He extended a delicate, seven-fingered hand. "Regardless of what is decided, it cannot damage our friendship."

As always, Chad marveled at the slim but strong grip. "No. Nothing can harm that."

The new arrangement made things much easier. Chad and Runs-red-Talking were allowed to do pretty much as they pleased while the rotating study teams gained access to two intelligent young humans. Meanwhile Mindy helped team members with their gathering and recording while they provided her with material for new shows.

The ratings for *Quozltime* remained number one in their time slot while Quozl toys and related products continued to sell well. Other companies tried to hire the genius behind the Quozl away, which resulted in regular unrequested bonuses and perks from her employers, who would do whatever was necessary to keep their star writer happy.

Mindy Collins was one very content young lady.

She shared her good fortune with friends and family. As for Chad, he had little time to watch the program. His Ph.D. continued to elude him and he had trouble finding jobs which would let him spend three months in the mountains. His sister had no such problem. Her producers were delighted to let her join the family at their summer retreat since she invariably returned with a stack of fresh new story ideas.

So Chad was more than a little surprised when Mindy announced one year that she would not be accompanying her parents and brother to the cabin by the lake. When he pressed her for an explanation she informed him that this spring there was simply too much work requiring her personal attention, ideas for new shows including Quozl Babies, revisions to existing material which hadn't been properly developed by the staff. With luck she would be able to clear it up in a few weeks. Then she would join them.

He was reading in the cabin's den, contemplating the next meeting with Runs-red-Talking and a new brace of researchers, when his mother announced that his sister had finally arrived and that his father was on the way to Boise to bring them back.

Chad finished the paragraph he was on, then frowned and looked toward the kitchen where his mother was working.

She moved slower now than when he'd been a child but if anything her cooking had improved.

"Them?"

"Mindy and her fiancé, of course. You mean you don't know? No, of course you don't know. You bury yourself so deep in your work it's hard to find you, and you're so forgetful."

"How long has this been going on?" He put the book aside and sat up, gazing out the window at the smooth surface of the lake.

"Going on? Oh, you mean how long has she been engaged? A little over three months, I think. His name is Arlo."

"Arlo." What could Mindy be thinking, bringing a total stranger here? Not that there was any intrinsic harm in that. Unless . . .

"What does he do?"

"He's in the entertainment business, like your sister. I think he's an agent of some kind. I don't know what he agents, but he seems prosperous enough, and your sister certainly loves him."

Chad didn't reply. As his mother said, he was forgetful. But right now his mind was very busy, and very full.

Though he tried to reserve judgment he disliked Arlo at first sight. It might have had something to do with the designer outfit he was wearing when he stepped out of the floatplane. Though the jeans were denim and the shirt cotton, they seemed better suited to a Beverly Hills party than a week or two in the woods.

It's your problem, not his, Chad was forced to admit to himself. Why shouldn't the guy dress stylishly? Just because Chad's own clothes were six or seven years out of date was no reason to condemn somebody else's attire. Mindy's fiancé probably had to dress that way to impress clients, or producers, or whoever the hell it was he was required to impress. Chad realized it wasn't the man's appearance that disturbed him.

It was the way he was looking around, craning his neck to

scan the forest, as if he was searching for something specific instead of just taking in the scenery. Chad asked his sister about it the first time they were alone together, hauling the garbage to the trash bin and compost heap in the clearing behind the cabin. That had been their joint task since they were children.

"How much does he know?"

"Arlo?" It was dark and she held the flashlight. The cabin was an island of light behind them. "What do you mean, 'what does he know'?"

"Don't hedge with me," said Chad irritably. "You haven't told him anything, have you?"

She didn't reply. They dumped their loads in silence. On the way back to the cabin she murmured, "He's my fiancé, Chad. We're going to be married."

"Then you did tell him." Somewhat to his surprise he felt more tired than angry. "He didn't believe you, of course."

"Not at first. I'm not sure he believes me now. But he will after he's met Runs-red-Talking and some of the others."

Chad halted. So did his sister, because he grabbed her by the arm and swung her around to face him in the dark. "You're not serious. You aren't actually thinking of bringing him to one of the meetings?"

"I have to, little brother."

"Don't call me that. I haven't hit you in fifteen years, Mindy, but you're convincing me that maybe I should start making up for lost time."

She shook free of his grasp. "Look, I'm going to marry the man, Chad. I can't keep something like this from him. It's too much a part of my life. What do you expect me to do? Tell him to keep the home fires burning every summer while I vacation fifteen hundred miles away with my family? What kind of relationship is that?"

"It's our relationship that concerns me now. You and I,

Mindy. You're crazy if you think I'm going to let you take him to a meeting.''

"How is Runs, by the way? I presume you've met with him at least once already this month.''

"He's just fine,'' Chad snapped back at her, "and so are the rest of the Quozl, and they'll stay that way as long as their secret is kept. That's why you can't bring your pet fashion plate along. Their secret is safe as long as he doesn't believe in them, and he won't believe in them no matter what you tell him unless he sees a Quozl for himself. I won't permit that.''

"You can't stop us.''

"Try me. Maybe I can't stop you physically but I can move faster than either of you through the woods. I'll warn Runs and his party, tell them what's going on. They'll flee back to the colony, which you'll never find, and we'll pick another place to rendezvous. You know what that would mean, Mindy. No more story ideas. No more free ride.''

She replied quietly, calmly. "If you do that I'll come up here with other people, not just with Arlo. Reporters, maybe. They'll come because I'll pay them to come. We'll find the colony, wherever it is.''

He eyed her aghast. "You wouldn't do that.''

"Is that a risk you're willing to take? How much of a gambler are you, little brother?''

She knew him much too well, he reflected. How could his sister consider betrayal on such a scale? She'd made friends among the Quozl, had spent long pleasant days with them. But she was right about one thing: he couldn't take the chance that she was bluffing.

She stood silently, playing the light over the surrounding brush, until he was ready to reply. He had no choice, and she knew it.

"You're sure he's trustworthy? That he'll keep the secret?''

"I trust him, if that's what you're asking. Chad, I'm trusting this guy with my whole life, with my future.''

It was a feeble guarantee. "I wonder how the Quozl will

react? First there was just me. Then you came along, and now there's to be three of us who know. What happens if the Council decides three is too many?''

"You think they might do something violent?" Mindy considered the possibility. "I doubt it. They've continued with the meetings because they believe them to be in their eventual best interest. They haven't threatened or harmed us for the same reason. They'll leave Arlo alone because to do anything else might expose them to danger. Besides, physical violence is anathema to the Quozl philosophy. It says so in the Samizene.''

"Don't count on that too much," he warned her.

She was staring past him, thinking aloud. "I wonder if they could even defend themselves. I'm not sure they know themselves." She looked back at her brother. "Relax, Chad. You worry too much. They'll like Arlo. He's a good person. A little Hollywood, but that's not his fault.''

"How very reassuring.''

"I'll handle him.''

And she did, of course.

Runs-red-Talking was as taken aback as Chad had been. But there was nothing anyone could do about it once Mindy's fiancé actually saw the Quozl. Contact transformed previous doubt into ready acceptance.

Arlo did a lot of staring and listening but said little. He and Mindy must have talked at night, but she'd brought her own tent and despite his concerns Chad had the grace to avoid eavesdropping.

As for the Quozl, their initial agitation faded as Chad and Mindy reassured them that this new human was trustworthy. The fact that he and Mindy were to be mated had more of a positive effect on the Quozl than Chad would have imagined. It troubled him that they were more understanding of his sister's situation than he'd been. Gradually he found he was able to relax and accept what had happened.

Until the end of the summer, when the evenings had turned cold. A noise made him glance out the bedroom window. He saw the floatplane leave the dock, taxi to the east, and then rotate, its engine revving as his father sent it careening across the smooth surface of the lake.

Supply trip, he told himself as he looked back at the book he'd been studying. Probably the last one his father would make before they winterized the cabin and left for another year. He didn't give it a second thought until his sister burst into the room. She gave him an anguished look, then rushed to the window to catch a final glimpse of the departing plane.

He put the book down carefully, marking his place. "What happened?" His calmness astonished him.

"Arlo. I can't find him. I thought he'd be getting ready to come with us."

Arlo had been sleeping in the den. Enlightened era or not, he and Mindy were still only engaged. Mother would have insisted on the proprieties being observed, so the happy couple had preempted her concerns by volunteering the temporary sleeping arrangement.

"I've looked everywhere," she was saying worriedly. "Even out back by the compost heap."

"That would be a good place to check, yes," said Chad studiously.

"Finally I asked Mother, and she said that he'd mentioned something about going into Boise with Dad, for a change of scenery."

"And he neglected to tell you? He's not going to find much excitement in Boise, but then for some reason I don't expect he'll be lingering there. Did he take his luggage?"

She hesitated, unable to meet his eyes. "Just his backpack."

"Didn't want to provoke any discomfiting questions. How thoughtful."

Mindy sat down in the single chair, put her head in her hands, and began to cry. There were no great racking sobs, only the softness of despair. Chad let it run for what he thought was a decent interval, then rose, walked over, and put an arm around her. After all, she was his only sister, even if she was a certifiable idiot. As he understood things, that mental condition was a common companion of being in love.

When the proportion of sobs to sniffles had reversed, he went into the bathroom and returned with a handful of Kleenex, waited while she mopped at her face.

"That's it," he told her. "Nothing we can do about it now. By the time we could talk Dad into making another trip, loverboy will be long gone." He laughed derisively. "Dad will put him down right at the airport. Somebody in a hurry couldn't charter faster service."

"But I *trusted* him." Mindy's tone and expression were agonized. "We're going to get married, goddammit. I made him swear to me, over and over, that he wouldn't tell, that he wouldn't say anything to anyone else about what I wanted to show him."

"Easy to agree to when you haven't been shown anything. Six weeks of meeting with aliens doubtless weakened his resolve. I suppose it would weaken anybody's. Your Arlo's no better or worse than anybody else, I guess."

"No! He's *better*."

"Yeah, right. So tell me, big sister, what's your lover likely to do? You know him better than I, or at least you think you do."

"I don't know," she mumbled disconsolately.

"Think, dammit. Is he likely to go to the *Times*? The tv stations?"

"I told you I don't know. He—might just sit and think about it for a while."

"Uh-huh. He struck me right off as a real thoughtful kind of guy. At least he doesn't know where the colony is. We can give Runs and the others that much warning. I suppose the key is whether he can convince anybody else to take his story seriously. He didn't believe you. Maybe, just maybe, nobody will believe him. If the Quozl can stay hidden for a couple of years, maybe he'll give up on it.

"We'll have to ask Runs for advice. His people are the ones at risk here, not you and I. Do you have the guts to come with me and help explain what's happened?"

He didn't expect her to agree, would have understood had she declined. She did not.

"I guess I owe them that much, after what I've done. But I didn't mean to, Chad! I didn't mean for anything like this to happen. I like Runs-red-Talking and all the others we've met and I . . ."

"Fell in love. Maybe the Quozl will understand. They like you too, Mindy. In spite of what you've done."

"Do you think they might react violently? I know what I've said about that, but this situation is different. Do you think they could actually hurt us?"

"I've no idea. I'm not sure they do, either. I suppose a lot depends on whether they've considered the possibility of this happening." He looked out the window. "There's a first time for everything."

They said nothing immediately, letting the excited group of Quozl scientists set up their field experiments and lay out their sleeping pads. Runs-red-Talking was not so easily fooled, however. He confronted his human friends on the second day, his huge eyes switching back and forth between brother and sister, ears cocked alertly forward, tail stiff and motionless.

"Something is in difficulty. Large, small?"

"Quite large, I'm afraid."

"Very large," Mindy added. She was resigned to whatever might happen.

Chad wondered if she might panic. It wouldn't do her any good. The slowest Quozl in the group could easily outrun her.

"What is this matter that has you so concerned that it grooves your face, friend Chad?"

"It's out," he said simply. "The secret. Your secret." He

turned to his sister. With both her brother and Runs gazing at her expectantly she had no choice but to respond.

''It's all my fault.'' She was on the verge of tears, but her voice did not quite break. ''I was engaged to be mated. My intended was named Arlo. I felt comfortable, felt good, about sharing my life with him. That meant sharing everything. You can't keep secrets from your mate. You . . .'' She did break down then. ''He swore he'd keep the secret. He swore! But now he's . . .''

''He left with our father,'' Chad explained when his sister was unable to continue. ''He left without telling anybody he was leaving and he took some of his baggage with him. He didn't come back. My father said Arlo mentioned something about an important meeting he'd forgotten and that he had to get back home quick. That's the last anybody saw of him.

''He's in the business, see, where knowledge of your presence here could mean a lot of money.''

''I understand.'' Runs-red-Talking spoke carefully so he wouldn't be misunderstood. ''And you think this Arlo person would truly do such a thing for money?''

''Everything was going so well,'' Mindy mumbled. ''We never fought or anything. I thought we understood each other. I guess—I guess he felt that if he'd talked about doing something like this I might have tried to stop him.''

''I sure as hell would have,'' said Chad fervently.

''We have survived other crises.'' Runs kicked thoughtfully at the ground.

''Not like this,'' said Chad tersely. ''Don't you understand? He has no intention of keeping your secret. As soon as he can manage it he'll be back up here with media representatives, magazine reporters, photographers.''

''Even if, as you suggest, none of these people believe what he tells them?''

"It won't matter." Mindy's sorrow was slowly giving way to bitterness. "He can hire photographers, people with detection equipment. He'll find you, locate the colony."

"We are well hidden and there are safeguards against electronic intrusion. This person may not find the finding so easy. But this is a matter for the Elders to debate, not you and I." He eyed Mindy sorrowfully. "You realize that this time more than my freedom may be forfeit."

"I said I was sorry, dammit! I don't know what else to say." She reached out to put an arm around his shoulders, realized that would constitute an uninvited Sama invasion, and pulled back, staring morosely at the ground.

Runs-red-Talking whistled sharply to alert the members of the study team. "We will inform the Elders, but first I need to apprise my colleagues of this new development."

Chad and his sister sat off to one side, watching the Quozl discuss what had happened. The conversation was carried on at a distance since the Quozl were aware that both humans had grown conversant with their language.

When they finished it was not Runs who spoke to them but Talks-through-Glass, the senior team member.

"This matter is grave. You gain status from telling us instead of trying to protect yourselves. Actions show better than words how you truly feel. I believe that you will help us if you can."

Mindy's tone was earnest. "I'll do anything to try and make up for what I've done."

"If anything can be done at this point," the zoologist murmured sternly. "Perhaps there are ways to stop your intended mate from returning with others to search out our home. What those ways might be I cannot say. We three are scientists to whom human psychology is a dead-end tunnel. It will be up to the human studies section to make suggestions and for them and the Council to decide how to proceed." He hesitated. "In order for them to make the best possible decisions they require the best possible input. That would include yours."

"Ours?" Chad was filled with a mixture of fear and excitement.

"You must return with us, to prove firstly that you truly mean to help and also to offer your suggestions and advice. That is little enough to ask."

"You won't be missed," Runs reminded his friend. "You're supposed to be camping here for many days. It is only a couple of days' hike to the site of the colony."

"So close?" Chad had always thought in terms of a week's walk.

"I would have taken you there years ago, my friend, except for the danger."

"You're actually going to take us to the colony?"

"You already know so much. What does one more revelation matter? Do you agree to come with us?"

"Of course we do." When no response was forthcoming from his sister, he prompted her. "Don't *we*, Mindy?"

"Yes," she whispered in a small voice.

He could imagine her thoughts. Once inside the colony the Council of Elders could do with them as they wished. On the other hand, if they wanted him and his sister dead, Runs-red-Talking and Talks-through-Glass and the rest could accomplish that immediately. There were five of them.

What were the Burrow Masters like? Despots, politicians, philosophers? It didn't matter. Runs-red-Talking and he had matured together in an atmosphere of mutual respect and trust. That trust had been tarnished. All they had left was the respect, and Chad wasn't going to jeopardize that. He would go to the colony to see if he could be of help, and so would his sister. If they had to bind and drag her.

"Give us a few minutes to pack up."

"That will not be necessary," Runs informed him. "You'll be provided for."

"It's not that." Chad was scooping up camping equipment, food, and other freestanding items. "If anybody came looking for us and found just the tent they might think some harm had come to us. If they come looking and don't find the tent they'll assume we're camping elsewhere until they *do* find something.''

"That's well thought through." Talks-through-Glass gestured approvingly. "The stories Runs-red-Talking tells of you seem true." His gaze flicked in Mindy's direction. "You, we are not so sure of."

"I don't blame you. Don't worry." She rose from her seat. "I'll prove myself. I've been so damn self-centered through all this, but I'll make it up to you, somehow."

"You cannot. You can only help us minimize."

XVII.

ACTUALLY IT TOOK two and a half days to reach the valley of the colony. They crossed several mountain ridges, all high, none particularly difficult, only to discover a place as devoid of infrastructure as the campsite by the river. It was identical to the several valleys they had just traversed, with nothing to suggest that anything other than squirrels and badgers dwelt in its depths.

But when one of the study team's members pressed an open palm and his right ear to a depression in an uneven-sided boulder, the rock suddenly slid aside with a soft hiss to reveal a smooth-walled, plastic-lined tunnel beyond.

Years of interacting only with Runs-red-Talking and later with groups of three to five Quozl had not prepared Chad to deal with the sight and smell of so many aliens in one place. A thriving population he expected. What startled him was the density. There were Quozl everywhere, rushing to and fro without bumping into one another, without so much as intruding on one another's Sama. Some kind of internal radar prevented collisions. They repelled like furry magnets.

And they talked. The noise was more overwhelming than the odor, a ceaseless high-pitched, breathy babble of male and female voices. In the enclosed tunnels and intersections it sounded like a million Buddhists alternately reciting the same mantra. He was reminded of the L.A. freeways at rush hour: everything moving slowly and methodically, the cars never quite smashing into each other, radios blaring and people talking above the overheated susurration of thousands of engines.

Not all was activity and purpose. In places clusters of individuals paused to talk and debate, ears and mouths moving rapidly. Juveniles chased each other, weaving through the crowds, while infants on the verge of pubescence peered warily at the incredible congestion over the rims of their mother's pouches. Adults paused at innumerable public mirrors to adjust their clothing.

Shocking and graphic enough to draw the two young humans' attention from the aliens themselves were the artworks that lined tunnel walls and dominated open places. None of it was reassuring. Chad had often discussed the barbaric, bloody past of the Quozl, but words were less threatening than sculptural depictions. More bloodspilling, disemboweling, and sheer sadism were on display than one would find on the screen at a rural drive-in in West Texas on a summer Saturday night.

And all of it was rendered with exquisite attention to detail and taste. The peaceful, pacifistic Quozl strolled amiably through corridors that dripped with blood.

He thought about asking Runs or Talks-through-Glass about a particularly gruesome bas-relief, had to remind himself he wasn't on a sight-seeing trip. For their part Quozl glanced in the direction of the visitors, did a number of stunned double takes, and quickly looked away lest they be considered impolite. A few so lost their composure they didn't care. They just stared.

What really shook them was when Chad put both forearms alongside his head and imitated admonishing Quozl ear gestures with his hands.

They were interviewed many times. The number of Quozl who had mastered English surprised not only Chad and Mindy but Runs-red-Talking as well. The linguists translated for the administrators and for those scientists for whom language was not a preeminent concern. None of the Burrow Masters spoke the tongues of Shiraz.

The senior linguists spoke better English than Chad, complete to relevant colloquialisms and slang. They sometimes drifted over into French, which they had learned from watching Canadian satellite transmissions.

Their room was small and cramped, though spacious by colony standards. While they were not watched it was made clear that they could not be allowed the run of the Burrows. Confusion and consternation among the general populace would be the result. Their brief appearance had caused enough of an uproar, which the authorities were having difficulty dealing with.

The measure of Mindy's contrition was that she did not once pull out her pad to sketch or make notes.

By the third day it was apparent to Chad that certain conclusions had been reached. Oddly enough, he wasn't worried about himself at all. For the benefit of the two humans the discussion was conducted in English as much as possible.

"Two solitary infants accidentally encounter one another." Short-key-Leaps was speaking authoritatively. "The course of two civilizations is altered as a result. One can plan forever, but individuals make fools of us all." His ears bent out at right angles as he resumed his seat.

"Once a heavy object begins to roll downhill it grows progressively more difficult to stop," said another member of the surface studies team. "If not slowed it acquires a momentum and purpose all its own." His gaze darted at Mindy for the barest instant. "I believe the correct English term is 'avalanche.'"

"This is what we are faced with." Short-key-Leaps rose again. Chad admired the ritualized choreography even as he listened intently to every word.

There was a brief pause as younger members of the surface study team translated for the five Burrow Masters present. Only when they had concluded did Short resume speaking.

"This is a thing grown too large to stop. If we could not halt it with logic in the past when it was of smaller dimen-

◇ **271** ◇

sions, we surely cannot stop it now." Both ears bent forward and down to momentarily cover his eyes.

"The colony is invisible to sight but not to instruments sensitive to certain levels of the electromagnetic spectrum. We can put on an electronic mask with no guarantee it will not be seen through. In recent years the Shirazians have developed the ability to measure extremely low level radiation. A casual searcher will not find us. A determined one eventually will. We cannot measure the degree of this renegade human's determination, nor can we gamble our entire future on it." He turned to face Chad and Mindy.

"It is generally agreed that knowledge of our existence here on Shiraz should have been kept from you for a minimum of another hundred cycles. That may no longer be possible."

He resumed his seat. There followed a period for meditation, in which Chad and his sister did their best to participate. At its conclusion one of the younger members of the surface study team rose. His English was not as good as that of Short-key-Leaps, but his tone was equally forceful.

"Been decided it has been. We cannot allow first-time widespread contact/knowledge of our existence here prematurely to be disclosed by this Arlo human whom we know not knows us not at all. Must therefore with great reluctance and/or sadness take the initiative somehow and make the contact ourselves before he can reveal/disclose us. In vanishment of time we seek leverage."

Tries-simple-Glow took his place. Chad was a bit surprised to see her. He'd imagined her to be a mere technician. Perhaps circumstances had raised her status.

She stared at him, whether out of curiosity or deliberate reproachfulness he had no way of determining. Age was revered among the Quozl and Mindy was older, but Mindy was the one guilty of betrayal. It greatly diminished her position among the Quozl.

Or maybe it was just, he thought with a start, that Tries-simple-Glow felt sorry for him.

It never, ever occurred to him that she might like him.

"What do you think, human Chad? Do we grab the horny bull?"

He made a stifled noise, kept his lips rigorously together lest he expose his teeth and thereby his brutal human nature. Some of the tension went out of him. It had no choice. A sideways glance showed Mindy with head bowed and her hand over her mouth. Evidently the Quozl linguists' mastery of human slang was not quite complete.

"It's a thought. You can't hide here forever. I've always believed that. If not Arlo somebody else would find you, maybe somebody we don't know and can't influence." He took a deep breath. "Personally I've always thought you were fooling yourselves, thinking you could stay hidden here for hundreds of years. Sure the area is infrequently visited, but wilderness areas everywhere are drawing more and more visitors every year. It's not like you dug in up on the Canadian Shield or under the Greenland icepack or something. Sooner or later one of your survey teams was bound to run into somebody. Or some mining company would've sent prospectors in here illegally just to check the prospects out. There's cobalt and chromium and all sorts of valuable stuff in this part of the country. Runs tells me you've been mining it yourself. A mining team might've found you by accident." He turned his attention to the senior Burrow Master present. There were a dozen Burrows now, according to Runs. As he spoke he dropped his eyes, deferential as any Quozl. He sensed the gesture was appreciated.

"Arlo's forcing wider contact. It's up to you to preempt him. How do you want to do it? Take out an ad on tv or in *USA Today*? Should we bring reporters here? The big papers and networks wouldn't come but I think we could cajole somebody from a local station into bringing a crew up. As soon as they put out the first pictures you'd have all the attention you never wanted."

"One avalanche at a time is enough to deal with." Short-key-Leaps spoke without rising. "So long as the exposure is limited to this Arlo person we are able to proceed at a pace *we* determine.''

Tries-simple-Glow indicated acknowledgment with a dip of her right ear, continued. ''We will commence with caution and necessary improvisation. It has been decided that two Quozl will go with you to make known our presence to human society. Your observers will see only two Quozl at first. This we believe, based on what we have studied of your people, will be more reassuring to them. We think it would be unsettling for many of your kind to learn immediately that thousands of Quozl are living among them. We have always believed this.

''The longer we can keep the scale and location of the Burrows a secret, the better it will be. It offers us flexibility in the event your people react violently to the revelation.''

''They won't,'' Chad said sharply, immediately regretting his impolite outburst.

Tries-simple-Glow muted her instinctive reaction. ''Can you promise us that?''

Chad relented, his reply resigned. ''No. I can't.''

''Then we must go cautiously. We can force the issue, but at our own speed. If more humans meet two Quozl, they will be much less interested in talking to this Arlo about other Quozl whose location he knows not and whose numbers he can only guess at.

''We also believe that this meeting should take place in a large metropolitan region far from the Burrows. It will draw all attention from this area, which can only be to the good. If we cannot delay another hundred cycles, perhaps we can delay a few. We can put the time to good use. Not only must humans be properly prepared for contact. So must our own people.''

''Let's do it in Los Angeles,'' Chad suggested after waiting a proper interval before speaking. ''We live there, we know it, and it's one of the centers of media activity. But how do we get a pair of Quozl from here to there without giving them away?''

"You drive," said Short-key-Leaps matter-of-factly. "It is vital that those who accompany you have the opportunity to observe."

"There are no cars here. There are no roads," Chad pointed out. "That's why we have to fly in and land on the lake each year."

"We could all walk out, traveling at night as much as possible," suggested Runs-red-Talking. "With Quozl leading, the darkness wouldn't be a problem."

Chad eyed his sister, who appeared dazed. Ignoring her, he addressed his thoughts to Runs. "That's something we've discussed before. The folks would understand. We'd tell them we want to see a lot more of the country. We could go into a small town. I could leave Mindy behind with your representatives, hitch to a bigger town, rent a car and come back for all of you, smuggle you into the car at night. Or maybe I could get a van. Yeah, and everybody could hide in the back. That'd work. That'd be perfect!"

"No," said Short-key-Leaps solemnly. "Another hundred cycles of privacy would be perfect. A hundred years for the anonymity of a van. Fate forces poor trades." His ears waggled.

"The two assigned to join you will travel with a small but powerful transmitter so that the Burrows may be kept informed of your progress, both physical and social. It will operate on an undistinguished frequency and will not alarm those humans whose business it is to monitor such things. It can inform, and if necessary give warning."

"You won't get much reception between here and L.A.," Mindy warned him.

Ears bobbed humorously. "Each of your relay satellites provides numerous subchannels for audio communication. Most are vacant. We will make use of one. Transmissions will be encoded and broadcast many times real-time speed. They will draw no attention."

"Have you decided," Chad inquired hesitantly, "who's going with us?"

◇ **275** ◇

The Master of Burrow Six spoke for the first time. Chad and Mindy had to wait for translation from Tries-simple-Glow.

"Against our better judgment but compelled by circumstance, Runs-red-Talking will assume this task."

Runs stiffened slightly, commented only with his ears. If he'd been expecting the reluctantly bestowed honor he'd hidden his hopes well.

"His personal experience with humans is unexcelled, however unfortunate. We must act for the best interests of the Burrows, not as we personally might wish. His companion will of course be female."

"Naturally," Chad murmured to himself. He knew the Quozl well enough to know that Runs or any other Quozl male would literally go insane if deprived of feminine companionship for more than a couple of weeks at a stretch. It was not a question of emotional deprivation. Hormones ruled the Quozl as thoroughly as they did humanity. The difference was that the Quozl had come to terms with the reality of their own physiology.

A young scientist rose. "This is Seams-with-Metal," said Tries-simple-Glow by way of introduction. "Among the surface studies team she is the agilest of mind if not the most experienced or intelligent. We believe that in this instance a talent for improvisation is more valuable than many other attributes, in which she is not in any event lacking. She knows your language as well as anyone. One area of specialization in which she excels is her knowledge of the methodology of native manipulation called public relations. Is this not appropriate?"

"Most," said Mindy, startled. She had clearly not expected this degree of sophistication among Quozl students of human behavior.

"Preparations must be made." Seams-with-Metal possessed a voice that sang like panpipes, Chad thought. Though he restrained himself it was clear Runs-red-Talking was more than pleased with the Council's choice of a colleague.

"We have our own to make. This will take a little time to set up." He thought rapidly. "We'll convince Mom and Dad we're going to stay out an unspecified number of weeks. They'll just nod. In fact they'll be glad of the time alone. I've thought for a number of years that Mindy and I were cramping their style.''

"Agreed," said Short-key-Leaps, "save for your use of the plural."

Chad glanced up in confusion. "What?"

"We have no choice but to believe in you, to believe that you truly want to aid us," the xenologist quietly explained, "but no matter how powerful our belief in this we still would not refuse reassurance."

Chad's reply was guarded. "What kind of reassurance?"

"The strongest kind." An Elder ear gestured in Mindy's direction. She was fully alert now. "Chad, you may leave to acquire such additional supplies as you will need for your extended walk. Meanwhile your sibling will remain here to confide in us."

"Look, if it's a hostage you want, I'll be glad to . . ."

"No, Chad." Mindy's expression was uneasy, but her tone was firm. "If it's me they want to stay, then I'll stay. That's the least I can do. You go tell Mom and Dad. You can carry back more stuff than I anyway."

"It will give her time to meditate," said Tries-simple-Glow encouragingly. "The philosophers believe it will do her good."

"Yeah, you go, little brother." Mindy favored him with a wan smile, hurriedly quashed it when she saw nearby Quozl turn away in disgust. "I'll stay here and meditate like crazy. Think of the story material."

"If that's the way you want it." He agreed reluctantly.

"No, it's not the way I want it. It's the way *they* want it. I'll be okay." She smiled again, this time with her lips tight. Then she drew him close and to his immense surprise, bussed him affectionately. "Just don't get distracted by a book or something and take your time hoofing it back here, okay? I mean, I know how courteous and polite the Quozl are, but don't forget one thing.

"I've also seen their artwork."

XVIII.

Chad made it to the cabin and back in record time. Mindy greeted her brother's return with unabashed relief despite all the bravado she'd displayed prior to his departure from the colony.

The four travelers left immediately, escorted partway by members of the surface studies staff including Short-key-Leaps. When the latter had gone as far as planned, they exchanged ritual farewells with Runs and Seams. So little visible emotion was involved that it was hard to believe the team members were consigning their fate and that of the entire colony to one young renegade and his comparatively youthful female companion.

From the point of farewell it was an additional five days' hike to the outskirts of the tiny mountain community called Bonanza. There Chad and his sister promptly battled over which of them was to remain behind with the two Quozl and who would walk into town to try and hitch a ride into Boise to rent a vehicle. Chad insisted he should be the one because he had more stamina, but Mindy argued vociferously that it would be far easier for an attractive young woman traveling alone to get a lift than it would for a bedraggled, luggageless young man. Condemned by his own traditional devotion to reason, Chad conceded her victory.

The following days were not easy for him. What, he found himself wondering, if his sister decided to abandon the entire plan and instead catch a plane out of Boise to rejoin her fiancé? If so, he could do nothing about it.

Several times he and his friends had to hide from passing hikers. Then the day came when the climber they were fleeing turned out to be Mindy. She hadn't been gone many days. Chad felt embarrassed by his earlier thoughts.

"It's parked on the north end of town." Mindy looked back the way she'd come. "I came as far up the last road as I dared."

Chad studied the dirt track that ran below their camping site. "A van could come up that."

"A van, maybe, but I rented us a motor home instead." At his surprised look, she added, "Why not? We'll travel just as fast and there'll be plenty of room for our friends to move around and still stay out of sight."

When informed of what she'd done, Runs-red-Talking and Seams-with-Metal were pleased.

Chad had to admit when he saw the big motor home that his sister had driven it as far as possible up the dirt road leading out of town. It was a twenty-four-footer, brand-new and loaded with extras. Though Runs and Seams had both studied images of such machines they were still intrigued enough to poke at every button. The bathroom elicited an endless string of amused ear gestures.

Their interest had waned by the end of the second day. Runs was contentedly occupying himself with the reassembly of the microwave oven, which he had dismantled the evening before. Chad watched him manipulate the delicate, tiny electronic components as deftly as a jeweler setting a pavé diamond. Seams settled on a small side window and spent hours staring at the passing scenery.

Before returning to pick them up, Mindy had done some hasty shopping. The back of the motor home was piled high with clothing hastily gleaned from the teens' departments of half a dozen stores. Additional humor was generated as Runs and Seams tried on ill-matched but adequate covering. The results would fool a casual observer for a crucial moment or two, provided neither Quozl stepped outside the motor home.

◇ **279** ◇

Ears could be tucked into caps, but Runs-red-Talking's feet might be disguised only in ski season.

Seams selected a thin raincoat with matching hood which concealed everything except her face. Thus hidden she was able to sit closer to her window while watching the landscape flee by at sixty miles an hour.

Not that they ran much risk of being seen, since the highway they were driving was one of the least traveled in America. They took 95 all the way down through southern Idaho and into southeastern Oregon, then across to the wilderness of northern Nevada. Avoiding Reno and Carson City, they eventually cut back into California to connect up with state route 395 near the mountain community of Bishop. Hundreds of miles had been safely traversed without trouble.

Now they found themselves in country barren to human and Quozl alike, though their guests were impressed by the gray ramparts of the eastern Sierra Nevada. As Runs explained, the records indicated Quozlene was a world of hills and valleys, geologically ancient, too tired for tectonic dramatics. Its mountains were ground down and its canyons filled in. Not so Shiraz.

"Maybe someday I can see Quozlene," Chad said dreamily. "No, come to think of it your ships don't travel fast enough to make that practical, do they?"

"Generations live and die to accomplish the shortest journey." Runs spoke from his position on the bed in the back of the motor home. Clad in cap and coat, Seams occupied the passenger seat next to Mindy, her huge feet tucked up beneath the dash. They had left the Sierra foothills for the blasted expanse of the Mojave Desert.

"Shiraz is our world now."

Chad sat up to stare out the back window. "There's something you've never told me, Runs. Why you did it. Why you broke all the laws and made your way illegally to the surface."

"I wanted to see my world," he said simply. "The Burrows are comfortable but they're also throwbacks to ancient Quozl history. I wanted to feel soil beneath my feet, smell fresh air, listen to the singing of the little mammals that fly. I wanted to hear the hum of insects. Most of all I wanted to smell the trees, to feel growing bark and living wood.''

Chad was nodding to himself. ''I remember you spending a whole evening talking about nothing but the grain of a particular wood.''

''There is truth in trees,'' Runs informed him firmly. ''All the wonders of nature and the natural order are subsumed in wood. To study a tree is to study the universe. If it were possible we would make everything we use or own out of wood.'' He gestured out the window with an ear.

''Wider contact with humans would mean easier access to wood. You know of the law which bars study teams from bringing back to the colony anything but wood gleaned from fallen or dead trees.''

''I remember all the wood I brought you over the years.'' Not only local pine and spruce, he mused, but the little pieces of dogwood and purpleheart and buckeye and redwood he'd ordered from specialty dealers in L.A.

''It is a way of keeping touch with one's world, be it Shiraz or Quozlene or Azel or any other. For us the tree stands for life. If a world is home to trees it can be home to us.''

Chad remembered the linked rings that Runs had almost given him years ago. The Quozl were not simple carpenters and their wood not simple wood. Was he missing something important here? Were the trees of Quozlene more evolved than those of Earth, or merely different? The Quozl had achieved travel between the stars. What had the trees of Quozlene achieved?

Runs-red-Talking hoped for wider contact, though perhaps not the kind that almost occurred at the Exxon station in Independence. Mindy had gone to the ladies' room while Chad supervised the endless flow of dollars into the motor home's vast double tanks. Only when he removed the nozzle from the fill tube did he notice the little girl of about seven standing with her hands behind her back staring up at the side of the motor home. Carefully putting the hose nozzle back in its slot, he leaned out to try and follow her gaze.

Before he could, she turned and ran toward a mini-van parked at the inside island, yelling at the top of her immature lungs.

"Mommy, Mommy! Come an' see the big rabbit!"

Chad's body temperature fell a degree. He rushed to pay for the gas, ignoring the attendant's puzzled stare. Looking toward the motor home he could see nothing, but there was no doubt whom the little girl had seen through the tinted glass.

Fortunately she was utterly unable to interest her exhausted mother. Before she could, the travelers had fled the station for the safety of the highway.

Seams-with-Metal confirmed his fears. "Yes, the little one saw me. I am always interested in the refueling process and I grew careless."

"What harm in that?" Runs wanted to know. "Is not the purpose of this journey to reveal ourselves to humans?"

"Not in a haphazard manner."

The two fell to arguing. Chad understood them fluently and Mindy well enough. Like all Quozl debates this one was interminable, the subject under discussion often being lost completely as each participant sought to acquire status by out-apologizing the other. They had to avoid even the appearance of fighting. He wondered how they would handle possibly hostile human questions.

Runs had made a point. How were they going to announce themselves to the rest of the world? By calling up the local stations? "Pardon me, but my name's Chad Collins and my sister and I have a couple of alien visitors staying with us who'd be willing to do an interview. You'll send someone right over, won't you?"

Indeed they would. Interviewers in white coats wearing solemn expressions.

The truth of it was that neither human nor Quozl had given

much thought to the matter. Now that they were nearing Los Angeles, it was time to do so.

Chad was out of his depth and realized it. He intended to leave the mechanics of any confrontation to his sister. As head writer for a popular television show she'd probably been interviewed numerous times. She would know how to set things up, how to advise Runs and Seams.

The Quozl made excited sounds as the motor home turned off I-5 onto the 405, sliding down the interstate into the ocean of lights that marked the outer limits of the San Fernando Valley. It was after midnight and traffic was as light as it ever got in L.A. They attracted no curious stares.

"Are there any cities this big on Quozlene?" Mindy asked curiously.

"Oh yes." Runs measured his reply carefully. "Or so the recordings indicate. I have never seen them for myself."

Mindy eased into the slow lane after letting an eighteen-wheeler rumble past. "That's right. I keep forgetting."

She took the third exit after the Pass, winding through foothills among expensive new developments. At least she had a house, Chad reflected. They wouldn't have to try and hide the Quozl in his apartment.

It was a spacious tile-roofed two-story, much bigger than his sister needed but in keeping with her position and income. The extensive landscaping shielded the place on three sides. The lot was large enough to offer a modicum of privacy.

Which did not matter because the house was not empty.

"Hiya, sweets!" The brash hello greeted them as they followed Mindy into the tiled entry hall. "Where ya been? I expected you weeks ago."

Mindy strode purposefully into her den. "How did you get in here?"

Arlo uncoiled from the couch. "You gave me a key. We're engaged, remember?"

"I'm trying not to," she replied frostily.

"Now, sweets." His words were as reassuring as WD-40

to a cranky hinge. "No need to panic. I know what I'm doing. It's all for the best, believe me."

"You lied to me. You said you'd keep the secret. You promised, Arlo."

He looked past her. "Can't keep secrets very long if you're going to truck 'em all over the country. The one on the left I know." He nodded at Runs-red-Talking. "The female I don't recognize."

As Chad hurriedly shut the front door behind them, Arlo walked up to Seams-with-Metal and reached for her face with his right hand. The clumsy effort to mimic the traditional Quozl greeting was somehow endearing in its awkwardness. Though Chad wasn't prepared to credit the agent with so refined an emotion, another person might have called the attempt a sign of sensitivity.

Seams-with-Metal started to respond, then caught herself. "Who is this person?"

Walking past her into the den, Chad gestured derisively at the agent. "That's my sister's boyfriend, the one who provoked this trip. The one who's caused all the concern. Arlo, meet Seams-with-Metal."

"Charmed, pleased, delighted." The agent offered the familiar honorifics without artfulness. More with artifice, Chad thought angrily as he searched the den and the room immediately adjacent.

"Where are the reporters? Where's your hidden camera crew?"

"No reporters. That's not the way to do this. Not yet. I didn't want to go out on my own. I thought we'd all do it together, cooperate like."

"Like hell," Chad shot back.

"Don't be that way, man." Arlo turned to Runs-red-Talking. "I know that you see what I'm talking about. You can't keep hidden forever. Sooner or later somebody's gonna stumble on your place, wherever it is." Chad thought the argument was familiar. With a shock he recalled using it himself, when trying to explain things to Runs.

"It'd be much better to reveal yourselves at your own speed. Well, at our own speed. Because there's too much at stake here for me to just forget about it. So your speed and my speed are going to have to be our speed. But I've got your best interests at heart, believe me."

"What heart?" Mindy wanted to know.

Arlo looked pained. "Sweets, let's not forget who's made herself a nice little nest egg off our Quozl friends, shall we? All I want is a tiny slice of the action. And I'll do better by them than some Pulitzer-hungry reporter would, because I really do like the little guys. But this business of trying to hide in the ground for the next couple of hundred years is idiotico. Now's the time to stand up and say howdy, because of all the goodwill *your* show has generated." He was watching Seams-with-Metal.

"I didn't expect to do anything right away. I wanted to talk it over with you and your brother first. The Quozl too."

"You expect us to believe that?"

Arlo shrugged. "Kind of hard to, now. But yeah, I did. What I didn't expect was for you to bring company."

"I think Arlo is right." Everyone turned to Runs-red-Talking. Arlo beamed. "There. You see?"

"Runs, I don't . . ." Chad began.

"My friend," the Quozl said earnestly, "I have spent my whole life believing that wider contact with humans was vital to the continued health and development of the colony. My contacts with you and your sister over the past several cycles have only reinforced these feelings. The longer we spend hiding and afraid, the more difficult eventual contact will become. Already attitudes are stagnating, initiative ossifying. We must expand upward as well as outward if we are to become true citizens of this world.

"In this I know I am considered aberrant. The Council would disagree, though there are those in the colony who sympathize with my feelings. They dare not voice them aloud. Only I can do so, having made myself so invaluable they cannot do without me.

"Now that we are here, with a mandate from the Council to widen contact, I believe we should continue as planned. As friend Arlo has not revealed our existence we should be able to manage our introduction so very much more efficiently. I see no reason to change our plans."

Seams-with-Metal glared at him. "The Council thought we had been betrayed. If they knew otherwise they would surely change our instructions."

"But they do not know otherwise."

"We will use the communicator to ask them how to proceed."

"The great Looks-at-Charts was my relative. A scout uses his initiative. We will not use the communicator." His ears bobbed instructively. "I have removed several important components without which it will not function."

"You are a traitor."

"I think otherwise. I am convinced the future will vindicate this choice of action."

"No question about it." Arlo wore a broad smile, hastily lost it at the look on Runs's face. "I hereby offer my help."

"*Your* help?" Mindy eyed him dubiously. "How can you help?"

"It's an agent's job to assist his clients."

"Clients!" Chad couldn't restrain himself. "Where the hell do you get off calling yourself . . . !"

"Any new celeb who wants his introduction to the media managed properly needs an agent. The Quozl are gonna be the biggest celebrities of the millennium."

"I think I like you." Runs walked over to shake Arlo's hand. "I believe your friends misjudge you. I think you can help us."

"Wait a minute, wait a minute!" Events were moving too rapidly for Chad. Arlo eyed him accusingly.

"What's wrong, Chad? Want to keep the Quozl all to yourself?"

"That's ridiculous. I want only what's in their best interest, and . . ."

"I know what is in our best interest."

Everyone turned to look at Seams-with-Metal. In her left hand she held a small rectangular box, gripping it securely with five fingers. The other two pressed against a pair of depressions set in opposite ends of the object.

"This device is very powerful," she calmly informed them as sweat began to trickle down Chad's neck. "Within its effective radius it produces enough heat to carbonize bone. There will be nothing left to give away our presence."

"Now please, just a moment." Mindy pleaded even as she was retreating.

Seams-with-Metal was Quozl-calm. "This is the best solution. Only three humans know of our presence on Shiraz. All are present in this room. The individual who precipitated the crisis is also present." She stared evenly at Runs-red-Talking. "The elimination will be clean. I was instructed to take this opportunity if it proferred itself."

Runs appeared remarkably unperturbed. "You would be murdering five intelligent beings, yourself among them. No Quozl could do that."

"No sane Quozl. I am different. Why do you think I was chosen to accompany you, Runs-red-Talking? I am an aberration, not unlike yourself. I can carry this thing through. I have no wish to die, but am willing to perish on behalf of a greater cause." She turned to Chad and his sister.

"I apologize most extremely for this necessary action." That was the Quozl for you, Chad thought wildly. Polite to the end. "Your excision close to the colony might have provoked anxious searches of the vicinity. Here your passing will generate no outcry, result in no intimate inspection threatening to the Burrows."

"How do you know?" Mindy stammered, trying to bluff.

"Because we have studied your broadcasts and we understand how your procedures and minds would work in such an instance."

Still Runs did not panic. Chad marveled at his self-control.

"If you are different, as you say and as I have suspected, then you are more like me than you are the fossils who populate the Council. Therefore, you must suspect that the way I propose is the best for the future of the Quozl of Shiraz."

"I know nothing of the kind. I know only what I was instructed to do if it seemed possible. *Bis-mey-ohy-meene chaplo*," she finished in Quozl.

Her fingers dug into the depressions. Mindy screamed. Arlo dove for the fragile shelter of the couch. Chad closed his eyes and regretted that at the end he had nothing to say, to himself or anyone else.

A moment passed, another. He opened his eyes. Mindy stopped screaming. Arlo peered over the back of the couch.

Seams-with-Metal untensed and began to inspect the device. Runs-red-Talking strolled over and gently but firmly took it from her limp fingers. Instead of resisting she eyed him curiously.

"I do not understand why it failed to function."

"It failed to function because I discovered it and divined its purpose some time ago," Runs explained. "I removed several critical but tiny components, much as I did with the communicator. Did you think I spent the entire journey down here disassembling kitchen appliances?"

Mindy slumped in a chair, resting a hand on her forehead. Arlo started to let out a whoop, thought better of it, and kept silent.

Seams spoke quietly, ever polite. "It was never off my person. That means you had to invade my Sama while I slept. Without permission."

"Not an impossible task for one as different as myself." Runs smiled with his ears, the gesture expansive and unmistakable. "Those who provided you with this device may have forgotten that prior to escorting surface study groups my profession involved the repair of complex electronics." He put the now harmless explosive device on an end table. "Dysfunctioning this was a simple matter for me."

She took a step toward him. "Where is the missing component?" Chad held his breath, expecting to see for the first time one Quozl commit physical violence on another.

Runs's ears continued to bob humorously. "Somewhere in the depths of a large river hundreds of human miles to the north of here. It will never be found. In the unlikely event that it is, it would be remarkable if its origin or function was suspected by the finder."

Seams-with-Metal stopped. "I agree. Therefore, I must accept what you have done. Alternatives must be considered." She turned to confront Arlo, who had finally emerged from behind the couch, and said as if nothing had happened, "If you can assist us in making successful wide contact we will be ever grateful."

"Wait, wait!" Mindy rose from her chair, an expression of disbelief on her pretty face. "You just tried to kill us!"

"I know. It is a failure I regret. I could possibly slay one or two of you before I was myself incapacitated. This would be a futile gesture as the third would remain. Therefore, I am obliged by tradition and the instructions of the Samizene to put failure behind me and participate to the best of my ability in the next best course of action. This involves the cautious expansion of contact." She turned back to Runs-red-Talking.

"You have achieved what you desired. I regret it most surely. Now, tell me how I may be of assistance."

"I do not know myself." Runs looked over at Arlo. "What does our experienced friend suggest?"

Friend? Chad took the seat his sister had vacated and tried to steady himself. Meanwhile Runs-red-Talking and the Quozl who had just tried to blow them all to bits cheerfully began discussing approaches to announcing the Quozl's presence to the rest of mankind.

Mindy stumbled over to join her brother. "Look at her." She indicated Seams-with-Metal. "How can she change positions like that?"

"The Quozl don't believe in wasting time on the unachievable. When they decide to go with the flow, they do so unreservedly. We don't have to worry about Seams-with-Metal anymore. Now if *Runs* had agreed with her we'd all be talcum powder by now.''

Having recovered rapidly from the near-assassination, Arlo was letting his thoughts race with possibilities.

"Basically you guys are and always have been primarily concerned about the kind of reception you're going to get once you announce yourselves, right?''

"That is correct,'' said Runs. "The goodwill generated toward Quozl by the television program will help, but we cannot be sure it will be sufficient to overcome all human xenophobic attitudes.''

"Right. But I think we're on the right track talking about the show. It suggests to me that the best way to deal with this is on an informal basis.''

"You can't announce the presence of alien beings on Earth 'informally,' '' Chad said sarcastically, but Runs and Arlo both ignored him.

"We need to keep the authorities out of it as much as possible,'' Arlo was saying. "Put you across to John Q. Public before the brass hats have time to react. I could sneak you into the White House, but that doesn't have the right feel.''

"This isn't a product to be sold,'' Chad reminded him.

"The hell it ain't, Chad. You don't know much about the real world, do you? *Everything's* a product to be sold. Soap, cornflakes, philosophy, radial tires, religion, the value of the yen versus the buck. Everything. And that's my business.''
He started to give Runs a friendly tap on the shoulder, at the last instant remembered what it meant to enter a Quozl's Sama uninvited.

"You don't show up declaring that you want eternal peace and friendship with all mankind. You don't sit down to negotiate long-winded treaties. You *sell* yourselves. Mindy's show gives us a built-in audience to start with. Advertising, PR; that's how you put yourselves across to Earth.''

"It may be so,'' Seams conceded. "I have studied this.''

"No drawn-out negotiations." Arlo was racing now. "You bypass the governments, and go straight to the people. We'll make you so popular so fast that the xenophobic types won't be able to lay a finger on you."

"You're as crazy as Runs is," Chad blurted in frustration.

"Crazy?" Arlo grinned at him. "I'm in a crazy business, Chad. You have to be a little crazy to make it work. But give me one thing: I know people. I know what buttons to push, what strings to pull. Animated aliens, real aliens—the public doesn't care if you sell it to them the right way. You want to make successful contact," he said to the two intrigued Quozl, "you don't go for the cover of *Newsweek*. You try for the *Star* and the *Enquirer*. You do the right talk shows, show up at the important openings. Believe me, the politicos will beg to be seen standing next to you."

"Possibly the most important event in human history," Chad muttered, "and you're trivializing it."

"Of course I am. Now you've got the idea, Chad. That's how you make friends and important contacts quickly. Something that's perceived as trivial isn't perceived as a threat. Take religion today. The more people trivialize it, the weaker it becomes. We want the public to think of the Quozl as trivial, as all flash and no substance. As entertaining, but harmless." He cocked a quizzical eye at Runs and Seams.

"You're still not sure about all this, are you? Okay, I'll prove it."

Chad felt control slipping away. Years he'd spent meeting and talking to Runs-red-Talking, then introducing his sister, only to have this comparative stranger, this verbally facile, exceedingly shallow person, take over. He could see it happening, see it in the way Runs and Seams paid close attention to his words. And there didn't seem to be a damn thing he could do about it.

That was not what mattered, though. What was important was whether or not his sister's fiancé was right.

Arlo was mumbling to himself. "You'll need to be incorporated, of course."

"Incorporated?" Runs's ears bobbed and dipped.

"Don't worry, I'll handle all the details. We'll need lawyers, accountants, you'll need a business manager to handle the colony's income. There'll be plenty of that, and not just from the show." He glanced in Mindy's direction but she was too numb or dazed to object. "My fee will be small. Minuscule, really. Considering your prospects that'll be plenty. You can always be sure of a good agent, Runs, because if you fail he fails."

The Quozl looked back at his old friend. "Does he tell the truth?"

Chad wanted to lie, to yell, to eliminate Arlo altogether. Instead he said, "If there's money in it for him I think he'll tell you the truth, yes." He looked at the man, only a few years older than himself, whom he hated and on whom they were going to have to rely. "How are you going to prove to them that this is all going to work, like you just said you would?"

Arlo exuded confidence. "By taking them out tomorrow and introducing them to humans who've never seen a Quozl before."

Mindy looked dubious. "Just like that?"

"Yes. Just like that."

"If you're lucky you'll just start a riot, not a war."

"We'll start nothing of the kind, sweets. Because there's one place where we can all go together where Runs and Seams can stroll around in plain sight. Where their presence won't provoke any excitement or even much comment. Where they can talk to other humans without having to hide themselves, as freely and as often as they like."

Chad stared at him. "You're not just crazy. You're certifiable."

"There is no such place," Mindy said with finality.

"Oh but there is, sweets. A place where everyone blends in. A place where the out-of-the-ordinary doesn't stand out. Not even a Quozl.

"A place called—Disneyland!"

XIX.

MINDY STARED AT Chad. He considered his sister. That left Arlo to do the talking.

"It's a park," he explained to the puzzled Quozl. "A special kind of park. People there dress up in costumes, like your scarves and jewelry, only more so, to look like imaginary characters. Don't you get it? You're already known as animated characters from the *Quozltime* show. The humans who go to this place expect to see something like you walking around. Everyone will assume that you're short skinny humans in special costumes. They'll have to, because they can't assume anything else. You can ask whatever questions you want to ask, act however you like, without anyone even suspecting that you're visitors from another world. The only problem you'll have is that little kids will want to have their pictures taken with you."

"We're not visitors." Runs-red-Talking corrected him politely but firmly. "I was born here. Shiraz is my world too."

"Shiraz, yeah. I like that. Has a swell exotic feel to it. What do you say? Ready to go?" He concluded with a prideful flourish. "I can even get us comp tickets."

Runs-red-Talking pondered several minutes before turning to Chad. "What do you say, old friend? What do you think we should do?"

"I think it's the craziest thing I ever heard of." He took a deep breath. "I also think it might work." Arlo looked vindicated. "If there's one place on the planet where Quozl might be able to walk around incognito, as it were, Disneyland's it. The only problem is that your English is almost *too* good.''

"That's right," said Mindy. This is wild, she thought, absolutely wild. She regretted having missed the exact moment when they'd crossed over into unreality. "You have to talk like this," and she forced herself to speak in a high, childish squeal.

Seams-with-Metal listened carefully. "I have studied broadcasts from many parts of your country, but that is an inflection I do not recognize."

"It's not a human accent. It's the way the Quozl sound on my show."

"It sounds ridiculous," said Seams with great dignity. "It is too loud and too sharp. Another Quozl would find it degrading and impolite."

"But you're not going to be talking to other Quozl. You're going to be talking to humans. Kids will expect you to talk like that. It'll help you maintain your anonymity."

Seams-with-Metal's expression twitched. She considered thoughtfully, then said something in a perfectly puerile comic voice. "Is that what you had in mind?"

"That's perfect, that's remarkable!" exclaimed Mindy. "Even better than the professionals who do the show."

"How about that?" Chad's tone was desert dry. "Maybe they can even get a job doing voices for you." He wondered if his sister realized they were dealing with a galaxy-sized incongruity. "They're very good mimics."

"I can talk that way also." Runs promptly demonstrated. "Tell me, do I sound sufficiently like a Quozl?"

Mindy was properly abashed. "All right, lay off. Though I suppose I had it coming."

"I'll drive." Arlo headed for the garage. "My Eldo's got smoked windows." He smiled at the two Quozl. "You guys can sit in back and look out without anybody spotting you. Once we get there it won't matter."

It was a weekday and the gigantic parking lot was more

than half empty. Mindy and Chad exited the car full of apprehension, but Arlo was in high spirits. Runs-red-Talking and Seams-with-Metal joined them, having put aside their camouflage clothing.

As they emerged from the car, a station wagon overflowing with two families cruised past, the driver hunting for just the right parking place. Children gestured in the direction of the Cadillac and its occupants. One mother smiled and waved.

"See," Arlo told them delightedly. "Everybody accepts you for what you look like, but nobody knows you for what you really are. It'll be like that all day."

They picked up their special tickets at guest relations, which enabled them to enter quietly without having to stand in line at the regular turnstiles. One guard eyed them uncertainly but allowed them to pass without comment at a whisper from Arlo. Chad was sure he could feel the man's eyes on his back as they passed beneath the train bridge and into the park proper.

Seams and Runs were beginning to relax. They found the park fascinating but less so than its inhabitants. For the first time they were surrounded by humans, and they were trying to absorb everything at once. Languages and colors, shapes and sizes, actions and reactions. Despite Chad's warnings Seams-with-Metal finally couldn't stand it any longer. She extracted her recorder from her belt and began making records of their surroundings.

His concern proved unnecessary. No one paid her any attention, though she did draw an occasional curious glance from one or two camera buffs since the device she was using more closely resembled a crystal ashtray than a camcorder.

"Everything in your culture is repressed," Runs commented. "There is no place for proper sublimation except in your games. As these involve actual physical contact they would not be suitable for Quozl. They are in any event insufficient for your psychological needs because they truly help only those who participate in them. You must listen to our philosophers, Chad. They can help your people."

"Great idea!" Arlo was watching the crowd, reveling in the success of his suggestion. "We'll get your philosophers a show of their own, prime time. They'll put Dr. Ruth and Donahue on the sidelines."

"Slow down." Chad didn't share the other man's enthusiasm. "Formal contact has to come first, then wider public exposure."

"Wrongo, Chad. You got it backward. Don't you know anything about popular culture?"

"Only what I read in the papers and see on the tube."

Arlo was satisfied. "Precisely my point."

By that afternoon even Chad was starting to relax a little and enjoy the excursion. From time to time Seams-with-Metal would seek out a secluded corner. The others would screen her while she relayed up-to-date details of their progress back to the Council in Idaho. The failed episode with the bomb had already been discussed and discarded. Perhaps some on the Council regretted her failure, but they did not linger on it. The Quozl accepted, and moved on.

Her communicator seemed much too small to Chad to be capable of linking with a communications satellite high in orbit. Runs explained that the technology involved utilizing any nearby reflective surface to boost signal strength. Metal was best but glass or plastic would do.

As Arlo had predicted, passing children squealed delightedly when they caught sight of two of their favorite characters. They swarmed over the Quozl, deluging them with questions, running their tiny fingers through short soft fur, and demanding to have their pictures taken with them. Parents smilingly obliged, marveling aloud at the detail and quality of the two costumes.

"Aren't you hot in there?" one asked Runs-red-Talking.

"In where?" Runs looked frantically to Chad for help.

"In that costume." The plump, red-faced visitor from Iowa kept trying to see behind Runs, squinting in his search for invisible zippers and fasteners.

"He's used to it," said Chad hastily. "He's from a hot climate."

"Yeah, well, I hope he's getting paid right. Looks pretty uncomfortable from here. A real tight fit."

"It is," Runs admitted agreeably.

Later they stood and relaxed beneath the trees of the central square. The crowd swirled around them. Seams-with-Metal had put up her recorder.

"I think they truly like us."

"Of course they like you." Mindy was holding Arlo's hand. "Most of these kids have been watching you cavort on tv for years. They know that all Quozl are cute, cuddly, and helpful."

"And stupid," Chad couldn't resist adding.

His sister frowned at him. "Not at all. It's a kids' show, so the Quozl portrayed have to function on a level kids can understand."

They did have trouble with one middle-aged man who stared long and hard at the Quozl while his three children briefly clustered around them. As his wife led the kids away, he lingered behind. Chad noticed him staring and sidled over to him as Arlo and Mindy walked off with Runs and Seams.

"Something interesting?"

"What?" The man blinked at him, then nodded in the direction of the retreating Quozl. "Did you get a look at those two costumes?"

"Oh, the Quozl? Yeah. My friends and I know the actors wearing them."

"You do? Well, you tell them those are the best damn costumes I ever saw. I'm in makeup and effects profession-ally. I watched them while they were talking and I've never seen an oral prosthesis that good, not even Rick Baker's stuff. You can see right down their throats."

"They are good jobs, aren't they?" Chad's voice fell to a whisper. "Don't say anything to anybody, but we're trying out some new things, to see how acceptable they are to kids. You know, how well they fool them, like that."

"They fooled me."

A voice made him turn, reluctantly. His wife was yelling at him to come and help with the kids. He vanished in the opposite direction, still looking over his shoulder as his family tugged him away. To Chad's great relief they did not encounter him again.

As it turned out it wasn't someone well versed in makeup or costuming who finally confronted them later that evening as they entered the fantasy animal world of Adventureland. He wore a large safari suit, immaculately cleaned and pressed, and was accompanied by a slimmer gentleman who looked out of place in suit and tie. They came up quietly on Chad and his companions as they studied the bric-a-brac for sale in one of the innumerable gift shops.

"Excuse me? Are you all together?"

Startled, Mindy eyed the man in the business suit. "Yes, we are." Her brows drew together. "Who are you?" She noticed the large individual in the safari suit. He was standing behind them, screening the encounter from the rest of the crowd.

"We're with park security." The man's tone was courteous, his demeanor pleasant. "We'd appreciate it if you'd come with us."

Chad looked around, panicked, but there was nowhere to run. Not that it mattered. If they did bolt, park security could be all over them in minutes. And the same fence that kept people from sneaking into the park would surely be adequate to prevent anyone from slipping out.

Runs-red-Talking and Seams-with-Metal could easily outrun any human, but they would hardly be better off lost in the wilds of downtown Anaheim. What Chad couldn't figure out was what had gone wrong.

"Excuse me, sir, but have we broken some kind of law?" Arlo stepped forward. "We're not doing anything wrong here that I can see. We're just enjoying the park like everyone else."

"Not quite." The security man pointed at Runs and Seams. "These two are supposed to be Quozl, aren't they?"

To his credit Arlo didn't hesitate. "Well, sure. Lots of kids like to dress up. So do these two. Something wrong with that?"

"*Quozltime,*" the man explained as solemnly as if he was reading out a writ for murder, "is not produced by or in any way connected with the Disney organization. Quozl are not licensed Disney characters. Consequently we feel they are more than just out of place in the park."

"Geezus." Arlo slapped his forehead. "I didn't think of that." He turned on Mindy. "How come you didn't think of that, sweets?"

She stood numbly, unable to formulate a reply.

"We'd appreciate it if you'd come with us, please," the security man was saying. "Quietly, so as not to disturb any of the other patrons."

"Hey, we're sorry, we apologize." Arlo was talking fast but Chad feared it would be neither facile nor fast enough. "We didn't think this would upset anybody, really. Why not just let us leave?"

"I'm afraid it's not quite that simple. You've been under surveillance for a while. We've observed children run up to you asking for autographs and to have pictures taken with you. We need to find out why you're here, if you're doing this on your own or if there's some commercial purpose to your presence. Promoting another studio's production on our property, for example."

"Hey, it's nothing like that, really," said Arlo desperately. "We're just here because . . ."

The voice that interrupted him was high and squeaky. "We didn't give any autographs," Runs insisted.

The security man eyed him strangely. "That's very good, but you don't have to stay in character any longer."

"We're not promoting anything," Mindy insisted.

"No?" The man in the safari suit pointed at Seams-with-Metal. "What do you call those?"

"Quozl," said Seams, trying to help and not knowing what else to say.

"Really quite good." The other man murmured to Arlo. "I have to insist you come with us."

For once Arlo had nothing to say. Chad stepped forward. "Okay, we'll come with you. I'm sure we can clear all this up in a few minutes."

The security maven smiled again. "I'm sure we can."

They were escorted through the crowd to a back room, thence down a set of stairs into an underground passageway. Crowd noises were replaced by the sounds of workers chatting and the soft hum of electric carts moving supplies and people from one end of the park service complex to another. Runs-red-Talking whispered to Chad.

"Very pleasant. Barren, but otherwise not unlike parts of my Burrow."

"What do you think's going to happen?" Mindy queried her brother.

"Why ask me? I don't know. Maybe they'll just ask us some questions, have us sign a few forms, and kick us out. Don't worry. It'll work out okay."

He didn't believe that, but saw no point in saying so.

Eventually they entered a spacious, aboveground office in another part of the park. The two men who'd escorted them stood silently nearby while another smiling individual lectured them firmly but politely about the no-no's of using the park to generate interest in another studio's characters. Chad and Arlo looked suitably contrite while Mindy hovered in the back with the Quozl.

Instead of being dismissed, they were taken after the lecture to another office, where a woman explained that to satisfy company formalities they would be asked to provide certain information. Then they would be allowed to leave.

Chad was starting to feel hopeful that they could get away. Names and addresses were no problem. Agile wordsmith that she was, Mindy improvised identities for Runs-red-Talking and Seams on the spot. The woman dutifully entered these fictions in her computer.

"That's all," she said finally, smiling up at them. Chad and Arlo managed to smile back while the Quozl turned away. "Except," she added, "for pictures."

"Pictures?" Chad felt his smile fading.

"To complete the records. I'm sure you understand. If you'd just step over here a minute?"

She led them to the back of the room where they found themselves confronting a large instant camera of the kind used by motor vehicle departments to take the pictures that go on driver's licenses. Chad hesitantly allowed his face to be immortalized. He was followed by Arlo, then Mindy. Runs-red-Talking whispered to Seams-with-Metal, his earrings tinkling musically. The woman was beginning to get impatient.

Staring expressionlessly straight ahead, ears erect, Runs stepped up to the designated line. One of the security men grinned at him.

"All right. Enough, already. It's a great outfit but it won't look funny in the official files. So at least take off the head."

Runs-red-Talking had spent his whole life initiating action instead of reacting to it. Possibly that was uppermost in his mind now. Or perhaps he was simply tired of the game.

For whatever reason, he replied by saying, "My head doesn't come off."

Mindy closed her eyes. Arlo sighed and sat down heavily in a nearby chair. Chad groaned softly. As for Seams-with-Metal, she waited quietly to see how the humans would react. Ever observing, Chad noted.

The man in the safari suit was anxious to return to his regular post. "Look, staying in character is fine for the kids, but there are no kids here and we really do need a serious mug shot."

You had to give Arlo credit, Chad thought as the agent stepped forward. He never quit trying. "Give us a break, guys. These costumes are all one piece. You can't just take the heads off, and it takes hours to set 'em up right. We were counting on doing an appearance elsewhere tonight.''

''Not my problem,'' safari grunted. ''Take 'em off.''

''What if they refuse?''

The man in the business suit frowned. ''Can't they talk for themselves?'' He leaned over to peer closely at Runs-red-Talking. Runs-red-Talking stared back interestedly. ''How do you do the eyes? Magnifying lenses, or some kind of transparent overlay?''

This was not how it was supposed to happen, Chad thought tiredly. There should be bands playing, fireworks exploding, important people making speeches and shaking hands with revered Quozl Elders.

''They don't come off. They aren't wearing costumes. These are real Quozl, ambassadors from the Quozl colony on Earth.''

Business suit didn't miss a beat. ''Just when I thought you people were going to cooperate.''

Chad eyed the door, wondering if it was worth making a break for it. He decided against it. What would be the point? They couldn't get out of the park.

''Do you have a first-aid station here?''

Safari sounded insulted. ''Several. Why? Somebody sick?'' Business suit looked suddenly alarmed even though neither he nor his partner had laid a hand on their charges.

''Nobody's sick.'' Chad tried to be patient. ''If you have X-ray facilities we can settle this once and for all.'' Business suit looked dubious, so Chad made it easy for him. ''One exposure. Then we'll let you take your mug shots.''

Arlo chimed in helpfully. ''We'll even pay for the work.''

The two security men exchanged a glance. Then safari shrugged, which seemed to settle it.

He returned to his post and left the tidying up to business suit, which was a pity since he missed the reaction of the young technician operating the X-ray unit. As he refused to believe his own work they had to wait and repeat the procedure twice with additional witnesses. Then all hell broke loose.

While it was breaking, Runs and Seams insisted on a few moments of privacy. Both were nervous and uneasy, not because of the exposure but because it had been too long since either had engaged in intercourse. Chad and Mindy kept watch outside the storage room while the Quozl went about their important business.

Meanwhile the security man consulted with the medical technicians, who called in the park administrator, who intended to have them all carted off and fired until he saw both the Quozl and the film, who then contacted his superior, who called in additional expert medical assistance, by which time the already closed-for-the-day park saw the extraordinary sight of more vehicles arriving than were departing.

Lines of communication no matter how private or supposedly secure tend to leak like fifty-year-old steel pots. The reporter who chose to take a chance on the ridiculous found himself recording the scoop of the century, complete with pictures. The first official press conference to deal with the presence of alien life on earth was held in the Disneyland executive offices, a venue that would have pleased Dali and Bosch if not presidents and premiers.

Runs-red-Talking and Seams-with-Metal answered the questions put to them freely and thoughtfully. So did Mindy and a reluctant Chad. As to the exact location and size of the colony the Quozl were purposefully evasive. Everything was monitored by the Council of Seven during Runs-red-Talking's frequent trips to the bathroom, the Quozl bouncing the necessary signal off the glass window of a large 1890s peanut wagon stationed strategically outside.

By early morning administrators, reporters (others having gotten wind of what was happening and showing up), Quozl and friends were exhausted. Both vehicular and aerial police escort was provided to convoy the visitors from elsewhere back to Chatsworth. A permanent plainclothes watch was posted around Mindy's house, which only mildly intrigued her neighbors. Everyone knew she worked in film and tv, so such oddities were to be expected. They whispered about wild parties and drugs without suspecting a hint of the truth.

Runs and Seams had no difficulty falling asleep in Mindy's guest room. In contrast their human friends found it hard to get any rest, tossing and turning uneasily.

Meanwhile the neighbors allowed as how their assumptions might have been wrong because Mindy's front lawn began to sprout tv cameras like chickweed. If not for the presence of a small army of plainclothes police and FBI they would have walked right up to peer in the windows. By the time the sun cast its first baleful glow through the smog someone was waking up the mayor, since it had been decided it was his place to alert the federal government.

Arlo, however, was one step ahead of them all. He was taking full advantage of the fact that no one had yet thought to screen outgoing as opposed to incoming phone calls. As much as Chad disliked his sister's fiancé he had to admit that he knew his work.

When a delegation including the senior senator from the state of California, two members of the House of Representatives, several people from the governor's office, and the mayor showed up at the house at six A.M., they were informed by the police lieutenant on duty that the inhabitants had taken themselves elsewhere. Under proper escort, of course.

"What the hell do you mean 'proper escort'?" The senator was incensed. "Why didn't you keep them here?"

The lieutenant wished he was somewhere safe. Down in the gang zone, for instance. "No one said anything about keeping them here. They aren't under arrest or anything. And the aliens insisted, sir."

"Idiot!" The senator whirled on an aide while the representatives caucused. "Where did they go?"

"I don't know," the woman confessed.

"Well, find out."

"Hey." Everyone turned toward the urgent voice. "Hey, everybody. Have a look at this."

One of the reporters who had set up on the lawn as close to the front steps as the police would allow was gazing at the monitor attached to his cameraman's equipment. The sun was bright and he had to shield the screen.

"Isn't that them?"

The senator shoved his way to the front of the rapidly swelling crowd while police tried to keep everyone else back. Across the front yard other cameramen were rapidly switching their own monitors.

It was a widely viewed show. Not as big as Donahue or Walters, but popular. More importantly, Arlo had a contact with the host, who at first was understandably suspicious of a fraud. When proof was offered in the form of copies of the X rays taken the previous night and a brief sprinting demonstration by Seams-with-Metal, he agreed to an unrehearsed appearance.

"This had better be for real." The host was giving her makeup girl fits, pacing endlessly backstage minutes before airtime.

"Just wing it," Arlo advised her reassuringly.

"Everyone'll think it's a gag. I'll be laughed off the air. I won't be able to get a job hosting a cooking show in Muskogee."

"It's for real." Arlo was watching Runs-red-Talking and Seams-with-Metal grooming themselves. "In fifteen minutes you'll have more proof than you'll ever need. Just whatever you do, don't stop."

Actually it was more like twenty minutes before every reporter in Los Angeles descended on the station, fighting, bribing, and trying to pull rank to get inside. One network anchor suffered a broken leg in the crush but was too excited to file suit. By this time the studio audience had tumbled to the fact that this "interview with aliens" might be something other than a joke, and watched enthralled as the nervous host tried to question Runs and Seams in her normal penetrating yet folksy fashion.

When it was the turn of the studio audience to put questions to the guests, something like realization bathed them in its warm, reassuring glow. Around the country people set aside squawling infants, shopping, fast food, and work to crowd around television sets of all sizes. While Middle America watched and a representative sample of it put questions to bona fide aliens, an army of reporters battled with hard-pressed security men and plainclothes police in the hallway outside the studio.

"Where exactly do you come from?" asked a mother of three on vacation from Nashville.

"We'd rather not say." Seams-with-Metal's intricate ear gestures were lost on the woman and the rest of the audience. "It would not matter anyway. It is so far distant you could not find it in your night sky."

"How do you like it here on Earth?" The questioner was a machinist from Detroit. Chad was thrilled to observe that, like the others, he was smiling as he asked his question.

"What we have seen of it so far we like very much," Runs told him politely. "But we are concerned about what humans will think of us."

"You shouldn't be." The hostess rushed her microphone to within pickup range of the heavyset woman from Reno. She was positively gushing. "My children have watched your show every Saturday for years, and they love you!"

It was as Arlo had predicted and Chad had hoped. The audience was confusing fiction with reality, to the eventual benefit of the latter.

"It's not our show." Runs indicated Mindy and proceeded to explain. It didn't matter. Either no one in the audience believed him, or else they simply didn't care. The actuality of the Quozl fascinated them. How could characters on which popular cartoons were based be anything other than friendly? How could anyone listening to them talk possibly think of them as "invaders"? Why, the very thought was ludicrous!

All anyone had to do was look at them, listen to their high, whispery voices. Not only were they harmless, they were *cute*.

"How long have you been here?" was the next question.

For the first time, Runs-red-Talking hesitated. He whispered to his companion. Seams-with-Metal heard him clearly though not even the studio mikes were sensitive enough to pick up his words. She replied equally softly.

"Approximately fifty of your years," he informed the questioner.

That provoked murmurs from the audience and hurried work by the few reporters who had succeeded in gaining entrance to the studio. Clearly everyone had expected the Quozl to say something on the order of a few weeks or, at most, a couple of months.

"How could you stay hidden for fifty years?" a young man inquired.

This time Runs didn't pause. "We can be inconspicuous."

"How many of you are there?"

Chad didn't hear the answer. This was better, much better, than some lingering, solemn government interrogation. Everything was out in the open. Fear and innuendo and rumor needed dark enclosed places in which to grow. Everything Runs-red-Talking and Seams-with-Metal said was going out via relay live to the rest of the country and around the world.

The host descended from the tiers of audience seats to thrust her microphone at the two Quozl. She was completely relaxed now. With a start Chad realized she might as well have been interviewing any pair of celebrities about their next picture. He looked around and, as expected, found Arlo smiling back at him and nodding knowingly.

"So you're worried about your reception? Let's go with that. Tell me how you feel about that."

And so it went. The show ran ten minutes over, twenty, half an hour and on into a second full hour of overtime while network programmers frantically tried to clear their schedules to make room for the unprecedented live-action drama. It would be remembered that the first unarguable indication of widespread Quozl acceptance came in the form of women around the country calling their respective stations to protest the preemption of their favorite soaps for those "silly-looking aliens from another world." As Arlo had predicted and hoped, by presenting the Quozl in this manner to the general public they had passed beyond uniqueness to achieve banality.

Eventually technicians from the CIA arrived and sealed off the studio feed, but by then the Quozl had been on the air for more than two hours. It was too late to pretend they didn't exist.

As he squinted at the upper level of the studio Chad could make out the anxiety and frustration on the faces of the newly arrived government representatives. They were arguing among themselves as they gestured in the direction of the stage.

Meanwhile the host had been informed that the show was no longer going out over the air, though she was not told the reason. Now thoroughly enjoying herself and at last aware of the historic import of the broadcast just concluded, she turned a final time to her audience.

"I'm afraid we've gone over our allotted time, but I know all of you join with me in welcoming our new friends. How about it, America? Do we let our visitors who've nowhere else to go stay here on Earth?"

The roar of approval that resounded from the audience induced the reporters present to scribble and dictate furiously, while the government people could only wince. They hadn't lost control of the situation because thanks to the speed with which the Quozl and their friends had moved, they'd never been in control.

The audience response was heartwarming but not official, as Chad discovered when they attempted to leave the studio only to find themselves surrounded by police and speechless men in gray suits.

"You're going to have to come with us now," one of them informed him solemnly.

"But we don't want to go with you." Mindy was equally earnest.

"Lady, do you have any idea what this means?" The man flashed an open billfold at her, tucked it back into his suit.

"I've got an idea, but it doesn't matter. We don't want to go with you."

As he spoke the man's gaze continuously swept over the rapidly swelling crowd. Word of the Quozl's presence was spreading fast.

"We have to keep you away."

"Away from what?" Chad demanded to know. "The rest of the people? Why? They *like* the Quozl."

"This isn't a game," the man responded. "I've seen the X rays that were taken. These creatures are for real. There are more of them and they said on that damn show that they want to stay here. That's not something you decide by voice vote in a television studio."

"Why can't we go back to my place?" Mindy inquired. "You can keep just as close a watch on them there as anyplace else."

"Not necessarily."

To his alarm, Chad found that the phalanx of government operatives was edging them slowly but surely in a definite direction. He could not have escaped that ring of arms and bodies had he tried. That was when Runs-red-Talking spoke up.

"If you are thinking of taking us to some kind of compound, we'd much rather stay with our friends. Surely you won't try to take us somewhere against our will?"

The man from the agency appeared nonplussed. Obviously he hadn't expected the cute furry aliens to make demands of their own, much less press anything resembling a legal claim.

"Nobody's forcing anybody to do anything against their will," he mumbled uncomfortably, suddenly wishing someone else was present to give orders.

"That's good," Arlo chirped, "because otherwise it would look very, very bad in the papers."

"That's right. It would," agreed the tall, well-dressed stranger standing close to him.

"Who the hell are you?" the agent demanded to know.

"My name's Akers," the stranger said.

Chad could see the agent wavering as he recognized the newcomer. Jack Akers was the evening anchor for CBS News. A senator or governor the agent could have handled. They were merely elected. But network anchors were worshiped. Or as his father would have warned him, *You on delicate ground, boy.*

Under the circumstances and given the speed with which events had unfolded, the government had moved fast. Just not quite fast enough. Between the two-hour show and the number of important reporters present, they couldn't take Chad and his sister and Arlo and the two aliens and stick them in a hole in the ground somewhere far away where they could interrogate them at leisure. It was too late to label them state secrets.

While the anchor chatted amiably with Chad and Runs-red-Talking, the agents in charge of the tardy operation conferred among themselves and by radio with superiors. Eventually the taller one confronted Chad. His expression was exquisitely neutral.

"You can go back to your house. But all of you will be under twenty-four-hour surveillance from now on. No more unapproved nocturnal excursions, no more random tv appearances."

"Fine," said Mindy, "so long as we stay at my house and not at *your* house." She and Chad and Arlo pushed their way through the clutch of agents, searching for the Cadillac, Quozl in tow.

As they departed, the agent felt a hand run up the back of his thigh. He jumped, turned to say something, and was startled beyond measure to see Seams-with-Metal sauntering past. As she did so, she turned and gave him a slow, unmistakably sensuous wink.

For an instant he not only forgot why he was there, he forgot who he was. Seams-with-Metal analyzed his reaction, and was pleased.

Perhaps, after all, this was better than being able to have set off the bomb.

XX.

THEY FINALLY HAD to disconnect Mindy's old line, but the government demonstrated its belated efficiency by quickly installing half a dozen new ones. While they were usually tied up by visiting agents and representatives, those living in the house were not forbidden to make use of them. Jack Akers saw to that.

The guard which had originally surrounded the house had to be extended to seal off most of the immediate neighborhood as word of the aliens' presence spread. So dense was the security that it took half a day for Chad and Mindy's parents to make their way through. They had a pleasant visit, tried to return to home and work, only to find themselves deluged with requests for interviews and comments by the swelling army of reporters. At least their father was able to escape. Not even the most powerful news-gathering organization could force an interview in the cockpit of a 747 at forty thousand feet over the middle of the Pacific. Their mother found sanctuary with relatives.

As for Arlo, he was in heaven, fielding an unending stream of requests for endorsements, personal appearances, movie and book rights, and all manner of promotions aimed not only at the Quozl but at Chad and Mindy as well. The figures being thrown at him usually existed only in the realm of fiction. His only regret was that none of it could be conducted in privacy, since everything coming into or going out of the house was intercepted and screened.

Excerpts from the tv interview appeared on every broadcast, sometimes exhaustively analyzed by hastily engaged "experts." Magazines and newspapers competed to see who could put out the most special editions. A repeat television appearance, if it could be arranged, would certainly be the most viewed broadcast in the history of the medium.

Runs-red-Talking and Seams-with-Metal handled all of it gracefully. All those years of contact with Chad and Mindy, of monitoring television transmissions, had served the Quozl well. Not only could they respond smoothly to any question, their English was superior to that of the majority of their interviewers.

These consisted largely of government specialists. Chad and Mindy were subjected to their share. As Arlo was new to contact and hardly knew the Quozl, he was largely left alone, which gave him plenty of time to make and sign deals.

Within two weeks the colony was wealthier, at least on paper, than any enclave in the United States.

As soon as one cluster of investigators concluded their work another arrived to take its place. The President made it on day four, shaking hands all around while a compact boom-box hastily blared "Hail to the Chief" in the background for the benefit of a carefully screened group of reporters. Showing that he'd done his homework he even made an attempt at the traditional Quozl greeting. Seams-with-Metal gently showed him the correct way to place his fingers.

It made for terrific television.

Chad took his turn somewhat dazedly, though it was evident the President's smile was not for him or his sister but for the visitors.

"Interesting, shaking hands with someone who has seven fingers," he said jovially to Runs-red-Talking.

"Interesting," the Quozl replied, "shaking hands with someone whose hands are furless."

The President laughed heartily, a familiar, reassuring laugh. "I haven't as much time as I'd like. I have other things to do. I just wanted to tell you that on behalf of the American

◇ 313 ◇

people you're welcome to stay here as long as you want, that as a free country with a tradition of accepting refugees regardless of race, creed, color, or point of origin you are welcome to apply to become citizens like anyone else.''

''They're not refugees, Mr. President,'' an aide whispered, but the President ignored him. He was in his element, the camera lights intense on all sides, and thoroughly enjoying himself.

''In fact, I intend to suggest that a bill be entered in Congress to waive the usual waiting period so that you may apply immediately for American citizenship.''

''Wait a minute. They aren't sure they want to stay here. They might want to move now that they don't have to hide themselves anymore.''

The instant Chad spoke, it struck him that he was admonishing the President of the United States and that as a third-string research biologist for a mid-range biotechnology firm he might be somewhat overstepping his bounds.

Arlo winked at him, which helped a little.

''Well, I am sure, Chad,'' the President replied without sacrificing one scintilla of that brilliant smile, ''that our new friends will examine all the alternatives carefully before making any final decisions. I merely wanted to let them know how welcome they are.'' He turned back to the Quozl. ''You do like it here, don't you?''

''Yes,'' said Runs politely. ''I understand that there are also some pleasantly cool empty regions in your neighboring tribe the Soviet Union.''

Chad turned pale, but that was nothing compared to the reaction among several of the President's aides. Then he noticed the position of the Quozl's ears.

''Just kidding, Mr. President. Did not anyone inform you that we Quozl have a well-developed sense of humor?''

Color returned to the President's face. Someone laughed nervously. It spread, and even the Chief Executive was not immune. Runs-red-Talking and Seams-with-Metal looked on quietly, observing.

"I didn't have time for more than a quick briefing." The President wiped at his eyes. "We're certainly in for some interesting days ahead, aren't we?"

"I hope so," said Runs. "Several of our Burrow Masters would very much like to meet with you."

"Ah yes, your colony leaders. *That* much I was told. Amazing how you manage to keep in touch with them with that tiny communicator of yours. But we can talk about such things another time.

"Meanwhile surely there must be something we can do to make you feel more comfortable."

"Our thanks to you, Honored Elder," Seams replied, "but right now we are doing well enough and require nothing special in the way of assistance."

"But the process that will lead to the establishment of a Department for Quozl Affairs is already in motion. Preliminary funding has been approved by both Houses. Surely you could use just a billion or two?"

Both of Runs's ears dipped forward. "Your thoughtfulness is greatly appreciated, Mr. President, but we really are able to manage on our own. Hopefully in the future we can take advantage of your generosity of spirit. We do not wish to become a burden to your people."

The Chief Executive was mollified. What charming little folk, he mused.

One of the men standing close to him addressed the silence. "By the way, you haven't been too clear as to your exact numbers." Chad recognized the Secretary of State. Or maybe it was Interior; he wasn't sure. "Are there several dozen of you here? Several hundred?"

This time Runs looked not to Seams-with-Metal for advice but to Chad, who shrugged tiredly. "You can't hide anything much longer, Runs."

The Quozl bent an ear toward the official who'd posed the question. "As of last counting the Burrows were home to approximately sixty-three thousand, four hundred and twelve Quozl, including infants in pouch."

◇ 315 ◇

A stunned silence settled over the room. Chad wasn't immune to the effects of the pronouncement. Come to think of it, he never had asked Runs just how many Quozl there were in the colony.

"That many." The Secretary's mind was churning. "And all underground."

"We have managed adequately," Seams-with-Metal commented.

"I should say so. My, my." The President did not look as shocked as his aides. Perhaps, Chad mused, he was thinking of future Quozl votes. After all, if they became full-fledged citizens . . . It was not beyond the realm of possibility. At this point, nothing was beyond the realm of possibility.

He recalled times when Runs-red-Talking had spoken of the rigorous Quozl approach to population control. If such control resulted in an underground population of sixty-three thousand, what would happen when such controls were removed?

"We hope to call on you for assistance in the future," Seams was saying, "and to offer what little we can in return." It was no more than typical Quozl politeness, but it clearly pleased the President. So did her next words.

"One thing only we would request."

The Chief Executive was completely relaxed now. Someone was asking him for something. "Just tell me how I can be of assistance."

"We do not wish to be restricted to this one small burrow. We want to be able to move about freely, to go where we wish. It is vital to our health."

Chad listened to the bold-faced lie and fought to control his expression. He couldn't help but wonder if the Quozl had decided to present their request in this fashion or if they'd been coached by the ever-prescient Arlo.

"Naturally we don't wish to jeopardize your well-being in any way." The President was at his paternal best. "You will be allowed to go wherever you wish—militarily sensitive installations excepted, of course." An inadvertent moan rose from one corner of the room, from the vicinity of assistant head of the National Security Agency. The President took note of it and smoothly modified his response.

"I hope you won't think it forward of us to insist that you have an escort with you wherever you travel, to prevent you from being mobbed by adoring citizens. There exists in this country a real danger of people becoming too friendly—and though it pains me to say so, there are also those who might pose a danger to you simply because you are presently the object of much public attention. This is something I am familiar with firsthand. So you require protection for two reasons."

"Are we already so accepted, then?"

"It all happened so fast." The President smiled down at Seams. "If I may say so, you are not what many people expected in the way of visitors from another world."

"What did they expect?"

The President looked thoughtful. "Something less—attractive. People are not only surprised by your appearance; they are also pleased."

Arlo had been right all along, Chad thought. Now they couldn't be spirited off to some dungeon for interrogation and vivisection. Not after having been on tv nationwide, not after having given dozens of interviews, and especially not after the President himself had just guaranteed their right to travel when and where they wished—albeit under escort. Wide exposure was the strongest armor.

When they learned of the Quozl, other governments protested vigorously at what they perceived to be an American monopoly on alien contact. The State Department replied ingenuously that they had nothing to do with the Quozl selection of a homesite. This muted but did not halt the complaints.

Meanwhile Runs-red-Talking and Seams-with-Metal traveled as inconspicuously as possible around the greater Los Angeles area, observing, studying, recording, relaying information to the Burrows, and shaking hands with astonished adults and delighted children. Watching the reactions of humans to Quozl, Chad was convinced not only that the Quozl were going to be accepted by the populace at large, within a few years they were going to be able to run for public office.

So it was somewhat of a surprise when their presence was finally challenged. Not even the President could alter certain laws by executive fiat. The challenge would have to be met through the proper channels, like any other objection to the law.

The source was a small fringe group with questionable policies but plenty of money. They had the reluctant backing of several small reputable scientific organizations.

What they said was that it was scientifically and morally unconscionable to allow sixty-three thousand unstudied, unexamined aliens unrestricted access to the rest of the planet. There was sotto voce talk of communicable diseases. The protesters insisted that if nothing else, each Quozl be individually examined and passed before being allowed onto the surface. In addition they proposed restricting the Quozl to a proscribed reservation where they could be observed and monitored.

In short, they requested everything Chad and Runs had feared from the beginning.

The President's good intentions notwithstanding, the Quozl basically had no rights.

The controversy did not slow the financial tidal wave that swelled the coffers of the corporation Arlo had established in the colony's name. Everything was cleared with the Burrow Masters and Arlo left to take care of the details. Meanwhile government technicians were still trying to locate the site of the colony. They kept digging fruitlessly around the Collins's vacation cabin. Chad knew they would stumble across the Burrows eventually, but for now the Quozl were grateful for the delay.

It would be much better, he decided, to settle this first serious controversy before the colony was located.

They were actually going to have to appear in court. The

whole thing was ludicrous, which was entirely in keeping with the basis of contemporary American jurisprudence. The government attorney brought in to assist them was sympathetic and helpful. A shame, this business, she told them, but something they were going to have to go through with. A formality. Chad wasn't so sure, Arlo less so.

"I know it looks absurd," she was telling them. "The media are having a field day with it. But short of the President declaring a national state of emergency, we're going to have to follow the law. I can't tell you how embarrassing this is for the Administration." She looked curiously across the room at Runs and Seams.

"I'm afraid a declaration of good intentions isn't sufficient to contravene recognized scientific method. The Quozl are going to have to prove some things."

The Soviets immediately offered the Quozl unconditional asylum. After consulting with the Council of Elders, Runs and Seams graciously turned them down. They would happily sit in court to prove themselves to any and all human skeptics.

The group which wished to see the Quozl's movements and activities restricted engaged some impressive legal talent. Thoughtful scientists found themselves locked in uneasy alliance with xenophobes and pseudo-Luddites.

As he sat in the hearing chamber listening to the opposition propound its arguments, Chad saw visions of barbed-wire enclosure surmounted by gun towers and mines.

The government attorney was rebutting eloquently. "Is this any way to treat harmless visitors cast helpless upon our shores? You have heard their story. They did not expect this world to be inhabited. Instead they discovered us, we garrulous, quarrelsome humans. They cannot go elsewhere. They wish only to remain and be good neighbors and friends."

Everything you say may be true, the opposition subsequently conceded, but none of it was provable. As to the true nature of Quozl intentions and Quozl purposes there was only the word of the Quozl themselves. That, and the testimony of two young adults untrained in observation and analysis.

Runs-red-Talking and Seams-with-Metal listened to the debate silently, occasionally taking time to retire to a private cubicle. Ostensibly they were contacting their superiors for advice, when Chad knew they spent more than half the time copulating. In deference to the peculiar sensibilities of the American public, neither he nor the Quozl chose to mention this particular Quozl need.

In their concluding argument the opposition pointed out that the Quozl had entered the country, as it were, illegally, which observation drew more than a few guffaws and comments about "illegal alien" jokes from the resident media. That particular objection was overcome the following day when the President signed a hastily composed directive permitting unrestricted immigration from any location greater than five hundred thousand miles from existing U.S. borders.

The opposition then argued that if the Quozl were allowed to spread freely throughout the country, they would surely become a burden on an already straining welfare system. The government attorney countered with income figures supplied by Arlo which proved that per capita the Quozl were already the wealthiest minority in the country. They could support themselves quite nicely without any assistance from the government, thank you. Among the more visible contracts Arlo had secured for them was one with Weyerhaeuser and another with Georgia-Pacific. The two forest-products giants had engaged the services of the Quozl based on assurances from Runs-red-Talking that tree-farm output could be tripled with a little instinctive Quozl input. Nor was that the only area of forestry in which they proved themselves useful.

Quozl began to appear on posters alongside flat-hatted, shovel-wielding bears.

The opposition could see which way the hurricane was blowing, but hewed to their position against mounting odds. They held one card the government had not yet been able to trump: there was still no proof that humans and Quozl could exist safely side by side without harm to old ladies and little kids. Until such time as proof could be provided, caution dictated restricting the visitors to their present area of habitation, with severe restraints on their movements. It did no good to point out that Chad and Runs-red-Talking had been friends for fourteen years. One twosome did not a society make.

The government attorney committed a grievous blunder by admitting that the Quozl were reasonably happy where they were. The opposition pounced immediately. In that event, why not leave them where they were until such time as safeguards could be ensured? What harm could there be in exercising a little caution? Study and analyze first, and then if everything turned out as everyone hoped it would, all fine and good.

This argument struck many as eminently reasonable, and the opposition found itself blessed with new friends and support. If the Quozl truly intended to be good neighbors, why would they object to such a policy? Where lay the harm?

It lay, Chad knew, in the possibility that the government and the public might grow comfortable with the status quo.

The simple "formalities" droned on week upon week, until the weeks turned into months. The Quozl's initial novelty was wearing thin as the public accepted their presence and turned its attention to news of greater immediacy. Indifference strengthened the opposition. Something had to be done, and quickly.

It manifested itself in the expression the government attorney wore as she entered the hearing room one smoggy morning. Her makeup looked especially fresh and her face was devoid of the usual strain. In response to Chad's inquiry she merely smiled and directed him to sit back, relax, and watch.

Neither Arlo nor Mindy was present today. Of the Quozl, it was Runs's turn to be present for consultation. Seams was talking on the communicator.

When the government attorney called another witness forward no one took particular notice. The formalities had seen hundreds of experts in every field called by both sides to press conflicting claims.

The elderly woman who strode to the front of the room was dressed plainly. Her back was straight and her hair short. Runs was suddenly alert, sniffling the air. Chad eyed his friend uncertainly, unable to detect anything out of the ordinary himself.

"You have known the individuals in question for how long?" the attorney was asking the woman. Chad began to suspect when she announced her place of residence, but said nothing, hardly daring to breathe. By now Runs was on his feet, every sense alert and searching.

"And what do you think of your old friends?" the attorney inquired.

"Best friends I ever had. Ornery, just like my Willie and me. Don't know what I would've done without 'em after Will passed on. That's rough country up there. A tough place for an old woman to make a living."

"Would you say, Mrs. Greenley, that you've had any problems with your friends in all the years they've been living with you?"

"Nothing serious. Mostly they've been a joy to me and mine." She gazed around the hearing room. "Without their help I doubt I'd be here today."

"Thank you, Mrs. Greenley. Tell me something. What have they asked of you in return for all their help?"

Chad could see that the opposition wanted to object to this line of questioning, but they were slow to see where it might be leading. So they made the mistake of saying nothing, waiting like everyone else in the room to see what might develop.

"Not much. Just to share my roof, play their music, and raise their young-uns."

"Do you think they've been as friendly and helpful as any normal couple?"

"Your honor, we object." The opposition's chief counsel was on his feet.

"Overruled." The presiding magistrate surveyed the room expectantly. Everyone was tense, on edge, eager to see what might happen. The puzzled opposition counsel sat down, muttering to his colleagues.

"Please answer the question, Mrs. Greenley."

"Oh, they've been more than that. They look after me just like I'm one of their own." She had to raise her voice to make herself audible over the sudden whir of camera autowinders as alerted reporters began snapping pictures like crazy.

"So in all the time you've lived together," the government attorney concluded, "you've had no serious arguments with these live-in friends, no fights. You have contracted," and she stared pointedly at the opposition's scientific advisor-in-residence, "no unusual diseases from living in intimate proximity to them."

"Nope." The old woman was utterly unperturbed by the lights and her surroundings. "In fact what with them to help with the heavy chores I'm probably healthier than I've been in my life. It's hard up north in the winter, when the sun don't shine much and an old lady gets lonely."

"If you had to characterize your friends briefly, Mrs. Greenley: what they've meant to you, how you've come to think of them after all these years, what would you say?" As she concluded, Seams entered the room, sniffling guardedly.

She didn't have to think long. "Same thing I'd say about my grandkids: that they're a blessing from the Lord."

The government attorney looked sated. "*Thank* you, Mrs. Greenley." She turned to the back of the room. So did everyone else, those with difficult angles craning their necks in hope of a better view. "Would the members of Mrs. Greenley's *family* please come forward."

Underscored by a rising murmur from those in the chamber, a cluster of figures shuffled into view. There were a young man and woman accompanied by several children. There were also unseen figures clad in light overcoats with hoods. Such attire looked out of place in Southern California.

So did the cloth wrappings which swathed oversized feet.

Seven were so dressed. By now the oversized feet had been noticed by many in the crowd, but that didn't lessen the gasp of surprise that filled the room when all seven divested themselves of their overclothes.

Runs-red-Talking and Seams-with-Metal were not the only Quozl in Los Angeles after all.

"The old woman came forward voluntarily," the assistant attorney informed Chad and Mindy in an excited whisper. "Naturally we didn't believe her at first. Since this started, our office has been bombarded with nut calls. But because we're a government bureau we're obligated to listen to all of them.

"The longer she talked the more convinced we became that she might have something, though we weren't sure what. She knew stuff that hadn't been made available to the public at large, things you couldn't just pick up from watching tv. So on a hunch, Ellen," and he nodded in the direction of the beaming, triumphant chief government attorney, "sent somebody from the office up to check out her story."

A second assistant chimed in enthusiastically. "Old lady Greenley had been following all the news reports. You might not think it to look at her, but she's got her own satellite dish. Seems like everybody in that part of the world has one. When this bunch decided to try and seal off the Quozl, she decided she had to come forward. She wanted to help."

The other assistant thought to add an apology. He had to raise his voice to make himself heard above the uproar that had engulfed the hearing chamber.

"We kept it from you two because Ellen wanted it to be a complete surprise, and because they," and he indicated the seven Quozl assembled before the bench, "insisted on doing it that way."

Amidst the pandemonium Runs and Seams stood quietly, gazing across at the equally silent cluster of Quozl. Greetings had already been exchanged by means of hand and ear gestures. The aliens ignored the babbling humans as the court administrator vainly attempted to restore a semblance of order to the hopelessly excited audience.

Runs addressed himself in high-speed Quozl to the grizzled male who was clearly the patriarch of the group. Of those near enough to overhear, only Chad and Mindy understood any of what was being said.

Runs and the old Quozl began by complimenting each other on their appearance and jewelry. Then the Elder said, "You see, new friend, that the Council of Elders was and always has been wrong. All this might have been avoided."

"That is no certainty, Most Honored of Elders." Runs was correctly deferential to a Senior even though he happened to be the greatest criminal in Shirazian Quozl history. "The time was not deemed right by the Council."

"Though you felt otherwise." This from the patriarch's companion, a female of equal age. "You felt instead much as we did."

"No." Runs protested strenuously with both voice and ears. "Unlike you, I did not flee the Burrow. I sought no contact. It simply happened. What followed was something I did not and would not have initiated."

The female made an impolite gesture with one ear. "Your posture betrays you. Your mind does not out-argue your spirit. There is too much life in your Sama."

The young couple which had accompanied the two old Quozl into the room stood silently off to the side, corralling their children and waiting patiently.

"You should not be alive, High-red-Chanter." Runs still found it hard to believe he was really talking to the infamous renegade of recent history.

"If not for the old human female, both Thinks-of-Grim and I would not have survived through the first cold season."

Chad addressed them in Quozl. "If you could speak in English, it would be helpful. You're going so fast I can hardly follow you, and no one else in the room knows what is going on. Do you know English?"

"Exceedingly well," High-red-Chanter declared.

When the Quozl turned to English it grew suddenly silent in the room. Arguments ceased as everyone turned to listen. Reporters, politicians, police, and legal aides sat and watched enraptured.

"I am High-red-Chanter," the old Quozl announced in as stentorian a voice as any Quozl could muster. "This is my mate, Thinks-of-Grim. These are our offspring, and their offspring.

"Almost immediately after we settled on your world I determined to free myself of the monolithic social structure under which all Quozl labored. I felt myself stifled by a restricted environment maintained by unsupportable rationale when an entire new world beckoned. I did not have the courage to leave until I encountered a potential mate who felt similarly."

"Dead," Seams-with-Metal was murmuring. "Both should be dead."

"I don't follow," Chad said.

Runs tried to explain. "These are the legendary renegades who abandoned First Burrow many cycles before I crawled to my mother's pouch. It was assumed that they had been killed by the elements or by hostile surface carnivores."

"Such would have been the case," High-red-Chanter admitted freely, his exceptional sense of hearing allowing him to overhear every whisper, "if not for the aid freely rendered us by Most Honored Elder Greenley."

"They were freezing," the old woman explained. "I didn't know what they were, but that didn't much seem to matter at the time. They needed help, and I never turned anybody away from my door, no matter what they looked like. After they warmed up and we got to tryin' to talk, they just seemed to want to stick around for a while. Little Cindy liked 'em right away, and they took to her. She learned Quozl before she learned English.

"Me, I was glad of the company. Lonely after Willie died. They told me some of what they was and where they'd come from. When Cody James there married Cindy, she told him.

They came to live with me and we all kept the secret. Thinks-of-Grim there, she helped raise Cindy, and she and High helped raise my grandkids.''

The shy young woman spoke up. "It was good, always easy. Many's the time when I was carryin' my last one, Judity, I wished I coulda borrowed Thinks-of-Grim's pouch. Don't have to hold a baby or wash it when she's safe up inside you.''

"The Quozl may look funny," said Cindy's husband, "but they're just regular folks. We've lived with 'em, farmed with 'em, and my kids have played with them for a long time now.''

Mrs. Greenley was nodding approvingly. "That's my family. Kids and grandkids. Some of 'em got long ears and some of 'em don't, but they're all kin.'' She looked defiant. "Ain't nobody gonna tell me where my grandkids can and can't live.'' A jaundiced, experienced eye fixed on the opposition's chief counsel. "Is this still a free country, bud, or what?''

The chamber dissolved in final chaos as reporters streamed out to file reports and rush videodiscs to the nearest transmission facilities. For a while the presiding magistrate pounded his gavel on his desk and attempted to restore order. Eventually he put the gavel aside and relaxed. It was much more fun to watch the young Quozl playing with their human counterparts.

So in the end it was not the wandering explorer Runs-red-Talking or his friend Chad Collins or the Council of Elders that cemented the success of the first widespread human-Quozl contact, but the old renegade musician High-red-Chanter and a bunch of prepubescent humans and Quozl. The reasoned arguments of the opposition could not contend with video images of human kids and Quozl cubs playing happily together.

Chad congratulated Runs, Mindy almost hugged Seams before remembering that the gesture might precipitate a fight instead of delight, and the government attorney accepted the adulation of the press. The xenophobes in the audience stormed out spouting defiance and vowing to refile, but nobody paid them any attention. They were too busy taking pictures of the impromptu playground the children of both races had established in front of the magistrate's desk.

Most of the reporters had fled to file their reports. Only a couple remained, representatives of small local papers that could not hope to compete with the giant syndicates or the networks. They hoped for an exclusive detail or overlooked item that might be worthy of a story later.

One was aimlessly interviewing Cindy Greenley for lack of anything better to do, even though he knew the real news of the day was already burning modems from L.A. to Tokyo. Still, there might be something. Occasionally patience was rewarded, even though the young woman seemed more inclined to talk about her family and the berries and fruits she'd canned for the upcoming winter than about her newsworthy friends, the Quozl.

She was combing the long blond hair of a stolid little boy of six while keeping an eye on the rest of her brood. Off to their left the two youngest Quozl danced and wrestled with the two elder Greenley grandchildren. The Quozl were much faster, but the human kids were stronger.

Searching for an angle, the reporter asked what it was like before she married her husband, before he came to live on the land with her mother and the Quozl. He expected a simple, bucolic response because that was the only kind he'd received thus far.

"Quiet, mostly." Cindy Greenley brushed at a persistent cowlick. "I liked Cody right away, though. He was just like me and Mom; country but liberal, ready to try anything once." She added offhandedly, as though she was still talking about her canning, "Mom was right about it being lonely up on the farm, but it got better after High and Thinks showed up. High's a very good lover. Made the winters pass a lot easier."

Chad had been listening indifferently. Now he turned sharply. Mindy had retired to the women's lounge. Arlo was outside, entertaining lawyers, offers, and reporters. The older Quozl chatted seriously with Cody James while the children of both races played off in a corner. There was just Cindy Greenley, her little boy, and the reporter, with himself standing nearby.

Why had the woman kept her maiden name?

The reporter's expression was unreadable. "Excuse me, ma'm. I don't think I caught that last part."

"You mean, about the winters passing easier?"

"No, no. Before that."

"Oh, You mean about High being a good lover."

"Yes." The reporter was very, very alert now. "You mean that in the platonic sense, of course. Because the Quozl were good with the children, and helpful in times of difficulty."

"No, that's not what I meant. There was a time when I would've found something like this hard to talk about, but living with Quozl for a while you just naturally come to understand certain things. Suddenly what used to confuse and trouble you doesn't anymore.

"When I said that High was a good lover I meant exactly that. It was before Cody and I tied the knot." She smiled beatifically. "Far as that goes, ask Cody what he thinks of Thinks. She can play more than that funny flute of theirs." A frown creased her face and she looked meaningfully around the room. "You mean what with all that's come out, nobody's realized that humans and Quozl are sexually compatible?"

The reporter smiled. "No. Somehow that little item has managed to be overlooked. Mrs. Greenley, are you sure about this? You're not making something up just to tease me?"

"I don't tease, mister." Her smile changed. "If you ain't sure, go have a little private chat with Thinks-of-Grim or Seams-with-Metal."

"Thanks, not right now," the man replied, though a stunned Chad saw him glance involuntarily in Seams's direction.

Chad remembered the time when the Quozl biologist had chased Mindy, remembered the looks he'd received from female Quozl study team members. He'd put it all down to normal scientific curiosity, and perhaps a great deal of that had been involved. But if Mrs. Greenley was telling the truth, there was much more to it than that. Much more.

"Perfectly safe, of course, if you follow my meaning," the young wife was saying, as though it were the most natural thing in the world instead of the greatest scientific-social revelation since the arrival of the Quozl themselves. "I don't pretend to understand how it all works, except that they're not all that different. Cody's done more looking than I have and he says that their works are more adaptable than ours. I guess they're just a lot more, well, flexible in such things than we are."

"Didn't you find it—unnatural?" The reporter's eyes were the size of Ping-Pong balls.

"Mister, on a cold night when it's pitch-dark you don't find anything warm and reassuring unnatural. If everybody made love in the dark there'd be no prejudice in this world." She paused. "The only thing you really notice right off is all that fur. After that you just stop thinking."

"Is this for publication?"

Chad hurried over, looking around wildly to see if anyone else had overheard. "No, it's not for publication. You can't."

"The hell I can't." The man pocketed his recorder and skittered toward the exit, dodging Chad's halfhearted grab. Not that he could really stop him.

A gentle hand came down on his arm and he turned to find himself staring into the bright green eyes of Cindy Greenley.

"Really, it's okay. Why shouldn't everyone know? They'll find out sooner or later."

He slumped, envisioning the screaming but decorous headlines. What would the general reaction be? Calm and accepting like the Greenleys', or would it give fresh ammunition to the xenophobes?

"I mean," she was saying in her soft, almost Quozl-like voice, "they *are* mammals. Intelligent and caring. Cody and Momma and I came all the way down here to help people realize how happy humans and Quozls could be together. We're compatible, Mr. Collins."

"Compatible, yes, but . . ."

"It is for the best."

Turning, he found himself less than a foot from Seams-with-Metal. "As the woman says, it must all come out eventually."

"Sure. After free travel for all Quozl has been approved. After you've been made citizens. After the colony is so dispersed you can never be locked up in one place again. Once this hits the wire services, the sensationalism, the fear will . . ."

"Fear of what?" Cindy Greenley sounded genuinely puzzled. "Fear of infection? Fear of rejection? Fear of a new kind of life? I should think the knowledge will make the Quozl more popular than ever, not less."

"Humans will have to invent a few new words, reflect on new concepts. We will help. Willingly. That is what humans want. That is what humans have always wanted," Seams said with assurance.

Chad gaped at her. "You knew. You've known all along."

"My specialty was human studies." An ear bobbed and earrings jangled musically. "We had the old specimen, then good recordings of you and your sibling. The differences were clearly not insurmountable, to put it precisely. The Burrow Masters know, as do the senior members of my department. The rest of the colony does not. If they did it would be impossible to enforce the law against surface visitation, for curiosity's sake if no other. They will have to be informed."

"But who would've thought . . . ?"

"It is not something a human would consider, but it is of primary interest to Quozl. Until we reached Shiraz we were convinced we were the only intelligence in the universe. We were shocked to discover it was home to intellectual if not social equals. It was far less surprising to learn that we are compatible in other ways.

"There will be great astonishment on Quozlene when the news is carried there. To do that we must build another ship.

◇ **331** ◇

That is the sign of Burrow maturity. Azel did it, and Moszine, and even Mazna. Shiraz too will send out its ship, only it will carry back the greatest news of all. The news that we are not alone, that we have friends. Compatible friends. It is a secret we will share with you. Humans will accompany Quozl on the long journey back to Quozlene. Perhaps your grandchildren. Perhaps mine thrice-pouch removed.

"History makes its own rules. So says the Samizene."

A smooth, seven-fingered hand lightly gripped his shoulder. "Now tell me one thing truly, friend Chad."

He twitched, startled by the unexpected violation of his Sama. "What?"

Huge violet eyes gazed deeply into his. "Weren't you ever curious about it?"

Beautiful amethyst eyes, he thought. All Quozl had beautiful eyes. Their iris pigmentation was much more intense than that of humans. The corners of her mouth twitched, the closest any Quozl ever came to a recognizable smile.

"It is impossible, friend Chad, to fear those you can love."

He let her lead him through the chamber. Mindy watched curiously as they disappeared into a storage room. As they closed the door behind them, Chad rested a hand on Seams-with-Metal's fur. It was as soft as the finest chinchilla.

"You know," he murmured dazedly, "we might be able to keep up with you scientifically, but I'm not sure about everything else."

XXI.

HUMAN BEINGS ARE highly adaptable creatures. After the initial flurry of jokes died down, a complacency took over which ensured the Quozl's acceptance. Television crews, reporters, politicians were welcomed into the Quozl Burrows, though at Chad's suggestion the finest and most extreme examples of Quozl art were initially concealed from visitors' sight. Acceptance still preceded understanding.

The corporation which Arlo had providentially established continued to rake in enormous sums on behalf of the colony as the Quozl were compensated for everything from product endorsements to personal appearances. Quozl experts were dispatched to assist foresters from Finland to Ecuador. Inevitably they traveled first-class, conversing freely with their human fellow passengers. Many leaped at the chance, as Runs-red-Talking and High-red-Chanter had done illegally, to see more of their homeworld.

Nor were they only in demand for commercial purposes. Quozl music became wildly popular, while a serious party simply wasn't an "A" party without at least one Quozl couple in attendance. They mingled easily, their natural curiosity and famed sensuality making them the center of attention wherever they went. They could eat and enjoy many human foods, though alcohol only made them ill. They preferred fruit-flavored drinks.

There were some problems with certain religious groups. After all, if God had made man in his own image, where did that put the Quozl, who were clearly at least as intelligent as any human? The debate was not restricted to one side of the relationship, for certain Quozl philosophers had difficulty accepting the fact that not only weren't the Quozl not the only intelligent creatures in the universe, the other ones were bald giants with tiny eyes and nonexistent ears and feet.

When the extent of crowding at the Burrows was made known, there was an outpouring of sympathy for the poor, claustrophobically confined Quozl. Offers poured in to set up new Quozl communities elsewhere, offers which the Quozl accepted with honest thanks. Everyone wanted a Quozl community in their town. The result was that the Quozl diaspora took place much more rapidly than anyone, least of all the Quozl themselves, could have foreseen.

At first the Quozl had trouble filling all the requests, but with access to the surface came a relaxation on birth control, and the fecund aliens were quickly able to plant families everywhere from central Australia to the Swedish taiga. Their presence was always welcomed, never resented. They ate moderately and their agricultural skills enabled them to generate a surplus of food wherever they settled. They were the most productive refugees in history.

Their ability to tolerate cold made them much in demand as workers in the northernmost climes, and their delicate, seven-fingered hands brought them high wages and great admiration in those industries which required consistent digital skills. Give a Quozl a place to copulate, a little food, access to art, and the company of friends and it would make you rich, so the popular saying went.

In a surprisingly short time the sight of Quozl in their brilliantly hued bodysuits, trailing chromatic scarves and flashing jewelry, was a common sight. They became honored citizens not only of the United States but of most other countries as well.

No matter where they went or what they did, they were always unfailingly, sometimes embarrassingly polite.

They didn't merely mingle, they melted, acquiring property, prestigious degrees, and credit cards. It became popular to adopt young Quozl. Given the traditionally tenuous nature of the extended Quozl families, this was easy to do. Quozl and human alike delighted in the ease with which the offspring of both species matured side by side.

When the occasional cry was raised that the Quozl were going to conquer the world by simply outbreeding their hosts, the Quozl in those sensitive regions immediately and of their own accord reintroduced birth control procedures. They would not expand where they were not wanted. But since growth zoomed wherever the Quozl settled, such complaints were not very much heard. They were the ideal immigrants.

The paranoia that had existed among Quozl Elders seemed to vanish overnight as they found themselves received with honors wherever they traveled. It was a great relief. Clearly there was plenty of room on Shiraz for two intelligent races, especially when they complimented one another so well. It helped immensely that the Quozl were not clannish. They spread unobtrusively through human society.

Eventually what had once been a joke became reality and Quozl ran for public office. Their self-control and politeness was everywhere appreciated and admired. Quozl officials were not prejudiced for or against anyone, including fellow Quozl. They were also quite incorruptible, though their decisions were as subject to debate as those of any human.

By this time it was no longer possible to conceal the true nature of their art and history. Instead of revulsion it provoked curiosity among the general population, which under the guidance of Quozl philosophers began to re-examine its own background in a new light. After all, humans had their own traditional aberrations. Americans insisted on owning handguns, Latin Americans took most of the afternoon off for siesta, and the French revered Jerry Lewis, so who could criticize the Quozl for portraying violence in their art when their actual social behavior was impeccable?

Integration was finally considered complete when the Quozl,

in their own deferential, courteous fashion, began making human jokes in mixed company.

Instead of feeling threatened by the Quozl, humanity felt protective toward them. They were fast but fragile. And very, very friendly.

By the time Chad reached middle age the Quozl were no longer a novelty. It was difficult to imagine what the world had been like before their arrival. Unable to work at his chosen profession (and with no need to) he withdrew into the upper level of the Quozl corporation. Arlo remained its nominal chief executive while actually sharing duties with his wife, Mindy. As the first human to make contact with the Quozl, Chad was an international celebrity, too valuable to waste his time shuffling petrie dishes in an obscure laboratory.

Somewhat reluctantly he wore the mantle the press had woven for him, drove the fancy car and lived in the private compound. Uncomfortable in a crowd, he was compelled to learn how to deliver speeches. Public relations demanded it. His advice was sought constantly by giant corporations and private individuals seeking to do business with the Quozl.

Small wars stopped. With their understanding of violence the Quozl were able to provide insights which made such conflicts appear foolish to any would-be participants. Combat lost its appeal while interest in sublimated forms of violence soared. Mankind retained its competitive spirit without the companion bloodshed. As the Quozl explained, war was a disease of the individual human psyche, rooted in the imbalance between the sexes. The tendency was inherited, but also curable. By their very existence the Quozl proved that war was not the inevitable consequence of advanced technology.

Human history showed them that every single conflict could be traced to sexual frustration or motivation, including those originally thought to have been fought over religion. Mankind found such revelations difficult to face, but that is the nature of truth. It is invariably uncomfortable, but far easier to accept with the help of friends.

XXII.

STRANGE TO BE back in the Burrows after so many years, Chad thought as he made his way down the corridor. It was a restricted area, but nothing on the planet was off-limits to Chad Collins. Celebrity had its privileges.

It was equally strange to have white hair and have to walk with a cane because of bursitis, but that was also truth. He didn't worry about bumping into a Quozl in the dim light. No Quozl lived in these Burrows anymore. They had dwelt underground out of necessity and not by choice. Now they lived in places like Kiev and Rangoon and Vladivostok.

But the Burrows were not devoid of life. The technicians and curators who maintained it as an entertainment park and museum were always around, busy at their tasks. The colony had been turned into a major tourist attraction that was visited by millions every year, with rides and moving sidewalks and audiovisuals. The economy of Boise, the nearest large city, had boomed, and the tiny town of Bonanza which had long ago played host to a clutch of oddly matched hikers had finally lived up to its name.

The art which lined the walls and dominated the open places in all their garish, gory glory were reproductions. The original Quozl works had traveled to new homes with the Quozl as they migrated, or else they now reposed in honored niches of the world's finest museums. The old Burrow workshops were now filled with Quozl artists who churned out decorations for homes, city squares, and private collections.

There was a surprisingly large market among humans for the most depraved and bloodthirsty works the artisans could produce. Or perhaps now that the Quozl have helped us to know ourselves it was not so surprising, Chad thought.

Having initially encountered mankind-at-large in a place called Disneyland, it was not so ironic that the original colony site should end up as a similar sort of facility.

Within the Burrows, trained Quozl demonstrated ancient Quozl rites and donned archaic costume not only to delight visiting humans but also to instruct their own young, who had been born on Shiraz and knew of a planet called Quozlene only through recordings. To them it seemed a lonely place, a world inhabited by Quozl alone, empty of clumsy, powerful human companions.

It had all turned out so well, Chad mused as he shuffled along his chosen route. Not at all the way it had been depicted in dozens of old movies and books. Everyone had underestimated the affection two intelligent races could have for one another.

Not to mention other things not even guessed at.

Besides serving as a venue for entertainment and education, the old colony had one other purpose. it was often utilized for ceremonial occasions. The Quozl loved ceremony and delighted in re-enacting their colorful if bloody history, rich as it was in ritual and pomp.

Today would see the investiture of a new Senior Elder. There were only seven of them, a tribute to the old Council of Seven. Though not wholly ceremonial in nature, the office was something of an ultimate honor. It carried no power with it because there was no Quozl nation. Only Quozl history and Quozl art.

Age was still respected, and the honor of the office lay in the respect paid to it, much as Catholics looked to the Pope and neurotics to their favorite astrologer. Mindy would have enjoyed this, Chad thought to himself. In the old days she'd have fashioned a new script out of it. There was no longer a *Quozltime* show, of course. In the presence of real Quozl it was not needed. The Quozl were fine actors in their own traditional and in human plays, save for the fact that nothing could induce them to smile.

There was no longer any Mindy, either. She had passed away five, no, six years ago. Arlo was in poor health and unable to attend but sent along best wishes anyway. All their differences and initial dislike aside, he'd turned out to be a pretty decent brother-in-law. Chad had never married—been too busy, somehow—but he had several nieces and nephews, who doted on their famous uncle.

The back route led him to the VIP lounge where he was able to watch the investiture surrounded by people and Quozl almost as famous as himself. It was fascinating, violent, and satisfying, as with most things Quozl. It was rich with elaborate chants, mock battles (which originally had not been mock), splendid costumes, and ancient music. All this he was comfortable with.

What he found hard to accept was Runs-red-Talking, who was the object of all the attention. He could only think of the now graying Quozl as he'd first seen him, lying motionless at the bottom of a mountain pool, gazing thoughtfully toward the sky as he slowly drowned.

But he didn't drown, Chad reminded himself. I pulled him out. For this.

He stood down there, the center of attention, ears bent, his enormous feet platformed on the sandals of office. Television crews manned both by humans and Quozl sent images and a running commentary around the world. An investiture of one of the Seven didn't happen every day.

When the ceremony was over, Chad hobbled down with the rest of the dignitaries to pay his respects. He could sense the eyes on him, hear the murmurs as he was recognized and people stood aside so he could pass. It was useful to be famous.

Runs-red-Talking beamed from beneath his formal attire as he spotted his old friend approaching. His ears, while weak, managed to bob by way of greeting. There were many cameras focused on them.

Only when the media began to focus its attention elsewhere did Runs lean close to whisper. "Now that we are done with this nonsense you must spend some time with me." His voice was still high and Quozl frail.

"It's been a while, hasn't it?" Chad was aware that two premiers and a president were waiting awkwardly in line behind him, anxious to shake the hand of the new Senior Elder.

"Come back tomorrow," Runs told him. "We'll make a journey. Let's go back to the old river."

"To the shrine?" Chad asked, referring to the impressive monument that had been raised by the frog pond.

"No. Too many tourists there. Let's go farther upstream, where we used to camp."

"I'd like that. Worlds change, civilizations rise and fall, but nature is a constant. She knows how to take her time. I fear she's taken most of mine."

"Mine as well."

They parted, with Chad agreeing to return the next day. In fact, he ended up visiting for several days, enjoying balmy mornings and hot mountain afternoons in the company of his old friend. Despite the plethora of people anxious to wait on two such famous personages they still managed to find time to themselves, to sit alone by the river and reminisce.

Eventually the last day dawned, as last days inevitably do. Chad would take his private plane back to Los Angeles while Runs would retire to his ceremonial post at La Paz. They did not let sentiment cloud their parting. They were too old and too wise for that.

"It worked out well, didn't it, Chad?" Runs asked.

"Well enough, though unexpectedly so."

"I wish the original elders could see how things have gone. I wish all the landing crew of the *Sequencer* could see. Death can be such an irritation."

Chad forgot himself for a moment and smiled, but quickly

quashed it. "Time to say goodbye again. I know you will bring respect to your office." They gripped hands and Runs's ears dipped. The handshake lingered and Chad frowned. "Was there something else?"

For an instant Runs-red-Talking seemed to hesitate. Then he said with conviction, "No. Nothing else. Farewell. Visit down south when you can."

"I will. I promise."

Runs-red-Talking watched his old friend limp down the corridor. As if in response to an unvoiced call a young human materialized at the controls of an electric transport. He helped the old man into the passenger seat and whisked him away, along with a cartful of memories.

Runs turned to go, only to find his way blocked by another vehicle. It was small and entirely self-contained. It had to be, because its occupant could no longer walk. The new Senior Elder stared through the dim light. Then he dipped his ears very low, blocking his eyes and offering himself in the ancient posture of complete helplessness. His tone dripped submission, and gladly.

"I am overwhelmed with honor by your presence, distant relation."

"Uncover your eyes." The voice was so thin it was almost inaudible, even to another Quozl. "I try never to miss an investiture."

Runs lifted his ears, straightened proudly. "How may I honor?"

"Talk with me awhile. My days used to be precious. Now the moments are."

They chatted of inconsequential things, Runs realizing he would remember this conversation for the rest of his life. Eventually he was emboldened to ask a question which had troubled him all his life.

"You could be a Senior Elder. You are due great honor, yet you refuse it and choose to dwell instead in comparative anonymity. The younger generation which would adore you lives largely in ignorance of your very existence. Why? I apologize profusely for my impudence.''

The electric chair whined as its occupant turned to face a large open place. It was in the process of being renovated. Soon it would receive a reproduction of the immense sculpture that had once occupied it, complete with fountains and growing plants. The quiet continued for so long that Runs feared the other might have fallen asleep.

Such was not the case, however. He was merely engaged in silent contemplation.

''I choose not to accept great honor because I do not deserve it.''

''Honored Senior, I plead difference with you.''

''Plead all you like. You won't be the first.'' Aged eyes peered searchingly into Runs's own. ''How can I accept honor, having once killed an intelligent being?''

''There were reasons. There was justification.'' Runs knew the story but felt compelled to make his point nonetheless.

Another drawn-out silence followed before the husk of a voice murmured, ''Perhaps. Tell me, Senior Elder, for I have questions of my own: what do you think the reaction will be on Quozlene when the Shirazian ship arrives six or seven generations from now to inform them of the colony's success? When it arrives with a mixed crew?''

''I cannot imagine.''

''Try. And do not take too long. Remember that my moments are precious.''

''It is my hope and that of everyone that they will take to humans as readily as humans took to us.''

''That is how I believe. That is how I must believe.'' A vast sigh filled the corridor and for an instant Runs-red-Talking was afraid. But the voice came again. ''Sometimes I think intelligence counts for nothing, luck for everything. It is good to know we are not alone, even if our only friends are barbaric potential killers.''

''It can be unsettling,'' Runs admitted, ''but also useful. There have been many discussions: among scientific staffs, among Burrow Masters. Where humans can evolve there may also be other intelligences, less tractable, more belligerent still. If such a thing can be imagined.''

"Yes, and those colony ships which never reported back to Quozlene may have run afoul of them. I am familiar with the arguments.''

"We will find out, but now we can do something about such cases, should it be proved they exist. Because while we cannot fight, we now have friends who can and will on our behalf.''

"That is the critical question,'' whispered the voice from the chair. "Will they?''

"I can only speak from my own observation, my own life and experiences. I am confident that they will.''

An ear might have bobbed in agreement, but the movement was so slight Runs could not be certain he'd seen it.

"It was all worthwhile, then. Everything that happened. Even the way it happened. A different individual here, another reaction somewhere else, and Shiraz might have turned out tragically. This is still very much the humans' world, though we are more secure now than ever. It is best to let them think they are still in complete control. Their primitive pride requires it. They cannot cooperate unless they believe themselves to be in command. So be it. We have grown beyond such pettiness. It is the result that matters.''

"We have the Samizene,'' Runs pointed out.

"Truth. They are improving, though they still allow their unbalanced sexual natures to dictate to their minds. At least now they can envision a common destiny. We have helped put an end to their silly tribal conflicts.

"In ten to twenty cycles the first Shirazian generation ship will enter underspace with a full complement of human and Quozl. They believe that we are helping to spread them through the galaxy. They do not see that it is the other way around, that this is how it must be. They cannot help the fact that they are human and not Quozl. But with time and tutelage they will improve.''

"It is a hard thing, to deceive one's friends," Runs murmured.

"They have secrets of their own they choose to keep from us. There can be fairness in mutual deception. What matters is that they think they are in control. It is the safest way. The Quozl do not need to stand on the top of the mountain. We are far too busy taking its measure. Simpler to let friends do the hard climbing and tell us what lies at the peak.

"We live where they grant us permission, which is more than ample. In return for their aid and friendship we give them knowledge, therapy, sympathy, and interstellar travel. They will go with us to found a grand galactic union in which they may declare paramountcy, if they so desire. We will stand aside and let them bare their teeth, ever courteous, ever polite. That is the way of the Quozl."

"If they knew this there are those humans who would fight us."

"Fight what? The great majority would not permit it. They like us too much. It is far better to be cute, cuddly, and lovable than to wield a bigger gun or sharper sword. We obey their laws and hew to their restrictions, we leave all major decisions to them—while we advise quietly and deferentially. We do exactly as they command, which is just what we want."

Runs-red-Talking had not become a Senior Elder through lack of understanding. He knew what the other was talking about, comprehended fully. It was all there for anyone to see, in the Samizene, and in Quozl history. It all made sense.

It made so much sense he even understood when the old scout broke out in a wide, glistening grin.